THREE
STAR FIX

Joseph Jablonski

© 2002 Gardenia Press

THREE STAR FIX
Copyright © 2002 by Joseph Jablonski

ISBN trade paperback: 0-9722349-2-6
Library Of Congress Card Number: 2002110630

For inquiries or to order additional copies of this book, contact:

Gardenia Press
P. O. Box 18601
Milwaukee, WI 53218-0601 USA
1-866-861-9443 www.gardeniapress.com
books@gardeniapress.com

To Darlyn

Author's Note

Three Star Fix is a work of fiction, the principal characters fabrications of my imagination. The ships and ports are genuine, however, and many of the encounters typical, some even borrowed from sea-stories I've heard. This sea-story takes place during a tumultuous period in our maritime history, when ships waddled out of port loaded to their marks with bombs for Vietnam, when owner's reps lurked in the union halls with envelopes of cash, looking for crew. It was the end of an era; of a class of ships-steam-driven, break-bulk freighters-which, like the four-masted schooner, no longer plies the world's oceans; of a pre-AIDS time of innocence when a dose of clap was no more feared than the common cold; of young men and women questioning, as they should, their parent's convictions and their pastors' sermons. I gratefully acknowledge my shipmates through the years, men and women of the Merchant Marine, all you mates and engineers, sailors, oilers and cooks with whom I have sailed through foul weather and fair, who have shared your stories and listened to mine. I know well the appeal and the difficulties of the life we chose, and find there, as a writer now, a wealth of inspiration and material.

I thank the United States Merchant Marine Academy, it's faculty, staff and administrators, for educating and feeding us, and for looking the other way from time to time. I thank my Kings Point classmates-Phil, David, Paul, Ed, Tyler and hundreds more-and your beautiful wives and families-for your inspiration, and especially for your life-long friendships. As you know, this is your story, yours and every frightened novice to this business of moving ships across blue water, whether maritime academy cadet, navy swabbie or smooth-faced wiper; anyone who ever hoisted a seabag, fisted onto a rail and climbed the gangway of a ship bound for ports whose names we couldn't pronounce, headed for adventures we never could have predicted. Adventures in many cases far less believable than this fictionalized rendition. I thank the Masters, Mates and Pilots Organization, and my brother and sister deck officers and captains, for holding the course on our primary task of safe navigation as the ships grew, the crews diminished, cargo values increased and pressures to perform miracles intensified.

Humble gratitude to Bob & Marcella Jablonski for being superior in every way to young Jake Thomas's parents, for the undying love and prayers you have always provided to your children's projects, no matter how ill-advised; to my brothers and sisters, nieces and nephews, their spouses and significant others-especially those of you who have read or listened to a chapter or two and commented. I thank my children: Peter, also a Kings Pointer who, with Lucinda and classmates Chris Gasoriek, Hank Demarest and others, have either read chapters or talked with me about them; Tasha and Scott for listening to me drone on, mile after mile, the last twelve chapters during that roadtrip to Wyoming; Anna for the inspiration you unknowingly provide as a committed artist; and to Katerina, for the games of cribbage and volleyball and your irreverent sense of humor.

I thank all of you (and if I forget to name you, I apologize) who spent valuable hours marking up chapters, bringing light to the arduous process of crafting fiction. In the beginning there was Gail Kingsley, Hannah from New York, Margaret Donsbach, Kim Steffgen and Liam Cullen, now deceased, plus
Rachel and others who came and went from our critique group. I especially thank my editor Laura Vadney, and good friend Jon Rombach for your invaluable encouragement and criticism; Gardenia Press for believing in this story; and, later, Jack & Debra Robertson, C.W. Metcalf, Kelley Kievet and Thomas Rude, Leslie Cumming, Crofton and Duffy for reading subsequent drafts, advising on marketing or contributing to the creative process. I thank my tennis pals Jennifer and Suzanne and Linda and others for your reading and marketing opinions, and for letting me win a match from time to time.

To Darlyn, my wife of many years, I thank you for your uncompromising perfect pitch and for showing me how what I kept thinking good enough could be better.

Like one of my many sea-voyages, moving Three Star Fix from concept to bound book has been a passage I'll not forget. To all of you who have in some way shared this journey, to the fictional characters of my story, and to what has become, in certain instances, a blending of the two, I thank you.

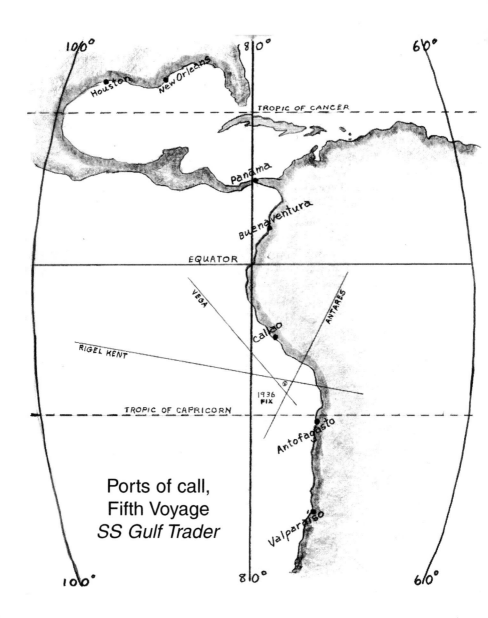

Ports of call,
Fifth Voyage
SS Gulf Trader

Crew List of the SS Gulf Trader
Voyage 005
Commencing in the Port of New Orleans
July 18, 1967
Captain Henrick C. Isenhagen, Commanding

01 Chief Officer..Paul O. Hunt
02 Second Officer...Franklin B. Potter
03 Third Officer...Donald J. Campbell
04 Third Officer..Antonio X. Petrocelli
05 Deck Cadet...Jacob J. Thomas
06 Boatswain...Arnold B. Jones
07 A.B. Seaman..Robert Fletcher
08 A.B. Seaman...Irving Jackson
09 A.B. Seaman...Spencer T. Dority
10 A.B. Seaman...Edgar M. Fryar
11 A.B. Seaman..Raul Huezo
12 A.B. Seaman...William J. Sarutzki
13 Ordinary Seaman...Thomas B. Michaelson
14 Ordinary Seaman...Timothy J. MacCaffrey
15 Ordinary Seaman...Samuel S. Simmons
16 Purser..George P. LeClair
17 Chief Engineer..Edward P. Hammond
18 First Assistant Engineer...................................George A. Coleman
19 Second Assistant Engineer............................Anthony F. Markezich
20 Third Assistant Engineer...............................Terry C. Moorehouse
21 Third Assistant Engineer...............................William O'Grady
22 Engine Cadet...Walter V. Miller
23 Oiler..Ben B. Clausen
24 Oiler..Lawrence T. Forster
25 Oiler..Richard G. Lauritsen
26 Fireman...John R. Leedham
27 Fireman...Alexander K. Merritt
28 Fireman...Herman A. Woolpert
29 Wiper..Roy Acherman
30 Wiper..Fredrick A. Litchman
31 Wiper..Paul O'Leary
32 Steward...Thomas L. Scrugham
33 Chief Cook..Vernan D. Nauck
34 Second Cook/Baker.......................................Alphonse A. Norton
35 Third Cook..Betty O'Laughlin
36 Bedroom Steward..Frank A. Findley
37 Utility/Saloon..Harry White
38 Utility/Messroom..Stephen Jefferson Arnold

New Orleans
July 18 - 21, 1967

The taxi bounced over the tracks and swerved to a stop next to the gatehouse in front of the Nashville Avenue docks off Tchoupitoulas. I set my bags on the asphalt—a seabag and a small handgrip with black and green plaid cover, and the old Navy sextant the Academy had loaned me—then paid the driver with my last twenty. He drove off and I turned, nervous, the back of my shirt wet with sweat. Behind me was New Orleans, where I'd just spent an anxious night at the YMCA; and behind that my first nineteen years of life in a village in Nebraska where telephones were connected in five-house party lines and the priest blessed new John Deeres on the rare occasion when someone actually bought one. Ahead stood a small, concrete-block building with a metal gate that lead directly to the door of a huge tin-sided warehouse. I rubbed the toes of my shoes on the calves of my khakis, gathered my bags and walked past the guard who barely glanced at my papers.

I picked my way between rows of pallets piled high with cargo on one side, wood crates on the other; dodging the kamikaze forklifts and waving when the longshoremen yelled. There was no path and I had little to guide me besides instinct. I walked through a wide doorway, emerging from the shadows into the bright sunshine dockside, my eyes blinking, adjusting slowly to the sight of the ship lying before me like a piece of fiction. She looked nearly new, freshly painted a light gray. Her superstructure towered above the scores of men swarming her decks. She lay no more than twenty yards away, so close my inexperienced eye could not find her ends. My gaze drifted upwards and found the nameboard. Gold-leaf letters against varnished wood spelled out *SS Gulf Trader*. I breathed easier. At least I'd found the right ship.

Long gray booms with black ends were swung out over the dock, lifting pallets of cargo, swinging them inboard and lowering them into the holds. Forklifts screamed by, tines at eye level, into the warehouse and out, lumbering side to side with the weight of the pallets. Bulky men shouting, cursing, hollering insults and smoking fat, black cigars looked at me, some smiling as they passed.

I stood there gaping, wishing myself invisible to this chaos. My heart thumped against my ribs and I felt an unaccountable yearning for this life. This is where my dreams had led.

* * *

I had bawled like an orphaned calf my last day at home, stuffing socks and shirts and books into my seabag, eyes too blurred to see what I was doing, arms moving helter-skelter. When I finished packing, I stopped crying and grew real sullen. Damned if I was going to let my old man see me cry. My mom sat in my one chair over by my small desk, sobbing, saying over and over like a mantra, "I don't know why you had to say those things. Father Henry never did anything to you. And now your dad is so ashamed. You don't care who you hurt."

She had a point. I'll give her that.

* * *

The *Gulf Trader* lay in the Mississippi River—like me, fidgety with excitement. She rolled from side to side as loads were lifted and landed. She surged fore and aft, straining against slack spring lines as a tug pushing a raft of barges, his engines roaring, passed. She was bigger than life and yet lively; a monster, barely tethered, crawling with hundreds of raucous, big-bellied men.

I inhaled deeply and tried to calm myself. Ahead, the gangway stretched between dock and ship like a narrow bridge from safety to risk, from known to unknown—a pathway to great and dangerous adventures. A sailor stood on the main deck with a knife in his hand doing something with the ropes holding the net that looped beneath the gangway from the dock to the main deck. He wore jeans and a white tee shirt, was thin and dark with black hair oiled back, hawk-nosed, officious, a cigarette dangling from his lips. A young man, not much older than me, thinly built with blond hair that fell to his shoulders, had his right foot on the platform at the base of the gangway, a dirty brown seabag over his shoulder. The sailor finished with the rope, carefully slipped his knife back into the sheath he wore on his belt, looked up and gestured with his head. The blond man walked aboard.

Following his example, I hoisted my seabag over my shoulder, fisted onto my sextant and handgrip, and climbed the metal steps of the gangway. The ship rolled slightly onshore, like a welcoming dip. Lacking experience with an unsteady firmament, I grabbed the rope rail and continued up, reached the upper platform and stepped aboard, feeling for the briefest moment like Billy Budd or a young Marlow or Jack London himself.

I found myself in a narrow passageway between the gangway and the house, a passageway that formed a bottleneck between the forward and after decks.

"You must be the cadet," said the dark-haired sailor with the sheath knife, stressing both syllables and using a long "a" so it came out "kay-dett."

"Yes sir," I answered. "Name's Jake. Jake Thomas. Cadet." I held out my hand as my dad had instructed me in the days when we still spoke.

"Put your hand down, boy. I don't shake hands with cadets and I don't really give a shit what your name is."

I looked at him, unsure how to respond.

"A-a-and, who are you, sir?" I stuttered.

"Fletcher," he answered. "I'm the A.B. on the twelve to four watch. Any luck at all, you and I won't have much to do with each other."

He walked aft, limping slightly.

A jowly, cigar-smoking man in a tight uniform held up a clip-board, motioning for me to sign. I took it and the pen, unset-tled after my encounter with the sailor, but determined to move always forward, and boldly wrote *cadet-midshipman* under order of business.

"Through that door and up the stairs on your left, there, buddy," said the watchman.

Dragging my bags over the foot-high sill through the heavy metal door, I stepped into a linoleum-tiled passageway just large enough for two men to pass if one turned sideways. Off it were many doors. The walls—bulkheads they were called—were painted a pale, sickly green. The ship smelled like antiseptic cleaner and cigarette smoke. A sign with the word *Boatswain* in phenolic letters identified one room; *12 to 4 A.B.* another, *4 to 8 O.S.* a third. I came to a staircase and struggled up, my bags dead weight. Up the stairs, I found a foyer with a desk in the center. A dark-haired man wearing thick glasses sat smoking and typing.

"Jake Thomas, cadet," I said.

"George LeClair," he answered, pushing his glasses up on his nose and squinting. He shook my hand. His left eye twitched.

"I'm the purser. Your room is up there and around to the right." He pointed back to the stairway. "Here is some paper-work you need to fill out. Just return it later today."

I found my room and set my bags on the floor. The engine cadet, who I didn't know well, was already aboard. His name was Walt Miller—Wally—and he was a year ahead of me at school. His bags lay on the upper bunk so I took the lower. Still wear-ing the midshipman's khaki uniform I had dressed in that morn-ing, I washed my hands and face, brushed my teeth and set forth to meet the mate and captain.

For a deck cadet reporting aboard his first ship, the captain is God the Father and the chief mate Jesus Christ. Raised Catholic, I carried with me a great fear of both those deities. But I was strong and healthy and knew how to work. I'd been raised with an overdeveloped sense of propriety and I knew the value of "yes, sir" and "pardon me, sir."

The chief mate—known as "the mate"—sat in his cargo office wearing a rumpled khaki shirt with three gold bars on the shoulders. The sign on his desk said *Paul Hunt* and he was my boss—a regular guy, more or less; certainly not Christ-like in any sense I could detect. When I entered, he glanced up from his task of digging at his cuticles with a small knife, gave me a once over and stabbed the knife into a corkboard on the wall. Roughly, as though angry at having been interrupted, he snatched a piece of paper off his desk and handed it to me. I noticed his fingers bled.

"Cadet," he said.

"Yes, sir. Thomas is the name. Jake Thomas."

"I know your name, son. I saw the telegram from the Academy Training Representative. Here. This is the cargo plan for number five hold. I want you to go into the 'tween deck and make sure they're separating the Buenaventura flour from the Callao flour. And hurry back. I got plenty of work for you."

I wasn't at all sure what it was I was supposed to be doing, but I considered it vital. I recalled hearing the words *'tween deck* in my Cargo Operations class, but had no idea what one looked like, much less where it might be located. Asking around, I found number five hold aft of the house, climbed hand over hand one level down a vertical ladder, and discovered from a burly but kind-hearted longshoreman that I was standing on the 'tween deck—"the *upper* 'tween deck," he said, distinguishing it from the spaces below. He glanced at my cargo plan, confirmed this was the space and handed it back. I thanked him, then looked about. I scarcely knew a pallet from a pulley. Crates and boxes and bags of flour were neatly stacked on all sides. A pallet with what looked like an axle was landed on the half of the square that was closed. A forklift driver speared the pallet, lifted it and drove it into the far corner where he raised it higher than a man could reach, the diesel motor running at high speed, and jammed it into the very top of the ten-foot space. I climbed like a kid on a jungle gym around the cargo in that hold until I found bags of flour designated for Buenaventura. It was separated from the Callao cargo by sheets of butcher paper with the word *Callao* stamped all over it.

* * *

God knows how long I was gone, but I finally returned to

the mate's office with something in the way of information. He barely glanced up as I handed over my drawing showing where the cargo was stowed, what separations I saw, and what space was still available. I noticed the knife was back in his hand and the area around his cuticles bleeding. He saw me looking at them.

"You like knives, kid?"

"I've got one." I didn't know exactly what to say.

"Know how to sharpen a knife?"

"More or less."

"Here, give me your hand."

I held my right hand out. He cut a slit across the top of my index finger, then looked up to see what sort of reaction I might have. I pulled my hand back, watching the blood seep from the small slice.

"Didn't feel a thing, did you? That's a sharp knife for you."

I nodded. He looked at me with a crooked smile and a sort of crazed look in his eye. After a moment of strained silence, he blinked once and said, "Don't bother the Captain till tomorrow. And next time you go into a hold, don't take all day. Now go on. Stick with the third mate and don't get hurt."

I walked out of his office wrapping my handkerchief around my finger to stop the bleeding, vowing to myself to work hard and to learn this business quickly; considering what exactly is the proper reaction when your superior slices your finger with a knife, thinking maybe someone with a bit more gumption would have hauled off and slugged him.

On deck I wandered for thirty minutes wondering how I'd find the third mate since I had no idea what he looked like. I dodged the pallets of cargo moving into the holds and the empty cargo hooks flying back out, finally figuring out the offshore side of the ship was a lot safer than the onshore side. Once there, I made my way aft until I stood in the relative quiet of the fantail looking upriver. A man in khakis wearing a billed cap approached.

"You look like a cadet," he said.

"Yes sir, I am."

"I'm Don Campbell, third mate." He stuck out his hand. I shook it, trying to recall what my father had said about the importance of a handshake being not too firm, but, God forbid, not too weak either.

"Nice handshake, cadet," smiled the man, his blue eyes twinkling. "Your dad teach you that?" He was red-faced and boyish, shorter than me by a good four inches, but solidly built with a trimmed red beard.

"Matter of fact, he did," I said.

"So what's your name, boy?"

"Jake," I said.

"Welcome aboard, Jake."

He looked at me closely, as if sizing me up.

"All right, let's go," he said. "Stay close, but not so close that you clip the heels of my shoes. And watch your head. Your main job for the hour left on my watch is to not get hurt. Your second job is to ask questions. You can ask exactly two questions every ten minutes, which gives you a total of ten before I get relieved. You'll never remember more than that anyway."

* * *

I asked my ten questions, received answers to some, strange looks to others. Soon enough, the workday was finished. Wally, my roommate, had just showered when I walked into our room. He wore a towel around his waist, and strutted around like a barnyard cock.

"Been to the French Quarter?" he asked, smiling.

"Last night for a few minutes."

"I was down here last year. Drinking age is eighteen. Bars stay open all night. Women everywhere. Lot of them naked."

* * *

I felt like a complete hick in downtown New Orleans—like somehow with all the new experiences, I was living in a heightened level of consciousness—gawking at the crowds on Canal street, staring at what I thought to be erotic photos of nude women in the glass cases in front of the strip joints, listening to the clouds of jazz that floated up out of the clubs, curious about every damn thing.

We drank beer at a bar called Moses Attic, where we met up
with two cadets from another ship. We were all from the same
maritime school. I knew one of them, a black-haired guy from
Baltimore named Bruno who lived in my battalion but over in
first company with the football team. The four of us walked up
and down Bourbon Street, wild as a small squadron of AWOL
sailors, ducked into one of the strip joints without paying the
cover, and hooted like geese when a girl with bright red hair
slipped off the pasties covering her nipples and wound herself
around a steel pole. The place was packed with loud men and
foggy with smoke. Around midnight, we stopped into an oyster
bar on the corner of Canal and Bourbon Streets and sucked
down a dozen slimy oysters. Wally, who looked like a cross
between Jiminy Cricket and Howdy Doodie, promptly ran out
and barfed them back up again—one by one, still flopping, they
were so fresh. Drunk and dizzy and chattering like squirrels,
Wally and I said good-bye to our two classmates, caught a cab
back to the ship and collapsed into our bunks at 3 a.m.

* * *

I was up at 7:30, a little hung over, but still able to put down
a plate of greasy eggs and hash browns. The mate had an endless
number of consignments he had questions about and kept me
climbing in and out of cargo holds like a monkey. That night,
after a shower and a short nap, Wally and I returned to the
French Quarter and partied like condemned men.

* * *

The sailor's life suited me. I loved the freedom and adventure on the one hand and the security of knowing I had a bunk
and prepared food—three hots and a cot, as Don Campbell put
it—on the other. I missed my family—my Mom and four brothers and four sisters, all younger than me. I even missed my dad
in spite of how he and I couldn't be together in the same room
more than thirty minutes without yelling at each other.
    After breakfast on the third day, Mr. Hunt, the mate, told
the eight to twelve third mate, an effusive man named Antonio

Petrocelli whose main characteristic, from my point of view, was how much he sweat, to post the sailing board. I accompanied him down the stairs to a small locker near the gangway. One would have thought he had been asked to build a new ship or prepare to go to the moon. With elaborate motions and much huffing and sighing, he removed the black sailing board from its tiny locker near the gangway, cursing Mr. Campbell, the 12 to 4 third mate, for not putting the plastic bag with the chalk and erasure exactly where it belonged. I dug around a little and found them for him and Mr. Petrocelli purred like a cat, happy to have these tools with which to complete his assigned task. While I watched, he scratched and screeched on the black board in a fine hand, the news the Gulf Trader would *Sail for Houston at 0001 hours on July 21. Sailor's Callback 2300 July 20.* Then he carefully carried the board outside and hung it on its hooks at the head of the gangway. When he finished, he stood back like an artist admiring his work.

* * *

The mate knocked me off at noon.

"We're sailing tonight. Y'all take care of any business you might have ashore," he said. "Just be sure you don't miss the ship."

I stayed aboard till Wally was ready. He and I walked down the gangway around four and caught a cab to a Canal Street gin mill—Wally's term—as if the only unfinished business we had was to drink beer. Wally had been there before. It had no windows, which made time stand still, was dimly lit, and stunk of spilled beer and cigarette smoke. A long wooden bar curved around and made a runway where women pranced back and forth in their underwear. We sat near the door. It was early—before five—and the room was mostly empty. A thin-legged, dark-haired girl with heavy breasts danced lethargically along the runway, doing a silly little bump and grind, caught up in her own thoughts. She wasn't beautiful, at first glance anyway, but I found myself attracted to her. Maybe it was her naked breasts and thighs, I don't know. I was only nineteen, with little experience in these matters, and could hardly be accused of being discriminating. Her face was angular with high cheekbones and a strong, thin nose. She seemed melancholy or preoccupied, both qualities that made me want to hear her talk about herself.

Wally and I nursed our beers while our eyes, burning from the smoke, grew accustomed to the dimness. A couple of guys sat almost opposite us at the other end of the bar. Three or four seats away sat a loner, gaping at the girl with an expression that reminded me of hunger. Every time she danced by, she turned to face him, then squatted and edged her hip over while he reached up and stuffed her bikini panty with a dollar bill like it was food—a light salad maybe, or a vegetable. I watched her face as his hand touched her most intimate area. She faked a smile of thanks, removed the bill and tossed it onto the bar, then moved on.

What the hell, I thought. A job's a job. Maybe she thinks that too.

"I know that guy," said Wally, quietly.

"You mean the guy that just stuffed the money into her g-string?"

"Yeah."

"No kidding. Who is he? What's he like?"

"A guy from school. Flunked out last year. Total asshole. But he's got a roll of bills and will probably buy us a beer."

Wally called his name. I don't remember it now. Bob, I think. He bought us beers, anyway, and that was our goal. And he continued to stuff dollars into the girl's g-string, so she spent plenty of time nearby, and that wasn't so bad either. Hours passed. Other dancers came and went. Bob told us he had his engineer's license and was sailing regularly on ammo ships to what he referred to as "that hell-hole, Saigon."

"What are your draft numbers?" he asked.

"Three hundred two," said Wally, smirking like he'd won the lottery.

"Twelve," I said.

"Good thing you're in college," he looked straight at me. "Or you're a dead man."

I nodded. Three boys from my hometown—population fifteen hundred—were already buried. Jim Daniels and Ralph Edwards and the youngest Kutska boy. All friends. Guys I'd played football with. Regular guys from regular families. Henrietta, the red-haired librarian, had been adamant about me going to college.

"Even if you don't die over there," she'd said. "You'll get a leg shot off or come back addicted to hashish." The woman knew about everything. I never argued with her.

"Whatever you do," she said. "Stay in college. I don't have much money but if you ever need any of it, let me know."

Henrietta pushed books across her big oak desk the way Big Al Swoboda pushed Schlitz across his sticky bar—books by Hardy and Conrad and Dickens and Tolstoy and London and Melville. I'd sit in the rocker across from her, reading, the only sound the ticking of the old clock I occasionally wound that sat on the mantel above the door. From time to time, I'd sigh at a particularly vivid passage, stop reading and stare down the broad front steps out the door of the library, across the expanse of lawn down the road that led out of town, watching the snow fall or the grass turn green or the yellowed leaves flutter to the ground. Books, and the library, became my refuge during those tumultuous high school years when it seemed I couldn't help but piss people off.

* * *

Soon it was after nine. When we told Bob our ship was sailing at midnight, he hit his forehead with the palm of his hand like the two-bit actor he turned out to be and said "Shame y'all leaving. I'm having a party tonight with women you wouldn't believe. My building is a dormitory for TWA stews."

"Stewardesses?" The word conjured visions of amoral young women just hoping to meet someone like me.

"You should see them. And you wouldn't believe how friendly they are."

My ability to suspend disbelief in the face of the most obvious clues to the contrary is testimony to the strength of a young man's strongest desires. Wally looked at me as if some very important part of my brain had come loose when I suggested we go back and give the old man a cock and bull story about needing to miss the ship for some highly urgent reason and could we please catch it in Houston. Bob said he thought it was a fine idea, though, and wrote a phone number on a napkin as he was leaving, saying he had to get ready for his party. Never occurred to us there was anything strange about him walking out at nine-thirty to get ready for a party in his own apartment at ten.

After Bob left, I worked for a half-hour convincing Wally I wasn't completely nuts and that, "Jesus Christ, you only live once, and you'd damn well better grab opportunities when they come around because life is short and what the hell, all he can say is no."

"He can say a lot more than no," Wally answered. "And don't forget, you get eighty-sixed off this ship, you'll get handed a one-way ticket to Saigon."

"Eighty-sixed?"

"Means kicked out; asked to leave."

It was after ten when we walked up the gangway. The mate sprawled in his chair, a glass of scotch in one hand, cigar in the other, listening as we told our tale of meeting my cousin on leave from Viet Nam and could we catch the ship in Houston, sir. I embellished it just enough, I hoped. He laughed when I finished, pointed up to the captain's room with his cigar and said. "You kids got some kinda balls. Go ask the old man. He'll be up at eleven."

We walked up the two flights to the chief engineer's state-room and found him sitting in his office in a dirty white boiler suit, overhead light off, a Heinekens on his desk, half-width reading glasses on the tip of his nose, scouring an engineering diagram with a magnifying glass under the light of a swing-arm lamp. His name was Hammond, Chief Hammond. He was tall and lanky with a shank of straight brown hair that hung to his eyebrows and made him look boyish. A man of few words, he had an honest, straightforward manner that I liked.

Wally told our story—surprisingly well. Chief Hammond peered over the top of his glasses, smiled a little, waved and said, "I don't give a shit. Talk to the skipper."

The door to the captain's room was closed, so we climbed the remaining three flights to the bridge. Mr. Potter, the iron-haired second mate with the ministerial countenance, was already there, testing the navigation gear in preparation for sailing. Watching him answer telephones, flip toggle switches, and activate the radars, I would have thought we were on a space mission rather than a two-day voyage to Houston. At eleven-fifteen, the captain stepped quietly into the wheelhouse. I had seen him only twice before. He had been seated both times. I was surprised he was three inches shorter than my six foot one height. His hair was crew-cut, accentuating protruding ears with giant lobes. He glanced quickly—almost suspiciously—about the wheelhouse, walked over and spoke a few words to the river pilot who sat, a brown beret cocked jauntily on his head, smoking and humming in front of one of the radars, playing with the controls. The pilot seemed jovial compared to the captain who stood ramrod straight, unsmiling, his shoulder boards pale yellow in the fluorescent wheelhouse light.

Captain Isenhagen walked to a small table on the port side of the settee, poured coffee into a porcelain cup with the word CAPTAIN on it and mixed in two heaping spoonfuls of sugar. He sipped it, seemed to like it all right, and walked to the front rail where he stared out over the Mississippi. He lit a Chesterfield. I walked over and stood next to him as respectfully as I could and quietly told him our story. After I spoke, he stood there, eyes narrowed, motionless except for occasionally lifting the cigarette to his lips and inhaling. Finally he looked at me and said, "Do you haff enough money to get to Houston?"

"Yes sir," I said.

"All right. Be there by eight Tuesday morning or I vill call the ATR and report that you missed the ship."

When I realized we'd been given permission by the captain, my new father figure, I said, overly exuberant, "Yes sir. We'll be there. Thank you, sir."

Wally and I flew out of the wheelhouse and down three flights to our room. We tossed some clothes into a bag, ran out and clattered down the stairs to the main deck just as a gang of sailors walked by like a chain-gang heading aft. One of them, an old black man I had not yet met, said, "You young-uns watch yo'sefs now."

* * *

Wisps of fog were beginning to blow off the river as we

opened the doors to the Yellow Cab. Not sure where to go, we returned to the bar on Canal Street where we had met Bob, thinking he probably lived in the neighborhood. Less than two hours had passed. The dark-haired stripper was still there but was finished working and sat alone on a barstool, dressed in a short black skirt and white blouse, sipping a drink with a red cherry in it, smoking. Two girls danced in high heels along the bar, one pale with spiky blue hair, small sagging breasts, and a scar on her stomach; the other with a long tattoo—a snake whose tongue reached up toward her crotch—curling down her left leg.

But we had important business. Wally dialed the numbers on the napkin. He got a no such number message. He called information, but Bob wasn't listed. I got twenty nickels for a buck and Wally tried a dozen combinations of the numbers, muttering, "The bastard's probably dyslexic—if he can read at all." After midnight, we gave up and moved over to sit near the stripper.

Wally moaned, "The tugs are probably pulling the ship into the river now."

"I can't believe I just missed the sailing of my first ship," I said.

"Probably not too many people can say that," said Wally.

"I feel like such a jerk."

"You should," said Wally. "Still, can you believe that son of a bitch gave us bogus numbers?"

"You said he was an asshole."

"Why would he do this though?"

"Because he's an asshole."

The girl—her name was Antoinette—asked what had happened. We ordered a round of Jax. Looking at her sitting there in the dark bar, I found her significantly more attractive dressed than she had been naked. She knew Bob, of course, and laughed, said he touched her panties more than she did. I felt a weird jealous twinge, but laughed anyway. She felt sorry for him, she said, because he was always alone. He showed up three or four times a week, usually early in the evening, like tonight. Then he'd disappear for months at a time.

"Says he works for the CIA, but I've heard CIA stories before. The double-oh-seven syndrome, we call it. That and 'I'm a photographer. Are you a model?' are popular lines." Her brown eyes sparkled when she laughed.

"Does he hit on you?" asked Wally.

She shrugged. "I'm a stripper. If guys don't hit on me, I'd better go into social services or something. I've never given him my number or let him walk me home though."

"Can't blame you," said Wally, completely serious. "What a fucking loser."

Wally ordered whiskey with beer chasers. I'd had enough to drink, though, and just wanted to talk to the girl. She had grown up with her mother in a bayou town west of New Orleans and was studying architecture at Tulane but thought she'd been a courtesan in a previous life and "wouldn't mind trying my hand at that."

"Your hand?" I asked.

"Among other things."

Her only fear with regard to working in this place was that one of her professors would stop by some night. We talked for a half-hour. Finally, she yawned and said she was leaving.

"Hey, we got lots of time to kill. Mind if we walk you home?"

She hesitated. "I make it a practice to never date customers."

"Well, we're not exactly customers," I said. "And this isn't much of a date."

"You're right." She laughed easily. "Let's go. There's been a couple of muggings on my street lately. I don't mind the company."

She lived deep in the French Quarter, she said, seven or eight blocks off Canal down a dark street near the river.

* * *

I held her hand as we walked and tried to ignore Wally, who was drunk and chirping like a chipmunk—which is exactly what he looked like. We hurried along Canal Street, entered the French Quarter at Bourbon Street and walked through loud groups of late-night drunks a couple blocks till we turned right. The fog thickened as we cut over east toward the river.

Wally drifted away from time to time as we walked and I

would reluctantly let go Antoinette's hand to go find him, bring him back, return and take her hand again. The light from the streetlamps diffused into the fog and the closer we got to the river, the fewer people we saw. The street, Antoinette, Wally, everything seemed fictional now and a little bit dangerous. We walked past the door to a clinic of some sort advertising, "FREE CONDOMS. PREVENT VD."

"You ever have sex with guys you meet in the bar?" I asked, shivering.

"That's none of your business. I'm certainly not going to have sex with you tonight if that's what you're asking," she said.

"No, I was just wondering, I guess—you know, if girls ever have sex with guys they don't know."

"They do. They're called hookers and they charge money for it."

I nodded, thinking she didn't have to be such a wise-ass. We walked quietly a half-block or so, watching Wally fade in and out of the fog up ahead.

"Sorry," she said, nuzzling my ear. "Guess I've forgotten how it is to be with tender-hearted farm boys."

I smiled.

"Do you have a girlfriend?" she asked.

"I guess so."

"Have you had sex with her?"

"Not exactly."

"Have you made a commitment to her?"

I thought about that before answering.

"That's the deal, isn't it? Commitment."

She stopped suddenly and looked at me. "This is my apartment." She reached up and kissed me hard.

"Usually just the promise of commitment is enough," she smiled. "I'd invite you in, but my apartment's small."

"I'll look you up when we get back to New Orleans," I answered.

"There you go," she said, smiling. "A commitment. You're learning. I'll look forward to seeing you."

Her door opened and closed, and she was gone like a screen actor when the movie's finished. I blinked, shook my hands as though wet, and went to look for Wally.

When I found him, he was leaning against a lamp pole like a cartoon drunk, puking. I laughed and sat on the curb, waiting till he finished. The night seemed colder now and darker. It occurred to me that Wally being drunk and me responsible for him might have just cost me an opportunity to lose my virginity—a goal I'd set for myself and the sooner the better. But that's why cadets were sent out two to a ship—to look after each other. It was a sacred duty and I figured Wally would repay the favor before the voyage ended.

Wally eventually stopped retching. He groaned and wiped his mouth with his handkerchief. We struck off toward Canal Street. He stayed either ahead of me or behind me, but couldn't seem to match my speed. The fog was thick and the street deserted. I worried about losing him.

He was twenty feet ahead of me when I saw the silhouette of two men like cardboard cutouts—large, fully formed—emerge from the murk. The knife in the taller one's hand glimmered as it caught the light from the street lamp behind me. He cut off my path while his shorter sidekick went for Wally. Two thoughts struck me simultaneously. One, protecting Wally was my responsibility. Two, these guys weren't going to get a nickel from us, I didn't care what.

My assailant was my height and young. His long black arms were gawky and his legs kept moving back and forth as though he were running in place. I wanted to tell him to stand still, for Christ's sake.

"Gimme a nickel," is what I heard him say, although I suspect that might have been a projection of the exact amount I'd already decided he wouldn't get. He held the knife awkwardly, in a clenched fist, point up, like how my little sister Marcy held a knife when she attacked a piece of roast beef at my Grandma's house at Sunday dinner. In my mind's eye, I could see the Captain's face on the darkened bridge, cigarette smoke trailing out the corner of his mouth, looking with an unflinching gaze into my eyes, saying he would call the Academy if we weren't on the dock in Houston when the ship arrived. No question I'd get kicked out of school.

The mugger and I stood there, our faces not six inches apart, his eyes darting like little birds, mine focused and steady, for what seemed like minutes. I couldn't hear anything from Wally's direction, but knew I had to do something quickly when I glimpsed a vehicle with a light on top moving slowly toward us. I yelled, "police." The guy swung with his blade—like he felt compelled to but didn't know why or how and certainly didn't want to hit me. I countered just as clumsily with the arm holding my sports coat. His knife cut the inside pocket of my jacket, our only evidence from this caper. Otherwise, with the fog and the darkness and the alcohol, it could have been a dream.

My attacker scurried away and I ran toward Wally. His mugger was shorter and his beard pointed and mean looking. He had Wally's billfold in his hand and was about to take his money when I grabbed it from him and pushed him so hard he fell. I yelled again, "Police." It was a taxi and, to my surprise, it stopped. My legs worked fine till I was sitting in the cab at which point they jellied up and shook all the way to Canal Street.

Wally seemed sobered by the experience. Coming up on the bus station, the driver commented that all river traffic was stopped because of the fog. Wally and I looked at each other and I told the cabby to drive straight to the Nashville Avenue Wharf.

It seemed like we hit every red light on our way there. As we approached, we thought we could make out the deck lights of our ship and cheered wildly, shaking each other's hand, whooping and hollering and patting the driver on the back. He bounced over the tracks, drove through the open gate and onto the dock. We got out. The lights we had seen were dock lights. Our ship was gone and its absence blasted a big hole where I'd already shot a happy ending to this particular memory. Wally said it must have sailed before traffic was stopped and was probably navigating downriver by radar. He kicked gravel into the river, muttering "son of a bitch." We returned to the cab and drove to the Greyhound station, longing for our warm bunks, feeling like whipped pups.

Houston, Texas
July 22 - 25

My feet dangled over the heavy wooden stringer that ran along the edge of the dock. I looked up from *Crime and Punishment,* the book I was reading for my Sea Project, and shielded my eyes from the morning sun as an empty black-hulled tanker with oil and rust streaks down to its boottopping maneuvered in the turning basin. A big white and black tug pushed on the bow; a smaller red one pulled the stern to port. Once the tanker was headed downriver, the tugs repositioned themselves and pushed the tanker broadside into a little hole-in-the-wall lay berth over on the west side of the channel. Beyond it, we could see the Gulf Trader. Even at this early hour, the air was clammy.

Three seagulls fought life or death to perch on a piling fifteen feet from where we sat. They squawked and flapped until Wally, suffering from two nights of drinking, threw a handful of rocks at them. They apparently thought he was throwing food, though, and just worked harder to gain the perch. I watched them awhile, tried to relate their activity to things Raskolnikov was doing in the book I was reading, but my mind was blank so I gave up and ignored them.

*   *   *

We had slept like corpses for most of our Greyhound ride from New Orleans. Ed, a classmate who lived in Houston, and

who had just received orders to join an Isthmian Lines C-3 load-
ing cigarettes and beer for Subic Bay, picked us up at the downtown bus station, then drove directly to a bon voyage party he
had been invited to by friends he'd made during the two years
he'd spent in the army before getting admitted to the Academy.
We drove past brick apartment building after brick apartment
building, then turned off the boulevard into a treeless patch of
cul-de-sacs and ranch houses. The party was in a sick-green,
three-bedroom with a fenced backyard. We sat on metal lawn
chairs in weedy grass while one guy barbequed and another
tended the keg. I didn't know much about Texans, Ed being the
only one I'd ever met. Turned out he was hardly typical. Ed's
nickname at school was Old Pecker, since he was three or four
years older than everyone else in our class. His friends were
older, too. They were mostly couples and a few singles in their
mid-twenties.

I was hungry following the long bus ride, and the hamburgers, baked beans and potato chips tasted good. So did the beer.
As the evening wore on and we all guzzled too many plastic
glassfuls, one of the wives—a petite brunette named Gladys, her
hair ridiculous in a too-tall beehive—broached the topic of dirty
words. I had just finished reading *How to Talk Dirty and
Influence People* by Lenny Bruce and had been thinking a lot
recently about the power words carry with them. I stopped talking to Ed and Wally about how a cadet should react if the Chief
mate slices your hand with a knife and turned toward the group
to listen.

The women seemed to like this subject more than the men.
A leggy gal named Peg, wearing short-shorts and a halter, said,
"fuck," and I thought her husband was going to have a stroke.
Mary, who was single and seemed to be both the most liberal
and the most literate person in the crowd, said a couple of "c"
words that made me uncomfortable. One of them, *cocksucker*,
described something I didn't really understand. The repeated *k*
sounds made it harsh, almost violent. The word described something that sounded sexual but really gross—at least for one of the
parties involved.

I told everyone about Lenny Bruce and how he had been
arrested for using dirty words in his comedy routine. Gladys's

husband said, "good." Mary and Gladys asked what word he had used. I wouldn't come right out and tell them but, getting into the spirit of things, I bet everyone they couldn't guess. No one else had read the book. The guessing started with conventional dirty words. There was giggling among the women, and growling from some of the men. Wally, who sat next to the keg so he didn't have to walk so far to refill his class, badgered the husbands for being uptight while Ed, our local friend, just laughed. After some incorrect guessing, I hinted the word started with an "m" and had twelve letters. No one could guess. Finally, one of the husbands said, "Just say the goddamned word so we can get back to a more interesting topic."

When I said *motherfucker*, you'd have thought the hand of God had just descended and turned everyone to salt. Women clasped their hands over their mouths; men mouthed the word, thought about it and turned red with anger. Ed grabbed Wally by the arm and motioned to me with a flick of his head to follow quickly. In the car, he said, "Damn man, we are lucky to get out of here alive. You got to watch what y'all say around Texans. They don't mind whoring and drinking and gambling, but they keep their women real separate. 'Specially their mothers."

I didn't say anything. Seemed like no matter what group I got thrust into, I figured out how to offend it and get booted out. Probably how people get to be like Raskolnikov, I thought. Any maybe not all that uncommon for merchant seamen.

* * *

Once the tanker was pushed clear of the turning basin, an old bulk carrier that had undocked not far from where we sat moved in to be turned. The Gulf Trader stood marking time downriver, her hull freshly grayed and her clipper bow smart with its gleaming black lettering and anchors. She was beautiful.

An hour passed and the Gulf Trader was finally alongside running out her lines. Wally and I tried to look as energetic as possible, climbing the gangway even before the sailors put out the safety net. I felt more than a little shame-faced at having missed the ship, and didn't say much that day. I did make the first of several resolutions I would break this voyage: to make my sea-project a priority, quit drinking so much, and get more sleep. I heard a few comments from Paul Hunt, the mate, about how slow I was moving. Others, notably Don Campbell and George LeClair, commented on my red eyes. I ignored them.

My hangover faded as the day progressed. Over the course of the next three days, I showed the mate how I could work, climbing in and out of cargo holds without being told, looking at web frames and bilge suctions, kicking shoring, inspecting separations, and taping available cubic so the mate could decide how many more cases of canned salmon or crates of household goods he could stuff into a space. I was on the bow and the stern twice each watch with the mates heaving in spring lines, setting stoppers and figure-eighting the lines around the bollards. I liked going to the bow alone and took to sitting on the forward bollard on the starboard side for five minutes or so to rest and look around whenever I went up there. Sometimes I would stuff the paperback copy of *Crime and Punishment* into my back pocket and read a few pages, then sit looking around at the ships and the waterway and the cargoes. It became my refuge from the hectic life of the ship in port.

After breakfast each day, and again before getting relieved at four, I would run down the gangway to read the drafts. At the end of each watch, I would double-step the six flights to the bridge to tap the barometer and sling the psychrometer, then write it all up in the deck log. I liked the jobs even if I didn't always understand why they had to be done. I liked most of the people. I liked that I could eat three sirloins at Sunday dinner or four hamburgers Tuesdays at lunch. I especially liked that my father wasn't around to yell at me. I wasn't going to get booted off this ship. It was my new home, my only home, really, and I liked being here.

* * *

Houston in July is hot and sticky as the inside of the slaughterhouse I worked at my senior year of high school. I walked ashore the first night, but the mosquitoes swarmed me once I got away from the ship, and I didn't much care for how far I had to walk to reach a store or a bar. Back on the ship, I found a breeze on the stern that carried the bugs away, so sat and wrote letters to my folks and to Melissa, my girl friend. I'd called my Mom from New Orleans to let her know I'd made it there OK but didn't talk to my dad. I told her I was sorry for the trouble I'd caused. She said maybe I could call again sometime before we sailed foreign and talk to "your father." She'd talked to Father Henry. Tried her best to patch things up; make them right for her family. I could picture her humility as she explained to the old boar; could picture his imperiousness as he advised her it was common for young men to reject their religion. Just not like I did. Not with what he considered to be such anger and disrespect.

I'd learned to keep my mouth shut. Didn't, for example, say I'd been drinking when I blew up. Just drinking beer and playing baseball on a Saturday afternoon. Not drunk like my dad got every night in his Lazy-Boy, or like Father Henry was when our baseball flew up onto the front porch of the rectory and smashed through his living-room window.

I was the one who chased the ball up the steps onto the porch. The unlucky one, maybe. The one he called "that no-account Thomas kid" when he looked at me with those rheumy, blood-shot eyes. Saw me there and lumped me in with my old man; with trouble and the good-for-nothing losers our little town had no shortage of. Maybe we were all drunk. Drunk like the men around there got. Stinking, fall-in-the-gutter, say stupid things drunk.

* * *

After writing the letters to my family—in which I apologized and told them I loved them—and to Melissa, I sat and looked around at the Houston ship-channel. There was nothing pretty about this waterway. It smelled like rotten eggs and had black chunks of tar and brown turds of oil floating on the surface or lying in little piles at the shoreline. Factories and refineries belching smoke lined its banks. A rusty old tanker drifted slowly downriver, and a couple of small, underpowered tugs blew chunks of soot and thick black smoke from their stacks as they labored to push fuel barges upriver.

Houston was an oil port, and the channel was choked with tankers off-loading crude and back-loading gasoline, diesel, jet-fuel and lubes from the refineries.

Wally went ashore with some of the engineers the second night, but I found a phone booth and called my folks to let them know I was OK. We had only one phone at home in those days— number 415-J. Being a party line, the neighbors had the extensions and one heard old Mrs. Underhill's asthmatic breathing at some point during most calls. My mom, the Great Communicator, answered. We talked as if nothing had happened. She sounded lively and in good spirits; and wanted to hear every bit of news about what I was doing and how I felt and were they feeding me. What can a young man on his first ship tell his mother, anyway? That he walked a stripper home the other night? That his roommate puked up a dozen oysters, but was feeling better, thank you? That he still hadn't gotten laid, but it was right up there on his list of things to accomplish?

"I hated missing mass last Sunday, but I'm planning to go next chance I get," I said.

Nobody said anything and I felt like a jerk. Then my mom started crying and Mrs. Underhill's breathing grew louder and next thing I knew my dad was talking. He said it was hot there, and the price of corn was up some. His new business was taking a lot of time but he thought he could make a go of it with help from his dad. Then my mom got back on. I told her I loved her and that I would definitely find churches to go to in South America. Finally, I said good-bye to everyone including Mrs. Underhill and hung up.

* * *

Our schedule called for us to sail for Cristobal, Panama at 0800 Wednesday, July 25th. On Tuesday, at the afternoon coffee break in the ship's saloon, the mate and the Chief engineer decided the cadets and the officers should go for dinner that night to a Mexican restaurant named Boyds.

We left the ship at six. I liked feeling part of a group, a group of brothers of the sea, and here we were off the ship, comrades in arms, celebrating a final meal together before beginning this great and adventuresome voyage. Everyone seemed excited to be going ashore together. Paul Hunt and the Chief engineer lead the way. Then came the First Assistant—Wally's boss, man by the name of Coleman, third mate Don Campbell, purser George LeClair with the twitching left eye and coke-bottle glasses, and one of the thirds, Terry, freshly graduated from one of the state academies, who was just a couple years older than Wally.

Boyds was a waterfront bar-restaurant-dancehall-saloon— the worst waterfront bar on Navigation Avenue, according to George LeClair, the purser. It had an acre of asphalt that was half-full of pickup trucks, most of which were fitted with gun-racks and had confederate flags stickered onto their rear bumpers. I had been warned against coming here the first night in when I'd asked what there was to do around Houston. Being with the people who had warned me made it OK though. We strode into the bar, telling jokes and laughing.

Don Campbell said, "Seamen's bars are the same all over the world. Exactly like this."

Nudes on black velvet hung along the walls, a wooden ship's wheel with a clock inset in the hub sat on the sill above the black swinging doors that led to the kitchen; faded orange life rings were suspended randomly from the ceiling. Don pointed to a guy with oily black hair and a gold chain supporting a gold anchor around his neck sleeping with his head back and his mouth open in a booth in the corner.

"Even him," Don said. "He's in every one of them."

After drinking a beer and meeting the owner, a big-boned Mexican woman named Maria, we moved into the dining room. Maria had powerful arms, large breasts and hips, jet-black hair and red lips. She flirted outrageously with Chief Hammond, pointing to his crotch and once even raising her blouse and flashing her large tits—an act that provided me no end of pondering since I'd seen so few before. He said she was forty, which surprised me because I thought that was old, and Maria looked pretty damned good. She'd saved the fives and tens she'd earned as a young girl servicing horny Texans in a border town outside Brownsville. Saved enough to make her way across the border and rent an apartment and get a job putting together burritos in a side-street café. A cowboy with emphysema liked her beans and married her and brought her to Houston. She remained faithful as a pet to the guy till he died—smiling, according to the Chief—leaving her enough money to buy Boyds.

She seated us and asked our names. I told her mine. She moved her finger slowly across the cleft in my chin and said, "Cadete will be a good lover. He has a pussy in his chin." I turned red while the others laughed. She stared straight at me with a semi-serious, wise look and I could see she wasn't really joking. I hoped she was right. If I didn't get naked with a woman one of these days, though, what did it matter?

Maria served authentic, family-style Mexican food with lots of tortillas, plates of stringy beef and chicken, beans and rice, peppers and onions and cheese and olives. I mixed everything together on my plate, rolled it into a giant, floppy, flour tortilla, topped it with salsa and sour cream, and thought it the best meal I'd ever eaten. Closest thing to ethnic food I'd had before was Chef Boyardee ravioli. This was ten times better than that. The stringy meat had been marinated in vinegar and something spicy, and the beans were nothing like the Van Camps I'd grown up eating. None of it was like anything I'd eaten before. Maria poured rounds of tequila shooters from a jug with a little worm in it, while empty bottles of a Mexican beer called Del Negro stood like brown bowling pins at one end of the table. By the end of the meal, my head sweat from the peppers and my tongue stumbled from the tequila.

Dinner conversation ashore was different than on the ship. "Seamen afloat talk about women; ashore they talk about ships," said Don Campbell, whispering. "Just listen."

"We should make twenty knots, no problem," said the Chief.

"Calling fifteen ports in twenty-two days will be tough on sleep," added the mate.

"How long do we stay in Valpo?" asked the young third.

"Four days are scheduled," answered the purser. He looked over at me. "The sailors consider Valparaiso paradise. You cadets have to be careful in Valparaiso."

Everyone laughed knowingly, winked and elbowed one another. Wally and I just listened. There was much to learn and to understand—all the union practices and work-rules and company policies. The names of people from the industry got repeated so often they took on celebrity status—usually because of some outrageous behavior like drinking a fifth a day coupled with an uncanny ability to perform some shipboard task, like without ever looking at a cargo plan tell the mate exactly where some weird-shaped heavy lift should be stowed. There were names of cigar-smoking union bosses boarding at payoff to arm-twist the sailors into contributing to the political fund; names of cigar-smoking, pot-bellied port captains who made unannounced 5 p.m. visits to the ship to see if the mate was drunk; names of cigar-smoking, pot-bellied, scotch-guzzling port engineers who slipped bottles of Johnny Walker into Coast Guard inspectors' bags to ensure the ship sailed on time. Something about these ships and the people who worked them had the eerie feel of a parallel universe.

* * *

When we finished eating, we sauntered back into the bar like a posse of satisfied hombres. It was after nine, and the band was tuning their guitars. The barstools were mostly full and the rectangular wooden tables were filling up. Five or six Germans sat together belting out drinking songs. A group of Norwegian sailors, all with thin blond hair and blue eyes, argued loudly, arm-wrestling at another table. Single Americans or Brits in pairs sat on the barstools, smoking and talking quietly. Fletcher, the A.B. who hated me, sat next to two Brits near the corner where the bar jutted out into the dance floor. He said hello to the chief mate when we passed but turned his back on the rest of us.

Maria presided over the place from a raised dais behind the bar. Dressed in a green skirt frayed at the hem and a bright red blouse, she looked and acted like an Aztec Princess, barking at the waitresses, sliding beers the length of the bar, filling orders for the mixes to go with the hard-liquor customers had brown-bagged in. Small groups of unaccompanied women filtered through the door, sitting at the bar or sliding into one of the hard wooden booths along the wall. The room was large. We found an empty table near the center and sat. The chief and first engineers were whiskey drinkers and had brought Southern Comfort from the ship. The mate liked his scotch and ordered soda water to mix. Wally and I stuck with our Del Negros, but also belted back the bourbon the engineers kept in front of us.

The band wore black. Black hats, black belts, black boots, black shirts, and black jeans. Against the black were bright silver buttons or burnished silver buckles or silky silver bandannas. Their instruments were black and silver as well, and their hats had brims that extended six inches all around. The musicians were lanky—like Texans are supposed to be—except the bass man who was almost dwarfish. They finished tuning up and started playing and we settled in for the evening.

Men outnumbered women at least two to one. Most of the women were older than me, smoked with almost desperate motions of their fingers and red mouths, and were small around the middle with breasts that seemed too large. As a group, they had a thin-lipped, hard look I found kind of scary. I was getting bored listening to Wally rattle on about the condenser job he'd helped with that day when I noticed two girls and a short guy with a big cowboy hat enter. They sat at the end of our table. The cowboy was drunk and seemed angry. He kept turning to one of the girls, pounding his fist on the table and making loud comments like "—I don't give a damn about—" or "—don't you tell me—." Once I figured out which girl he was with, I walked over to ask the other to dance. Her name was Adeline. She wore a short skirt and white boots up to mid-calf. She might not have been beautiful, but in the dark bar with the evening and beer wearing on, she was plenty all right. Plus, she was more than happy to get away from the cowboy. After we danced a couple times, we sat by ourselves in an empty booth in the corner by the front door. Adeline couldn't say enough bad things about the cowboy. The "little bastard" was so jealous that Clementine, her older sister, could hardly answer the telephone without getting "the fourth degree." She was afraid to leave him even though he'd already "roughed her up" a couple times. Her mother had called the police once but the tone in Adeline's voice gave me the feeling her family had been down this road before.

"God, that man is so wound up tonight. Ah do not *know* what his problem is."

The evening wore on and Adeline and I got comfortable with each other. We pressed close during the slow dances and she had some moves during the fast ones I'd never seen at the sock

hops in my high school gym. In the booth, we graduated to sitting on the same side and kissing. She kept putting my hand on
her right breast, which made me nervous since Wally, who was
drunk and apparently had nothing better to do, pointed and
laughed every time it happened.

It was near midnight when I noticed the cowboy and
Adeline's sister dancing a slow dance. He looked ridiculous
being so short and wearing such a huge hat. Clementine was at
least as tall and wore boots with heels besides, so when they
danced what you saw was a short guy whose Stetson cut his partner in the neck.

The two English seamen and Fletcher laughed and carried
on. Everyone in the place was good and drunk. I'd watched
Fletcher some during the evening and noticed he had a disconcerting habit of facing one direction but looking at someone off
to one side or the other. As he whispered something to one of
the Brits, I could see his eyes were really looking out at the dance
floor. The Brit laughed, turned and said something as
Clementine and the cowboy danced by. The cowboy let go of
Clementine, grabbed the front of the Brit's shirt and jerked him
off the barstool. Maria got there amazingly fast and stepped
between the two of them with, of all things, a rolling pin. God
knows where she got it; most likely she kept it at hand beneath
the bar. Next thing we knew, the cowboy was out the door and
Clementine at our table.

"Son of a bitch," said Clementine, adjusting her tight, low-
cut blouse. "You see what he did, pickin' a fight with that cute
English guy just 'cause he noticed mah boobs. Now he's being
kicked out of a sailor's bar, no less."

"Ah'm stayin', Clem," said Adeline. "Ah will find my own
ride home. Ah am not getting into a truck with that little bastard
agin, and neither should you."

"Addy, what in the hell am I supposed to do? You know
what'll happen if I don't go home with him."

At that moment, the door, which was between us and the
band, swung open and the cowboy walked in. I don't know if
anyone but me saw him since the dance-floor was full but he was
a magnet for my eyes. In my lust-drunk stupor, my reactions
were slow and I didn't say anything about the cowboy reappear-

ing. The girls continued talking. As he crossed the floor toward
Fletcher and the two Brits, I noticed he held something big and
black in his hand. When I realized it was a gun, I raised my arm
to point, but froze; the yell I'd intended stuck and became a gasp
for air. A twilight zone amber light engulfed the scene and
movement became slow motion, high-noon clear. The two Brits
and Fletcher all twisted slowly and together like puppets and
looked directly at the cowboy. The Brit in the center, the one
who'd said something to the cowboy earlier, had what I thought
was a wise-ass, British look on his face. Fletcher had an honest-
to-God smile while the other Brit's face was distorted, I suppose,
with fear. The cowboy raised the gun, his mouth ugly with rage.
Maria loped toward them, panicked, her arm outstretched, a yell
on her lips. The band played a Merle Haggard tune, but when
the lead guitarist saw the weapon, his mouth, which had been
wide-open singing, stayed that way as the gun popped. I saw it
all. A small dark hole appeared in the seaman's forehead. I froze,
but others, less drunk or more experienced, moved quickly.
Don, the third mate, appeared out of nowhere, grabbed my
arm—still raised in a point—and led me out through the back
door where I bent and puked. Squad cars with lights flashing and
brakes squealing arrived as we got into the taxi that stopped for
us across the street. Next day, the Houston Post ran a short piece
on page seventeen about *another sailor murdered* at Boyds on
Navigation Avenue.

* * *

I'd never liked fighting in high school. Gene, my baseball
coach, once told me, "you'd a been a helluva athlete if you
had a little more fight in you." Seeing one man take the life
of another, seeing him raise that pistol as easily as he'd raise
his finger, hearing the pop of the gun the same instant as the
bullet smashed into the other guy's brain, haunted me and
for days after I felt like I'd been slugged in the gut. I had bad
dreams for the better part of a week—always with Fletcher
smiling his evil grin, looking out the side of his face. I promised myself one thing after that—I'd never hurt someone
because of a woman. Speaking of which, I wished I'd gotten

Adeline's phone number. I think she was up for some action, commitment or not.

Houston to Cristobal
July 26 - 29

The next morning, a dull, heavy pounding against my door woke me. I groaned and looked at my watch. Six-thirty. I closed my eyes. Wally yelled out "Yeah?" from the top bunk. The door flew open and I popped up, startled and awake. A hulking figure blocked the light from the hallway.

"All hands, cadet," said the man in a voice pitched ridiculously high.

"We're awake," I answered. He closed the door without a sound.

"What was that?" asked Wally.

"They call him Tiny Tim. He's an Ordinary Seaman."

"Extraordinary, I'd say. The guy blocks the whole door. What's he weigh, anyhow?"

Early morning conversation was the only source of conflict between Wally and me at this point in the trip. Wally woke up talking. I didn't. I ignored him, lay there a moment or two, then crawled out of my bunk and stepped into the head as if it was just another morning.

A vision surfaced of the murder I'd witnessed the night before. The short cowboy stood with his gun leveled at the British sailor seated on the corner barstool.

"Jesus, Wally. Remember last night?"

"Just what I was thinking about. Let's sail this big iron boat. We've had enough adventures for awhile."

"I came out here looking for adventure."

"Yeah, well, you've found it."

* * *

We were scheduled to sail at eight. All hands were called to turn to. Everyone had a job, even us lowly midshipmen. I did my bathroom routine, then dressed in clean khakis and walked across the foyer to the mate's office. He sat at his desk, knife out as usual, intently cutting something on his desk, oblivious to me. I looked at his desk, disgusted.

"Found it on the dock this morning," he said without looking up. "Couldn't resist dissecting the little critter."

I could see he had cut off the arms on the cockroach's right side and was watching as the bug pushed itself around in a circle using the appendages on its left side. The roach threatened to crab under a pile of papers, so the mate stabbed his knife once, twice, three times, through it's back into his desk. He looked up, grinning.

"I'm told you saw the shot last night."

"I did."

"Any bad dreams?"

"Reminded me of how we killed steers in the slaughterhouse. One shot between the eyes, the look of betrayal and the front legs crumpling. Had a little trouble going to sleep, but no dreams."

He looked at me a few seconds. "You were smart to leave the farm. No future shooting things in the head."

I looked down at the dead cockroach. His eyes followed mine.

"Not much future in this, either," he said. He looked at his knife then back at me.

"Can sailors carry guns?" I asked.

"Nope. Can't even have them aboard. The old man carries a pistol or two to protect himself from the crew but no one else can have a firearm. Not even me or the Chief. That's the law."

He extracted his knife from the body of the roach and

swiped the bug into his wastebasket.

"Glad I was there last night, though. What about you?"

I didn't answer. The guy was weird. He sent me to the bridge, which was my assigned station for mooring and unmooring. Mr. Potter, the crotchety second mate, was already there bustling about the wheelhouse.

"Grab the wheel, son," he said. "We're testing navigation gear. Make yourself useful."

I put both hands on the ship's wheel. It was like a steering wheel in a car but had spokes and was smaller in diameter. I turned it left till it stopped, then back hard over right, watching the rudder angle indicator above the forward windows move off zero or 'midships all the way to thirty-seven degrees, which is hard over. Mr. Potter snapped at me for allowing the rudder to travel all the way to its stop, saying, "don't two-block the rudder or we'll have to call for a diver." I thought to myself if that's the case, why is it designed and built to travel thirty-seven degrees? But what did I know? I was only a cadet. Under Mr. Potter's close supervision—and I do mean close—I moved the short red levers in the wheelhouse and on both bridge wings from left to right causing the deep-throated whistle to blow. He cursed me roundly for not knowing how to brew coffee. Seemed like everything was so damned specific on a ship. Do one thing just a little differently and all hell broke loose. I had never made nor drunk coffee, so how was I to know you put in ten of the little red caps of grounds for a twelve-cup pot? The five capfuls I'd used made something that looked to me like coffee—not "virgin piss" as he called it.

Mr. Potter told me to run up the flags for sailing. I hadn't a clue what to do.

"Young man, is this your first ship?"

"Yes sir, it is."

"All right then, why didn't you tell me? You can't be expected to know anything. I will however expect you to pay attention to what I tell you."

He pointed toward the pigeonholes that ran across the wheelhouse just above head-level aft of where the helmsman stood.

"Get the pilot flag. *Hotel.* There in the *H* hole."

I pulled a red and white flag out of the pigeonhole marked *Hotel.*

"Go run it up on the offshore side."

His detailed instructions continued and soon I was on the port bridge wing shielding my eyes as I looked at the flags crackling at their halyards in the stiff breeze. I walked to the edge and looked down, surprised at how high above main deck I was. A parade of crewmembers was coming aboard then, saying last goodbyes before the ship sailed foreign. Women accompanied some: wives or girlfriends, I figured—maybe even a mother or two. A few kids walked as far as the gate with their seaman dad, then sheepishly bid him farewell. The women all cried through their goodbyes but I sensed one or two weren't that unhappy to see her man walk away. I saw Don Campbell, the third mate, dressed in jeans and a white shirt. An attractive black-haired woman held his hand in one of hers, her other hand clutched tightly by a pretty little girl. A boy two or three inches taller than his sister held Don's other hand. I was only fifty yards away, so I could see plainly as he picked up his son, hugged him, set him down, did the same with his daughter, then turned his attention to his wife. The kids seemed to be giggling, but even from a distance, I could see tears streaking the woman's face. She and Don embraced and stood motionless as a sculpture. Then she pushed him away, turned, grabbed one hand from each of the children and walked toward the parking lot, never looking back. Don stood there a moment as if counting their footsteps, then turned heavily, adjusted a brown shoulder bag, and trudged through the gate toward the ship.

The pilot, a heavy-set, red-faced man, arrived on the bridge at seven-thirty sharp, wheezing and blowing like a bad lawnmower. The Captain shook his hand and told him to "go get your eggs, Mr. Pilot." I took him down so I could eat as well. The saloon bustled with people hurrying to sail. After two long weeks on the coast, the ship was full of cargo, fuel, lubes, fresh water, and victuals—full and down, the mate said—and ready to sail foreign. Harry, the black waiter with fuzzy white hair, wore a spotless serving jacket stiff with starch. He was a nervous man who did an obsequious little two-step shuffle when he took orders or served food. This morning, with the saloon full of officers, plus a pilot, a port captain and a port engineer, Harry was beside himself. He shuffled before passing through the swinging door into the galley. He shuffled at every table and even shuffled once in the middle of the floor as though a thought had caught up to his feet. He got orders wrong on normal mornings. Today, with a full house, it was a disaster. I ate my eggs scrambled even though I always ordered over easy since I liked slopping up yoke with toast. The pilot just shrugged and reached for the syrup when he got hotcakes instead of oatmeal.

When we finished eating, I escorted the pilot back up the seven flights of stairs to the bridge. It was slow going since we had to stop at each landing while the pilot caught his breath and complained about no elevator and bad feet. Once we made the bridge, the pilot collapsed into the captain's chair, a big-armed thing, padded, and covered with yellow naughahyde sitting on a four-inch steel pole that extended up out of the deck. He gestured toward a dark, early morning thundercloud drifting in from the southwest. I stepped out onto the bridge wing with the bell-book in hand, ready to keep engine-order times and note tugs names and navigation markers and anything out of the ordinary. Mr. Potter had written out strict instructions for proper bell-book keeping and I knew he would check my work closely. I peered over the railing down sixty feet to the main deck. The booms were cradled, but the decks were littered with dunnage and lashing scraps—the larger pieces, according to the mate, to be stacked for use in the backload ports, the smaller chunks jettisoned at sea.

As I watched, the sailors and mates swarmed out of the house like a police squad—a dozen or more—some moving toward the bow, others to the stern to undock. Tiny Tim, the giant ordinary seaman, followed the gang out the door by sixty seconds or so. Once outside, he stopped, looked forward and aft, drained one beer then another, tossed the bottles over the side and lumbered forward. I wondered briefly if I should mention it to someone, but decided against it.

The captain, wearing four gold bars on his shoulders, and the pilot with a black beret he'd taken from his bag and set rakishly on his head, their knowledge and experience Godlike in my estimation, walked together out of the wheelhouse near to where I stood on the starboard bridge wing. The sailors took lines from the tugs both forward and aft. The captain gave the order to single up. Lines were slacked, their eyes tossed off bollards by the linehandlers ashore, then one by one winched aboard. Soon only a headline and a spring were attached to the dock forward and a stern line and spring aft.

The rain cloud had moved over the harbor and an offshore breeze rattled the flags on their halyards. I felt the first drops on my face and closed the bell book around my pencil to keep the page from getting wet. The captain ordered, "let go all lines" over the P.A. mike, and the pilot told the tugs to take in the slack and be ready to heave the ship off the dock. Minutes later, after hearing "last line" and "all clear" from both the bow and the stern over the bridge loudspeaker, the tugs responded to the pilot's orders by whistling and tightening their towlines. The rain fell harder and a bolt of lightning flashed followed quickly by a clap of thunder. The captain and pilot walked into the wheelhouse. I followed and closed the door to the bridge wing, almost breathless with anticipation. We were sailing for Panama. Sailing to a foreign port named Cristobal and then on to other ports whose names I couldn't even pronounce. Knowing the ropes were cast off; seeing the berth move away as the tugs pulled us out; feeling the power burst as the engine came half-astern—all those things produced in me not only a powerful sense of freedom, but also an unsettling sensation of uncertainty. I had never before not had my feet on firm ground.

* * *

Thus began my life as a mariner, with lightning flashing and thunder cracking. The wind blew around the points of the compass as the storm cloud flew over the harbor like a wraith trailing a sheet. The pilot worked the tugs at full power to keep the ship steady in the turning basin. Once we were turned, we let go the tugs. The pilot ordered half ahead and we picked our way in and out of traffic down the Ship Channel and through Galveston. At the sea buoy, the captain shook the pilot's hand and signed his slip. The pilot ducked his head and one shoulder into the carry-

ing-strap of his bag and I escorted him down the outside ladders
to the main deck. He climbed hand over hand down the pilot
ladder that lay flat against the ship's side, surprisingly quick considering his bulk, then stepped nimbly into his boat, turned and
gave a full-arm wave up at the captain eighty-five feet above him
on the bridge wing. From that moment, we were on our own. A
small group of men—and one manly woman named Betty who
helped cook—protected from an unfriendly environment by a
hull of thin steel. As the pilot's launch dieseled away, I sensed an
almost palpable sigh of relief from the two able-bodied seamen
leaning against the rail. The rain-cloud flew away east, fresh sea
air blew across the ship and a half-rainbow formed, one end of it
touching the breakwater, the other disappearing somewhere in
the Gulf of Mexico.

* * *

The mate directed me to work on deck that afternoon
with Boss Jones, the boatswain. He was a tall, shirtless black
man whose muscles rippled across his broad shoulders and
long arms and through his stomach. His face was long—
almost horsy—with long teeth and a broad nose. He looked
to be in his mid-fifties, but powerful, with a younger man's
confidence.

Boss Jones had sailed boatswain for nearly thirty years.
He always sailed with Captain Isenhagen even though the
two men were seldom seen together. Boss Jones assigned me
to work with two sailors off the 12 to 4 watch: an ancient
black man named Irving Jackson and Fletcher, a man I did-
n't like, and even feared.

We tossed dunnage over the side, tightened the turnbuckles on the lifeboat falls, lashed the gangway and stowed
mooring lines. The mate, I discovered later, made his rounds
also—alone. He rifled through the rooms and lockers looking for booze. Whatever he found—beer, whiskey, or gin—
he hauled out and tossed over the side. Later, after things
had returned to normal, Boss Jones said, "The man got a
mean Baptist streak in him."

The captain, on the other hand, raised in Europe,

believed men needed a glass or two in their day, didn't really even trust a man who wouldn't take a drink. But he was busy with navigation and communication matters that morning, and had no idea of the havoc about to be effected on his ship and crew by this new mate.

* * *

I was unprepared for the peacefulness of being at sea—particularly after all the excitement in port. Although the water appeared flat calm, the ship moved through it with a rocking motion like a tended cradle. I'd never slept better. The food was good enough—meat, potatoes, gravy, limp vegetables—and plenty of it. I stepped outside regularly to expand my lungs with the sea-air that seemed scrubbed and bubbly—nothing like the burnt plains dust the wind whirled around where I grew up. I once thought the wind at home, dry and hot out of the south during the summer and a biting howler from the north when the days turned short, was why the men in my town drank too much. One couldn't just walk outside into something pleasant. The summer sun fried the dusty air; the wind drove it through one's clothing, into one's pores where it became mud. The Nebraska winter was like living in a freezer, the wind forcing the frigid air into openings in one's clothing or through the layers of Melton wool we called coats. I figured if I could breathe in a few draughts of sea-air every day for the rest of my life, other problems would just disappear.

Of all the subjects I had to study on this ship—Rules of the Road, Ship Construction, Cargo Operations, and others—Navigation interested me most. When the pilot-boat was clear of our ship, we set a course of Southeast or one hundred thirty five degrees to run along a track drawn on the chart by the second mate from Galveston Sea Buoy to the Yucatan Channel. By the time I came up on watch early the next morning, we could no longer see land; only water and sky, and a pencil-line dividing the two. No buoys, no lighthouses, no point of land, nothing. There was a purity out here—visual and otherwise—I would never have imagined.

The celestial navigation portion of my sea project required

me to shoot morning and evening stars and, when I could work it into my schedule, noon. Then there were daily azimuths and amplitudes to measure compass error, sun-lines with running fixes, occasional sights of the moon and planets and Polaris just so we'd know how difficult the solutions to those were. I'd done well in navigation class at school, but now that I was confronted by a practical application of that knowledge, I knew I hadn't learned enough. I spent my first watch poring through formulas in Bowditch, then familiarizing myself with the tables from the Nautical Almanac, H.O. 214 and H.O. 249. As I understood it, the theory of celestial navigation went something like this: in the middle of the ocean, no land in sight, the navigator imagines the stars and planets on something called the Celestial Sphere. Earth is a sphere also, a sphere in the center of the Celestial Sphere, which rotates around an axis that extends north to Polaris and south through some very distant point. The Celestial Sphere rotates in the opposite direction to the earth and therein lies the navigator's challenge—to measure the exact position of a heavenly body at an exact moment in time—something navigators couldn't do before the invention of the accurate chronometer.

Practically, it works like this: the navigator measures the altitude of, say, the sun, notes the exact time of the sight, then does certain mathematical calculations. The results allow him to bring the sun down from the celestial sphere to earth, plant it in a particular place on the earth—as though it were a lighthouse—corresponding to its position on the celestial sphere at the exact moment its altitude was measured, then take a bearing on that lighthouse and draw a Line of Position. One's ship lay somewhere on that Line of Position which, unfortunately, is quite long—roughly as long as the world is round. Where two Lines of Position cross, a fix results. As I would learn later in the voyage, the more Lines of Position the navigator lays down, the more confident he or she feels about knowing the true position of the vessel. Three, as it turned out, is a minimum standard.

On the second day, I brought my sextant to the bridge. I carried it in a varnished wooden box a foot by a foot by six inches deep, which I set on the chart table and opened. Letters etched in white into the black index arm read *U.S. NAVY, BUREAU OF SHIPS, E.T.S. SEXTANT, MARK 2, MOD. O.* The telescope was stowed separate from the sextant. It was about ten inches long and screwed into the adjustable collar in line with the horizon glass. It was an "erect image type" and had a spiral focusing mechanism I adjusted for my right eye. The sextant frame was triangular. The lower arm, called the limb, was cut with notches or teeth, each of which represented one degree of arc. The tangent screw engaged the teeth and was released from them when the index arm moved. The micrometer drum turned for finer gradations of minutes and seconds. The index mirror mounted on the index arm, the horizon glass on the frame. Both were fitted with adjustable sun-filters. The handle was designed to be held in the right hand while altitude adjustments were made with the left.

I took it out of its box, fitted the telescope, swung the arm back and forth, turned the micrometer, and polished the dust off the filters and the mirrors. Mr. Potter watched me but didn't say anything at first. I set it down carefully on the chart desk, as if it were something magic.

"OK, son," said Mr. Potter. "There it is. That's what keeps you and me and the Captain one rung above the sailors and the engineers. Let's take the error out and teach you how to use it."

In spite of significant effort, after two days I had little in the way of usable navigation to show for my work. I liked the mathematics—called spherical trigonometry—and loved learning the mythology and astrological significance of the star placements. Practically though, I struggled. By the end of the second day, I laid down a two-star fix. My Lines of Position (LOP's) came from Aldebaran, the blazing red Follower of Pleiades, the seven sisters; and Canopus, a bright blue-diamond once worshiped as a God by ancient Egyptians. They crossed five miles south of our track—and seven miles south and east of Mr. Potter's five star pinwheel. The captain grunted when he saw my position. He grabbed my navigation notebook and looked at my sight reduction for Canopus.

July 27	Canopus
GMT	8h 24m 03s
8h 20m	15° 18'

4m 03s	1° 01'
GHA Aries	16° 19'
assumed longitude	92° 41'E
LHA Aries	144° 00'
AL	35° 00'N
Hc	55° 45'
Ho	55° 50'
A	5T aL 35° 00'N
Zn	233° assumed longitude 92° 41' E

"A two star fix iss not as good as a three star fix," he said finally, setting down my book and fixing me with his gaze. "But it iss a beginning. I am pleased to see you put on the chart what your numbers tell you—regardless how far away from the second mate's position. Do not cheat or lie at navigation. It iss far too important. If you do not know where the ship is, say so."

* * *

My idyllic notion of life at sea came to an abrupt and startling end our second day out. The story, pieced together from hearsay is this: Captain Isenhagen received a call sometime after midnight from the boatswain who told him that Tiny Tim O'Brien, 4 to 8 Ordinary Seaman, "has got a fireaxe and is going room to room looking for something to drink. The crew has barricaded themselves in their messroom. One man is missing. Young Tommy Michaelson, the eight to twelve Ordinary. We believe Tim has got hisself a hostage."

The captain called the mate on the phone and told him that since he had thrown everyone's booze over the side, he could go ahead and handle this problem himself. The mate came directly to our room—it was 2:20 a.m.—knocked on the door and opened it. He entered quickly and closed the door behind him, startling me awake.

"Did you say you're looking for volunteers to help tie down a three-hundred pound sailor with a fireaxe and a hostage who's smashing doors in the crew's quarters?" asked Wally, able to go from snoring to intelligent conversation in the flicker of an eyelid.

"That's right, fellahs. We got us a wildman down there and someone's got to round him up."

"Tell you what, Mr. Mate," said Wally, who didn't work for him, would not receive a fitness report from him, had already taken a dislike toward him, and had a penchant for sarcasm. "This doesn't sound like a job for an engine cadet. Fact is, it doesn't sound like a job for a deck cadet either. Sounds to me like a job for about six large men with machine guns. I'm going back to sleep, and I advise Jake to do the same."

I smiled at Wally's retort and shook my head.

"I'll help you, Mate," I mumbled.

"All right, cadet, come to my office when you're up."

"Take your key," said Wally, "Cause that door's gonna be locked tight as the hand-hold plates on a boiler soon as you walk out."

I dressed quickly and left my room. The lock clicked the instant I closed the door. I walked across the foyer to the mate's room. Mr. Hunt was busy gathering materials. He handed me a small coil of rope and a medicine bottle he'd taken from the hospital. I opened the bottle and sniffed. It was filled with whiskey. He carried another medicine bottle with whiskey in it and slipped a set of handcuffs into his front pocket. I was glad to see he left his knife sitting on the desk.

We left his office and cautiously descended the stairs. Two levels down, in the crew's quarters, we saw damage. Doors fireaxed open hung ajar on broken hinges. A bloodstain ran along the light green bulkhead at elbow level like a red stripe. The mate instructed me to lead the way, but I deferred to him.

"He might listen to you, mate. No one's gonna listen to a cadet." My opinion of this mate was falling fast.

"All right." he said. "Follow me. And don't be afraid to give him that whiskey if he charges us."

The mate walked cautiously forward. His words "charges us" gave me pause, but I followed him anyway. Each room showed evidence of a mad search. Clothes, mattresses, pictures, sheets—everything helter-skelter. The mirrored doors off the medicine cabinets were ripped open and small containers of Colgate and aspirin and Vitalis lay scattered about as though a windstorm had blown through the shelves of a small pharmacy.

"Looks like Tim got the mouthwash and cologne," the mate whispered.

"What?" I tried to figure.

"Those things both have alcohol in them," he said without looking back. "That's what a drunk on a ship goes for when he thinks all the booze is gone. I've seen it before." He seemed to enjoy this.

At the end of the passageway, he slowed his pace and motioned me to do the same. He poked his head around the corner and drew an audible breath. "Kee-rist, will you look at this."

I looked. The corridor was trashed; the doors axed open. Clothes and mattresses lay scattered in the middle of the hallway; patches of blood stained the walls. Tim was most likely somewhere in this passageway since the messroom was at the end of the hall and the door to that, as the captain had told us, was blocked.

We crept forward, the mate with his handcuffs, me with my rope; both of us holding bottles of whiskey like offerings to a god. Focsle by focsle, we made our way, peering cautiously into each room. We passed the 4 to 8 AB's room. No one there. Then the ordinary seaman's room, then the 12 to 4 AB's room, then the quartermaster's room. All seemed empty although I kept expecting Tim to jump out of one we'd already passed—behind me—trapping us between him and the blocked door to the messroom. I hedged by waiting for the mate to pass a doorway before creeping up to look inside.

The 8 to 12 ordinary seaman's room was next to the blocked messroom door. That Ordinary's name was Tommy Michaelson. He was my age, more or less, with long blond hair. He had walked up the gangway in New Orleans just ahead of me and was making his first trip to sea also. We had talked, one night on the bridge, when he came up with a new can of Folger's and a bottle of Pine-sol for cleaning. He asked me about my job. I told him. He asked how one became a cadet. "By going to a maritime academy," I said. He had never graduated from high school though. Besides, Louise Boudreaux, his girlfriend in La Porte, Texas was pregnant.

The mate and I continued forward, looking, I figured, like a pantomime from a cheap thriller. Midway down the corridor, the mate held up his left hand to signal I should stop.

"Listen."

Sure enough, I could hear labored breathing coming from the end of the passageway.

"He's in Michaelson's room," said the mate. I hated to think about what we find there.

We inched forward. The breathing grew louder. The breaths were fast and raspy—like a file on metal. The mate raised his voice.

"Tim, this is the chief mate. I want you to come out of that room with your arms in the air. You are in a lot of trouble. The coast guard will investigate this and you'll probably be put in jail. Do you understand?"

I don't know how Tim felt about that, but I thought it was a stupid thing to say to a large and dangerous animal still carrying a weapon.

The hacksaw breathing stopped but the silence following was worse. We were two feet from the room now and I was terrified. The mate reached the doorway and peered around the sill, past the door that lay on its side half in and half out of the passageway.

"Oh Christ," he said.

Being taller, I looked over the top of his head. Tim sat, naked, folds of flesh glistening with sweat, in the middle of the room on Tommy Michaelson's arm, which was, thank God, still attached to Tommy's body. Tim cradled the fireaxe in his lap. He appeared to smile, as if that would make up for his transgressions. His eyes were small and swine-like, but dilated. His thin blond hair was plastered down the sides of his head and across his face. Blood was spattered about him, particularly on his hands and arms.

"Mate, get this elephant off me," Michaelson said. He sounded more angry than hurt.

"Tim, get off Michaelson and put down that goddamn fireaxe," instructed the mate. Tim stared back blankly.

Mr. Hunt said, "You do what I say and you won't get hurt. First, stand up. Slowly, now. Do what I say, Tim, and I'll give you whiskey."

Whiskey. Magic word.

Tim grinned weirdly. He set the axe down gently as if, after destroying half the ship, he suddenly was afraid of breaking something. He stood, surprisingly agile, put his hands under Tommy Michaelson's shoulders and picked him up as easily as if he were a doll.

"Let me go, you goddamn gorilla. You're just an ordinary seaman like me," said Michaelson.

Tim's lips twisted and he let go of Michaelson's arm. Michaelson ran past me and the mate, down the passageway and around the corner. His arm and shoulder were blood-soaked, but he ran fine. I figured if a wild-eyed lunatic with a fireaxe had just released me, I'd run pretty well too. I turned to watch him, glad he was free, wondering what it had been like being held hostage.

Tim moved toward us and I instinctively backed away. The mate had not bothered to tell me where we were taking this monster. I held the whiskey in front of me just in case Tim got past Mr. Hunt. We were a strange sight, I figure, me and the mate moving slowly, step by step, backward, each of us holding up a small bottle of brown liquid as a naked giant, blubbering spittle from his mouth, grunting and gurgling, flabby arms outstretched, pleading for the whiskey, matched our pace step by step by step as we rounded the corner and continued down the passageway.

"Go open up the hospital," said the mate suddenly.

It was on the next deck up, the business deck, where the purser had his office. I left the mate and ran up the stairs, then realized I didn't have a key, so ran back down to Mr. Hunt who removed the keys from his belt loop and handed them to me without turning around. I ran up and unlocked the door. The mate was right behind me with Tim after him, hands out-stretched, whimpering. Mr. Hunt led Tim into the hospital and handed him the whiskey like a bone to a good dog. Tim stood beside us now, which felt very weird—like watching a movie and having the actor, who just happens to be a crazed killer—jump off the screen and into the next seat. Sweat splattered off him like raindrops and his odor was disgusting. He blubbered like a baby as he lifted his large head and drained the whiskey. It was enough to make me seriously consider quitting drinking.

"Now, lay on that bed, Tim. We have to handcuff you."

As his body adjusted to the alcohol, Tim regained a semblance of humanness.

"Mate, I'm all right now. I just can't live without a drink now and then. I'm addicted. Every man in my family is addicted to alcohol."

The way he said that sounded kind of reasonable, and really sad. I couldn't help but think of the men in my town who struggled to keep jobs and family together, acting like drunkenness was natural as a head cold.

"Lay down now, Tim. I got to strap you to this table."

I thought the mate was making another huge mistake here so I started backing toward the door. I figured you offer a gorilla a banana you might get him back into his cage, but talking him into lying down so you can tie him up is another matter altogether. With two days left till Panama, I'd have kept Tim nice and tipsy, then let the authorities have him. Turned out the captain agreed with me. He stood in the doorway with the purser and the boatswain behind him. He wore heavy black boots and a pistol in a holster on his belt. Authority dripped off him and he had a German accent besides.

"Mr. Mate, you vill please give Tim a bottle of whiskey and ve shall leave him here in the hospital. Do not strap him down."

"Captain, I can't give him a whole bottle."

"Then you vill join Tim on his plane ride home from Panama."

"Cadet, go get that bottle of Jim Beam from my bar," said Mr. Hunt.

When I returned, Tim sat smoking a cigarette, a towel covering his lap. I thought he looked like a regular guy, just really big and stupid. George LeClair was rummaging through the cabinets for Merthiolate to treat Tommy Michaelson's wounds. The captain stood off to the side, motionless but observant. We filled Tim's bottle with whiskey. The mate promised he'd have food delivered and would bring more liquor any time he called. The purser took what he needed and locked the cabinets. We left Tim alone in

the room and closed the door. The boatswain posted a man
to stand by with a radio in case there was trouble or Tim
needed something.

* * *

Two days later, on a dazzling blue sky blue water morning
with shimmering drops of crystal spray shooting up off the glistening white rocks of the breakwater, flying red, yellow and blue
flags from our halyards, we steamed like a victory parade past
Cristobal Mole and tied up. A doctor and two security guards
boarded with the agent. I stood, quietly watching, as, a few minutes later, Tim stumbled down the gangway, handcuffed, one
guard in front of him, the other behind, his head forward looking at the rungs, his life, in my opinion, wasted.

Cristobal, Panama
July 30

Except for the doctor, the two hulking security guys with pistolas on their belts, and the agent—one Fernando Estaban who I would get to know better northbound when it was me with trouble—no one boarded the ship at Cristobal until Tiny Tim, shackled and manacled, took his last walk down our gangway. The sailors lined the rail like the brothers of the sea they were. They seemed to bear little ill will toward the huge man for breaking up their quarters and terrorizing the ship, although no one said much beyond, "luck, brother." Paul Hunt, the mate, had the good sense to stay out of sight.

I thought of myself as I watched Tiny Tim stumble off; of my dad silent and grim after my flare-up with the priest, driving me south of town, stopping and silently waiting, staring at the broken white lines along highway ninety-two till I got out. Of my mom sitting crying, little pieces of her heart scattered around my room along with singleton socks, broken pencils and a couple of empty Pepsi bottles.

I had fifty miles to hitchhike to Grand Island where I could catch the bus to Omaha. Only thing he said was "don't come home until you can fit in better." Until I learn to drink more, I thought, but didn't say anything. Didn't even say goodbye. Got out of the car, pulled my bags out, turned and walked up the road while he sat there, watching me. Drinking gin, I figured. Thinking to himself he'd failed again.

As the agent helped Tiny Tim into the police vehicle, I vowed I'd never again leave in disgrace. The car with Tiny Tim drove away and out of the blue, a memory I thought I'd erased forever crowded my mind like an unwelcome guest. I was ten, walking past the feed store the Saturday morning my dad was fired. I was collecting for the Omaha World Herald and stood across the street behind a flowering crabapple when it happened. Dad drank then too, although he was young and good-looking and thought he could get away with it. Thought throwing ninety mile an hour fastballs for the town team would protect him. He stormed out of the Feed Store, looked up and down the street, muttered something and marched back in. Seconds later, he was back out, this time with Roger McCluskey, the owner, behind him. Roger was the kindest man in town, so I knew this couldn't be easy for him. Roger kept putting a hand to Dad's shoulder. Finally, Dad walked away. Walked to his car, got in and squealed tires driving away.

* * *

I glanced at my watch. Eight-thirty. Morning in Cristobal. Below, on the wharf, crowds of longshoremen created a complex roar that rose to the deck. With Tim gone, the hoards of smallish, brown-skinned fellows climbed single-file up the gangway. Each wore flip-flops and carried over his shoulder a purse woven from strands of old mooring line dyed blue or red or yellow or green as though the color brown—their color—was unacceptably plain. I stood gaping. Cristobal was my first foreign port on my first foreign voyage; these stevedores my first foreign people.

I walked up a flight of stairs to the mate's cargo office, the cubicle perched just above main deck on the port side of the ship, designed to make him as accessible as possible while the longshoremen worked cargo. Mr. Hunt sat surrounded by people, everyone talking at once. He spotted me, waved me over, said a few words and sent me on deck with an abrupt gesture of his cigar. I was to help the third mate open hatch covers. Our cargo for Panama was in holds two, three, four and five plus some guns in the special locker in number one. Mr. Petrocelli, the 8 to 12 third mate, overweight, bald on top with clownish tufts of black and gray hair above his ears—bullied his way through the crowd of longshoremen like a whale through a school of fish. I followed directly in his wake. When we reached the masthouse for number two, he struggled up the ten-foot vertical ladder, grunting and complaining. Once on top, he unlocked the control box and moved the levers while I watched the heavy metal hatch-cover split at its seam, the two parts buckling, the center lifting and the whole apparatus rolling aft. My job was to holler if the wheels came off the track.

After opening that one hatch, Mr. Petrocelli decided I was probably trained well enough to operate the controls myself. From that point on, I climbed the sides of the resistor houses while he stayed on deck, smoking his beloved Marlboros and issuing constant instruction to me and everyone else who came within earshot.

* * *

I had spent much of the past two days in serious consultation with Don Campbell, the 12 to 4 third mate I was coming to regard as my closest friend on the ship besides Wally. He advised me about sex in Panama, sex in Buenaventura, sex in Callao, sex in Valparaiso and sex in general. Embarrassed, I told him I was a virgin and appreciated when he didn't laugh. He told me a little about his first time; that it had been in a whorehouse in New Orleans. Maybe it wasn't so odd after all, I thought, this business of a young man paying for his first time. He was full of what I thought sensible, manly advice.

"Don't worry too much about catching that first dose of clap," he said. "Most everyone in this business gets at least one dose. It's not much worse than a cold what with the antibiotics they've got today.

"Always take a bottle of beer up to the girl's room with you. Use it to clean up with afterward. Safer than the damned sewage they call water around here.

"Don't get too drunk or you'll wake up broke—I gay-ron-tee. Stay aware of where you are and what's going on. Besides, contrary to what you might believe, the less alcohol you drink, the more fun you'll have in bed.

"Don't, for Christ's sake, lose your head when you fall in love. And don't look at me like it won't happen. If you don't fall in love with one of these senoritas down here, you're a cold-hearted son of a bitch. Happens to everybody at your age. Mine too. Just don't do something stupid like miss the ship and get married. No matter how strong that passion is, believe me when I tell you it'll wear off—and a lot sooner than you'd like to imagine.

"Watch your money or the slimy hand of a pimp will get it. Keep most of it in a side pocket or a shoe. And no matter what, keep a twenty in the *other* shoe for taxi fare back to the ship."

I wanted to ask really basic how-to questions and even tried but Don brushed them aside.

"You'll figure it out," he said. "And if you can't, the girls will enjoy teaching you. That's the beauty of paying for it when you're young—you have fun and learn something to boot. Shame there's not something similar for women."

I thought a lot about Melissa, how she kept telling me her love would redeem me, that if I loved her, the sex would free me from the confines of this culture of rural Catholicism. I didn't see any real point to the love part, though. I thought sex ought to be enough. Melissa didn't quite see it that way. She was younger than me but had tried casual sex. Decided she needed some commitment. Something at least resembling commitment. Like the stripper I'd walked home. Maybe like most women. But, again, what did I know?

* * *

I stayed busy on the ship all that morning. After the hatch-lids were opened, the mate handed me the key to the special locker in the forward end of number one upper 'tween deck where we carried the surface mail plus small lots of high-value cargoes including a shipment of guns and ammunition. Several broad-shouldered men in tight olive-green with blue berets worn smartly over the left eye showed up at the cargo office around nine with documentation. They were all taller and bigger than the average Panamanian—almost a different race. They accompanied me up the port side through the watertight doorway into the forepeak, then through the double locked door into the iron-mesh special cargo locker. I had a copy of the manifest showing exactly how many pieces were there, how many rounds of ammunition, what caliber and everything else I needed to know. The cargo was padlocked in wooden boxes small enough for two strong men to comfortably lift and carry by the stout metal handles fitted into a recess in each end of the box. The manifest showed we had two hundred Colt forty-fives—not exactly rabbit guns—plus several miscellaneous pieces along with the leather holsters and ammunition to go with them. The men with me were impatient and pushy, and I surprised myself by growling at them when more than two tried to enter the locker at one time. This wasn't a neighborhood grocery. Seemed a little odd the mate had entrusted me, a green midshipman, to do this job alone. But then, after the Tiny Tim fiasco, nothing he did surprised me too much.

By 11:30, all the guns and ammunition were signed for and off the ship. After lunch, the chief mate told me to see if Don Campbell, who was on watch, needed anything. If he didn't, I was free to go ashore. Don and I went to the bridge while the longshoremen scooted down the gangway for their mid-day siesta. In the chartroom, Don pulled the harbor chart out of the chart desk, flopped it open on the chart table, and showed me exactly which berth we were tied up to. He penciled in the specific path I was to take to get to the best whorehouse. By the time he finished, I was confident I couldn't possibly get lost. He suggested I go early to beat the rush and "get the lady of your dreams."

* * *

A thundercloud rose up around two and drenched Cristobal while I slept. I was vaguely aware of the wind whipping raindrops against my window. Shortly past three, I woke, showered, pulled on clean underwear and white jeans that I discovered later were too tight, stuffed the forty dollars I'd drawn from Mr. LeClair into my pocket and ran down the gangway three steps at

a time. The longshoremen were massing on the dock in preparation to board for their afternoon shift. I walked past the bow
where I looked up at Don Campbell, who was leaning over the
side checking headlines, half his body visible above the rail.

"Protect you, my son," he shouted, making an exaggerated
blessing with his right hand.

I smiled and waved, thinking I still needed to deal with the
question of sin and guilt, but figured I would have the opportunity soon enough. I turned left into an alleyway between two of
the warehouses and headed toward the gate. Water from the
afternoon downpour glistened on the asphalt. The sun beat with
renewed vigor and the heat had already built back up as though
no rain had fallen. Lavender and bright yellow flowers—wild
orchids—grew from every crevice in the asphalt. A faint stench
of rotting vegetation mixed with the smell of sewage.

The gate into and out of the port was manned by a young
guard—he looked like a boy—wearing a uniform similar to those
worn by the men who had taken the guns off the ship. He sat on
a chair in front of a pink stucco building joined to a similar building across the road by a heavy iron gate hooked open so vehicles
and pedestrians could pass. He read a newspaper and looked at
me, his dark eyes round and bright, as I walked by holding up
my shore pass. He held his fingers to his lips and shrugged, asking for a cigarette. I motioned to him I didn't smoke. He
shrugged again and resumed reading.

Outside the gate, I looked around and tried to visualize the
chart Don had marked up. In front of me stretched a street with
large stucco buildings, some white, others yellow or pink. I
walked past them. The signs above the doors indicated they were
used as agencies for shipping companies. One was a customs
office. Uniformed men lolled in front smoking, sardonic looks in
their eyes, guns that resembled my old single-shot four-ten leaning almost too casually against the side of the building.

Don had told me the bar I should go to—it had the most
beautiful women, he said—was the Texas Bar. I knew it was just
up the street to my right, but I felt rich with time. I don't know
if it was fear of intimacy or curiosity about the newness of this
strange city or what, but I decided to wait—at least till dark—
and go exploring instead of whoring.

So, rather than turn right onto a street that would have taken me directly to the Texas Bar, I turned left and walked down an alley bustling with shops and vendors with pushcarts selling jewelry and skewers of meat and cold drinks. One shop sold radios and electronic goods from Japan; another displayed bright cotton dresses from India; a third was stuffed floor to ceiling with Panamanian crafts. There were others, all operated by dark-skinned, black-haired people I figured to be Indians from India. Seemed curious they would operate stores in Panama. I spent an hour wandering through the shops—buying nothing, of course, since my meager funds were earmarked for something far more important than trinkets. I was fascinated by the Panamanian handicrafts, in particular the colorful Molas, a reverse-appliqué cloth, roughly fifteen inches by twenty, sewed by Indian women from the San Blas islands, used as clothing in place of painting their bodies—a cultural improvement brought them by Catholic missionaries. I decided if I had any money left Northbound, I'd buy these as gifts.

Finally, tired of shopping, I continued up the street to a plaza. There was a large church, a couple of government buildings, food stalls, more small shops.

People congregated on the benches or stood in groups talking to their neighbors. I changed some dollars for black market balboa with a young man who acted like he could get me anything, so long as it was illegal. Then, thinking to explore further, I picked an avenue that looked interesting and charged ahead.

Streets in Cristobal radiate out from the port and from the various plazas. The street I'd chosen went straight briefly, but soon curved, first to the right, then to the left, then again to the right. Thinking to make my way toward the Texas Bar, I turned off the street on which I had departed the plaza, then turned again off that street. Finally, I admitted to being completely lost.

The sun was setting as I walked—sweating profusely now—into another plaza. Long red and purple rays of sunlight beamed horizontally between the church and the vicarage and illuminated an open-air café where old men sat on crude benches in sleeveless under-shirts and straw fedoras, smoking. I bought some cooked meat skewered onto a stick from a man with a wooden cart that had a built-in charcoal brazier—but no refrigeration that I could see. My first bite was hot and spicy and I considered for a moment whether I was eating dog or goat or rat or crocodile. It was lean and tasty and not too tough, so I decided I didn't care what it was and finished it, licking the juices off my fingers. A vendor selling cerveza and Coca-Cola had something to say to everyone who passed by. I bought a beer from him, listened for a while to his exuberant Spanish, then walked over to sit on a park bench. People strolled by—old and young, men and women, lovers and friends—some arm in arm; others holding hands. Boys with boys, girls with girls, boys with girls; it didn't seem to matter. Everyone touched someone else. Mothers nursed their children; old men talked—incessant sounds of Spanish. Two uniformed soldiers stood in the shadow with guns, ominous and unsmiling.

Time passed. I sat. I fell into a mesmerized state of semi-consciousness I was given to, looking across the plaza at the church, remembering Sunday sermons of the I am the Shepherd, You are the Sheep variety that particularly infuriated me, vaguely aware of the people around me chattering in their unfamiliar language. The sun had set when a shout startled me awake. I rose, looked about, decided the shout was not meant for me and, without thinking, walked down yet another street that branched out of this plaza. Dark night came swiftly and I was soon lost. I thought about hiring a taxi, but was afraid I'd be short of money. Besides, I wasn't sure the driver would understand "Texas Bar."

The street I now walked on took me into a residential district. The houses were French Colonial—a style I could identify since only a week earlier I had walked through the French Quarter in New Orleans with the architecture student from the strip-club who had explained certain characteristics of that style. I liked the intricate ironwork, the small balconies, the painted shutters, the textured stucco. People spoke to me or followed me with their eyes as I passed. I had no idea what they said since I didn't speak Spanish but I knew I was an oddity here. An old woman with no teeth—maybe a grandmother or a witch—sat in a doorway and cackled as I walked by, startling me.

What in God's name am I doing here, I thought to myself. This isn't where I want to be. A young boy approached out of the darkness, his skin so dark I could see only his white eyes and the reflected light on his smooth cheeks. He spoke in Spanish. No comprende, I replied. Fuckee fuckee, he said. I'd not heard that before but it sounded universal. He held up his hands so I could see, and pumped the index finger of one hand in and out of the circled palm of the other. Again, universal.

Who is this, I wondered. Maybe an angel sent by God to help me in my quest. I believed, briefly, this had all the earmarks of something "meant to be" as my mother would say. Let go, let God. I had been brought to this place, to this boy—a guide— away from the sordid Texas Bar, with its unruly ships' crews and painted women, by some holy providence that looked after innocent Catholic boys on their quest for a first sexual experience. I figured he was about to lead me to the most beautiful woman imaginable and said "Si."

He led me down a dark pathway marked by a wall of damp plywood on one side and stones and small bushes on the other. The pathway twisted and turned. I tripped once, so the boy grabbed my hand and we continued, the touch of a stranger odd. The path smelled of urine, old charcoal and rotting weeds. The holiness of the adventure began to fade. My hands were clammy and I was anxiously squinting into the darkness when a building appeared, blocking our path. There was no light, but when the boy rapped softly against the thin wooden door, a candle flickered to our right, revealing a window. The door opened. A girl stood in the doorway, but with so little light, I could not tell what she looked like. She and the boy spoke staccato Spanish, then the door opened wide and I was invited in. He held out his hand and demanded *cinco denairo*. I knew enough to give him five dollars, thinking this the right price. He pushed me in, closing the door behind me.

* * *

The candle burning in a primitive wall-sconce above a simple, unpainted wooden dresser provided the only light. My eyes adjusted slowly to its surreal flickering that made nervous monsters of both the girl and myself against the bare ochre wall. In the center of the room stood a single bed covered with a white sheet. Above that, on the wall, hung a picture of the Sacred

Heart of Jesus. The floor was wood. A white porcelain washbasin and a pitcher sat on the dresser. Electronic voices hummed and buzzed in another room. Most likely the girl's parents, listening to a radio while their children worked. But, I thought, what did I know? Less than nothing.

The girl was plain looking, short and dark-skinned. She had pulled her black hair tight off her small face and braided it into a long, single piece. She had a low forehead, thick nose and shapeless, fat lips. I was not attracted to her—not physically, not intellectually, not emotionally.

She took my hand and pulled me over by the dresser where she unzipped my jeans, then motioned for me to remove them. I didn't like the idea of standing barefoot on her floor, so rather than remove my shoes, I thought to pull my jeans over them and wear them while I did my business, then pull my pants back on and make a quick exit. My left shoe caught in the pant leg and I stumbled to the floor, trying to catch myself with my left arm. I shook my head and tried to smile. The girl giggled against her fingers.

With my shoe stuck, I couldn't move my jeans either on or off. Sitting on the wood floor in the flickering candlelight in my underpants, I freed one shoe, removed it; then freed the other and got it off as well. Finally, I got my pants off. The girl sat on the edge of the bed trying not to laugh. I stood, still wearing my white jockey shorts. She reached into the hole in front and grabbed my penis. Her stubby little fingers were clammy and I gasped. She examined me, then bathed the entire area with a cold washcloth as if prepping me for some medical procedure. I watched it shrink and wondered what other indignities fortune had in store for me that night.

Satisfied I was clean, she rolled her shirt to her neck, exposing two small, rubbery breasts with nipples that looked like pencil erasers. She unbuttoned her jeans, slid them down her short, chubby legs and let them fall to the floor, perhaps the only thing she did even hinting of sensuality. She wore boy's jockey shorts—indistinguishable from mine—and red socks that folded back, low on her ankles. Not exactly sexy lingerie, I recall thinking. Not exactly what I'd had in mind. With her thumbs hooked into the elastic waist, she queried with her eyes whether or not I wanted them removed.

How am I supposed to know, I wondered. I motioned for her to take them off. She did and there it was: hidden in a tiny patch of curly black hair, a strip of pink like a piece of raw meat. I probably gasped. This is the part of the female body I've spent so much time fantasizing over? This?

That was it; what she was selling. It was mine for the taking; mine for five lousy bucks. She lay, dark eyes probing, passive, exposed, vulnerable; chubby brown body naked from rolled up blue sweater to rolled down red socks. I looked at my penis. It was roughly the size of a couple pieces of bazooka gum, chewed and shaped between the fingers of one hand. I couldn't recall it that small before—at least not in the past few years. I leaned over her. She stroked it as I supported myself above her. In spite of everything, I may have actually felt faint sexual stirrings when I happened to look up. There, staring from the wall, were the sad brown eyes of Jesus Christ asking me what the fuck are you doing here, anyway.

And that was it for sex and romance. I stood and dressed as quickly as I could without making an even greater fool of myself. She lay, quiet, watching me zip and button and retie, neither accusing nor happy nor sad. I hoped she didn't blame herself and would make good use of the money. I walked to the door, opened it, mumbled good-by, and stumbled up the path out onto the street where I heard again the old woman cackle—the old grandma witchlaugh that I ran from till I heard it no more.

* * *

I felt like crying, like one of the losers Wally was always going on about, like I was a failure in the most important sense of what it meant to be a man. The street on which I was walking—running, really—changed. Instead of pavement bordered by French Colonials, it turned into a river of ragged asphalt flanked by tumbledown shacks. I tripped on a chunk of asphalt and fell on my face. I sat up, looked at the scratches on the palms of my hands, wiped my tears off my cheeks, stood and walked. People sat, drinking, talking, playing games. Old men, young men, women with children, young women giggling. The older ones gestured as I passed, the infants played in the dirt, ignoring me. I sensed I didn't really exist, that I passed through their lives, invisible.

The street deteriorated to a gravel and dirt road. People walked or stood in groups on the side—most of them barefoot, all of them thin. Some herded goats; others carried chickens or vegetables or fruit. There was nothing here I could call a house. Instead, bits of temporary privacy gained from blankets stretched across sticks or wires. Some of the shelters had walls of plywood or cardboard; others—the nicer ones—corrugated metal roofs. Fires in braziers and simple kerosene lanterns burned along both sides of the road—like a bivouacked army—tended by women wearing bright skirts and plain white blouses, cooking and boiling water for their families. A cacophony of odors wafted from the shacks: burned oil and something that smelled like corn, charcoal fires, waste. Women cooking for their families. Like my mom cooked for us. Kids everywhere. Why so many, I wondered. Catholics. The South American religion. Kids on top of kids. The Lord will provide. The Lord will love them. Just have them. Have more.

I walked and walked—unthinking, without awareness. The clapboard huts had disappeared now and the hair at the back of my neck, wet with sweat, tingled as my instincts warned me I was on the margin of civilization. Groups of young men stood on either side of the road, some holding tiny transistor radios to their ears. Most had small, pointed beards, many smoked—what, I didn't know at the time. I liked the raw sweet smell of it though.

When I thought about the value of my few dollars here, I turned and stepped rapidly back toward the kerosene lights. Four men followed me. I strode purposefully past the clapboard shacks, staying in the center of the road, glad I was tall. They ran after me. I broke into a full sprint. I ran and ran, propelled by the footfalls behind me until I found myself back among the French Colonials, panting. I slowed to a walk and turned. No one there. A young boy with large white eyes approached. It was him—my guide from earlier, barking for his sister while their folks watched the news. He saw it was me, smiled, bowed and backed away. I felt like a fool. Brother and sister. Like my sister Sarah and me shoveling sidewalks and mowing lawns—only different. Totally different. His eyes spoke. Why do you have more than us, why don't you share? Do you really just want to fuck us? I cursed my upbringing for this guilt. I wasn't there to share my culture, or learn about theirs. I was there because I had dollars in my pocket and wanted to trade those dollars for sex. The old woman still cackled as I entered the plaza. I bought a coke and sat, glad to be somewhere I recognized, thinking myself safe.

Two young men in jeans and white tee shirts shuffled toward me.

"Hey, Joe, cool, man. Got any smoke, man?" He hung onto the word man.

"Don't smoke," I said.

"Look here, man. You want some smoke? You want ta buy some weed, man? You want some Panamanian weed for yo' friendships in the states, man?"

"No thanks, man," I mimicked him. "Don't use it, man."

One of them, the one who hadn't spoken, moved to my left side. The talker had a face that started wide at the forehead and narrowed to a pointed goatee. His constant smile was an evil grin. I felt surrounded by danger.

He said, "Hey, man, you look here, man."

I stood abruptly, vaguely aware of something happening. The man to my left, the one who had moved there to sit was rifling through my wallet. He had picked my pocket. I grabbed the wallet and yelled "Thieves." The man on my right, the talker, smiled, but the smile was menacing.

"Be cool, Joe. Be cool, man. Fuck you, American man." He gestured obscenely, then turned, and both ran for a darkened alleyway.

My knees trembled. I sat on the bench and shook my head to clear it. I looked through my billfold for the fifth time. It was all there. Thirty bucks plus the local balboa.

I looked around, wondering what to do. It was nearly ten. I felt lost and my goal of lying with a woman that night seemed unattainable. I didn't even know how I would return to the ship. Across the plaza, a tall black man held court. He looked familiar. It was Boss Jones, the ship's boatswain. Dressed in a sparkling white shirt with a heavy gold chain around his neck, he towered above the Panamanians. He was engaged in animated discussion

with a street vendor. As I walked toward him, a sense of
redemption washed over me like a waterfall.

"Ka-dett." He smiled. The word had a paternal sound. I
hadn't worked with him much yet, but heard the sailors say
things like "Best boatswain in the Gulf. Best boatswain in
the NMU."

"What a young boy like you doin' here in de' plaza wid de'
ol' folk when he should be in de' ho' house wid dem young
girls?"

"I was headed there, Boss. But I got lost."

"You got lost?" He looked at me, his eyes wide. "Lost?" He
lifted his head and laughed, then laughed louder, finally roaring.
The Panamanians nearby looked at him in awe.

"Ka-dett. You looka here. You out lookin' fo' dat firs' piece
o' tail an' you got yo'sef lost?"

To listen to him, one would have thought nothing on earth
could be funnier. The man could scarcely talk. I was miffed. The
way he laughed at a little thing like getting lost, I was just glad
I didn't have to tell him about my other experiences that night.

"Come wid me, Ka-dett! You come wid de' boss-man. I's
gon' d'liver you direct to de' whorehouse. You done found
yo'sef a guide."

* * *

I followed him down a dark street. Tall as I was, I nearly ran
keeping up. He turned left, then right. I heard music. We walked
past a bar with the door open and girls standing in the doorway.
I saw another doorway, more girls, another, and more. Sailors
milled about, laughing and cursing, drinking and smoking,
singly and in groups.

It was nearly eleven. Low-wattage streetlights glowed against
the dark tropical sky; flashing neon advertised booze and girls.
The open-fire braziers of vendors cooking meat cast weird shadows. The door to every bar gaped open, mouth-like, dim bar-
light illuminating the silhouettes of the girls in the doorways,
chattering with each other and flirting with the sailors. Men
pissed against the sides of buildings, guzzled beer, pushing and
shoving. One young man, frailly built—more boy than man—

swung at a burly bald guy wearing an earring. The sailor laughed, dodged the awkward blow and dropped the boy with an easy punch.

The women all wore short skirts or short shorts and tight blouses. In my youth and state of need, I thought them beautiful, sexual, sensuous. All of them. Every single one. They did what they could to entice men into their bars: raised the hem of their skirts, bent to show their breasts, undulated their hips. Modesty did not exist. The girls worked at being erotic, but would abandon that in a moment if they thought quick exposure of a nipple or raising the skirt and pulling aside the skimpy panties might work better.

"Fergit all dis' trash," said Boss Jones. "We's gon' to de' bes' whore house what got de mos' boo'ful girls fer yo' firs' piece o' tail. Y'all want a classy girl."

Well, yeah, I thought, why not. Ahead, across a narrow street, I saw red neon flashing TEXAS BAR. Loud guitar riffs floated out the double swinging doors. Over the top of those doors stood a woman who could have been an Amazon. Crimson lips and blue-black hair, she looked like a devil-woman.

"Dat de' place, ka-dett. Dat de' Texas Bar. You gon' find de' girl o' yo' dreams."

The woman saw me as we approached. She swung the saloon doors in on herself.

"Oh, God," I said. Smoky red light outlined her long legs spread slightly, wearing a skin-tight top and a black skirt that barely covered the area between her legs. Her waist was narrow and her breasts jutted straight out. She had high cheekbones and large, almond eyes. Her hands rested on her hips, her large, made-up eyes bore into me. I wasn't at all sure I had what it took.

Boss Jones seemed to feel my hesitation and nudged me ever so slightly, as if by adding his masculinity to mine he might bring me to the level of this woman before us.

"Dat's Maria," he said. "She hep you out all right."

I left Boss Jones and stepped into the street. Random thoughts flicked through my mind like an eight millimeter newsreel: my girlfriend Melissa offering me love's redemption, the Virgin's heel smashing the serpent; black-frocked priests predatory and unsmiling.

A metamorphosis happened as I crossed over. I thought: this is it, God. I've waited long enough. You've stopped me, and guilt has stopped me, and fear has stopped me, and I've stopped myself, but nothing's going to stop me now.

Maria moved slowly, a sensuous, hypnotic dance meant only to arouse. She stretched out her arms, crushing me into those breasts. We didn't get inside the bar. She pushed me against the doorjamb, ground her pelvis against mine, placed my hands firmly on her butt and swirled her tongue in my mouth till I was panting like a mutt. My mental processes ended. My only feeling was a strong male impulse: I wanted this woman. We stood in the doorway, a couple mold, grinding slowly together, scarcely breathing. As we passed through the doorway, I heard Boss Jones behind me lift his head to the stars and drown the old grandma witchlaugh with a roar.

* * *

Inside, the Doors' hypnotic music that made me want to spin slowly blasted from speakers and I became aware of people moving like primitives. I saw skinny Wally, drunk as a goose, arms and legs akimbo, hopping and leaping with a woman who must have weighed one eighty. I recognized others: a sailor here, a cook there. Jerry, the young third, at the bar. Everyone had a woman, everyone acted like he'd been at sea for months.

Maria led me through the cacophony of the dance floor up the rickety stairs to her room. I was like a hot coal, glowing with passion. She stopped at the landing halfway up, reached into her purse and handed me a fat stogy, hand-rolled in cheap paper, stuffed with dope. She lit it and I inhaled deeply and mindlessly, inhibitions gone. I had never before smoked—had never before inhaled anything but air. I swear the stuff spun me into a dream world, actually altered my perceptions. Standing there kissing this woman's wet mouth, drowning in sensation, I glimpsed a strange and wonderful vision of voyaging south across the Isthmus, across the Equatorial Parallel, deep into a Southern Continent where hurricanes spin backwards, where pleasure mixes with dance with color with music; where women with wild hair raise their skirts and men go unzipped, where even death

signifies more than just heaven or hell. I inhaled again and saw
sailors and whores whirling on the smoky dance floor beneath
me and thought, for some reason, of Dorothy and Oz, murmuring to myself, "This sure ain't Kansas."

Dante's Upper Hell came to mind: a whirlwind of passion
and noise, red lights shining through smoky haze, bodies of men
and women with no spiritual or emotional connection dancing
like demons and me with my escort, my feminine Virgil, whose
job it was to guide me through this maelstrom, up the stairs to
the sanctuary of her room, then instruct me in the ways of love.
We scarcely crossed the threshold of her room and fell into her
bed before ripping away enough of each other's clothes that I
could touch her breasts and we could fit together those body
parts that produce such intense pleasure. My first sex flashed by
like a dream, Maria on top, covering me with her sweat, insert-
ing me with a flick of her fingers, purring like an animal, her lips
smeared red, her dark eyes dull, her naked breasts against my
chest, her pelvis pressing mine, circling slow and rhythmical.

After the first one, I lost track of orgasms or what she was
doing. I knew only how it felt, and threw my arms over my head
in surrender, wondering why people ever did anything else.
Finally, Maria gasped, burrowed into my shoulder with her
teeth, whimpering, and rolled off. Seeking air, I turned toward
the open window with red neon flashing through. In my stupor,
I heard my guardian angel, Boss Jones, roaring "Ka-Dett, Ka-
dett" over and over and over again. Maria slipped out of the bed,
walked to the window, leaned out, yelled, "Fuck you," and
slammed it shut. The noise stopped. She turned toward me and
said: "You cadet-boy. You sleep here." I probably smiled.

* * *

Maria and I kept each other going most of the night. When
I'd drift off, she would wake me and I'd do my best until she'd
mutter something in Spanish that I figured meant "get off me,
you oaf, so I can get some sleep." Then I'd sleep awhile until, at
some level of unconsciousness, I'd recall that intense pleasure
and roll toward her and kiss and lick and touch around on her
until her arms would pull me into her sweating body. Finally, we

both slept like dead, arms and legs entwined about each other and the drenched sheet. In the early morning, the sun just up and already threatening heat, birds chirping through the window once again open, Maria woke me and pushed me out of bed. I fell to the floor, then got up and saw her lying on her back, the nubs on her grapefruit breasts pointing to the ceiling and those legs slightly apart. I climbed back on top. It was nothing like the night before, but in those days, after that first taste of sex, I was like a crazy person. I threw all my money on her bed but she cursed me in Spanish, gathered up every peso and jammed it back into my pockets.

"You crazy cadete'. You don't know nuthin'. How can I take your money, you so dumb? You the worst lover I ever had. You come back, I teach you how to fuck."

"Maria, I'll come back and marry you and we'll make babies."

"Fuck you, cadete'. I don't want marry you. You too dumb. You a lousy lover. Go back to your ship now, pronto."

"Maria, I love you."

She threw my shoe at me. I pulled on my clothes, kissed her hard and left, forgetting every precaution Don Campbell had taught me. I clanged down the back fire escape, out through a back gate, up an alley between buildings and into the street. It was all I could do to keep from jumping and clicking my heels together.

Cristobal, Panama
July 31

The early morning sun shot lightshafts between the build-ings, and just like that, it was hot. Windows and doors were shuttered closed and the street was nearly empty. Three old women with rudimentary brooms pushed dirt off the sidewalks into the gutters, bending to examine any minute thing for value. From behind me, a gravelly southern voice called out.

"Hey, cadet. Hold on a goddamned minute."

I turned. George Coleman, the first engineer, stood there with one arm raised, the palm partially open.

"Morning, first."

"Mornin', shit. This fuckin' place stinks."

His blue trousers were dark at the crotch, and he slumped against one of the aluminum posts that supported the stained blue and dirty-white canvas awning above the entrance to the Texas Bar. Something yellow ran down the left breast of the plain white shirt he wore. A shock of brownish-blond hair fell across his face to mid-cheek.

I walked back toward him and got a whiff.

"Whew," I said. "You're right about the smell. Rotten night, huh?"

Wally had told me about this guy. He was the ranking engi-neer below the chief, and Wally's immediate supervisor.

According to Wally, he was a drunk and a redneck and, worst of all, the way Wally saw things, a loser. He got rolled regularly and often returned to the ship broke. He kept his job in spite of this self-abuse because day after day he worked like a dog in the steaming engine room, no matter how drunk he'd been the night before.

"Hell, last night wa'nt so bad. Ah may have drunk one too many beers."

He released his hold on the aluminum pole, staggered, then recovered, worked his right hand vigorously in his back pocket, extracted his wallet and looked inside.

"Goddamn nigra thieves." He spoke in the slow, deliberate drawl certain classes of Southern white men use to pronounce their imagined superiority over nearly everyone.

"Piss me off, these people. Hundred and fifty dollars— gone." He shoved the wallet back into his pocket.

"Let me lean on your shoulder, there, cadet, until I get my strength back. How you? Feelin' strong? I'll be strong soon. Hell, I can out-work, out-drink, out. . . well, maybe not out-fuck seein' as how you cadets never stop once you get goin'. But I sure as hell can outwork and outdrink you."

I reluctantly let Mr. Coleman lean on my shoulder. The odor coming off the man gagged me. I realized he was still drunk.

"Ah got me a family. Two kids, a verra nice wife. Mah dawg's named Bull."

"You got a dog named Bull?" I asked, not hearing him clearly.

"No, goddammit. Blue. Blue. Mah dawg is Blue."

"Blue." I said nodding, thinking fine, blue.

"We got us a house down in southwest Houston."

He rattled on as I rolled my eyes. "Nice goddamn house. Single-story, three-bedroom. Split-level, they call it. Verra nice neighborhood. In the suburbs. Full a' God-fearin' white folk— not that ah got anythin' against nigras, long as they know their place. We got us a family room downstairs with a paneled bar. God damn!" Thoughts of his bar excited him. "All carpeted. You jis' wun't believe it. Green indoor-outdoor carpet. Indoor AND outdoor. Wet bar, it got, fully stocked mahogany cabinet. Color TV. Verra nice carpet. Hell. I got me a boat. I water the lawn."

Christ, I thought, this guy's not only heavy, drunk and smelly, but boring as well. We moved forward, step by step, painfully. I tried to visualize last night with Maria to take me away from his stench.

"The wife says I like my booze too much, cadet." He chuckled as if sharing an inside joke. "I jis' can't stop drinkin'. I forget where I am and what I'm doin'. I hit the wife sometimes and the boy and mah girl, too. Like my ol' man usta hit me. Whap! Right 'cross the face." He slapped at an imaginary person. I muttered a prayer of thanksgiving for my dad. He might take drink now and again, but God bless him, he was never violent.

Small, noisy black birds hopped from ground to branch to roof to wire.

Like a bird on a wire. I thought of Leonard Cohen's song. *Like a drunk in a midnight choir. I have tried in my way to be free.* Free for what? Get drunk and hit people? Hit your family, for Christ's sake?

Two locals who had apparently slept in the street folded their cardboard and relieved themselves against the sides of a building. A very young man with long, black hair swept across one eye—probably a sailor off one of the Greek ships I'd noticed when we entered the harbor—lay on bare ground in a narrow alley between two buildings. I thought of the rats I had seen darting along the corners of a building the night before. The sickening smell of human waste permeated the air. Two women with brooms, heads wrapped in black cotton, walked slowly by us, their faces registering nothing.

"That alcohol causes a lot of problems, I guess." I tried to sound sympathetic. Usually a mistake, with a drunk.

"Alcohol don' cause no problems. It jus' sits in a bottle. It can sit fer days and weeks and not cause a single goddamn problem. Ain't nuthin' wrong with a bottle of booze."

On top of everything else, a philosopher. We went through the gate into the dock area with scarcely a second glance from the gate guard who once again requested by pantomime, a cigarette. George Coleman yanked the remainder of a pack of Marlboros from his shirt pocket and threw them on the ground at the man's feet. He scowled but picked them up. We continued through the gate.

As we neared the ship, Fletcher the A.B. caught up and passed us, saying nothing. He turned and looked back briefly and scornfully, then continued to the ship and up the gangway.

"Now that fellah there," said Mr. Coleman pointing. "He one bad apple."

I said nothing. Seemed like a lot of bad apples out here.

By the time we reached the ship, Mr. Coleman seemed almost sober. Mr. Potter, standing the 4 to 8 watch, bespectacled, dressed as always in pressed khakis, stood at the head of the gangway, arms folded, looking like a Presbyterian minister. He looked at me but said nothing as George Coleman walked past him, nodding like drunks nod.

Panama Canal,
August 1

Wally stirred when I walked into our room. He was lying on his side on the top bunk facing the door. His green eyes popped open; he looked toward me a couple seconds, stretched, and was wide-awake. He had been called at six and it was a few minutes past that now. Our transit time was 0700.

"I feel like shit," he said. "Why can't I stop at six beers—or eight or ten?" He sat up and burped.

"All right, tell me about it," he continued. "Tell me how she was beautiful and you did it seven times and because you're Catholic, you plan to marry her."

"That's pretty close to right. How 'bout you?"

"I was there, in the Texas Bar, behaving myself. I saw you go upstairs. You could have at least picked a good-looking one. Hope she didn't charge you."

Wally seemed a little out of sorts. I assumed it was because I had gone ashore without him.

"She was beautiful and you know it. What do you mean behaving yourself? I saw you flailing about on the dance floor with that amazon. What'd she weigh, anyhow? And no, she didn't charge me."

"Liar. So I like my women large. What's it to you?" He let himself to the floor, stepping directly on my pillow on his way

down, turning toward me and grinning. I ignored it. He pulled
on his coveralls. "Didn't happen to run into the First on your
way back?"

"Matter of fact, I did. Still drunk. Pissed himself. Got rolled.
What a prize."

"Like my old man—or what's left of him." Wally sighed. "I
don't know. There but for the grace of God go any of us, I suppose. Just hope that's not you or me in twenty years. By the way,
you got a letter."

I looked at my desk thinking I really liked Wally. I hadn't
told him much about my dad yet. His dad had left home when
Wally was young. Mine had hung in there—something I appreciated a lot. He'd taught me to hunt and fish, had coached my
baseball team, attended all my games. A fat envelope lay on my
desk with my name written in a flowing feminine hand. I picked
it up. A hint of scent. Her scent. I missed a breath. The name
Melissa, my girlfriend from home, scrolled large in the upper left
corner; no return address. Planning to read it later, I folded it
and stuffed it in my pocket.

A sharp rap, our door burst open.

"C'mon cadet." It was Mr. Hunt, the chief mate. He wore a
rumpled shirt with shoulder boards. His skinny legs with black
socks and shoes stuck out of baggy shorts like Popsicle sticks.
"Ready to go to work? Party all night, pay the piper all day. And
I'm the piper. I gotta be on the bow going through the locks.
You can be there with me. Tugs at seven. Eat later."

After the mate left, I lay down fully dressed and dozed until
Wally splashed water in my face. It was a few minutes past seven
when I walked out of the house headed for the bow. The sun had
already climbed a quarter of the way up the sky and the air was
sticky. On the bow, the deck gang was heaving in mooring lines.
Boss Jones, the boatswain, stood like a primitive god at the
winch, shirt off as usual, black skin gleaming as he worked the
controls. This was my first time on the bow unmooring, so I
stayed back and watched. Something I didn't understand initially was happening. Some labor problem. Boss Jones and his
sailors had either inadvertently misunderstood the mate's orders
or were purposely disobeying them. The mate told the gang to
take in one of the spring lines. A broad-shouldered A.B. with a

scar on his cheek slacked a headline instead. Mr. Hunt swore. He ordered that line heaved in again. The sailors stopped off the line and took it to the winch drum. The boatswain ran the winch the wrong way so more line paid out. The mate marched up to the boatswain, stood as tall as possible which made him, comically, only five inches shorter, stuck his face up to the boatswain's Adam's apple and yelled. All work stopped. The boatswain smiled, looking both vastly superior and infinitely more powerful, turned on his heel and walked off the bow.

"Vat iss going on up there, Mr. Mate?" The captain's voice boomed over the loudspeaker.

The mate, nervous, kind of hopped over to the speaker box. "The goddam boatswain just walked off the bow, captain. I want to fire him."

"Get the lines in, Mr. Mate," came the master's voice.

The sailors stood in a small group on the starboard side of the bow, mumbling amongst themselves. Without the boatswain there to direct them, they ignored the mate. After five uncomfortable minutes and more exchanges between the mate and the captain, the boatswain returned. Mr. Hunt touched each line he wanted heaved in. The sailors continued making mistakes: stoppers were applied wrong and slipped; the winch was run at slow speed and the boatswain refused to run it faster, calling it a safety issue. The lines slithered through the Panama chocks so slowly you could count the fibers. The mate snapped at me to go help. I walked over and stood near old Irving Jackson, the raisin-skinned 12 to 4 quartermaster. He spoke continuously under his breath as we flaked a line on deck.

"Yas suh, yas suh. Dis mate, he got trouble now. He got trouble. Lor', lor', dis mate got hisself trouble."

I watched him closely as he talked. Everything that happened today seemed slower than normal and somehow larger and more interesting than before. I assumed it was the marijuana Maria had given me.

I couldn't figure from Irving's bluesy lament what was happening but I had a sense of bad voodoo when he said "sumpin' real bad gon' happen to some body on this here ship. You jis' wait 'n see if ol' Irving Jackson don't speak da *truf*."

He talked on, mostly under his breath, as I walked over to

the port side to watch the last lines creep through the panama chocks. The tug passed a snowy-white eye with a dense weave I recognized from my seamanship class as Sansome. The sailors looped it over a bollard and the mate yelled into the speaker "tug fast." I walked over to the starboard side to stand next to Irving Jackson who was leaning out over the bulwark looking down at the tug pulling us off the berth.

"Irving, why is the crew angry with the mate?"

"Ka-dett, ka-dett, you don' know nuthin' and thass good. Bes' not to know nuthin' sometime. Dis mate done disrespec' dis crew when he dump the booze over the side. He done disrespec' dis crew when he dump the booze. Dis crew ain' gon' fergit."

"You mean they're angry because he threw all the booze over the side?"

"Ka-dett, you don' worry. The crew like you fine. We knows you got to work wid dis mate. We knows that, ka-dett. We don' hold 'gainst you nohow. Dis mate, he didn' treat Timmy right, he didn' purtec Tommy Michaelson. He don' know how to be a mate. Dis mate, he one fer you to look at and say, mm-hmm, da mate do that, I know's not to do that. Da mate don' do that, mos' probly I should do that. You gittin' what I'm sayin'?"

"Yeah. Just do the opposite and I'll be doing the right thing."

"Thass it." He laughed and slapped me on the shoulder. "You got it, son. Jis do the opposite a' the mate and you be fine."

The bow of the ship turned to port and we moved toward Gatun Locks. As we neared the locks, the mate sent me and Irving Jackson aft to lower the gangway. I thought we should hurry but Irving had one speed—deliberate. The gangway had never been secured after undocking this morning so it was rigged and ready. I arrived first. The boatswain had shown me where the switch was so I walked over ahead of Irving and ran the gangway down to the water's edge. A dirty-white canal boat, diesel engine knocking badly, slipped under the gangway and a single-file of Panamanian line handlers boarded.

I leaned against the rail, watching them. They were all slim, dark-skinned men wearing khakis and hardhats and carrying col-

orful woven purses over their shoulders. Then I saw her—out of
the blue, I saw Maria. She was boarding the ship with the linehandlers. She turned her head up and looked straight at me and
smiled her most I-am-a-woman-and-I-like-it smile. I grabbed
the handrail hard and muttered something like "What the—"
Irving Jackson caught my arm and I turned to look at him—just
for a moment—then turned back and she was gone. I walked to
the head of the gangway and peered carefully under each line-
handler's hardhat. I knew I had seen her. It had not been a
vision. It had been her—a flesh and blood woman. I would have
sworn to it. But she was not aboard. I returned to the bow.

We approached Gatun locks. The linehandlers anticipated
every order, then carried it out with a minimum of effort. They
coiled and flaked heaving lines—two on the port bow, two on
the starboard—then erected portable cardboard huts so they
could nap or gamble or just sit out of the sun and talk. The canal
boatswain, distinguished from the others by his yellow hardhat,
instructed his men with a jerk of his head or a wink. Locomotives
motored silently along on either side as the ship nosed into the
lock. The linehandlers tossed heaving lines to counterparts on
the wingwalls who loosely bowlined the eye to a small circum-
ference wire-rope, then dropped everything so the wire could be
hauled aboard, its eye tossed over a bollard and the locomotive
secured to the ship. We took one locomotive on each bow forward and one on each side aft. The linehandlers threw off the
tug's line and the tug backed away gracefully as the bow glided
slowly into the lock. I sat in the hot sun on my favorite bollard
watching. Boss Jones ran the winch, ignoring the mate like he
was a speck of rust on the devil's claw.

The ship's sailors operated the winches for the canal linehandlers. Irving Jackson stood a few feet from where I sat on the
bollard, daydreaming of Maria. When I looked up, a collision
with the massive lock gates appeared imminent.
    "Mate, look ahead," I jumped up, pointing. "We're going to
hit those gates."
    "Don't worry about it, son," he drawled. "That pilot has got
everything under control. See there. He just ordered the loco-

motives to brake."

The trains whistled, then squealed their brakes, tightening the wires and stopping the ship. Less than twenty feet from the gates, we were dead in the water.

"Gates closing," sounded the radio voice of the second mate aft.

In minutes, the ship began to rise to the level of the second lock. The mate explained what was happening.

"What we're doing here, young man, is climbing from the level of the Atlantic Ocean up to the level of Gatun Lake. We usually anchor in the lake to allow the northbound convoy to pass. Then we'll cross the lake and sail down through Galliard Cut to the Pedro Miguel and Mira Flores Locks which will drop us to the level of the Pacific."

"What lifts us up and lets us down?" I asked.

"Water. What else?"

"Must take mighty big pumps to move all this water around."

"No pumps Jake. Gravity. When the gates aft close and we're locked in, a huge valve opens, and the lock is flooded with water from the lake. Once we're up to the proper level, the gates ahead open and we move forward into the next lock. We get locked in there, the gates close, another valve opens and that lock is flooded with water which lifts us on up to the level of that lock and so on and so forth. Operation of this here canal depends on one thing. Know what that is?"

"Water?" I said timidly. He frowned, probably thinking this new midshipman of his wasn't particularly bright.

"Rainwater." he said. "You know that cloudburst yesterday shortly after noon? Well, those have got to happen regularly down here or the level in the Lake drops too fast and the whole damn canal could shut down."

Ahead, a crack of light appeared between the two massive gates. The locomotives acknowledged an order by whistling and moving forward, towing the ship ahead. The gates opened into a recess in each wingwall and the ship surged ahead toward the next lock.

"It's nearly ten, cadet. Why don't you mosey on back to the galley for a bite and bring me a coffee and doughnut?"

"Sure, mate. Be glad to."

There was a holiday feeling on the ship. Sailors leaned over the rail, coffee mugs in hand, watching other ships and talking. Engineers found jobs in shady spots on deck, out of the hot engine room. The cooks prepared extra food and brought it out to the Panamanian linehandlers who traded their woven purses for a pan of stringy beef or a bucket of coffee, milk and sugar. The sun was more than halfway toward its zenith, the air pleasantly warm. We moved into the center lock, passing lightposts holding banks of stadium lights. Ahead, I could see Gatun Lake, mysterious and calm, in deep jungle.

Irving Jackson was on the bow with Boss Jones—why, I wasn't sure, unless to act as a witness in case the mate decided to badger the boatswain about the trouble earlier. Far as I could tell, Mr. Jackson's only duties were to stand at the railing and look over the side. The boatswain, on the other hand, ran the winches for the canal linehandlers. Fletcher arrived on the bow to relieve Irving at ten. Surly as ever, he grumbled about the bad coffee Simple Simon, the ordinary seaman, had made. I walked aft down the starboard side with Irving shaking his head the whole way.

"My oh my," he said. "That man can't say a good word 'bout *no* man, *no* time."

The ship passed an observation post where small bleachers had been erected. A group of people—Americans, I figured—sat watching us. Most wore short pants, bright cotton shirts and billed hats. We stopped to look. I waved. Mr. Jackson stood there and smiled.

"Yassuh," he said, looking at them. "Nice lookin' group a' white folk there, sure is, sure 'nuff is. Nice they could come by to watch us."

Then I saw Maria again. She sat in the center of the group, waving at me. She wore a blue top open at the throat, and a blood-red scarf tied in her black hair. Her lips were dark and shiny. I could see her as clearly as I could see the fat, pale white guy in the green and black Panama shirt next to her. I kept my eyes trained exactly on her and waved and shouted, "Maria, Maria. Hello, Maria."

Irving Jackson grabbed my arm. "Say there, ka-dett, you feelin' OK? Who you wavin' at, anyhow?"

"Irving," I said, "look, there in that group of people. See the dark-skinned woman sitting there in the middle?"

He looked. "Dark woman in the middle a' them pale faces? Noooo. Say!" He looked at me seriously. His left eye was phlegmy and streaked with red. "You ain't hittin' the bottle, are you?"

"She's the one I was with last night, Irving. Look, she's come to see me off, to wave goodbye. Can you believe it?" I turned again to wave but we were moving away rapidly now. As we slowed for the next lock, one of the locomotives moved into the line of sight between us.

Irving Jackson and I continued aft. My heart pounded as I thought of her, and I knew I'd better talk about something else or I'd get aroused.

"Irving, what will the sailors do now?"

"Oh, mos' likely dey won' do nuthin' in purticler. Nuthin' in purticler." He laughed and slapped his thigh. "Ha ha. Sailors ain't zackly revlootionists, know what I mean, ka-dett? This mate jis won' see da coperation he might think he should be gittin', that's all. This gang all perfessionals. We all perfessionals. We knows our job. We made a point dis mornin', that's all. You can rely on one thing. Dis boatswain ain't gonna do nuthin' to fuck up dis' cap'n. He ain' gon' do nuthin' to hurt dis cap'n. This cap'n bout' good as gold. You wantta learn to be a cap'n, you watch ol' cap'n Isenhagen. He the bess."

We were almost at the house now. The ship had been lift-ed to the level of the next lock and we drifted forward. I sat on the wooden bench lashed to the rail outside the door to the house while Irving stepped inside. We passed the lock gate on the starboard side. It was huge, over fifty feet wide and deep as the lock. When it opened, it snuggled perfectly into a recess built in the concrete wingwall. Our speed increased. I was amazed a giant steel ship could travel so fast with concrete walls less than ten feet away.

"Now then," Irving said when he returned, holding up a thick ceramic mug. "You see dis' here mug? You see dis mug I got my coffee in?"

I nodded.

"You ever seen one a' dese mugs over in da officer's saloon?"

"Can't say I have."

"You won't neither, 'cuz da officers on a ship drink outta cup and saucer while da unlicensed drink outta mugs."

He took a swallow of his coffee and lit a Lucky Strike. His face was a prune; purply brown with lines and little pouches in his forehead and cheeks. He was thin and wiry, and I could see the intelligence in his eyes.

"Mugs and cups and saucers. Thass jis' one way o' keepin' da crew separate. Dere's other ways. Oh yeah. You kin bet dere' is. You got yurselves a nice saloon wid mahogny bulkheads and some a' dat dere fine cut glass wid da pichers a' dem bootiful womans cut into it. You got yurselves nice little tables wid white tablecloths and all dat dere cryssalized finery while we sits on old wood benches and eat off sumpin' like you'd find in a old caferteria. Plus we got rough-ass knives and forks and dese mugs. You gittin' what I'm tellin' you, cadet?"

"Yeah. Yeah. I see."

"OK, then, so you knows there's always jis' a little friction between da officers and da crew. Always a little, sometime a lot. The crew be lookin' fer respec. They need their hunnert dollar bills at payoff and their rest and clean linen, but the unions provide that. What unions don' provide is for the officers to respec dem. Now, see here, ka-dett, that mate, Mr. Hunter or whatever he call hisself, he in his right to go 'round and throw over people's booze. He in his right as mate. But dere wasn't no kinda trouble. Nobody was gittin' drunk, nobody was fightin', everthin' was cool. He had no call to toss over da booze is what I'm sayin'. He did that 'cuz' he mean. He a mean man. He did it to show the crew dis-respec, to show 'em he da boss, that he do as he please and nobody kin say nuthin' 'bout it."

I nodded. The ship rose so rapidly, the concrete wingwall seemed in a free-fall.

"Besides, when he done that, he 'dangered the crew because Timmy, he got to have dat alcohol. It like his medicine. You don' jus' take a man's medicine away. You understandin' dis, ka'dett?"

"Yeah, I see."

"So, the crew feels very disrespect by dat dere mate, Mr. Hunter, whachacallhim. Very disrespect. That why they fucked around on the bow today. They won't do that agin, cuz' it would hurt dis' capin, but they wantta show dis' mate he cain' jis do what he pleases."

I brushed my hand across the top of my head, wet with sweat, looked at Irving Jackson, saw a shriveled man, wondered if he'd had a wife somewhere along the way, or children; what he did when not on the ship. I couldn't really imagine him anywhere else.

"All right, so tell me about the boatswain and this captain."

"Oh, yeah. Dat a story all right. Dat a real good story. An' I de ony one what kin tell it straight."

Before he started, I walked into the house, poured coffee into a china cup, set it in a matching saucer and picked out two sugar doughnuts with a napkin. Irving and I took our time walking back up to the bow so when I handed the coffee to Mr. Hunt it was cold. At least, I thought to myself, it's in a cup and saucer. He was busy talking on the bow phone, so I walked over to the starboard side of the windlass, stood by Mr. Jackson and listened to the story of Boss Jones and Henrick Isenhagen.

Isenhagen had emigrated from Germany to New Jersey before the war because he was Jewish on his mother's side. His father's family had Nazi friends and his parents' separated over politics and young Henrick followed his mother's family to America against his father's wishes.

He'd graduated from the German Maritime Academy in Hamburg and had raised his license quickly to Chief Officer. At the US Coast Guard licensing center at South Ferry Park in Manhattan, he'd obtained a U.S. license and took a chief mate's job on a ship called the Willamette Victory. This ship loaded ammunition in Sunny Point and sailed with a fleet bound for Mermansk, a small port near Leningrad through which America supplied the Russian war effort.

Young Isenhagen felt the need to continually prove himself during those early days of his career. He was tough on his men, "purtickly mens of color." Mr. Jackson paused and looked at me, his right eyebrow raised, to make certain I understood.

Jackson sailed on the Willamette Victory as well, rooming with a young able-bodied seaman name Jones. Jones had no first name far as Irving Jackson knew. He was tall and thin, sturdy as an oak mast and brash as new brass bearings.

"That man could bend metal. He could lift two hundred pound blocks above his head," he said. "I ain't never seen that man put a beer or a glass of whiskey to his lips but I did see him take three women up to the rooms above the Florida bar in Callao one night."

Isenhagen regularly tested Jones by giving him difficult and dangerous jobs, or jobs that demanded great skill, that others struggled with. He set him to luffing tackle, worming and parcelling wire rope and painting over the side in a boatswain's chair with the ship underway. Jones could throw a long-splice into eight-inch poly faster, according to Irving Jackson, than any man alive.

Approaching the coast of England in heavy seas, their ship was holed by a German torpedo. Water flooded number two. Isenhagen was determined to save the ship. He took his sailors into the hold and worked to stop the leak. Irving Jackson, on the masthouse running the winch, lowered timbers from number one and rolls of canvas and bags of cement. A temporary bulkhead was built. High seas lashed at the ship making work nearly impossible. Isenhagen and Jones worked side by side.

"The ship be pitchin' and rollin' like a wild horse. I's perched like a scared goose on that mast house, looking straight down into the mouth of hell. I sees a big timber wash up against the mate, breakin' his leg like a chickenbone. Jones sees that and nex' thing I knows, he shoutin' sumpin' up at me and all I sees is the whites o' his eyeballs and his mouth workin' like one o' them there silent movies where the black man be scared. I don't hear nuthin' but the wind howlin' through the rigging worse than roundin' the horn in the old four master's. I hold my hands up to let him know I can't hear him so he sends a man up to the bridge to tell 'em the mate is down and the bulkhead let go. Water be floodin' the hold. We takes a list and lays way over to port. Well, that cap'n, he had enough a' that kinder news. He sends the man back wid the order to abandon ship and one by one, the sailors struggle up out a' that cargo hold."

He moved his arms and legs up and down as if climbing a ladder.

"They fought their way up from the lower hold to the lower 'tween deck to the upper 'tween deck and up and over the side o' the coaming to the main deck." His eyes were popped out as if he were watching it happen all over again. He paused, then blinked to refocus and looked over at me.

"There be a time in ever' man's life, ka-dett, when he wunners, you know, what the fuck is goin' on. You git what I'm sayin'? When it seems that the worl' is jis' too fucked up! When you says to yo'sef, my Mama *never* tol' me nuthin' 'bout dis. Well, dis' one a' them times for po' ol' Irving. I stood watching man after man haul hisself up outa that death-trap of a cargo hold, water swooshin' this way an' swooshin' that, the ship rollin' and yawin' and buckin' 'til finally no one but Boss Jones and Isenhagen be left down there. I kin see Isenhagen hurt real bad, an' I be thinkin' to mysef, now what? You git what I'm sayin' ka-dett? Dis one a dem times you damn sure wish you was somewhere else, but you ain't. You there. You got trouble and you got to deal with da situation. Jones, he jis' look up at me on dat resistor house, knowin' I can't hear him and probly can't help him and kinda shrugged. Then, he picked up Isenhagen like he a sack a' yams, broken leg and all, threw him over his shoulder and started up the ladder.

"I want ta tell you, ka-dett, I never seen nuthin' like that, an' I never specks to see nuthin' like that again. Here this man, walkin' up da side o' dat hold like a fly, wid anuther man slung over his back an' actin' like it was nuthin'.

"Dey gits to da top, where Boss Jones got to climb up over the fuckin', you know, coaming, an' what you 'speck happens, but the ship buck like it got somethin' pers'nal gainst these fellers and Isenhagen damn near falls. Boss Jones, he jis' catches Isenhagen's hand as the man be slippin' off his shoulder, and hangs on and pulls him up over the coaming onto the deck.

"I be shakin' my head, thinkin' to myself, lor', lor', dere be two men won't never fergit dis' sperience. Boss Jones carry that mate down the deck an' laid him in dat lifeboat gentle as a sleepin' chile, legbone pokin' out his blood-stained khakis. I crawls in nex' and Jones lower the boat, and climb down the 'barkation ladder down the side a' the ship and into the boat." He shook his head back and forth.

"So, you think this cap'n and this boatswain ever gonna be anything but bone-deep brothers of the sea? I doubts it, ka-dett. They been through way too much together fer some honky-ass chief mate to come between them."

As we talked the ship sailed out of the final lock and entered Gatun Lake. Irving and I stood at the stem of the bow and watched the anchor drop with a roar and a cloud of dust. The captain squawked something on the radio. The mate looked at the boatswain and pulled his hand across his throat, the boatswain set the brake. Irving attached a black anchor ball to the foremast and heaved it up and we were anchored. I looked over the gunwale and saw the chain stretch tight, then slack back as the ship settled aft and the giant flukes dug their way into the muddy bottom.

We had anchored near the shore where the jungle was so thick I couldn't see the ground. Monkeys chattered at us from the treetops and brilliant birds—scarlet parrots and hyacinth macaws with two-foot tails shrieked and flapped their wings. The mate sent me aft to "eat or nap or jerk off or whatever you cadets do over lunch."

I stopped by my room, changed into my swimming trunks, grabbed a towel and a pillow and went up to the flying bridge. Wally was already there, his freckled body limp, asleep in a deck chair. I sunk into the other chair, leaned back and dozed.

Warm drops of water against my skin roused me. The rain fell harder and the wind started to blow. I lifted one eyelid enough to see Wally's chair was empty. My watch said one-twenty. I lay back and closed my eyes, enjoying the feel of the warm rain against my skin. The wind backed and increased. Lightning crashed nearby. Thunder followed almost immediately and the soft warm drops were suddenly pellets against my body. I still could not bring myself to move.

Below me, the wheelhouse door slid open, then, after a

moment or two, closed with a thud. I wondered who would have stepped out onto the bridge wing in the middle of a rainstorm, but lacked the energy to lift my head or even open my eyes to look. That changed when I heard the captain roar, "Ass far ass I am concerned, Mr. Mate—" before his voice was drowned by the howling wind. My eyes snapped open and I jerked my head around. There, at the far end of the bridge wing—maybe 40 feet away—stood the captain and the mate. The cloud behind them darkened and lightning bolts fell like hurled spears. I could see the fear in Mr. Hunt's face. Thunder cracked as Captain Isenhagen's hand jabbed forward, his finger stopping just short of touching the mate's chest. Mr. Hunt's head seemed to tuck further and further between his shoulders, turtle-like. The storm raged and the captain railed against the poor mate for five minutes or so as I watched, hidden partially by the mast, my eyes wide.

Then it was over. The harangue ended and the storm moved aft. The sky lightened, the lightning and thunder became more distant. The captain turned on his heel and marched into the wheelhouse. The mate slipped around and down the stairs like a scared rat. I stood in my bathing suit dripping, slackjawed, my hands clenching the rail in disbelief.

The ship continued on its path through the canal. We had anchored only a couple of hours while the northbound convoy passed us on their way to Gatun Locks. Now we were once again moving through the jungle toward the Pedro Miguel Locks. I stood at the rail looking first at the tops of the trees glistening with the raindrops, then far down at the shoreline. A crocodile slithered off the mudbank into the water and disappeared. A large bulk carrier less than a mile ahead maintained its distance. A muffled burst of thunder behind me made me turn. The storm was still a living, breathing creature; a round black cloud emitting lightning bolts, huffing and puffing its way across the lake and into the jungle. A rainbow followed, but quickly faded.

I went below, stunned by the show I had witnessed. Alone in my room, I toweled off, put my khakis back on and returned to the bridge where I stayed while the ship locked through Pedro Miguel and Mira Flores, dropping to the level of the Pacific.

After eating a quick sandwich, I took the two pilots down to the gangway and watched them descend into their boat, turn and wave, then disappear into the sitting compartment. I stood watching as we picked up speed heading south through the Golfo de Panama, mesmerized by the water moving faster and faster beneath us. I walked to the bow and sat on my favorite bollard. The sun set. A brief twilight passed and stars flooded the sky with specks of light. A light breeze fanned my face as the ship moved ahead and I felt peaceful there alone in the night, but also a tingling of anticipation. Having passed through the Panama Canal, I sensed I was on the other side of the world; that I'd left that part of the globe—like the left side of the brain—dedicated to and dictated by common sense and virtue and hard and fast rules. I felt I'd entered the other side, a shadowy place of magic and illusion, where things I had no experience with were commonplace. The sort of place where, as Irving Jackson had said, "yo' Mama never tol' you nuthin' 'bout this."

Balboa to Buenaventura
August 2-3

Sitting out in the black night, immersed in stars, listening to the water gurgle alongside the hull, I caught myself nodding off. I got up and slowly climbed the outside stairs to my deck, entered the house on the starboard side, slipped quietly into my room, threw my clothes on the floor and crawled into bed. Wally was already in the upper bunk snoring, another habit of his that annoyed me. Now that we'd been roommates for two weeks, we were both on each other nerves for little things. The habit that annoyed me more than anything was his disgusting tendency to pee on the floor in our head. He liked to talk when he peed— most other times as well. When he talked, he turned to his right to be better heard, causing urine to splatter over the right side of the toilet bowl and onto the linoleum. Generally, I liked Wally. Some things really didn't signify—another term out of Wally's personal lexicon—and I was doing my best to distinguish between what did and didn't.

I was nearly asleep when I remembered the letter from my girlfriend. Jerking awake as though prodded, I reached up and toggled my bunk light back on. It had been so long ago that I stuffed the letter into the pocket of my trousers, I wondered if it was still there. I picked my pants up off the floor and my fingers traced out the bulky envelope. My heart raced.

I held the letter in both hands, turned it over and back, then sniffed it. Most girls from my town wore a scent called *White Shoulders*. Melissa preferred *Interlude*, which I thought was really cool, if for no other reason than it increased her mystique. Much as I liked it, though, it wasn't enough to push me over what she called the "Catholic edge" into the murky abyss of sex. Melissa wasn't Catholic. She wasn't much of anything religious. But she was a free spirit—possibly the only one in central Nebraska in 1967. Her parents were old when she was born. She came as a blessing and they had raised her like she was a cherished object: a jewel or fine porcelain. She'd had every toy, every hug and kiss, every encouragement—unlike me, who had been raised by a Catholic mother who believed the easiest way to heaven was through suffering; a disoriented father who woke every morning thinking about alcohol and nicotine; a convent of bitter nuns, and a bully of a priest.

My mother didn't much care for Melissa, whose sense of morality was just too different. Melissa had told me that when she was fifteen, one starry August night in the bed of her father's blue and white three-quarter ton dodge, a boy told her he would love her forever. She let him touch her and she touched him and the intimacy was so pleasurable that from that point on she saw no real reason to hold back. Six months before meeting me, he'd moved out of state and out of her life. Word leaked out and her reputation suffered some, but nature had provided her with a long-range view of life. Besides, living as she did thirteen miles outside of town, she wound up dating guys from neighboring villages who didn't even go to our high school.

I first dated Melissa during Christmas vacation of my freshman year at college— a little more than six months before joining this ship. It was my first time home since leaving in August and it was a big time for me and my friends: snooker at Big Al's, road-hunting pheasants, shooting hoops at the high school gym, all the time talking, comparing notes about school or girls or whatever. One Saturday night, I went to the polka dance at the VFW hall west of town. The Polka Kings played—Ron on accordion, Jerome on steel guitar and Eldon, who was my age, drumming and singing. Old and young, everyone danced and sweat and laughed and flirted, then slipped and slid out to their cars in the crystal cold night to drink whiskey out of the pint bottle and laugh some more—maybe wrestle with someone a little, or make out in the back seat of a car. Melissa was there. She was a junior in high school—in my brother Bob's class. I had been vaguely aware of her during my senior year of high school, but she was only a slow-to-develop sophomore then. That night at the VFW hall, I saw her dancing the Flying Dutchman—a wild whirl where three partners swing each other round and round as the music crescendos to a frenzy—with a couple guys my brother's age and my heart skipped one beat. Her shoulder length blond hair flew one way, her short red skirt the other and I was hooked.

I somehow let her know I was interested and before thirty minutes had passed, she had left a pimply-faced junior standing in the middle of the dance floor while we snuck out the front door. We were together the next four nights, took a break over Christmas, then resumed dating on the 26th. On New Year's Eve, we were in the basement of her house, her parents asleep two floors above us. The old grandfather clock up in the entryway had just finished its twelfth stroke and she and I were mostly naked. In spite of being monumentally— well, in my opinion—aroused, I refused her the commitment she sought. She thought I was afraid of sex. I didn't know what to say. She slipped back into her bra and buttoned her blouse, shook her arms at her sides and laughed her pixie laugh with her green eyes sparkling.

"I can't believe that goofy church you go to can make you resist me," she said.

We stopped dating after that. I was just too embarrassed. In January I returned to New York to finish my freshman year at the Academy.

I had been back in Nebraska for only a week or so in June when I saw Melissa drive her daddy's big white Buick through town. My friend Jim and I were dragging the main in his father's pickup, u-turning at the grain elevator at the west end, then, on the east side, just past Pearl's Café. Those seven blocks were pretty important geography back then, when I was slogging through my adolescent years, unsure of my capabilities and limitations, unsure of my beliefs, of my preparedness to go into the wide world, unsure of every fucking thing. Up and back, up and back, talking, talking, acting like mythological heroes, looking into the windows of the cars we met, looking for someone, for something, for *some thing* that would take us up out of our angst into what we believed would be the joys of adulthood.

Melissa drove by, alone, her blond hair pinned up above bare shoulders and I knew I'd found what I was looking for. She u-turned at Pearl's. I got out of Jim's pickup a block before that, crossed the street to the westbound lane and waited. She stopped, leaned over, all white teeth and smiling red lips and opened the door on the rider's side. It was a warm evening and she wore denim shorts and a yellow halter. Her skin was tanned and her breasts had doubled in size during the six months we had been apart. I ached for her. I was leaving for New Orleans in two days and this was it. My mind was made up. Tonight was the night. If telling her I loved her was part of the deal, well, probably I did love her. No Catholic Church guilt trip lack of commitment small town mothers were going to hold me back. We turned off the highway, cut the lights and drove down a dark, tire-track dirt trail to a quarter-section her father owned just north of the Middle Loup River Bridge. The fecund smell of fresh cut alfalfa was fuel to our fire. The moon was an over-sized yellow ball suspended like on a wire above a hill to the east and there were a million stars. We kissed and rolled in the soft dirt and grabbed at each other like reunited lovers before she told me she was having her period. Period. We could do anything except make love, but were too inexperienced to know what that might be. Thirty-six hours later, I was on my way to New Orleans, still a virgin.

On the ship, I lay in my bunk, holding the envelope, turning it over and over, smelling it, smelling her, wondering what she was doing, thinking about the missed opportunity that January night in her basement. Recalling the pleasure I'd had with Maria, I vowed to not make that mistake again.

I opened the letter. Such strong scent rose out of the envelope that Wally missed a breath, snorted and coughed, then resumed his rhythmic breathing.

Dearest Jake,
Will you really get this letter? Where are you? In Panama? I can't believe you will get this letter in Panama. What will you be doing? Sitting on the ship – in your room? At a dining table? On deck? Where? I miss you a lot. I miss your cheeks and your hands and your jet-black hair and the way you stutter a little when you talk. I miss kissing you (I haven't kissed anyone since you left). I miss touching your chest. I don't know what I miss most about you. I miss what you tell me about places I've never seen.

I want to say something. You know I have something of a "reputation". You also know, since I told you, I've been with another boy, you know, sexually, and I will admit I like sex and I like guys. With you – believe it or not – it's totally different. I don't just want to hold you and kiss you and lick your ear, I want to crawl inside of you and be you and have you crawl inside of me and be me. I don't know what that is, but I suppose it's love. I just know I miss you so much I can hardly breathe. I mope around here all day and my folks are worried and my mom thinks I should go see Doctor Miller.

I saw your mom in town the other day and gave her my biggest smile and waved and waved. I don't think she likes me much though. She kind of waved a little. Oh well. I think I can make her love me. Like I think I can make you love me. Just because you're a million miles away, don't think I can't reach you with love. I'm doing it now. I know I am.

I write to you a lot – but I don't send what I write. I have your address in Valparaiso or some place like that, so you'll get a letter from me there.

I like to sit up in the window of my haymow at night, looking at the stars, feeling the breeze against my face and smelling alfalfa. I think of you. I have that little picture of you in your dumb cadet hat and I sit here in the moonlight and look at it and think all sorts of things I'm afraid to tell you about since it would probably scare you or make you think there's something wrong with me. Well, let me tell you. There is. I am in love. Sometimes my tummy aches, I love you so much. I love you, and I love loving you.

Melissa.

I was stunned. I reread the letter, folded it, set it beside my bunk, picked it back up and read it again. Melissa loved me. The most beautiful girl I'd ever known loved me. I was so exhausted by emotion and a lack of sleep that I dropped off, waking at five when Simple Simon called me for morning stars, asking me why my bunk light was still on and would I mind if he read the letter I clutched in my hand since he hadn't gotten one.

With our schedule calling for us to arrive at the Buenaventura River on the morning tide, Sunday, July 30th, we ran on a slow bell south and a little east, looking toward a timed arrival of 0600. Buenaventura was just south of four degrees north of the Equator and our course there kept us far enough away from land that I had a clear horizon for navigation fixes and azimuths.

I couldn't focus on my navigation duties though. I walked around in a daze with the letter in my pocket thinking of where I could go to read it again. Mr. Potter, the second mate, rapped sharply on the door of the head on the bridge because I was taking too long.

"No masturbating on watch," he said, not a trace of humor in his voice.

I read it in the lazarette lying on my stomach on the pile of old rope down below the fantail, where the boatswain had sent me to help Irving Jackson bring up an extra mooring line; then again perched on my favorite bollard forward over the lunch hour with a pod of porpoise leaping near the bow. The sun shining through a thin layer of cirrostratus put a hint of a halo around it. The water was mirror flat. Flying fish left droplet trails as they jetted a foot off the water, looking for insects. I thought to myself I had never been happier.

That evening, I crossed Sirius, the dog star, brightest in the heavens, star of tremulous motion, with Canopus and Capella—all three first magnitude stars. Capella was believed to be identical in size to our sun but emitting two hundred and fifty times as much light. I'd shot it last, when the horizon was less clear. It crossed the other two far to the north. The Sirius – Canopus cross fell in very near the second mate's six-star fix—a pinwheel, as usual. Mr. Potter plotted his sixth line of position as I wrote down the time for Capella.

"That's not exactly a usable three star fix," he said when I'd finally laid down my fix. "But keep trying. Some people never master it. Just remember, if you don't, you cannot be the navigator which means you cannot sail as second mate which means you'll never be a master mariner."

"What is the difference between master and captain?" I asked.

"The Coast Guard grants the master's license. The company selects its captains from the ranks of its licensed masters. The exam for the license is the fourth extensive exam one must take in this career, following behind third mate, second mate and chief mate. Each exam takes as long as a week to complete. To set for one's master's license, one must have sailed at least one year as third mate, passed the second mate's exam; sailed one year as second mate, passed the chief mate's exam; sailed one year as chief mate, passed the master's exam. Depending on how one's career goes, this can take eight or ten years. The master mariner must know everything about this craft of sailing: how to splice wire rope, rig a jumbo boom, navigate a narrow channel, lash cargo, care for passengers, control his crew—preferably by humanitarian means. Of all his knowledge, though, nothing is more important than understanding the difference between a good fix and a mediocre fix. That is why we work toward mastery of the three-star fix."

Simple Simon's call with news the baker had fresh cinnamon rolls on the pass-through between the galley and the crew pantry included, almost as an afterthought, the captain's order for me to go directly to the port side pilot ladder—although Simple couldn't remember why. I dressed, brushed my teeth and ran down to main deck. Irving Jackson stood there coiling a heaving line for the pilot's bag while Boss Jones knelt tying the knot that secured the ladder to the padeyes welded into the deck. The ship turned gracefully to port as I leaned over the rail to look at the ladder. A small white boat with it's red and white pilot flag hanging limp above the deckhouse intruded upon the calm blue water as it approached down our port side. The day was glorious. First rays of sunlight beamed out above the hilly coastline.

Mists of vapor rose off the green roof of the jungle. I smiled at the boatswain.

"Good morning, Ka-dett," he boomed.

"Morning, boatswain. Morning Irving."

"Mornin' youngblood." said Irving Jackson.

"And did the woman in Panama meet with your approval, Mr. ka-dett?" asked the boatswain with just a hint of a chuckle. Irving Jackson did a funny little tap dance and bow.

"She was wonderful," I answered.

"Had a hunch you might like Maria," he said. He glanced toward shore. "As regards this god-forsaken doghole, may I point out there are serious risks involved with going up to Chancre Hill."

Irving Jackson, his sideman, nodded and shuffled and bowed and said "yassuh, you done got that right. Dere some risks on chancre hill, sho' 'nough, there be. Ha Ha."

"I would never lead a young man down a dangerous path," said Boss Jones. "But I personally have found the girls there to be fine, just fine. Take a little extra care, you know, ka-dett? A bottle of beer to wash up. Pick one what appears healthy, that don't, you know, smell bad."

"You shore don' want one what smells," said Irving.

The bow of the pilot boat nosed up against the side of the ship aft of the ladder. Irving Jackson lowered the heaving line. A black-skinned sailor wearing flip-flops and red gym shorts tied the pilot's brown leather bag onto the line, looked up squinting, and gave a thumbs up. The pilot stepped over the low gunwale of his boat, onto the bottom rung of the rope ladder, and climbed the eight steps to the deck.

I took the pilot's bag as protocol demanded and carried it to the bridge, the pilot following me. After a brief exchange with Captain Isenhagen, he looked at the quartermaster and said, "Steer zero nine five." Then he ordered half ahead and we moved briskly into the mouth of the Buenaventura River.

Frank Potter instructed me to plot positions as we navigated upriver so he could note them in the bell book. After passing through the small bay, we entered a narrow river and jungle engulfed us on both sides. The trees rose well above the bridge. Monkeys chattered. More of the brilliant birds I'd seen in

Panama cawed at us from the treetops. The water below was murky and still, and along the banks I saw dugout canoes, log rafts held together with leather straps, a flat-bottomed skiff with no gunwale. A small woman with uncovered breasts—heavy, as though full of milk—beat clothes against a rock near the bank on the starboard side. We moved slowly upriver—tentative—feeling our way through the shallow spots. I watched the pilot, an intense dapper man, shorter even than the captain, with dark skin, black hair and a trimmed mustache. He wore pressed white shorts, ink-stained at the front pocket on the right side, and a short sleeve white shirt with gold epaulets sewed onto the shoulders. The chart we were using indicated a muddy bottom, shallow in spots. The pilot had his own landmarks—certain trees, maybe, or an uncovered rock, or small inlets along the bank. We never bothered him with our fixes. He knew this water better than anyone. Occasionally, he spoke to Captain Isenhagen, who invariably nodded in response.

After picking our way at half and slow for forty-five minutes through a narrow place with jungle close enough to pluck leaves from the trees, we opened onto a broad reach along which sat the Buenaventura Docks. An ancient black and red tug powered up its engines and blew three puffs of black soot from its stack.

The sailors tied up quickly and quietly. The gangway was lowered and the safety net secured. According to Irving Jackson, the boatswain and Captain had talked, and there would be no further labor interruptions. An endless number of chattering longshoremen boarded and shuffled forward or aft to their assigned hatches and went to work positioning the booms, building their cardboard shade and climbing down into the holds. I helped Mr. Petrocelli open hatches. The sun rose higher. This wharf was carved from an equatorial rainforest. The air was heavy and full of moisture.

Giant, galvanized doors to the red-tiled warehouse slid open with a rattle-bang and within minutes the asphalt apron on the wharf swarmed with longshoremen carrying work gloves and peddlers selling Inca carvings, green gem-stones and gold trinkets. Paul Hunt approached me just after I had climbed down from the top of the resistor house at the forward end of number three.

"Cadet, I need your help today," he said.

"That's why I'm here, Mr. Mate," I answered, holding my hand against the glare coming off the superstructure.

He handed me a sheet of paper showing the cargo break-down in number five hold.

"Listen," he said, moving the chewed-up cigar stub from one side of his mouth to the other. "Ten bucks if you keep the longshores outta the beer in five lower-hold."

"That's a deal, mate." I answered.

I discovered early on I couldn't keep the longshoremen out of the beer. Furthermore, I figured the mate must have known that. They must have smelled it, because within minutes of uncovering the hatch, they had made a dozen holes down through the cardboard separator to bring up beer. Every long-shoreman in sight had a cervesa in his hand and stood there, smiling and toasting me.

I made a quick deal. If they stayed out of the hold and pro-vided a pig of ice, I would bring up enough eight-ounce bottles of Miller's High Life to keep everyone happy. Seemed logical. I preferred the role of bartender to that of policeman and, in this heat, cold beer was better than warm for everyone.

Wally asked me to wait for him to go ashore that night. The cargo from five was finished by four and by dinnertime I had chased the longshoremen out and closed all the hatchcovers. I figured I'd drank a six-pack or more, but sweat most of it out.

The mate handed me a ten spot when I went to his office. He said, "If you go to Chancre Hill and come back with a wart on your cock, don't blame me. In this port, you pay your money and you take your choice."

I raised an eyebrow and looked at the bill, wondering what, exactly, I would be buying with it.

After eating and showering, I stepped into khaki shorts, pulled on a summer shirt and walked out. Wally was already at the gangway wearing the straw hat he'd bought in Cristobal to keep the sun off his freckles. It hadn't rained that afternoon which meant we could expect a downpour that night. We walked along the cracked and pitted asphalt surface past the warehouses to the gate, where the guards didn't bother looking up from their card game. Outside the barbed-wire fence, a gang of taxi drivers accosted us, each with a better offer. I had looked carefully at the harbor chart this time, memorizing street names, even stepping off, with dividers, the distance to town, then up to Chancre Hill and back to the ship. I wasn't going to get lost a second time.

Wally leading the way, we blasted through the gauntlet of taxi drivers, walking purposefully and ignoring their chatter. We hoofed down the gravel road toward town talking a mile a minute when an old white Chevy pulled up and drove slowly alongside us. The driver wore a green banlon shirt and a Yankees baseball cap. His dark face was broken by a toothy smile.

"Me Juan. Me studente at Universite de Columbia," he said.

"Bonus nachos, Juan," said Wally.

"You are Amereecanos, no? I like Amereecanos. I hope to speak with you some Eenglish."

"Bono, there, Juan. Speak away. How the hell are ya?" Wally extended his hand.

"I ees very happy to meet you. Perhaps you want a ride to town? Maybe you want girl in Buenaventura," he said, as if, ultimately, there wasn't much else to talk about. "Colombian girl. Very beautiful." He kissed his fingertips.

"Where are the best girls?" I asked.

He pointed ahead and to the right where, in the distance, a steep dirt road led up a hill. A few small buildings sat on the shoulder where the jungle had been cut away.

"Very beautiful girls up there. Also," he smiled and shook his head slightly, "there is the government casa. Not so beautiful senoritas, but very nice, very clean. Muy bueno."

"But girls not so beautiful?" I said, amused that even the locals thought the government whores second rate.

Juan twisted his face into a frown and shook his head as if having a gas-pain. Then he brightened with a new thought. "Senoritas on the heel very bee-utiful. You weesh to ride in my taxi?"

"Yeah. We need a taxi," said Wally. "I don't know about my pardnero here, but I'm going out to the government casa."

"Take Wally. I'm not sure where I'm going."

Wally jumped into the cab, rolled down his window, smiled his Jiminy Cricket, gapped-tooth smile and said, "To hell if you're not careful."

"You need taxi later, you look for me. I weel be on heel waiting for you," said Juan.

"How do you know I'll be there?" I asked, smiling.

He touched his temple with his right index finger and rolled his eyes toward Wally. "I think you like beautiful senoritas."

The cab left in a cloud of dust and I walked into town. The shacks I passed—cardboard walls, tin roofs, cloth hung for a door—could hardly be considered buildings. A narrow stream containing what must have been human waste, considering the stink, ran along the side of the road. Street urchins, some completely naked, others wearing only shorts, stopped their play and held out their hands, palms up.

According to George LeClair, the Conquistadoras shipped gold to Spain through Buenaventura during the 15th century. In contrast to its present impoverished period, the city had enjoyed a golden age when a large cathedral and government houses were built, stone boulevards laid down and beautiful Spanish mansions constructed.

The marketplace was closing for the day as I strolled through. Vendors rolled their wares into colorful blankets, slowly and carefully, to make certain they missed nothing. They watched as I passed, hoping I'd buy something. I walked by a half-dozen stucco buildings used by shipping companies and their agents, eventually arriving in the plaza. It was like a poorly tended garden, the vegetation out of control. A statue of a military man on a horse stood in the center, his arm broken at the hand. Yellow and lavender flowers bloomed everywhere; small wooden benches and pathways for lovers sat partially concealed in the foliage. I bought a cervesa from a street vendor, selected a bench and sat to drink. Dim but ornate streetlights struggled to illuminate. Across from me sat the Catholic Church and a rectory. A cabildo stood alongside the rectory and next to it were other important looking buildings.

The bench I sat on was painted pink, its legs covered over with vines. Tiny green lizards played about my bench defying gravity by sitting on the vertical. Shadows of long brown rats ran like dark fluid along the edges of the pathways that led to the center of the plaza. The familiar smell of sewage and charcoal was overwhelmed by a penetrating minty fragrance that made me lightheaded. Couples walked by arm in arm, nuzzling and murmuring in low tones. Armed guards with black hair and small mustaches lolled smoking in the street nearby.

The Church was built of adobe and stone, and had been whitewashed so it gleamed in the evening sun. It had two unequal towers, one capped by a bronze dome with a cross at the very top; the other square and stolid—an elegant Quixote next to his Sancho. Bells hung in both towers and as I sat there, they began ringing as if for evening prayer. The roofs of the church and the other buildings were covered with blood-red tile, the adobe facades outlined in gold paint. Gold paint further defined a vaulted archway below which was an asymmetrical star-shaped window. Below that were large wooden doors, also arched. The doors opened onto an elevated platform from which huge steps dropped to the cobblestone street. Old men, women with infants, and a gaggle of raggedy ass kids sat on the steps.

A black-robed friar appeared at the top of the steps speaking in rapid Spanish and waving his arms. The peasants scattered slowly, looking tired, their heads turning to the friar as if hoping for a little something, then to the stone steps, to the job of descending, thinking, perhaps, of another hungry night in the streets.

Once the steps were cleared, the friar glanced about with a satisfied look, then disappeared inside one of the large doors that closed with a dull clunk. A cool breeze tickled the hairs on my arms. Twilight passed into full night. I felt secure and at peace in this plaza, before this edifice of a church. People moved about quietly. No one spoke above a whisper. Small black birds hopped from branch to bench to terrace looking for crumbs or insects. In the distance, I heard a child wail.

I sat for a long time, not moving. My breath grew shallow and my muscles limp. My mind considered Raskolnikov. I was deep into Dostoevsky's book now, put off by the edginess of a man descending into madness but also stimulated. I wondered idly which whorehouse Raskolnikov would go to were he in my shoes. Would he take the safe path and go to the government house or would he abandon sense, and risk contracting a disease for something as nebulous as the promise of female beauty? Was pleasure heightened because of beauty? Or only desire? And what about guilt? I thought about the eyes of Jesus above the Indian girl's bed. So guilt destroyed pleasure? Or only when desire was lacking? How much desire was enough to overcome a little guilt? I'd heard old men had trouble getting hard, thought again about the Indian girl I'd walked away from. Not enough desire? That had to be it. She lacked some erotic quality I needed to stimulate my masculinity.

These thoughts played in my mind like idle children. I remembered Mr. Potter calling Buenaventura the bunghole of the Rum and Romance Run. He said more than three hundred inches of rain fell each year, and even when it wasn't raining, the place was a hellhole.

Two of the streetlights went out as I sat, pinned to the bench. The cathedral, now dark and threatening, stood before me, a reminder of the authority that I, like Raskolnikov, was coming to question. Time passed. I couldn't move; couldn't decide. Then, like a slap, raindrops lashed across my face. I jumped up and without a second thought hurried toward the road that lead to Chancre Hill. As I walked quickly away from the cathedral, I recalled being a young boy, dipping the tips of the fingers of my right hand into the ceramic holy water font, crossing myself as I heaved against the stout wooden door, happy to exit the candle-lit church after confessing and reciting my penance, released once again from its power.

The asphalt street turned to dirt and gravel and the rain fell in sheets. I hurried up the hill, barely able to see the road as it wound around out of the town into the jungle. I slipped along in the mud, focused on the lights ahead, blurred as they were. The going was difficult and I thought to myself this seemed wrong, that falling into sin, which is what I considered my choice to be, should be easier. Finally, I reached a level place and I saw a row of small buildings. Each had an open-air patio covered with a tin roof. Naked colored lights—like Christmas bulbs—were strung from ceiling to pillar to ceiling to pillar and I could see, in the distance, people moving about. As I approached, I heard music with a quick, lively beat. Closer to the building, I saw sailors sliding through the mud from one patio to the next in search of—what—the perfect girl? More beauty? True Love? Mangy dogs slunk under the patios for shelter. Piles of trash littered the roadway. I walked past the first bar, the Cockpit, where I recognized members of the black gang from my ship. George Coleman, the first engineer, stood at the bar, so I walked on by.

The hand-painted wooden sign on the next bar said Wonderland. I stepped up out of the mud onto the corner of the patio. Three or four men sat in chairs next to tables topped with chipped yellow formica, strewn with empty bottles, whores standing nearby or sitting on their laps. A girl with eyes like a cat, green and almond-shaped, walked toward me wearing a short black robe, loosely tied. She took my hand and led me to a table in the corner. Old car speakers hanging from the wooden rafters played Jefferson Airplane. The music had a tinny sound as it and the rain reverberated against opposite sides of the metal roof. We sat at a table near the far end of the patio and I sensed the only thing separating me from the jungle were the Christmas lights hanging from the ceiling.

The girl sat on my lap, facing me, her legs straddling mine. She licked my ear and whispered Spanish words as Grace Slick belted out her song about ten-foot white rabbits. I put my hands to her hips and pulled her against me, trying my best to act like this was how things should be. What a weird world, I thought to myself. I had expected boundaries because I'd always had them; now, there were none.

"Cadete'," she said. "Cherry boy." She nuzzled my neck, her nipples rubbing against me. Her lips touched my cheek, then moved to my mouth. I held back at first, thinking of disease, then surrendered to the waves of desire and responded. I felt her transfer something—a little pill, I thought—from her mouth to mine. I rejected it at first, then, as she pressed her body harder against me, arousing me fully, I let go and swallowed. Her mouth tasted of peppermint candy.

She pulled away, smiling. "You want cervesa?" she asked, and a beer appeared.

"What is your name?" I asked.

"Alicia," she answered. She was different from Maria. In spite of her aggressive manner, she seemed younger and more innocent. Her black hair was boyishly short. She laughed at me, all white teeth and sparkling eyes, and handed me the beer. One of the sailors from the ship stood at the bar—drunk and obnoxious. He sent a glass of white rum to my table. I drank it and chased it with the beer. I was thirsty and it tasted good. Alicia had a bowl of nuts brought to our table. I ate a handful, then drank another beer. The sailor sent over another glass of rum and raised his own in a toast to—I don't know—me? women like Alicia? I didn't really care. The rain clattered on the roof. Jim Morrison sang Strange Days. My head was spinning and the nature of time seemed different, but I realized I felt no fear.

Alicia looked at me as if she understood and kissed me again, her passion heightened. My world seemed to shrink then, until it consisted only of this Alice and my desire for her. There was no thought, no guilt, no wondering about disease, no thirst or hunger, nothing but an animal longing to mold my body to that of the woman on my lap.

We moved from the patio to a small room behind the bar. I don't recall my legs working. I don't recall the sailor saying anything. All I know is I lay on my back on a sheet on a mattress with Alicia and we were both naked. The room was small—not much larger than the bed—and it was spinning. There were three nondescript walls and a dingy, rose curtain on a rod. I had no sense of time and our pleasure was childlike. Alicia kissed me and giggled, bit my ear and tickled me. When her teasing became too much, I would grab her, squealing and squirming, maneuver on top and thrust myself into her until she wrapped her arms about my head and her legs around my body.

This went on for what seemed like hours and hours through shifting layers of consciousness, until at some point, I found myself awake and stone sober, lying next to a sleeping Alicia, wondering how much time had passed and what all had transpired. I looked at my watch. The luminous orange digits showed five after four. Alicia's right leg and arm lay across my body as if to prevent me from leaving. I moved and Alicia curled even closer. I remembered the pill she had transferred into my mouth, then decided that for all I knew or cared, it could have been peppermint candy.

I felt relaxed, drained of desire. I wanted to return to the ship, to shower and lie in my own bed. I moved her arm and leg. She lifted her head, saw me and frowned, then burrowed with her mouth like a small night animal into the crook of my neck. I became aroused again. She purred like a cat, shifted her body and took me inside of her. I moved and she moved and we moved together. My thoughts toward her were tender, and briefly I considered her life here: her tiny, miserable room, nights with different sailors. I wondered what she would do when she was too old to attract business.

I kissed her, moved her silently off me and got out of bed. I slipped on my shoes and bumped along in the darkness to the toilet where I gagged from the smell. I peed into a long metal trough, slanted like a gutter toward a hole and poured the half-bottle of beer I had dutifully saved over my penis, working it into the folds—thinking to myself how ridiculous this seemed. I dressed and left the mate's ten dollar bill on the bed. Alicia lay there, quietly watching. She made me promise to return. I felt melancholy, thinking how easily promises were made when there was no chance of keeping them. I dressed, said goodbye and kissed her. Her cat eyes followed me as I left.

Outside, the jungle seemed alive and felt dangerous. I heard screeching and buzzing, imagined I heard a large animal moving nearby. I was afraid but felt I had no options, so started down the road when a car idled slowly up beside me. It was my friend Juan, like a guardian angel. "You weel find danger on this road at night, senor."

When he dropped me at the gate, I gave him what money I had left—maybe five dollars. On the ship I showered, then slept fitfully for two hours, dreaming of a man named Raskolnikov wandering along a road—narrow, with rungs and a rail, like a gangway—that provided a safe access through a jungle alive with vipers, wild orchids and large cats with women's bodies. At some point in the dream, I realized I was Raskolnikov and the further I went along that path, the more terrible and near at hand became the dangers lurking on both sides. Then the road ended and I was faced with a horrible decision. To remain in the safety of the road, I had to either turn back or stop and stay there. If I went ahead, even a step, I had to leave the road for the jungle. I stepped forward as I awoke, wet with sweat.

Buenaventura to Guayaquil
August 4

We weren't scheduled to sail for Guayaquil till noon. I was called for breakfast but it was straight up 0800 when I staggered into the mate's office, rummy and red-eyed. Cargo was finished and Mr. Hunt sat at his desk wearing his half-width reading glasses signing cargo documents. He told me to go work on my Sea Project till eleven when I was to report to the bridge to test navigation gear with the third mate. I didn't argue. My sea project consisted of an inch-thick book divided into sections covering Navigation, Rules of the Road, Piloting, Cargo Operations and the like. Wally, being an engine cadet, had to study boring topics like Steam Propulsion, Refrigeration and Deck machinery—which, of course, he loved.

I had good energy after my night on Chancre Hill, so I actually worked a couple hours on Rules of the Road, memorizing the Good Seamanship Rule. According to Mr. Potter, this Rule not only covered most situations that could develop at sea but also provided guidance to live by. It went like this:

Nothing in these Rules shall exonerate any vessel, or the owner, master or crew thereof, from the consequences of any neglect to comply with these Rules or of the neglect of any precaution which may be required by the ordinary practice of seamen, or by the special circumstances of the case.

In other words, according to this rule, one is not only responsible for the consequences of his actions, but also for the consequences that come as a result of not following certain precautions that would typically be taken by a cautious, totally uptight person, looking foremost in his world to forestall life's dangers, whether seen or unseen. In other words, in my opinion, to live as if one would live forever—rather than follow the life is short dictum. I doubted Raskolnikov would think much of this rule, but could understand why Mr. Potter liked it.

Mr. Petrocelli was already in the wheelhouse when I went up at eleven, bustling about with a duster in hand, brushing imaginary dustballs from the toggle switches to the navigation lights. I laughed when I saw him. Couldn't help it. I laughed when he made coffee, when he tested the steering gear, when he wrote his log, when he shot sunlines. Nothing was ever simple for Antonio Petrocelli. He never spoke with the captain without grousing about one thing or another: his eggs were too runny or the third engineer frowned at him or the longshoremen were pilfering cargo. The captain kept a poker face and listened but seldom commented. He spent little time on the bridge on Petrocelli's watch.

"You see," Mr. Petrocelli would say seriously after the captain left the bridge. "That's how to keep the captain from bothering you. Complain constantly."

We crossed the equator at 0840 the following morning. On my way to breakfast, the second mate instructed me to tell the boatswain to secure his lockers in preparation for the bump when we crossed the line. I did as I was told promptly after eating. The boatswain gave me a coil of small stuff and sent me around to lash loose gear in all the lockers. I didn't think much about it. If they told me we bumped when we crossed the equator, well, fine. Who was I to argue? Around eight-thirty, the mate found me in the boatswain's locker forward and told me to report to the bridge for my initiation. I went there directly. Including Wally and one of the Ordinary Seamen, there were three of us polliwogs on board. The mate had a little ceremony where we were blindfolded and turned around clockwise until dizzy, then, supposedly just at the moment we crossed the line, turned counter-clockwise like water in a drain in the southern hemisphere and paddled a couple of times with a ping pong paddle. He had out his little penknife and wanted to tattoo a dolphin on everyone's ankle but the Captain shook his head, disgusted. I took the whole thing in stride. We received our King Neptune certificates signed by the captain and stamped with the ship's official seal. Wally scoffed, but I thought they were cool.

After dinner that night, Mr. LeClair, the purser, with the high-water pants and twitching left eye, stopped by our table and invited me to stop by his room for a drink after watch. Wally had just made his umpteenth jerk-off comment about Melissa's letter which he had, that morning, yanked out of my hand as he walked into the head, then locked the door and read word for word aloud while sitting on the toilet. I was pissed about it as first, but decided it didn't really matter. Didn't signify; wasn't worth getting upset over. Glad to get away from Wally, I said yes, but after Mr. LeClair left the saloon, Wally rolled his eyes.

"Now that sounds like a barrel of laughs," he said.

Mr. LeClair had rarely spoken to me since the day we had been to dinner together at Boyd's, the Mexican restaurant in Houston where we'd seen the British sailor murdered. I walked by his office all the time since it was centrally located on what was called the business deck, but he seemed to be always typing and too busy to visit. Earlier in the day, when I drew on my wages, he was businesslike, but not unfriendly, snapping out my four - five dollar bills with a certain gravity, giving credence to the idea that we worked and, for that work, received money. I was still at the stage where what we did seemed to be such an adventure, I'd have done it for nothing.

In the saloon, which was the only other place on the ship I ever saw him, Mr. LeClair rarely spoke and ate with his head down. When he did venture to comment, he sounded shy and uncertain.

He was shorter than me and serious. He wore pressed khaki shirts with a black tie stuffed between his second and third buttons, had oily brown hair and wore black-framed glasses. His brown eyes bugged out behind thick lenses and his jaw was weak. His ears protruded, his nose pointed and thin. His neck appeared stretched and he was stoop-shouldered. The twitch in his left eye increased when he got nervous and he smoked constantly, seeming to exhale less than he inhaled.

On watch that evening, I plotted another two-star fix using Canopus and Aldebaran, both of which twinkled faintly and late through the high cirrostratus which caused even the second mate with his 4-power scope to have to wait until it was almost too late to have a usable horizon. Mr. Potter wound up with three decent stars and plotted them. He had a bee in his bonnet for some reason and spent the last hour haranguing about the evils of alcohol and prostitution. I listened respectfully as I could but would like to have told him he was wasting his breath. Now that I was deep into Raskolnikov and moving deeper into this sultry, southern hemisphere, I didn't want to hear preaching. At eight, I dropped down the stairs three at a time and knocked on Mr. LeClair's door.

"Come in," he said quietly, so I opened the door. His room was small, but obsessively neat. It smelled of stale cigarettes and old socks. He sat in a chair between a half-size refrigerator and his bunk, which was covered with a yellow spread. He was thin and his right foot was crossed over his left leg, then crossed around behind his left calf. A cloud of smoke engulfed him and a water glass with whiskey sat on the top of the refrigerator near his left hand.

"What can I get you, Jake?" he asked, exhaling. "I drink single malt scotch—though that seems to be a drink for older men."

"Bourbon, please, if you have it," I answered. "No scotch drinkers in my family, so far."

He stood, walked over to his dresser, the top of which served as his bar, plunked a couple of ice cubes into a glass and filled it with Seagram's. His hands shook as he poured and I noticed his thumb and index fingers were brown with tar. We made small talk for a while. Where are you from? How do you like the ship? Sure is hot. I watched him suck on his cigarette and blow smoke rings in the air. He stared at me as if sizing me up or wondering if he could trust me.

"How long have you been a purser?" I asked.

"This will be my eighth year."

"You must enjoy the job."

"It has its good points. At least I don't have to work in the heat and noise of the engine room, or freeze to death on deck. Plus, we occasionally have interesting passengers."

He kept shifting in his seat, pushing the butt of his palm against his lap as though trying to suppress an ever-present hard-on. I honestly couldn't figure out what he was doing and didn't want to ask.

"How did you become a purser?"

"My parents were—are—both academics in a Catholic university," he said. "My mom wanted me to be a priest and never forgave me for not being ordained."

"Did you study in the seminary?"

"I nearly finished. I entered at age sixteen and quit at twenty-one with less than a year to go."

"Five years? That is a long time. Why'd you quit?"

He inhaled deeply, then blew a perfect smoke ring that drifted slowly toward the ceiling. "Because I—well, I had sex with a woman."

I choked on my drink, and almost laughed until I saw how deathly serious he was. "Well, I mean—well, that—but you weren't even a priest yet. That shouldn't have prevented you from being ordained."

"Of course I knew that. I was afraid that after having had a taste of sex, I would want more, priest or not." He stuffed out one cigarette and immediately lit another with his burnished metal, flip-top lighter.

"It didn't turn out that way." He spoke calmly and quietly, his eyes closed. I had to lean forward to hear him. "But I was afraid it might."

"You mean you haven't had sex since that night?" I noticed a picture above his bunk of the Blessed Virgin holding the toddler Jesus. I finished my bourbon, amazed at how quickly this conversation had turned bizarre.

"I didn't want to have sex then," he said as though confessing. "The truth is, I didn't consummate the act." He looked up at me, bug-eyed, studying my reaction to this very weird news. All I could think was that this must be one stopped-up guy. I stood, walked the two steps over to his dresser and refilled my glass. I was coming to understand why men drank hard liquor.

"So what happened? I said, trying to act—I don't know—nonchalant, I guess.

He stared at me for at least a minute, one side of his black-framed glasses higher than the other. Then, as if deciding he could trust me, said: "I don't want you to think I tell this story to everyone who comes aboard this ship. One or two know it. It's not something I talk about. I hope you won't mention it to others." He drank and inhaled.

"I see by your information card that you're Roman Catholic. So am I, of course. My religion—or maybe how my parents presented it to me—has a lot to do with how I am. I—I think I've become more desperate lately. I just hope I can trust you."

He sat quietly again, inhaling deeply from his Kent and drinking—gulping— scotch.

"What is said here stays here," I said, thinking that sounded really corny.

He sat, eyes closed, as though trying through force of will to control himself. Finally, somewhat composed, he continued.

"We were in Naples, discharging jeeps. I inadvertently told one of the engineers I had never been to bed with a woman, that I was a seminary student. They didn't care at all about religious vocation, just focused on how I'd not had sex and decided to wage an all-out attack on my virginity.

"I had been helping a Yemeni wiper learn English. The engineers used him to lure me ashore. MacPhayle, the chief, was behind the whole thing. They knew I'd never fall for it if one of them invited me. We took a taxi to a house on a narrow street in Naples. The house was bright yellow with red tiles on the roof and over the shuttered windows. I should have suspected something, but the wiper and I had become friends. I was young—just twenty-four—and couldn't believe he would trick me.

"I should have realized something was wrong when the so-called restaurant turned out to be a house. The only people there besides the wiper and me were a motherly woman with a thick braid of gray hair and a busty blond named Jeanette Caposiena. The wiper had told me this restaurant was the finest in Naples and very exclusive. We ate beef with noodles and drank red wine. Everything tasted very good. With the wine, my guard was down. The older woman asked if we'd care to step into the sitting room for coffee and brandy. The wiper, being Muslim, didn't drink, but accompanied us to the other room for his espresso. Next thing I knew, the wiper was gone to the bathroom, the older woman had left to get coffee and I was alone with the girl. I became frightened. The girl was an enemy—evil and devilish. I tried the door. It was locked. I knocked and shouted. The girl sat, her legs exposed by her short skirt, patiently waiting. Finally, terrified, I returned to my seat."

The poor man's eye twitched violently as he spoke. His legs crossed and uncrossed and he jiggled his foot. His eyebrows rose and fell like wings. I refilled my glass, saying nothing.

"I intended to not go through with the lovemaking when I realized what was happening. After all, it was only a temptation. Unless I agreed to it, there was nothing the girl could do. I was sure whatever decision I came to meant nothing to her. I realize I am not an attractive man. She would be paid regardless.

"She stood calmly and put on music. She started moving; pulled me up so we danced together. I know I was clumsy but I loved how she felt. She removed her clothes, piece by piece— hardly looking at me. I watched. Finally, she wore only black underwear. I desired her. You can't imagine the agony I went through, realizing that I wanted her—like one animal wants another. I lusted after this stranger—a woman whose name I did not know. No love—only lust. I thought of Christ dying for my sins. I thought of His Agony in the Garden. I thought of vows I meant to take, swearing to never have sex. This was a Temptation. I know it now. I knew it then. Her body was warm and firm. I could feel her warmth. I needed her touch. I needed the warmth of that woman."

He stopped, his breath coming in short gasps. His brow beaded with sweat, which he wiped with a folded white handkerchief he pulled from his pocket. He stood, walked to his dresser, leaned against it a moment, then poured another drink. His hands shook worse than ever and the scotch splashed on the floor. The room smelled of cigarette smoke and liquor and something else—fear, maybe, or something sick.

"Excuse me for being so upset." He smiled weakly, as though making a stab at normalcy. "It was a critical event for me. You understand, don't you?"

When he returned to his chair, he sat for a long time, eyes closed.

I poured another Seagram's.

"I'm from a very intellectual family." He resumed his story—one I didn't really want to hear, but couldn't figure out how to escape from.

"My father teaches history at Tulane; my mother teaches also and writes for scholarly religious journals. My father always considered touching between people, including my mother and me, to be improper. I remember being very young and hearing her cry because he had scolded her for holding his hand on campus one day. I think she sort of dried up after that awful criticism. Fathers can make such horrible mistakes. They don't seem to understand the power they wield." He lowered his head and shook it. "Afterwards, I don't recall her ever hugging him. She rarely hugged me. I never saw the two of them display affection publicly. I don't even permit myself to think about whether or not they are intimate when alone. I suspect it's rare though—and terribly lacking in anything resembling pleasure or tenderness."

He paused again, looking far off, at his parents I figured.

"I wanted desperately to touch that girl—to feel her naked skin. I succumbed to her temptation. I made love to her like an animal. I pawed like a beast at her breasts. I ripped away her pants and had her there—right on the rug on the floor. If my father knew I had done that—" He choked back a sob.

"Lots of things we don't tell our parents about," I said quietly. "Did you enjoy it?" Mr. LeClair didn't answer so I repeated the question louder. "Did you enjoy making love to the girl?"

"I didn't finish." His eyes fell to the floor. "I wasn't able to orgasm. Everything stayed inside me. At the last minute, the guilt I felt kept me from consummating the act."

He sobbed openly while I—I'm ashamed of this—I wanted to laugh.

"I still consider myself a virgin," he said.

I looked at my hands, then stood and poured another full glass of whiskey. I was drunk and knew it. I wanted to leave, but the strangeness of his story held me.

"This act kept you from becoming a priest?"

He nodded, unable to muster the energy to speak. Sobs rose in his throat, were forced down, rose again. I thought I had never seen such a miserable human being. He swung his right leg over his knee, readjusted his glasses and lit a fresh cigarette. After several drags—pulled with such force one would have thought him a dying man on oxygen—he took a long drink of his scotch.

The ship rose and fell. It was a sweet, comforting motion that took me by surprise and made me want to sink deeper into my chair. Then the ship's whistle sounded—long and throaty.

"Fog," George said. "That time of year, I guess."

I stood, staggered a step over to the porthole, pulled back the curtain and pressed my face against the cool glass. Cat-whiskers of vapor streamed from the masthead light. I watched for a couple of minutes until the whistle sounded again, the house vibrating with its rumble.

"It'll blow every two minutes till either the fog clears or Don Campbell comes on watch," said George. "He'll silence the whistle. He detests it as much as the rest of us."

I returned to my chair. We sat quietly through two blowings of the whistle and another half-glass of whiskey. Finally, I spoke.

"Did you feel you made the correct decision—about not becoming a priest, I mean."

"My family has never forgiven me. My father hasn't spoken to me in years. Seminary friends still don't understand. I feel like I'm banished from good society, from the company of my class, cursed to sail these waters with society's dregs. For a time, I considered myself a sort of missionary. I thought I could do God's work even without being a priest. I have no charisma, though. No one listened to my preaching.

"In these ports, when we dock, I see other men—many of them married—go ashore in the evening, then return in the morning. I know they've been with a woman—just some woman, someone they've never met before. I lie in this bed, wanting so badly to go out there. I—I get erections that last all night." He pressed his hand against his lap. I turned away.

"I don't know what to do. I drink too heavily. I smoke too much. I indulge in every vice. I feel locked in this room."

"What do you do when you're off the ship—on vacation?"

His face brightened. "I make retreats—Catholic retreats. I go to a place where I'm permitted to live like a monk in a cell, to be silent, to meditate on the sins of the world—on my sins—to flagellate myself until the temptations leave and I feel safe again."

"You whip yourself?" The incredulity was strong in my voice and I sensed a change in the room. I told Wally about it later and he said it was the whiskey, but I'll never believe that. The overhead fluorescent dimmed and the only light in the room was from a small lamp with a reddish shade. Something happened to George's face. His eyes were more penetrating and unfriendly. I felt they could see through me. His glasses resembled horns, the rims rising above his head. His complexion was no longer pasty, but beet red. His tongue no longer looked human, but flat, like a serpent's. All I could think was its time to go. I struggled but could not rise from my chair.

"It's how I am satisfied," he hissed. "I like when the cords bite into my skin."

He stood and turned, lifting his shirt. Raised welts glowed scarlet and black against his skin. He sat again and stared at me, acting as if nothing was out of place. The hair at the back of my neck tingled and I had the sense of being in one of those nightmares where something really bad is happening but you can't move, just can't escape.

Then the foghorn sounded, blasting through everything like an Archangel's Broadsword. The overhead light was once again on and regular old George sat before me, no forked tongue, no horns. I shook my head to clear it and drank some whiskey. George looked goofy as ever, legs crossed, cigarette smoke billowing out of his mouth.

"Do you think you could be wrong about this whole thing?" I said.

"Yes. I think so. That's why I've invited you here. I want to ask for your help."

"Me? What can I do?"

"There's a whorehouse in Callao. I want you to take me to it. It's called the Trockadero. It's—." He paused. "It's a special sort of place. I think it might be just right for me."

I stared at him, numb with whiskey. My tongue felt thick and my voice sounded like a record turning too slow. "Why-not-go-your-self? I-do-not-under-stand."

"I've tried but I lack the courage. I need someone to take me there and force me to stay, force me to go into a room with a girl. I'll pay you. I'm rather desperate, you see."

He looked pitiful. "I-will-think-about-it," I said in my 33-speed voice. I set my empty glass on the dresser and somehow it fell to the carpet where it rolled against his foot as the ship settled aft. He picked it up without comment and set it on his refrigerator. I needed to be out of this room.

I stumbled through the door into the passageway, then around the corner where I opened the outside door and nearly fell crossing the sill. The fog, the darkness, the rushing water, the warm air, the overwhelming presence of natural things made me dizzy. I leaned against the rail, holding back the urge to vomit, feeling the wind on my face, picturing on one hand, Melissa—an angel in spite of her sexual adventuresomeness—sitting in her hayloft writing love poems; on the other, George LeClair, beset by the devil of religious guilt, a prisoner in a tiny cell with a framed Virgin on the wall, scotch in one hand, cigarette in the other, smiling his sickly, pained smile, living an ugly, fouled existence and doing his best to end it.

Guayaquil, Pimentel, Callao, August 5-9

I stayed aboard in Guayaquil Monday recovering from my drinking bout the night before with George LeClair. We had less than three hundred tons of cargo to discharge and load, most of which was accomplished while I slept. On Tuesday, everyone ate hamburgers and grease-soaked French fries at eleven-thirty, then turned to at noon to unmoor. An ugly, black thundercloud grew into a dark tower directly above the roof of the jungle across the river and the day's deluge began just as the sailors went fore and aft. No one seemed to mind. The mercury in the thermometer in the perforated white box on the bridge wing read 101 and the sun had not yet crossed the local meridian. Some of the sailors rolled up their pant legs and stripped to the waist, resembling a band of aging pirates. I was on the bow with Mr. Hunt, the mate. He seemed to have taken a liking to having me around. Which was good since he would eventually write my fitness report. The sailors more or less ignored him now but at least they didn't purposefully do things to slow down the operation. No one, including me, respected the man.

We sailed out the Daule River through the jungle past Puerto Nuevo and Puna Island with raindrops pelting us. At Posorja, the village at the entrance to Golfo de Isla Santa Clara Guayaquil, I escorted the pilot from the wheelhouse down to

main deck and stood by the rail while he climbed hand over hand
down the pilot ladder into his boat and waved goodbye. Once
again, we were at sea. I returned to my room and napped until
star time, then went to the bridge.

Mr. Potter was chatty for a change—about the heat and
about a letter he had received from his daughter who was attend-
ing college somewhere in Alabama and who had fallen in love
with a boy from the right kind of family up in Georgia. "Joja" he
called it. I was preoccupied with the letter from Melissa and the
conversation I'd had with the purser, so I didn't have much to
say. Plus, I couldn't care less about whether his daughter married
into the right kind of family or the wrong kind of family. I read
Crime and Punishment with a sort of hunger now and had gotten it into my head that, like Ralskonikov, I could consider
myself beyond the limits of conventional morality. I was
wrestling with issues like is it all right to kill someone for a hundred bucks and should simple revenge include torture while the
second mate talked about the importance of marrying into the
right kind of family. Give me a fucking break.

Wally humored me when I got on my Raskolnikov soapbox.
Generally though, he was too sarcastic to carry on a philosophical conversation. He had his own pet peeves—how his dad was
never around; how difficult it was to get those patriarchal dere-
licts to pay their kids' child support; the long hours his mom had
to work to support herself and him. He wanted to study law
eventually and doubted he'd ever swing too far out on the anti-
establishment limb. I wasn't so sure about myself. Campus
protests against the Viet Nam war were increasing. I didn't have
strong feelings about that war, but what I read put me on the
side of the protestors—if for no other reason than their battle cry
was *Sex, Drugs, and Rock n' Roll.*

We usually talked for a half-hour around ten, lying in our
bunks, before going to sleep.

"You never have told me why your dad sent you packing.
What pissed him off, anyway?" asked Wally the night we sailed
Guayaquil.

"Wasn't that big a deal."

"If you're going to be a revolutionary thinker, you've got to
be able to talk about your experiences. How do you think myths

are created?"

"Just something I said to Father Henry, the parish priest."

"Yes. Fine. And what was that something? Did you tell him you didn't care for his singing voice at high mass? Or perhaps he gave you too many Hail Marys for your penance. Wait. I know. You wanted a second sip of wine at Sunday Mass and he said no."

I lay there staring at the metal rectangles on the bottom of Wally's bunk a few seconds, then said, "I told him he wasn't my shepherd and I wasn't his sheep."

"Are you kidding me? You told him that?"

"You are such a wise-ass."

"Well, excuse my non-Catholic ignorance, but what's the big deal about this shepherd-sheep thing?"

"He said that was the premise of the Catholic Church. The priest as Christ's representative is the shepherd and we Catholics, his followers, the sheep."

"Oh, I get it. You telling him you're no longer one of his sheep is subversive. Eats away at his power."

"Something like that. Let's go to sleep."

"You're an independent thinker, Jake Thomas, which makes you potentially dangerous. You have just two problems. One, you don't know anything. Two, you mostly want to have fun."

"You're probably right about not knowing anything. But what's wrong with wanting to have fun?"

"I don't think fun-loving, uninformed subversives get taken seriously"

"G'night, Wally."

"Night."

A pleasant sort of calm seemed to settle into the ship. The joke was the sailors sailed, the engineers engineered and the mates mated. I liked working cargo with the mate. I liked working on deck with the boatswain. I loved navigation, even though Mr. Potter could be a royal pain. I considered development as a navigator to be the acid test in this business and I was frustrated at the difficulties I was encountering in moving from being a two-star navigator to one who could regularly put down a three star fix.

The sailors had started painting the house and had so much staging and so many ropes rigged from the bridge wings that the front of the superstructure looked like a kid's jungle gym. The engineers had ongoing problems—one of which, the compressor for the air conditioner, wouldn't impact us fully till we were northbound. They were careful to couch conversations in technical jargon whenever talking in front of deckies.

"Filament on the thermostat. . ." said the chief.

"Steam pressure in the gauge glass. . ." countered the young third.

"Fucking blower's undersized considering the ambient. . ." said the first.

Partially because of this jargon, I came to think of engineers as being somehow superior to mates. Until I happened to go into the engine room one morning to fetch something for the boatswain and saw Wally and George Coleman bouncing up and down on the end of a long cheater attached to a giant pipe wrench the chief engineer held in place. Looked low-tech to me. Wally's motto was "a marine engineer is better than nothing," but he didn't say that in front of the engineers.

We tied up the next morning at Pimentel, the tiny hole-in-the-wall port for Chiclayo in the Sechura Desert. The sun was brutal. The mate, who had sadistic tendencies anyhow, knew I'd been drinking with the purser, so worked me hard that day climbing in and out of cargo holds. By the end of the day, I was exhausted, dirt-covered and sweaty. I showered and went to bed early. Wally kept bugging me about having gone to Chancre Hill and how big, ugly things were even as he spoke growing on parts of my body and that my nose would be eaten away when I was thirty-one like Schubert or some composer he'd read about. I wished he'd quit talking about it. That night, I dreamt about Melissa. She had short hair and her name was Alice. She took drugs and had sex with lots of men but kept smiling through the dream as if it didn't matter. I woke around three-thirty in the morning gasping for oxygen and moaning. Christ, I thought, this business of sex and love and the consequences that go with them isn't child's play. And I hadn't a clue why that was so. I believed I should reasonably expect to get past my Catholic

upbringing, that I could overthrow it and be someone different—someone like Raskolnikov whose life and ideas I was
becoming obsessed with. Seemed to me I should be able to
cavort—a word I'd learned recently that seemed appropriate—
with South American whores or pretty much anyone without
guilt or consequences. Far as I could tell, sex consisted of insert-
ing a part of my body into a part of hers, shuddering and quivering a little and squirting. Didn't seem like that big a deal.

We sailed Pimentel early the following morning. Days and
nights blended into each other now, the routine of life at sea
always a welcome respite from the hectic times in port. At sea,
I shot stars on both ends of the four to eight watch long as I
had a clear sky and could see the horizon. I was obsessed with
achieving consistency as a three star fix navigator and knew that
nothing besides practice would bring this about. Between
breakfast and lunch, I helped the mate with cargo or worked
on deck with the boatswain. To satisfy his compulsiveness, Mr.
Hunt sent me every day into a 'tween deck or lower hold to
"check just one more time" on cargo separations or shoring.
Shoring seemed a big waste for most of the trip. I kept a baseball I'd found in my room on my desk since sailing Houston
and it had scarcely moved.
    "Just wait," the mate kept saying. "You'll see why we shore
cargo before this trip is finished."
    This close to the equator, the days were lovely: sun, a few
clouds, sparkling water, dolphins, flying fish. I liked going in and
out of the holds. They were black dark. I carried two flashlights
and wore gloves. The ladder leading into them led straight down
a trunk with exits at each level: upper 'tween deck, lower 'tween
deck, lower hold. I liked crawling around down there looking at
the cargoes, ever alert for signs of a stowaway—not uncommon
according to the mate, particularly northbound, when the ship
was bound for the states. I was deathly afraid of rodents and kept
a sharp eye out for rats but saw only one—about a foot long he
was, sitting in the bilge in number five eating kernels of corn, his
beady red eyes glaring maliciously at my light. The mate wanted
to know immediately if I ever saw evidence of rats so he could
send traps down, but tending rat-traps was about the last thing

I wanted to be involved with so I forgot to tell him about the little beast and found excuses to not go into five lower hold again. Very Raskolnikov, I thought.

On days when I worked on deck, the boatswain sent me aloft in a chair to help paint the face of the house. I loved that. I learned to tie a boatswain's hitch, to move up and down safely and to secure myself. I learned how it felt to spend hours high above the calm blue sea, wearing only a pair of old shorts, paint bucket dangling from my chair.

During the afternoon, I usually napped and did a few pages of my sea-project. In the evenings, after watch, I played cribbage with Wally or read Dostoevsky before drifting off to sleep. I ate a lot.

Our next port was Callao. According to George LeClair, this was the port city through which Lima received and shipped its merchandise. We had a lot of cargo to discharge there, and were scheduled to stop again northbound to backload. Mr. LeClair had avoided me since telling me his story. I figured he was embarrassed. I would be. That afternoon after coffee, I went to his office to pick up my Callao draw.

"Afternoon, Jake. How much do you need for Callao?" he asked.

"I don't know. I guess we're going to be there awhile, right?"

"Four days and four nights is what the schedule calls for."

"What do I have coming?"

"Let's see. You make sixty-five a month and you've drawn forty so far. You've been on here nearly a month now, so you should be able to draw twenty bucks."

"Twenty it is," I said. He fingered two tens from his pile, handed them to me, wrote the figure down in the Official Log and spun the book around for me to initial.

"By the way," he said, "I'd like to take you out to dinner tomorrow night. I know some pretty decent places." He didn't look up when he said it.

"Sure," I said. "Love to."

The next morning after breakfast, I went up to the bridge as we approached Callao. We turned east just before the guano-covered island of San Lorenzo, had the pilot aboard by ten-thirty and were all fast by a quarter to twelve. I worked with Don Campbell opening hatches through the lunch hour. The chief mate, looking harassed, and, as usual, ridiculous with his skinny legs sticking out of baggy khaki shorts, ran out on deck shortly after one and threw me some keys.

"Jake, open the starboard aft reefer compartment in five upper 'tween deck. There's beef there for this port and some for Valpo as well. Make certain the separation is clearly marked and the hatch boss knows what's what. Any questions down there, come get me."

Shortly after four-thirty, we finished discharging the beef in five. I made sure the compartment was clean and ready to back-load, then came up, reported to the mate and went to my room to shower and change. At six, I met the purser at the gangway. He looked like I don't know what, a spy from a comedy series maybe. He wore brown trousers, a brown turtleneck and a camelhair jacket. His black-rimmed glasses had lenses that turned brown in the sunlight and he wore a large cross on a piece of leather around his neck. He broadcast alcohol fumes, Jade East cologne, and mouthwash like a protective shield. I stood there momentarily, looking at him. Finally, I got hold of myself, said hello and we took off. I felt more like a social worker with a retard than a sailor ashore with a buddy.

Since it was early, George thought we should walk. I figured he was stalling, but was happy enough to agree. This was his ball game. Peru was different from either Panama or Buenaventura. It was drier, for one thing; and although the air was too foul to see much, I caught occasional glimpses of one or two of the snow-topped peaks to the west that seemed to split the sky. The streets seemed dustier, but there were more automobiles and nicer houses and shops. Lima, a sprawling metropolis, sat just up the road. According to George, it had been an important Spanish city in its heyday, with fortress-like government buildings, a massive cathedral and wide boulevards.

We passed the Texas Bar, the New York Club and the Broadway Lounge. Thin, short girls with flat noses beckoned from the doorways. A group of sailors staggered from the

Broadway Lounge over to the New York Club. After a couple
minutes, they were back out again, heading over to the Texas
Bar. I noticed George did his best to not even look at the girls
and I can't say I blame him. They were homely and the bars
seedy-looking.

   We hiked along the road that led through Callao, which was
a squared, ugly off little port, toward Lima. We walked along
with ox and mule-drawn wagons, old trucks belching diesel
fumes, loaded down to their marks with bales and casks and vegetables and animals alive and dead going both directions. In the
fields, we saw sugar cane, alfalfa, corn, coffee and carob; oranges,
lemons and other fruit. The Rimac River drained the snow off
the mountains and irrigated the fertile valley. People rode horses and mules, or traveled by car or bus, but most, like us, walked.
We saw short, stolid Indians with grave faces, sometimes bent
like beasts of burden with enormous bundles strapped to their
backs. We saw tall proud Spaniards, an occasional Asian, many
Africans and, of course, every combination. The people appeared
resigned and tired. I heard few human voices—mostly trucks
back-firing and donkeys braying. The fingers of George's right
hand never left the large wooden cross that hung from the
leather strip he wore around his neck.

   A small man wearing a straw fedora and white shirt, half
unbuttoned, approached us as we walked. His rodent eyes
darted over his shoulder and back again. He cupped his right
hand over his left like a squirrel with a sunflower seed. When
he opened his fist, the size of the golden ring sitting there
made me gasp.

   "You look. *Si*. Very nice. *Muy Bueno. Oro*. You buy.
Twenty dollar. Very cheap." He spoke like he moved – in
brief, energetic bursts.

   "Get out of here," said the purser. "We don't want any."

   "No, wait," I said. "Let me see that ring."

   The man handed me the ring, admonishing me with quick
movements to keep it from the prying eyes of—whom—I could-
n't tell. I looked about. No one but some shoeless kids that I
could see. I bounced the ring in the palm of my hand, feeling its
weight. It was heavy, stamped with an Inca chieftain on top and
18K inside the band.

"This is beautiful." I looked over at George. "Feel this. Feel how heavy it is. It must be real gold."

The purser accepted the ring with a grunt, then returned it almost immediately, uttering with disgust the single word, "brass."

"Are you sure?" I said. I turned to the rodent-man. "I'll give you fifteen dollars."

"Si. Fifteen dollar. OK."

"Your finger will turn green within the hour. I guarantee it."

"I'll give you ten dollars," I said to the man.

Irritated, he held out his hand. "Si. Ten dollar. You give."

"You're making a big mistake," said Mr. LeClair, almost angry. "There's no gold in that ring. It's worth about ten cents."

"Five dollars." I realized I was negotiating backwards, but wasn't sure what to do about it. "My final offer." The man rolled his eyes.

"Si. Si. Five dollar." He seemed to grow more paranoid with each step, which only served to make me think he was somehow legit—in a very illegitimate way.

I opened my billfold and saw two one-dollar bills in addition to the two tens I had received from the purser during yesterday's draw.

"Here." I held up the two one-dollar bills. "It's all I have."

This totally exasperated the poor guy. He threw up his arms and shook his head.

"Si. Two dollar. Give me."

He grabbed the money, called me a "fooking osschole," spoke animatedly in Spanish and disappeared around the corner.

I shrugged, polished the heavy piece of jewelry like it was an apple and slid it onto the ring finger of my right hand. It fit perfectly. The purser shook his head.

"No denying you got the best of that deal. Your finger will be as tarnished as my soul before the night's over." He laughed without sound or mirth.

The buildings thinned out and we walked on several blocks past a post office and a bus station, then finally drew up at a restaurant called the King's Arms. Inside, the floor was covered with a thin burgundy carpet poorly laid, its edges badly frayed.

Imitation gold sconces—the gold peeling—were spaced every five feet or so illuminating cheap paneling. The ceiling had fake wooden beams hung in three-foot squares. George appeared distressed by the seediness of the place.

"Stupid mate," he said. "Told me this was a great place to get a steak. Well, what do you think? Shall we stay or shall we go somewhere else?"

"Fine with me to stay, George. Maybe the food is good."

My steak was tender and the *pommes fritas* weren't greasy. George nibbled on the anchovy and squid appetizer—a bit too sophisticated for my plain palate—but only pushed the rack of lamb around on his plate, concentrating instead on the two bottles of red wine. I drank the wine sparingly, preferring coca-cola. We'd each had two Pisco Sours before the meal and the food and drink gave me a warm feeling. The sun had set. George said little as he finished off the wine.

I told George the restaurant reminded me of a job I'd had in high school cleaning my hometown movie theater. The walls of the theater were painted black and the lobby smelled like stale popcorn. I swept kernels off the scarred wood floor, cleaned the restrooms, and vacuumed the stained red carpet with a mechanical cleaner that never quite picked up all the old maids, no matter how often I ran it back and forth. Sometimes in the mezzanine, I found rubbers—new and used. I kept the new ones in a secret place in my billfold and occasionally left the used ones thinking someone might need to reuse them. It was disgusting work, but it motivated me to go to college. George said he'd never held a job during high school—that his parents felt work was beneath him. That he was born into the intellectual class.

I laughed. "No problem with that in my family. Got my first job when I was eight. My dad told me to tell the guy I was ten so he'd give me the paper route. I don't think it hurt anything, you know, going to work so young."

After the plates were cleared, George ordered coffee and I asked for another coke.

"I think I might just head back to the ship," he said.

"Fine," I said. "I'm going to that whorehouse you mentioned the other night."

"You're supposed to insist I go with you, dammit. Drag me by the feet."

"I'm not going to do that, George. I'll go with you, but I'm not going to drag you or anyone else somewhere you don't want to go."

"I'm afraid to go. I want someone to slip me a knock-out pill and drag me to a whore's bed. I want to awaken to find myself seduced, non-virginal, corrupted—in other words, normal." He laughed his mirthless, silent laugh.

"George, I'm a little too young to tell you how to live your life, but I would like for you to, just this one night, consider yourself a different person. Think that George LeClair is still on the ship in his bunk, drinking whiskey and sweating and worrying about his hard-on. Think that you're someone else—someone you've always wanted to be. An actor in a movie, maybe."

"I have to ask you a question," George said, suddenly deathly serious. He motioned for the waiter to pour brandy into his coffee. "I don't want you to laugh."

He stopped talking and looked hard at me. At least, I assume he was looking at me. With people wearing sunglasses, it's never too easy to tell.

"Do whores ever turn men down because they're too ugly?"

"You mean the whores or the men?"

"I mean if the men are too ugly. You know what I mean."

"Well, I don't think so, George. Why do you ask?"

"Are you sure about that?"

"I've never heard of it. A whore has a job. She works for money just like you or me. I don't know, maybe they charge more for someone who weighs three hundred and fifty pounds and they're worried about being crushed." The question struck me as being so ludicrous I couldn't help but poke fun.

George turned his entire body to the side and sat with his hands on his knees. He removed his glasses and rubbed his eyes. "All these years," he said. "All these years I thought even whores wouldn't want me."

He looked over at me. His eyes were red and puffed. An uncharitable thought surfaced that if prostitutes ever did reject customers, George might well be on that list.

"Let's go to the Trockadero," he said. "I don't want to waste any more time."

George paid for our meal and bought a couple pints of Pisco, the local fuel-like corn drink that flowed like liquid fire down my throat. He handed one to me, which I slid into my hip pocket without a word, as though it was understood exactly why I might need this particular poison. The words of Boss Jones rattled around in my brain: "All you need for da Trockadero is a strong dick and a weak mind." We stepped outside and got into the first cab. As we rode through the streets of Callao, George told me yet another sad story from the many in his life.

"After quitting the seminary, I resigned myself to either committing suicide—something I seriously considered—or getting another ship. This purser's job suited me, so I shipped on a Moore-Mac freighter down the East Coast of South America."

It was dark in the car as we honked and flashed and braked our way through traffic oblivious to anything resembling rules. I was glad I couldn't see George's face. His story hurt enough without seeing actual tears.

"I had an ulterior motive for wanting to return to sea. I wanted to feel the warmth and softness of a woman again. I couldn't get the image of her body—how it felt warm and how it aroused me to look at it—out of my mind. I thought I would never date because I am truly too homely. In spite of that, I felt I needed human contact. I had never received it from my parents. I, well, I even thought maybe I would meet a whore and marry her and have a family. I knew I would never meet and marry a normal woman.

"Then something happened that changed my life. We were in Santos. I was giving the crew a draw, and accidentally shortchanged a sailor named Mike. Mad Mikey, the sailors called him. I thought he was a truly evil man—a little like Fletcher, the A.B. but more volatile. He didn't like me from the beginning and had given me a very bad time of it almost from the day I signed him on. When he realized I had short-changed him twenty bucks—I'd done it out of nervous-ness—he flew into a rage and all but attacked me. I apolo-

gized and gave him his money. As he walked away, he said
'You're so ugly, a whore wouldn't bed you at twice the
price.' Those were his exact words."

George was quiet for a few moments after saying this. I
knew he was doing his best to work up the courage to continue. He pulled the Pisco from his pocket, unscrewed the
cap, drank two or three swallows like it was water, and
replaced the cap. The cab had left the district where we'd
eaten and now drove along a dark, very rough dirt road.
Ahead I could make out a large building with dim lights
shining from many windows.

George continued, "I know I'm not a handsome man. In
high school, I was skinny and had terrible acne. I don't know
how often I heard, growing up, comments about how ugly I
was, how no girl would ever kiss me. My own relatives would
kid me about how I would break cameras that took my picture. When my mother withheld her affection because of my
father's quirks, I came to believe fully I was undesirable in
every way and would never attract a woman. In my school, I
was a joke. I was afraid to tell my parents how others laughed
at me. I had no friends."

Christ, I thought to myself. What's crazier anyhow? Sex for
money or the cruelty this poor bastard suffered growing up?

George looked over at me. "You're absolutely sure a
whore will go with me?"

I just looked at him. For a moment, I was afraid he might
actually try to hug me or something; then I thought, well,
what the hell if he does. The guy needs human contact. I just
hoped he'd wait till we were out of the cab.

The taxi dropped us in front of a dark dormitory of a
building that sat like a mushroom in a field somewhere on a
side-road between Callao and Lima. A dim yellow light barely illuminated the heavy wooden door. A short man in a
black shirt urinated against the wall not three feet away,
oblivious to the stream of men entering and leaving. The
place lacked the drunken comedy of a seaman's bar. It was
more utilitarian, but worse, tending toward desperate. There
was a serious, businesslike aspect to the faces of the men
coming and going—as if coming here was part of the job of

living. Some intuition told me I wasn't going to like this experience much. In spite of the urine-stench, I inhaled deeply, and we entered the queue of men moving toward the door. In the sickly yellow light, I noticed a gleam from the finger of my right hand, and remembered my new ring. I rubbed it for luck. I was going to need it.

Callao, the Trockadero
August 9

I'd never seen a building quite like the Trockadero. It had
three levels of rooms overlooking a large central open space. In
the middle of the first floor sat a ticket stand—an octagonal kiosk
large enough for a man to sit inside. We walked toward it, on
foot-wide finished planks secured with fatheaded spikes and
scarred from heavy boots. The kiosk had a glass window with a
round hole for talking and, lower down, a half-round hole above
a smoothed groove in the wood for passing money and tickets.
Two winding staircases—one on either side of the kiosk—led to
a second level and then a third. The staircases were railed with
ornate iron pickets and covered by a broad wooden banister
butchered with words, symbols and initials. Scarlet runners lined
the steps, frayed and dirty with old stains. Tall, multi-paned windows at the far end of the room were partially covered by dirty-
white shades, some ripped, others broken and hanging. The
place had a rancid smell—like the non-refrigerated food stalls in
a tropical marketplace toward the end of a hot day.

Boss Jones had clucked his tongue when I told him I was
going to the Trockadero.

"Even bookmen got sense enough to stay outta *that* place,"
he said.

But I was only nineteen, and possessed of the sort of lust for experience that can lead to ecstasy or disaster—or both. Besides, I reminded myself, I'm here to help George expel his demons.

George LeClair stood there birdlike, arms back, neck stretched, head forward, looking like he could fly. The man in the ticket booth extended his hand through the hole in the glass, palm down, fingers waving. I thought he was greeting us, so I waved back.

"He's motioning us to come forward," said George.

Other men came and went. A group of four walked away from the booth, grimly counting tickets. This was a serious place, where serious business was conducted.

We approached the kiosk. "*Quanto es?*" asked the purser. The man listlessly tapped a fare sheet taped to his window. The purser spent soldioro, of course, but it equated to one dollar and twenty-three cents U.S. per ticket. I thought about Raskolnikov and the value of one human body. George bought four tickets. He kept one and handed me three. I accepted them without comment.

We walked up the stairs together. The balcony on the second floor wrapped around the open center space and looked down on the kiosk. Doors to the rooms were against the outside wall, opposite the railing. Some were open; others closed. Men milled about as though shopping, generally somber. Women in stages of undress sat in front of certain doors. One, wearing a purple baby-doll nighty sat on a bench filing her nails. Another, ridiculous in black bra and panties and weighing two hundred pounds or better, sat smoking, flapping her legs open and closed, smiling lewdly at the men who passed by. Wally's type, I thought grimly. Four or five Latino men queued up before the closed door to the room next to hers engaged in rapid conversation of seeming urgency. A young black man—probably a seaman off an American ship—exploded out of a room on the third floor and ran down the stairs yelling "Five more tickets, man."

"This place is something else," I said to George. I had wanted detached sex, but this? I didn't know what to think.

"I—I just can't believe this," said the purser, stammering. "I didn't know it would be quite so cold."

I decided to make the best of it. "What the hell, George. I'm gonna find the longest line in the place and go stand in it. At least we have that rotgut Pisco you bought. We've paid our money. Might as well go through with this. I'll meet you at the front door in an hour. If I don't see you there, I'll catch you back at the ship in the morning. I've got taxi money."

"I noticed a young lady across the way looking rather nice and, actually, a bit lonely," said George, pointing. "I might try my luck there."

I had never before met a man with so little self-confidence. He truly felt he might have trouble getting laid here.

I climbed the stairs to the upper balcony and looked down the walkway. Three girls sat outside their rooms. I walked by them. The first never so much as looked up. Her head in her hands; stringy, reddish-black strands of hair sticking out between her fingers, she stared at the floor. The second smiled and smoothed her black hair, turning her head coquettishly. Her teeth were yellow-brown; her emaciated body unattractive in a stained yellow negligee. The third was totally naked. She appeared to be in her mid-forties, which, at that time, seemed grandmotherly. Her flesh hung in folds around her stomach as if a row of pillows was piled inside her. Her right leg was crossed over her left and the fatty part of her left thigh rippled when she moved. Her right foot swung back and forth in what was meant to be a provocative gesture. Her head rested on her hand, which was supported by her knee: the Thinker's pose. She fluttered her eyelids at me, and for just a moment reminded me of Melissa, who sat that way at basketball games at home when she wasn't up cheering. I stopped and leaned against the railing, caught by her flirt and the reminder of a different world. The woman took my hesitation to be a sign of interest and glanced demurely at the floor, then up again. She gestured toward her room with a butterfly movement of her eyelids. Even that reminded me of Melissa. Christ, I could barely breathe. It occurred to me this was a place where an experienced man might explore the dark side of his erotic nature. But me? Why I didn't leave then and there, I will never know.

I tipped back my bottle of Pisco as I walked along the balcony. The burning down my throat felt appropriate. A large man with shiny black hair wearing a dark suit and white shirt open at the neck walked heavily up the stairs from the main floor, stopped on the landing, squinted at the rooms as though near-sighted, walked to a door, threw it open without knocking and entered the room. I heard loud voices and the thud of fist striking flesh. A smallish middle-aged American with a crew-cut and wide eyes flew out of the room head first, naked. His clothes followed and behind them the dark-haired Spanish man emerged, resolute, head held high, pulling a young girl trying her best to cover herself with her free arm. She couldn't be more than fifteen, I thought. I took another pull on my Pisco and kept walking.

Ahead, toward the center of the walkway, I saw what was unquestionably the longest line in the place. I walked to the end of that line, hunkered down and stood there. I counted those ahead of me. Eight. We all faced a door. Like the line to a bank teller. Breathing was difficult.

A quiet, dignified man in a worn linen suit stood ahead of me. He had white hair and a generous mustachio and was extremely well groomed. He reached into his inside breast pocket and pulled out a flask. He uncapped it, took a long drink, then turned without speaking and handed it to me, as though I had come to drink with him and pass some time. I took the bottle and drank, coughing slightly as the sweet liquor burned my throat. Boss Jones was right, I thought, murmuring "*graci*" and returning the bottle. At that point, I wasn't even sure I could muster a stiff prick.

The Trockadero looked considerably worse from the end of a queue on the third floor. A dense haze of white-blue smoke drifted toward the remains of what at one time must have been a beautiful chandelier. Now, crystals were missing; ordinary bulbs were screwed into sockets meant for ornate lamps. The entire chandelier dangled precariously from two black wires. The ceiling looked cancerous: large patches of dirty plaster hung down or were missing entirely, exposing great sections of lathe. The few ashtrays in the hallways were overflowing and cigarette butts lay in trails from different doors like popularity votes. The floor was gouged and scratched. Carpets were burned, frayed and ripped; paint peeled off the walls.

I was jarred from my reverie when the door to the room in front of me opened. A stout Spanish man exited and a small Oriental entered so quickly that the door closed before I could see the female creature inside. For all I knew, she could be a monkey or a goat.

The minutes passed slowly. I shared my Pisco with the man in front of me. He produced a second bottle. It was small and black and the liquor tasted bitter, like rejection. After drinking it, whatever it was, I no longer felt much of anything: no fear, no apprehension. A silence fell like a shroud over me and the building and all its contents. The light in the place seemed dimmed and I felt like I was in a church, but without contentment or peace. Maybe I felt disgust and loathing—or alienation and loneliness. I knew it as some deep human need that made me want to scream: something so dreadfully sad and disconcerting about the relationship between men and women that I stood there silently weeping.

The man in front of me noticed and handed me the small bottle once again. I drank, then washed it down with a slug of Pisco from my own bottle. The door had opened and closed three times more. One would leave; another enter. I was now fourth in line, with two behind me. I no longer looked about. Rather, I tried to focus on the task ahead. In my mind's eye, I became more animal, less human. Minutes passed, but time no longer seemed important.

Thoughts of the purser crossed my mind. I wondered what he was up to. I suspected he had taken his insecurities and fled as soon as he was rid of me and even now was in a real sailor's bar near the waterfront, eyeing the bottom of another glass of scotch. I didn't care. I couldn't seem to muster any real interest in him or anyone else. Eventually, my drinking partner entered the room and I stood before the door, next in line. The door, which had been painted green at some point in its dismal history, came to occupy all of my consciousness. The rest of the building was dark. I felt abominable and disgusting. Still, I didn't move, intent on going through with what I had come to do.

The door opened. Buttoning his suit-coat, looking dapper and fresh, the white-haired gentleman walked out without so much as a glance in my direction. I entered. The room was dark.

At first, I saw no one—only a rumpled bed near the far wall.
Next to it sat a crude nightstand with a dim lamp—the only light
in the room—and a much-used brown book that had a white
ribbon marker like a book of prayer or a bible. It had no words
on its cover. To my left was a stack of crates meant to serve as a
dresser. In the corner shadow, to the right of the crates, I noticed
movement. There she was, nearly invisible in the darkness: the
woman. Her back was toward me. She was naked and finely
formed. Long legs, rounded hips narrowing gracefully into a
small waist. Her right arm moved vigorously as she washed herself in a small pan of white porcelain, chipped and scarred in the
inevitable accidents of heavy usage.

There was a sink for disposal but no faucet. She bent slowly
and used a metal dipper to refill the small pan from a large wood-
en bucket. Her hair was sandy-blond—perhaps the reason for
her popularity. She turned enough that I could make out her silhouette. She was younger than me. Her breasts were small but
uplifted and round and lovely. She looked at me and smiled so
sweetly I feared my heart would melt. I wished at that moment
I were an artist or a photographer and could somehow capture
her standing there—a nude in the corner, washing.

She smiled, her long hair swept across one eye. In one
hand, she held the white washcloth near the chipped porcelain
pan while the other stretched toward me, palm down, beckoning with slender fingers. She seemed exquisite, vulnerable
and precious.

I did what I had come to do, then handed her all three
tickets. She accepted them with a pleased, slightly surprised
look and kissed me on the cheek—an act somehow more
intimate than whatever else we had just done. In a daze, I
walked out to the hallway and looked at my watch. An hour
and a half had passed. I was late for my meeting with the
purser. I ran down the stairs, tears blurring my vision. I did-
n't hesitate, didn't look for him, saw nothing but ran directly out the door. I ran and ran and ran. Finally, my heart
pounding in my ears, I stopped. A light rain fell. An ornate
footbridge to my left crossed the Rimac River and led to
some buildings. I walked halfway across, stood and looked at
the rushing black water for a moment or two, wondering

how deep it was and how cold, thinking briefly of the lone-liness associated with suicide, then continued across.

The streets on that side of the river were cobbled and dark. The rain fell in large drops now, strangely soft for a country so near the equator. I wanted to remove my clothing and let those drops splash away my sins. I continued walking, head down, unaware of a destination. A large stone building reared up on my left. I raised my eyes. Seeing a cross above the door, I walked up the stone steps. The door was locked. I beat against it, but received no answer. I sat down heavily on the top step, my head in my hands, the rain mixing with my tears.

Callao to Antofagasta
August 10-13

I stayed to myself after the Trockadero. In spite of having done a number of other things I wasn't proud of both on this ship and elsewhere, something about what happened at the Trockadero was too much for me to deal with. Wally invited me ashore the next couple nights, but I begged off, stayed in my room and read. The ship's library, meager as it was, with its paperbacks stamped *U.S. Merchant Marine Library Association*, all with the top halves of their covers torn away, rows of Mickey Spillane mysteries and Zane Grey westerns, yielded, from a handful of hardcover classics, a collection of stories by Joseph Conrad. I reread *Youth*, the story that had originally set me to dreaming about going to sea. I'd even memorized a few paragraphs from that story and used it in a high school speech contest. Rereading it reminded me how I'd been seduced by the idea of adventure. Lying in the open fields behind my house in May, the dirt freshly plowed, the sun an invisible warm cloth on my skin, reading from a stack of books on a Saturday afternoon, imagining myself somewhere exotic, in some city with bazaars and men with bright turbans. Good as the reading was, it was but a writer's reflections, however skillful, of life. I was glad to be sailing this ship.

I continued reading Dostoevsky as well. I was becoming

more and more taken by the idea that people voluntarily give up control of certain functions of their lives for seemingly arbitrary reasons. I understood that we all are born to certain parents in a particular country governed by a set of laws, customs, ethical standards and community practices. We become educated, but that process enculturates us rather than teaches us to think. I could see that at some level thinking could be considered a dangerous thing; that in general one is not taught to think so much as to learn proper ways of thinking—like etiquette almost—ways that keep people good citizens.

I wrote Melissa every night now, telling her what I was doing on the ship, what I was reading and even a little about what I was doing ashore. Not everything, of course, not down to the last detail, anyway. I mailed letters from every second port or so, though the purser warned me against it, saying they might take months to arrive. I told her I loved her in every letter and felt I did love her—that I wasn't just saying it because I was thousands of miles away. Wally kept telling me "absence makes the heart grow fonder," and that I was a romantic but that as soon as I saw her again, "with her buck teeth, crossed eyes and stringy hair," I'd regain my senses. Plus, I couldn't quite square up this love I felt for Melissa with my new sexual adventuring. I worried a little about how faithful or unfaithful Melissa was being to me, but again, couldn't get my mind around how I should feel. I knew she had dated a lot of guys back there—and not just from my town but also from Lynchburg and Arvada and Dillard. I didn't know if she was sexually promiscuous or just liked to date a lot. I didn't even know if I should care. She wasn't the type to put some guy's ring on a chain around her neck and claim to be "going steady" like a lot of girls. One of my dad's sayings was *What's good for the goose is good for the gander.* I understood now what he meant, but didn't know how I was supposed to feel about it.

We were scheduled to sail Callao at 1300, Thursday, August thirteenth. The final loads of bagged coffee were piled in the hold at number four and the longshoremen left the ship shortly after midnight. The captain had delayed the sailing since the chief engineer was having trouble with his soot blowers and running at slow speed increased the soot output of the boilers. Excess soot had already clogged up the ventilation system and the chief was afraid he'd have trouble with the air-conditioning if we didn't keep the soot build-up to a minimum.

Mr. Hunt, the chief mate, didn't have any work for me that morning, so, after breakfast, I walked out of the saloon and headed up the stairs toward my room to work on the Rules of the Road section of my Sea Project.

As I walked by the Purser's Office, Mr. LeClair said, "Excuse me, Jake. Got a minute?"

"Sure," I said, surprised. Since visiting the Trockadero, George LeClair had avoided making eye contact with me. I walked around the corner into his office and sat in one of the blue naughahyde chairs. George lit a cigarette—even though one burned in the black ashtray next to his typewriter—and turned toward me.

"I wanted to tell you about the other night," he began.

I merely nodded, smiling pleasantly. I felt I had dealt with what I considered to be the shame of it all, but I had been wondering how George felt about it. Two Catholics—one a self-flagellating ex-seminarian—in a whorehouse even hardened sailors didn't frequent. Something had to give. Judging from earlier conversations I'd had with him, I assumed the experience put him way over the morality line he seemed so determined to never cross.

"I feel I owe you an apology for not meeting you when I said I would the other night at the Trockadero," he began nervously, inhaling from first one then the other cigarette. "I've been waiting for an opportunity to tell you what happened."

I said nothing, expecting him to tell me that after we parted that night, he had walked directly to the front door and returned to the ship. George shifted nervously in his chair, one of those swivel types, black, with metal arms. The ship was quiet except for the whir of the fan hanging in the corner of his office.

"Something wonderful happened to me in the Trockadero," he said, attention centered on the cigarette he was smashing into the ashtray. "I—I became a different man. I kept going back, buying more tickets, going with different girls. I went with beau-

tiful girls, homely girls, fat girls, thin girls. I kept going even
when I could no longer perform—just to lie with another
human, with her arms around me, her breath warm against my
neck. It was wonderful beyond my wildest dreams." Tears
streamed down his cheeks. He stopped, removed his glasses and
wiped his face.

"I've returned the past two nights," he continued. "To one
particular girl named Elisa. Last night, she and I had a date. I
had to buy her out of the Trockadero, but it wasn't much. We
went out just like a regular couple. Don't laugh, but I've never
had that experience before—going to a restaurant with a
woman, looking at the menu, ordering, drinking wine, eating,
talking. Her English is excellent and she's intelligent. And beautiful besides. I was—I was in heaven."

My mouth must have dropped open, because George
looked at me quizzically—his head slightly cocked, thick-
framed black eyeglasses higher on one side than the other,
eyes bugged out. Finally, he spoke. "I hope you will understand why I didn't meet you."

"George," I said, not knowing whether to laugh or cry. "I
forgive you totally—totally. I think what you did is wonderful."
I got up and walked over to him, wanting to hug him but instead
only clapped him on the shoulder, feeling like I'd done something really good for a change, even if it was accidental.

I was not sorry to see the last line cast off the dock at
Callao. I wanted to sail south. After two nights of sitting in
my room reading Dostoevsky, I was restless. I could scarcely
set the book down yet found the story so disquieting, I
couldn't sit still and wound up pacing, book in hand. The
scenes were so vivid and Raskolnikov's thoughts and motives
and feelings so skillfully brought forth, I found myself living
in his dingy basement apartment in St. Petersburg, struggling
to survive; slowly going mad. When I wrote in my journal, I
strained to find language that brought life to the page. I
would write something—about the sea, perhaps; or a conversation I'd overheard—read it, cross out a few sentences,
rewrite, cross out, then close the journal in disgust.

We were sailing for Antofagasta, but all I could think about was Valparaiso. Excitement for Valpo was building on the ship. The sailors talked about it often. They called it a sailor's paradise—the port with the most beautiful women in the world.

"So, you dripping yet?" asked Wally every morning after he learned I'd been to the Trockadero.

"Not yet," was my stock answer. The idea of getting a venereal disease appalled me in spite of Irving Johnson saying, "dose a' clap ain't nuthin' more 'n a bad cold." Something about being sick in that part of my body was more than I could stomach. The days went by. Even though I wasn't sure what symptoms I should be looking for, there was no sign of anything not functioning properly. The purser had not been so lucky. He took me aside after breakfast the next morning and told me he had a dose—but that he in no way blamed Elisa for it. He was certain it had been one of the girls he had been with the first night. He felt terrible because he was sure he'd given it to Elisa and had no way to tell her. Since he was the ship's medical officer, he prescribed a round of antibiotics and pronounced himself cured a couple days later.

Antofagasta lay just south of the Tropic of Capricorn—out of the tropics into a winter season. The run there was just over six hundred miles. We would cover that distance during two nights and one full day. Paul Hunt was busy updating the sailors' master voyage overtime sheet. I had helped him set it up. It was a large sheet of paper—maybe thirty inches by eighteen—and had the names of all fifteen sailors, both third mates, the second mate and the chief mate. Neither the captain nor I got paid overtime. A record of overtime worked got submitted weekly by the deck delegate—Fletcher—to the chief mate who had the task of approving it or disputing it. The disputes got resolved by union patrolmen at the payoff port. Eventually, the mate transferred the totals to the master sheet. The numbers in the body of the sheet were added horizontally and vertically, the totals at the bottom and the right side were then summed into a single total. In the extreme lower right-hand corner was one number that represented all the totals going in every direction on that page. It struck me as an absurd system. Getting that number correct

seemed nearly impossible for Mr. Hunt who had to fill out a
master sheet each month. The mate was doing the sheet for July.
To keep me out of his hair, he stuck me on both ends of the
twelve to four.

After our departure from Callao, I reported to the bridge to
stand watch with Don Campbell, the twelve to four third mate.
Except for the chief mate, Don was the first person I had met on
board this ship. He was thirty-four, the youngest of the three
watchstanding mates and definitely my favorite.

We were piloting along the Peruvian coast, fixing our position by sighting landmarks or lighthouses through the crosshairs
of the azimuth circle, reading the bearings, then finding where
the lines crossed on the chart. I liked the work. Don forced me
to study the chart, pick out peaks or points of land or small
islands or the occasional navigation marker, then take the bearings and lay down the lines of position. He would compare my
fixes to those he got by radar. The watch passed quickly.

"Cadet, stop by after dinner tonight for a beer," he said as
we passed the village of Pisco which lay just inside the Peninsula
Paracas and behind which mountain peaks towered. "I'll show
you the Alpaca blankets I bought yesterday in Callao."

Mr. Potter announced his presence on the bridge at exactly twelve minutes to the hour by brusquely walking by me as
if I were infectious, going straight to the barometer on the
bulkhead in the chartroom and tapping the glass with his
pencil. Once he was satisfied a major blow was not imminent,
he went about his ritual of placing two number two pencils to
the right of the chart, setting an eraser at the top of the chart
and neatly and carefully arranging two triangles and his personal dividers at the bottom of the chart. The triangles always
bookended the dividers, their ninety-degree angle corners
pointing outboard. He set the small felt-bottom paperweight
shaped like a mermaid off to the side out of sight, as if those
tiny naked breasts might distract him from the job of watch-
stander on this underway freighter.

Don was a loner in a lonely profession. He seldom joined
in the saloon banter. When he did, his remarks were caustic

and cynical.

"If ah was pres'dent," one of the Mobile, Alabama engineers had said rather loudly one dinner hour as though everyone around him was another of the good ol' boys whose company he was accustomed to, "Ah wunt jis' prosecute them queer draft dodgers up theah in Canada, ah'd go up and cut their balls off."

Don's retort was: "Considering the fact you could even make a statement that stupid, I'm astonished you've even got an officer's license. Or did your *cuzzin'* happen to be the examining coast guard officer?"

"Hey mate," whined the third engineer. "We wuz jis' talkin'. Thass how we talks where ah am from. We din' mean nuthin' disrespeckful."

After watch, I stopped by my room to use the head, then went to Don's stateroom, which was directly above mine. A fresh breeze kicked up from somewhere to the south and a short, bumpy swell made the ride uncomfortable.

I had not been in Don's room before and was totally unprepared for it. He had decorated the walls with paintings, photographs and tapestries. Books—mostly thick hardcovers with titles like *History of the World* and *The Life of Vincent Van Gogh*—were strewn about open, face-down. Vivid red and blue and brown rugs covered the floor and a haunting music—Bach, he said—hung in the air like some ancient spirit. Incense smoking in a corner filled the room with an exotic scent. I stood in the doorway gaping until Don said, "Hey, hick, close the door before the Old Man comes over to investigate the incense."

I pulled the door closed.

"Come in, Jake. Have a beer. Hey, great name by the way. Makes me think of the Jake in Hemingway's *The Sun Also Rises*."

"It's a nickname," I said. "For Michael."

He cocked his head.

"Listen, I've wanted to have you up for a drink for some time now. I love talking to you cadets. Just haven't had a chance with all this in and out of port business. Here, take a look at my blankets."

"They're beautiful," I said. They lay in a stack near the far wall, white with black designs. Don pulled them one by one off the pile, explaining why he liked certain markings, what he looked for in the blankets and how comfortable they were.

"Six dollars each," said Don. "Buy them for your Mom or your girlfriend."

He handed me a Heinekens and sat, his feet on his desk. "Here's that beer. Now, tell me your life story—or at least something interesting. How do you like it on here anyway?"

His friendliness disarmed me. Here in his room, he seemed much different than he was on the bridge where he tended to his work and said little.

"I like it real well. I think I'm starting to catch on a bit."

"You're doing great. I've sailed with lots of cadets so I know what I'm talking about. You get along well with people, which is more than half the battle out here. You work hard on the bridge and on deck. I'm one to tell people what I think and I think you'll make an outstanding officer one day."

Don was short and solid with a beer drinker's paunch. His hair was brown with a hint of red and it curled slightly up over his collar. Behind his back, the engineers called him "hippy" but that was probably more because of his liberal views than the length of his hair. He had brown eyes, a short sharp nose, and ears that were pointed at the top. His beard gave him a werewolfish look, which fit his disposition as a loner. Whenever some remark set wrong with him, his cool blue eyes grew small and dark and he shot a piercing retort, as if to correct wrong thinking and right the world. He both intimidated and fascinated me—as did any man of action.

The ship's motion had increased since I left the bridge and we were bouncing uncomfortably now. I told Don about my family and he told me how well he liked this captain.

"Let's cut the bullshit," said Don as I took a drink. "What do you think about this goddammed war we're involved in over in Viet Nam?"

I thought about how to answer the question. Don's position seemed rather clear. "I wasn't taught to question authority. I read stuff and hear about others who consider our involvement there wrong."

"Well, that's a noncommittal goddamned answer," laughed Don as he downed half his beer and wiped his mouth with the sleeve of his khaki shirt.

"I take it you're against the war," I said.

A fire blazed briefly in his eyes. "I've been there. I've seen the children without parents and the parents without homes. I've seen boys like yourself from Iowa sitting in the bars telling stories of death and dope and sex and violence like no one before ever imagined. It is a war without principles, where everyone and everything is your enemy, where the lines are blurred and not even an illusion of safety exists after a time."

"What do you mean by that?" I asked.

"Soldiers are in as much danger there from friendly fire—from the bullets of a comrade as they are from the enemy. President Johnson knows we cannot win this war. His generals know we cannot win this war. Young men like you go there full of zeal and patriotism. Within a few months, they're strung out on drugs and booze and sex and disillusionment. They stay till they lose an arm or a leg or even their life. Those that survive will live with memories of human behavior that is so outrageous, many will wish they'd died. Mark my words."

"Wouldn't North Vietnam take over the South if we weren't there? They are Communists, right?"

"Oh for Christ's sake. Of course they're communist. So am I. So what? Listen, drink up and go get some rest. Tonight on watch, I'll tell you an Arabic fairy tale I like to tell my kids. It will help you understand how I feel about this war."

I was in a deep sleep when the ordinary seaman called me at 2330 and was still disoriented when I opened the door on the landing that led to the bridge. A small red bulb illuminated so the wheelhouse didn't flood with light, ruining the watch-stander's night-vision. I was a few minutes late and Don had already relieved Mr. Petrocelli. Don was busy working the radar.

"Christ," he said. "These fishing boats never end. Tell you what, Mr. Cadet, you get in here with a grease pencil and plot while I look over your shoulder and tell you that Sufi story I promised."

The radar was pimpled with targets. I nervously took the grease pencil and marked those targets ahead of us, suddenly wide awake. Mr. Potter insisted I watch whenever he plotted traffic, but he'd given me little chance for hands-on learning.

Don Campbell brought an easy-going competence to this job.

"A nation we'll call Southern was governed by an evil king," Don said, reaching over and pointing to a dot on the scope a point to starboard moving rapidly across our bow. "This king killed and taxed, raped and pillaged at will. The way he held onto power was by making his people believe the king who lived across the river in the kingdom called Northern was twice as bad as him and was plotting to come and take over their land.

"The king across the river, of course, was good as gold, enlightened, concerned with the welfare of his own people and wanted nothing to do with anybody else's land. Fortunately, he was strong enough to prevent the bad Southern king from crossing over and attacking him. The people in Southern labored for generations under this cruel despot, telling themselves in consolation: 'As terrible as it is here, at least we don't have it as bad as the people across the river.'

"One day, a child drifted downstream from Southern kingdom in a boat that had slipped its moorings. It drifted straight to the so-called bad kingdom in the north. A father's love for his children is stronger than fear though, so the dad got into a boat and sailed into the other folks' territory. He saw his son's boat against the Northern bank and a large crowd of people surrounding it. Mustering his courage, he rowed directly into the middle of them and pleaded for his son's life, offering them his own in exchange.

"Turned out, the Northern people were real fine folks who took him to the king, fed him, told him stories, gave him and his son gifts, and sent them home, begging him to return as their guest. This guy realized he'd been living an illusion. When he returned home, he tried to convince friends and family they had been wrong about everything, that they should rise up against their king and become part of the Northern king's domain. Naturally, no one believed him. His wife discovered he was to be arrested for treason, so he took his family under cover of night and escaped to the North.

"When he got there, the good king questioned him, found out the bad king was militarily weak and that it would be simple to cross over and defeat him and bring peace to that kingdom.

When he asked the man for his opinion of this idea, the man said, 'No, my people have lived so many years believing bad to be good and good bad that they would fight on the side of bad. Many would be slain. The blood of my countrymen and yours would fill our great river. If you won, you would have the task of re-educating an entire kingdom to your good ways. My people are content with their illusion. They are not ready for change.'"

I listened to Don as I plotted targets on the radar. I was learning what was called the r-t-m triangle. Those letters stood for relative-true-motion and provided a simple method of figuring another vessel's ETA (estimated time of arrival); CPA (closest point of approach), and whether the other ship would pass ahead or astern. Don helped with the markings as he spoke. He seemed completely at ease telling a story and working the radar at the same time.

"Sufi stories have lots of little morals running around in them. Let me tell you my take on it. You can think what you want."

He walked over to the window, grabbed the binoculars and looked at a boat fine to starboard. We were smack dab in the middle of the fishing fleet now. Don paced back and forth in the forward part of the wheelhouse watching the tiny white lights bob up and down. Both sea and sky were pitch black and the boat lights blended with the stars so that I lacked a sense of place, felt even more disoriented than I had when I walked into the wheelhouse at midnight. He interrupted his story frequently with helm orders: "five right," "midships," "steady," "five left," Our ship weaved back and forth through the fishing boats that seemed oblivious to the danger of a big ship passing through them at twenty knots.

"Some people believe our spirits are evolving as we journey through the universe," he continued. "They believe we start at a physical level where we like sex and lots of material stuff. Then we evolve to a higher plane where we desire knowledge or power. Eventually, we arrive at a spiritual plane where we leave temporal things behind and concentrate on our connection with what they call the Godhead.

"People need to leave their tribe and the illusions a tribe provides. That is not so simple. It means severing relationships, leaving one's home and family, sometimes divorcing. For what? No one knows at the time. Maybe nothing. Maybe a life of loneliness and growing old and bitter. We think we can take others with us. But we can't. We just can't. We mate and bring children into the world, but ultimately, we journey alone."

The night was dead flat calm, dark with a sliver-moon low in the west and stars that seemed too close to the water. I felt a little breathless by Don's passion. He was talking to me about myself. About how I'd been exiled from home by my priest and my own father.

"How do we know right from wrong and good from bad?" I asked.

"Before I tell you *that,* put down a position from the radar while I watch these last few fishing boats," said Don.

I took a range and bearing off a point of land we were passing and ducked behind the curtain into the chartroom, afraid I'd miss something important. My fix showed us a mile or so west of our track. This was good since it meant we were further from land and the possibility of shallow water. Don continued talking when I returned.

"A lot of people in our country live their lives under the delusion that we have some kind of lock on what is true. Sometimes I think everything I was ever taught was wrong. I was told that in order to be happy, I had to be successful. Hell, happiness was never really brought up. Only success. The point always seemed to be to earn lots of money to buy lots of things. If one had a big house, cars, television sets—the list goes on and on—then one would have lived a good life. It's all bullshit. All bullshit. Look at the religions we believe in. My dad was an Arkansas Methodist; my mom a Maryland Jew. Because there was no place for Jews to worship in my little town, we went the Methodist route. Dressed up every Sunday. Sat in the same uncomfortable wooden pew, listened to one inane sermon after another and were considered God-fearing people because of that. Yet, I don't recall anyone ever mentioning seeking the truth or looking inward as a means of discovering God. The Methodist minister told

us where God was, what he was. What I recall more than anything is sermons about the virtue of success."

He pitched his voice into a remarkably good imitation of a
southern preacher. "And look at Brothah Conaby ovah heah
with his bank that he inherited from his father and his farms that
he foreclosed from the unwashed heathen tenement farmers and
his big house with its Olympic pool and his Cadillac cars and his
Florida vacations: that is what you-all should strive for."

He reverted to his own voice. "Well, you look at his double
triple chins and pudgy fingers that hadn't worked in a generation, folded around a belly the size of a propane tank. Then you
look up at that stark picture of Jesus Christ hung above the altar
and you think, no way; no way does Jesus Christ want me to be
anything like Albert Conaby. But you're a kid and you wonder
why the minister and all these adults believe this crap, and you're
confused and you question your sanity, and you wish so much it
hurts that Jesus Christ himself would just come down and tell
you how he wants you to be. And so, you grow up dwarfed and
gnarled and contorted in your mind, because you see black and
you know damn well it's black, but everyone around you just
rolls their eyeballs and sings, 'Hallelujah, brother,' and tells you
it's white. You get sick inside, because you know in the deep
parts of your heart the bastards are all hypocrites. You know your
own father is either a hypocrite or just plain stupid. Then you
think maybe you're the idiot 'cause how the hell could an adult
be anything but perfect—especially your own father and Mr.
Jaspers Broome, the goddamned Methodist minister and Albert
Conaby, the double-goddamned banker. It cripples you. Sure
enough cripples you."

Don paused. The fishing boats were astern now, but something odd was happening on the surface of the water just ahead.

"There's something," said Don. "Surface luminescence.
Caused by billions of microbes. Large fish come to feed on
them. See."

A school of dolphin or some other large fish jumped and
dove, creating millions of glittering purple and pink sparks of
light. I had never imagined anything so beautiful and stood
silently on the bridge wing till the school of fish was well astern.

"Makes all my talk ridiculous, doesn't it?" said Don.

I smiled, happy with the stimulation, both natural and intellectual. "Not really," I said. "You might not be luminescence,
but I like hearing what you've got so say."

"I'll take that as a left-handed compliment and continue.
Look at our government. Read the Constitution and the Bill of
Rights and the Declaration of Independence. Think about what
men those were who built this republic, who penned those mas-
terpieces about human liberty, who spilled blood so those ideas
could become the basis for a people to live lives free from
oppression. Then look at what our government is doing with
those laws: how they've twisted and bent them. Look at the policies our government implements; at the countries it supports.
Everything's gone ass-backwards. We persecute those who want
freedom and support dictators. We take money from the poor
and protect the rich's so-called right to exploit the working class
and the land and the forests. We strip-mine the mountains and
pollute the seas. Thomas Jefferson must be one sad son of a
bitch up there watching all this craziness."

Don stopped abruptly—like a door slamming. He stepped
into the chartroom to check our position and returned to the
wheelhouse almost immediately. I was breathless. I had never
heard ideas like this; had never seen such passion. Don's words,
on top of what I had been reading about Raskolnikov's notion
of man's relation to society, forged a path of light through the
darkness of my mind in a way that hurt. I wanted to hear more.

"What do you believe in?" I asked after Don had looked into
the radar, satisfied himself I was doing the work and had
resumed pacing in front of the wheelhouse. I sensed his smile
from his tone of voice.

"That's a fair question to ask someone rattling on and on
about how fucked up everything is." He seemed gentle and at
peace now, his passion spent.

"Let's go out on the wing."

I walked behind him, out of the air-conditioning into the
night air that was sensuous and lovely. The dome sparkled with
southern constellations. Don inhaled deeply then pointed out
Corona Australis, the southern crown; Sagitta, the arrow;
Scutum, the shield. Jupiter, god of the heavens, hung without
twinkling low in the west.

"God, oh God," he said.

I was silent, overwhelmed by the night's beauty and Don's powerful words. We both leaned over the dodger at the far end of the bridge wing letting the breeze cool us.

"I don't honestly know if I believe in anything," said Don finally. "No, that's not right. There are things I believe in. There are things I believe to be true. Most of them come from my Granddad, Chaim, to this day a Rabbi in Baltimore. He and I have corresponded since I was twelve and was sent to visit him and Grandmom for a summer. I went every summer after that till I was sixteen. Granddad started writing letters to me that first year; offered me a dollar for every letter I'd send him. A week after I'd send him a letter, I'd receive one back, always with a dollar in it. Still get them. Still get the dollars, believe it or not. Never spent them either. Have got a pile of them and feel rich because of them and the knowledge they represent. He said the Jews believe in one God, just like the Christians and the Moslems. If anything, Jews are even more monotheistic than Catholics in that we don't muddy the God-waters with Jesus Christ and all the saints. Jews believe anyone can reach salvation, though; that Judaism doesn't have a lock on Truth. Your God and your faith can work just as well for you as mine works for me. We believe since all men are created in God's image, all men are equal; Jews aren't somehow better than Methodists; whites are not better than blacks.

"I personally believe that whether or not a person has faith—a belief in something or another—does not alter Truth. What I mean is that just because some old maiden aunt of yours believes with all her might that the Roman Catholic Church is the one true church doesn't affect whether or not that is true. Now, it may be true or it may be an illusion, an illusion that comforts us in the dead of winter when the wolfish wind howls outside our door and we question whether we will survive—but believing does not make it so. I believe, in general, that all the world's great 'isms'—capitalism, communism, Catholicism, General Motorsism—all are just large, powerful organizations whose main goal and function is to control as many people as possible. To increase their power and further their position in the world. Not to say they don't do some good. Most illusions help people in certain ways at certain times. But none of them, I suspect, has a corner on the Truth Market.

"Sometimes I have a feeling that God may be inside me and inside you and inside most of us in a way that, with proper guidance, we could become one with God and therefore Godlike. I believe that I'm capable of loving more than I do and I truly believe I should be motivated by love. I believe that I'm frequently distracted from what is important by the day to day mundanity and general craziness of the world."

Don stopped and turned his head outboard, then walked up and back a couple of times. "I believe I can't wait to get back to the states and see my family again, and that I'm getting sick of this life at sea."

He paused, stepped over to the wing repeater and set the azimuth circle on a light three points to starboard. He watched it a couple minutes then continued.

"I guess that's about it. See. There are lots of things I believe. What about you?"

I breathed deeply, feeling too young to add anything to this conversation. I noticed Jupiter had set.

"I'm becoming aware of things I never knew about before. Sometimes it seems like everything I was ever taught just wasn't quite right." I paused, thinking about how to say what I wanted to say—even if, like a second magnitude star, it wasn't brilliant.

"When I was home this summer, my parish priest and I had an argument. He told my dad and my dad drove me to the edge of town and let me off. Told me not to return till I could act like I belonged. So I came down here and got on this ship. I think now I needed to leave home to learn about myself and the world. On the other hand," I paused briefly, "I believe in families and hard work and a sort of inevitability of things. I'm basically patriotic and I'll probably always be a Catholic, no matter how long between masses." I smiled sheepishly, thinking of my mother.

"Growing up on the prairie is isolating. Questioning big, basic things was not something my family taught us to do. Back home, life has a simple, natural rhythm: you get married, have children, find a job in a small community nearby, get a church pew you're comfortable in, raise your kids, join the Wednesday night golf club and the Knights of Columbus. My family grows a lot of the food we eat, and my uncles talk about fishing and their tractors. We discuss politics some, but if push comes to shove, people support the politician who belongs to their party. You don't question America's policies, especially on something like war."

I stopped. A whisper of cool breeze from a couple points off the port bow touched our faces. Don stared ahead. I could make out his face, more wolfish than ever in the moonlight.

"Tell you the truth, that small-town life sounds pretty darned good right now," he said. We were silent again.

"What are you reading now?" he asked quietly.

"*Crime and Punishment*. It's part of my sea project. Raskolnikov thinks certain men—men like Napoleon, or, in our time, Mao or Stalin—because of their greater capabilities or some force of personality, are beyond the rules of society. He thinks you can do as you wish so long as you get away with it, so long as you win and no one stronger or smarter challenges you or defeats you."

"Forget that nihilist crap," said Don quietly. "It's all bullshit. All that Raskolnikov, Sartre, Camus, Nietsche stuff. It does no good for anyone. Maybe allows you to survive tough times, if you need some kind of philosophical crutch. Let me tell you how I think people should live their lives. You can tell me to shove it or whatever, but what I'm about to tell you will never hurt you or anyone else.

"Look at those people who had such great ambitions—and you can throw your Ayn fucking Rand in with the lot also. They had ambition for money or for monumental palaces or life and death power over millions of people. You look at each of them and ask yourself what did they do for the world. Maybe they were great men, but they were all men who caused death, suffering, devastation. We think Hitler was bad because he exterminated six million Jews and directly or indirectly caused the world to go to war, but he was a piker next to Stalin and Mao, who, between the two of them, probably killed off forty mil."

"When I think of Raskolnikov, I imagine life at a smaller, more personal level," I said. "Are all men bound by the rules we're given or should we judge for ourselves which of those rules are right?"

Don looked at me over the top of the dim light of the gyro repeater. The ship he had been tracking had passed clear down our starboard side. Even in this light, his eyes blazed.

"This is what you should base your life on. This is what I think you should base your actions as a man on. On love and kindness. It's that simple. Do things out of love and kindness—both to yourself and to others—and you'll almost always do the right thing. Do things for any other reason—and I include following orders and obeying laws—and you will find that you hurt others. I don't advocate some kind of panty-waist, do-gooder, life-is-beautiful, let's-all-hold-hands-and-sing crap either. I can no more abide cowardly men than I can stand snooty women. I am not religious. I don't preach the gospel of Jesus or the teachings of Buddha, good as those men are. You, today, from this moment forward, do things out of love for your fellow man or I will personally kick your butt next time I see you. Be kind, be helpful, teach people what you know, learn what they have to teach you. Listen to what folks have to say. Watch them. Observe how they live their lives. Succumb to temptation from time to time as your own chemistry dictates. You're not perfect. If there is a God, he knows that." He paused. "But there is no excuse for not being kind, for not sharing, for not helping out, for not doing things out of love."

Seven bells sounded. Three-thirty. Nearly time for our relief. I looked closely at my watch in the light of the stars, hardly believing the bells correct, the night had passed so swiftly. I almost ran into the wheelhouse to write up the log before Mr. Potter arrived. In bed later, my mind bubbled with the yeast of Don's words.

I passed that day in a fog. Twice, the mate asked me what was wrong, why I couldn't focus on work. After dinner that evening, Don invited me to his room for a beer. When I got there, I walked around looking at his photographs. Several were of the woman and children I had seen with him when we sailed from Houston. "That your family?" I asked.

"That's them." He lifted the picture of his wife off his desk and looked at it, then handed it to me. "Have a close look at a beautiful woman."

The woman sat on a small bench before a circular mirror. She wore a brown slip with the spaghetti strap off her left shoulder. Her right arm was up combing her jet-black hair. Her breasts were raised because of the position of her arms and her chin was tilted slightly so her hair cascaded freely down her back. Her eyes were fixed on her reflection. It was the most intimate picture of a woman I had ever seen and I was embarrassed to stare at it with the woman's husband in the room. She looked like a screen actress from an earlier time: classically beautiful, emotionally complex. I wondered where she was from. She appeared too exotic for a red-faced, beer-drinker like Don. I could see one thing: there was more to Don than I would ever have guessed.

"My wife is an Armenian Jew," he said as if guessing my questions. "Most beautiful women in the world. Rarely see a homely Armenian." He took the picture from my hand and looked at it a long time. I finished my beer and opened another.

"I first saw her in New York one spring day in South Ferry park my third year at the Academy. Fell instantly in love," said Don. "Told my granddad how I felt about her. He said marry her. And I did."

"I've never met a Jew before you."

"Not such a big deal, huh?"

I was quiet a moment, watching questions surface and rejecting them, not wanting to insult Don or appear too much a hick. Henrietta, the librarian, had given me a couple of books about the Jewish culture last year. I wanted to know more.

"Are you raising your kids in the Jewish faith?"

"Yeah. They go to Synagogue and all that. My son will do his bar mitzvah in a couple years."

I decided to jump in with my questions.

"Why have the Jews been so persecuted through the ages when they hold such liberal views?"

"Probably for that exact reason. If political leaders can't sell exclusive belief in one true God, they have a difficult time governing. Jefferson believed his greatest accomplishment was separation of Church and State. Christian kings in the Middle Ages could never get Jews to join their religious crusades. Jews pre-

ferred to stay home, raise their families, do business, make art,
live out their lives and let others do the same."

I knew I'd have to think about that for a while.

"I didn't know you went to the Academy," I said.

"She's the reason I quit." He gestured toward the picture
of his wife. "I was a second-classman, doing fine. Well, fine
might be a little strong. Let's just say I was tending to business,
passing my courses, staying out of trouble, looking forward to
a quiet first-class year as a zombo. I first saw her standing next
to a crabapple tree in South Ferry Park exploding with pink
blossoms. She wore a white cotton skirt the wind blew against
her legs. I couldn't take my eyes off her. I was like a stallion,
standing there looking at her. Maybe it was the spring season,
maybe it was my age, maybe it was her, maybe it was just plain
old love. When I saw her, I wanted to fuck her so bad I'd have
eaten dirt; I'd have walked the bottom of the East River; I'd
have balanced bananas on my nose or juggled eggs. I hadn't
talked to her ten minutes but I knew I would marry her. Fuzzy
romantic feelings are bullshit. Let me give you some advice
about women: almost a sure sign of love is wanting to fuck
them. I mean fuck them against a building in an alley, or in a
sand bank in the river at night, or against a boulder up on some
mountain. You want to have sex so badly and so often, you can't
drive five blocks to the grocery store without stopping someplace. It makes you crazy. We married less than a month later
and I quit school. That was fifteen years ago and I still can't
drive five blocks without reaching for her hand."

My eyes widened in response to Don's outburst. "Seems like
lots of guys out here have been divorced a time or two. To hear
them talk, you'd have to wonder if they like women or just think
of them as, well, as something to use."

Don smiled and looked at me as he finished his beer. He
reached into his ice chest and pulled out another, set it on his
desk and tapped the top of the can. "Not sure if I want to get
going on this topic," he said, opening the beer and tossing the
flip-top into the waste basket. "But what the hell. Here's how I
see it. Men are afraid to respond to women as human beings
because women are superior to men in important ways. Women
nurture. Men destroy. Notice there are no women in that list of

violent despots you reeled off. It must be downright sickening to a woman once she starts to look around for someone to father her children and sees one semi-useless, controlling, passionless sack of shit after another to choose from. Men are weak, fearful, dependent, lacking in virtue and generally cowards. All right. All right. Lots of men work very hard bringing home the bacon so their wives can raise the kids and keep a nice home. But aside from that, we father children and protect what is ours, but otherwise, we're sort of useless in this era of nature having been conquered—unless you consider hitting a golf ball or hunting elk or watching football on TV useful activities. Name five things a man can do better than a woman. Shovel snow, maybe, or replace light-bulbs without a ladder." He looked hard at me. "How many men do you know that really seem able to love?" Don laughed as though he'd said something funny, lifted his beer can to his mouth and swallowed.

I stood speechless.

"I don't mean to sound like an asshole, but it takes strength to be tender, to open yourself to the risk of being hurt. Men think sex is an end in itself, and maybe at your age, it should be. Think about this, though. Remember it when you're ready to start loving women. Picture a full-blown adult female, ready to love you and bear your children, wash your underwear, cook your eggs, clean your toilet and kill to protect your babies. Imagine her wanting to give herself totally to one person, to you. Imagine her naked with high, tight breasts and a nest of black pubic hair to get lost in; with firm hips, long legs and a red mouth. Imagine her standing before you, naked, body glowing with desire. Imagine her arms beckoning and her saying 'love me.'

"Most men run like scared jackrabbits. They run to a woman who might be weaker or less demanding, or they run to a bottle of whiskey or to a career or to a whorehouse or to their mother." Don paused and wiped his mouth.

"I shudder to think of all the inane things women have to put up with in men just to further the race."

Don finished his beer and smiled, looking like an elf.

"So," he said. "That's about it. That's the fifteen-minute version of life according to Don. I don't know what you have planned for the future, but let me give you one more piece of free advice. Don't sacrifice everything for some god-for-saken career, whether it's out here or anyplace else. Don't be afraid to walk away from a good job if it's interfering with living. Got that?"

Don's eyes were once again piercing. "That's what I tell every cadet. Usually that's all I tell them. You're lucky—or maybe unlucky. You got to hear the whole stupid philosophy. Now, go to bed. I need at least an hour of sleep before I go on watch." Don pitched his empty beer can into the metal wastebasket.

I sat there staring. Couldn't move. Couldn't get over what Don had said. Was it true? All the things he'd said about men? I shook my head, not sure why, maybe to clear it. Don had gone into his head. I could hear his strong stream of pee hitting the water in the toilet. I stood as he returned, fumbling with his zipper. "Kind of hard to just up and leave after all that."

Don just waved his hand and smiled.

Back in my room, Wally snored louder than usual. I didn't mind. I lay down, smiling, feeling smarter than before, more ready to live, but wondering to myself if life just continued to grow more complicated or if at some point it kind of leveled off or even became simpler.

Antofagasta, Chile
August 14

I logged the crossing of the Tropic of Capricorn at exactly 0334, Monday, August fourteenth. The captain was on the bridge. We rounded *Punta Tetas* an hour later and picked up the pilot just before 0500. Docking in Antofagasta was routine except for one thing. As we entered the harbor, a fine dust seemed suspended in the atmosphere. A layer of the stuff covered the deck of the Gulf Trader before the second headline had been figure-eighted around the forward bitts and Captain Isenhagen had ordered, "Finished with Engines." The boatswain had prepared for it by burlapping all the vent openings, but it was insidious and got into everything.

After we were fast, I pulled down the Hotel flag, which I had run up when the pilot boarded. I ran the company flag up the same halyard but had to pull it down and redo it because I'd attached it to the lanyard upside down. I took the azimuth circle off the port wing repeater, replaced the cover, then stopped to look around. This had to be the most God-forsaken geography I'd ever seen—worse, even, than the prairie in winter when snow blew against a dull gray sky, covering the fields and the houses and the animals and the people. Here, hills of sand surrounded the town and the harbor. The sun glared down as if angry that we would stop in a place so apparently unwilling to support life. This was Antofagasta, largest town in the Atacama Desert. According to Don Campbell, my new source for virtually all information, years pass between raindrops in the Atacama Desert.

I slid the charts off the chart table and into the top drawer of the chart desk, then put the bell book on the shelf across from the chart desk over by the deck log. Mr. Potter, as second mate, was in charge of securing the bridge. He was meticulous. I had secured it three times now, and had not yet gotten it right. His eyes missed nothing. A pencil left unsharpened, lying on the chart desk—particularly in the fore and aft position where it might roll with a list—warranted at least ten minutes on why secure ships are happy ships and "a bridge isn't ship-shape and Bristol-fashion till every pencil is lead-down in it's hole, every coffee cup clean, hanging captain first on it's proper hook, every ash-tray emptied."

The sailors were just finishing rigging the safety net when I got down to the main deck. I leaned against the rail forward of the gangway watching longshoremen, vendors and officials walk quietly aboard. No one smiled. Their faces were stony and dry, their actions quick. They were small in stature and they resembled nothing so much as hard brown nuts.

My motives for selling my ring to one of them were honorable enough. We were nearing Valparaiso, our turn-around port, and I had yet to buy one gift for anyone at home. Even if I couldn't go home, if I wasn't welcome there, I figured I still had to buy gifts. I'd mail them if nothing else. I had come to miss my family, including my father, but how could I buy gifts when the small sum of money I earned went for rum and romance? Besides, in spite of what Don Campbell had told me about ignoring Dostoevsky and his Extraordinary Man concept I wasn't quite ready to roll over and play dead. If I needed money, and could figure out a way to get it, then whether or not the getting fell within the confines of whatever rules were governing my behavior—and there weren't many—was inconsequential, to my way of thinking.

The man who bought my ring wore a blue, double-breasted blazer and stood out from the others like a proud jay in a flock of mangy sparrows. He was taller, his hair brighter, his shoes shinier, his fingers longer and his mouth more refined. He carried a leather valise filled with watches and transistor radios, ballpoint pens, bottles of perfume, whiskey and toiletries. He bought as well as sold. From the American ships, he purchased chocolates, Chiclets, chewing gum, blue jeans, banlon shirts, batteries, tools and anything with the word Yankees on it. Besides being in the business of buying and selling, he was obviously a superior man. He was fair game.

We had only a small amount of cargo for the port and were due to sail at midnight. This fit nicely into my plan. Once the trader discovered the ring wasn't gold, he didn't have much time to return to the ship to claim a rightful refund.

Shortly before lunch, I went to my room and took the ring from the top drawer on my side of the green metal desk. I polished it on the sleeve of my shirt and looked at it. It was handsome: rich looking and manly. It was the type of ring a big man with big hands could wear. The top of the ring was stamped with a fine Inca imprint—the head of an Inca chieftain who ate meat raw, threw spears legendary distances, drank Pisco out of a bucket and satisfied a palace-full of maidens. If I hadn't needed the money so much, I would never have tried to sell it, bad luck or not.

I slipped it onto the ring finger of my right hand and slid down the stairs on the handrails to the main deck. The trader sat on a bench on the onshore side of the house. He sat there for a reason, of course. Crewmembers had to pass by him every time they went ashore or ducked in off the deck for a cup of coffee or a snack. He displayed his wares on a piece of green velvet cloth and was normally set up before breakfast—so crewmembers could see what he had. He would leave after lunch, either for siesta or to visit another ship, then return after dinner to catch the men returning from shore after debauching themselves with money that belonged as much to their families as it did to them. They returned drunk, spent, guilty as hell. Salesmen everywhere know guilty men buy gifts. And seamen—except, I tried telling myself, for Raskolnikov wannabe's like me—could feel as much guilt as anyone. It was almost as if the act of buying gifts for family members far away was the ointment men used to massage their guilt glands.

She'll like that, a man would think to himself, picturing the little woman in her apron bent over the sink in the kitchen of their home as he looked at the tiny bottle of French perfume he had purchased after a night of revelry. That'll be nice.

I stopped at the man's stand and fingered the watches and browsed the photos advertising local handicrafts, always making sure the ring was visible. The trader was quiet but watchful. He saw the ring.

"You want a nice watch for your girl friend?" he asked

"Can't afford it," I said, fingering a dark-eyed doll. "You have lots of nice things here."

"You are cadete'?"

"Si," I answered. "No money. Senoritas take my money. Senoritas and this gold ring I bought in Callao."

"*Muy bueno*," he said. "A beautiful ring. May I see it?"

"Sure," I answered. "I'll even sell it to you."

"Ah." His face registered a hint of approval as he felt the weight of the ring and saw the 18k stamped inside. "Is gold?" he asked.

"Far as I know," I said. "Better be gold, much as I paid for it."

"May I take it to someone else who might know better than me about such matters?"

"Of course," I said, suddenly not so sure this was going the way I had hoped.

"And, by the way," he said, "how much do you require for this very fine piece?"

"Sixty dollars cash," I answered without blinking. The man lifted his eyebrows ever so slightly.

He walked down the gangway to the tallest and broadest of the longshore bosses barking orders at the forklift driver moving pallets of aluminum ingots back and forth from the shed to the apron where they were lifted aboard by the ship's gear. The man held up the ring and others joined him. Soon, cargo operations on the wharf came to a halt as the longshoremen crowded around the authoritative gang-boss inspecting the ring.

The ring passed from one bony brown hand to another, each of which would bounce it up and down as if that told some true story. They all chattered excitedly, and I noticed heads beginning to nod. Gestures were made toward where I stood at the head of the gangway, followed by men shielding their eyes with a hand, looking up at me, curious about the young gringo who somehow had obtained possession of such a valuable piece. Finally, the ring made its way back to the longshore boss who inspected it once more, looked again at me, nodded and returned the ring to the merchant.

The trader polished it carefully on his jacket sleeve and made his way back up the gangway.

"It is a very poor quality of gold, my friend," he said. "At most, it is worth but fifteen dollars. However, because you are a cadete', I will give you twenty-five." He held onto the ring—a good   sign,   I   thought.

"Oh," I said, "sorry. I paid fifty for it. Even thirty is not possible."

"OK. OK. Forty dollars."

"Forty-five," I sighed at the huge loss I was about to undergo. "Plus that doll there for my sister. Take it or leave it."

The man pulled two twenties and a five from his bankroll and handed them over. "You are a skillful negotiator. You may take the doll."

Don Campbell invited me to go ashore with him that night and sample *Sopa de Congria*, a soup made from the giant eels local divers speared in their caves just south of here, and Chilean red. He said teaching me to drink wine was the only part of my education he felt totally comfortable with. At four, when Don and I were in the mate's office talking about shoring needed for the pallets of ingots, the phone rang.

"It's the captain," said Paul Hunt. "Says he wants to see you immediately. What'd you do, anyway? He sounds pissed."

I hurried up to the captain's deck, stopping first in my room to wash my hands and face, cursing my foolishness in thinking I could get away with pawning false goods. Standing in the passageway outside his door with its green privacy curtain half open, I knocked and waited. I could see his stern face—a bit comical, actually, with his oversized ears protruding—and on his desk, the gold ring. Then I saw the trader, legs crossed on the settee, a beer in his hand. The gig was up.

"Come in," said Captain Isenhagen, his voice stern. I entered. "Senior Portilla, my very good friend says you have forty-five dollars of his." I saw immediately the captain was not a man interested in feeble excuses.

"Yes sir, I do."

"Then return it to him and take this worthless piece of metal out of my room." He nudged the ring across his desk as though it was despicable. "Local Customs officials have decided to detain and fine the ship unless the money is returned."

"I'll—I'll get it immediately, sir."

I turned on my heel and left. I was caught fair and square, and decided not to try to save face by pretending I didn't know the ring wasn't gold. I ran down the stairs, grabbed the money from my room and returned immediately.

"Here is the money and the doll, sir. I apologize to Senor Portilla. I would like to say that I would have gladly refunded the money had he come directly to me."

"Take your ring, young man. And don't forget, you are a guest in the fine country in which these people live. I don't think you're the sort who would steal from a man who has invited you into his home for dinner."

"Senor Cadete', please accept the doll as a memento of Antofagasto." Senor Portilla spoke.

"Thank you sir." I took the ring and the doll. "My apologies, gentlemen, for the trouble I've caused." I turned and left, red-faced, wondering if Raskolnikov would steal from the home of one who had invited him to dinner if it served his purposes.

The chief mate had told me to shower and go ashore when I was finished with the skipper. Don, the third mate, met me at the gangway at five. As we walked through the warehouse piled high with wooden cartons and pallets of aluminum ingots, I told Don what had happened in the captain's room. We showed our passes to the security guard and headed up a street toward a restaurant Don went to every time he landed in this port. He smiled and looked at the ring.

"Beautiful ring," he said, bouncing it up and down in his

hand. "How much do you want for it?"

"Very funny," I said. "I think it's bringing me bad luck. The first time I wore it was to the Trockadero—one of my life's low points—the other time today."

"So why are you wearing it tonight?"

"To test my theory."

We walked past rows of small, dirt-colored houses with thin dark men sitting out front staring at us. Naked black-haired children played in the streets—risking their lives whenever the mammoth, smoke-belching busses rumbled down the narrow streets, the driver honking and yelling and flashing his lights.

Antofogasta is not large and the restaurant was on the water a few blocks from the ship. It served seafood, lamb and wine on a wood patio that looked out over a cliff ninety feet above an unobstructed view of the ocean. This simple café, Don's favorite on the entire run, consisted of outdoor tables covered with red and white checkered cloths. The food was served from a small kitchen and storage area partially hidden by a curtain.

Don escorted me to his favorite table. It stood in the corner of the patio, on the ocean-side, directly above the drop-off. We sat. I looked down. At the bottom of the cliff, waves broke over a ragged outcrop of rocks, creating an intimate beach where we could see a young couple, heads close, arms entwined, conversing. To their left, a small steep trail—not much more than a lama path—wound amid large boulders and gnarled, wind-bent trees up to the level of town. The woman's jet-black hair blew about her neck. Periodically, the man would brush the strands from her face and nuzzle her hair. I thought of Melissa and felt an almost overwhelming sense of longing.

Don ordered wine—a Rose', he called it. I truly knew nothing about the drink, having experienced only Mogan David at my home for Christmas dinner and some vinegary red from a gallon jug one drunken night at school in New York. This Rose' sparkled pink in the clear fluted glasses against the checkered red and white tablecloth. We clinked glasses and drank, but neither of us spoke. I turned my chair to face the ocean. The bright blue of the sky was separated from the deeper blue of the water by a pencil-line horizon, ruler straight. The winter sun sat less than three diameters above that line—a brilliant yellow ball suspended above a blue table. The ocean looked as calm as the wine in our glasses. I drank often, but my glass seemed always full. Our first bottle was empty when the sun's lower limb rested on the horizon.

"This is just goddammed beautiful. Makes all the bullshit worthwhile. Watch the sun set now, cadet. That layer of dust surrounding us this morning infiltrates the atmosphere here making the sunsets nothing less than magnificent. Watch it. Feel it. Be it, for Christ's sake."

I said nothing. The lower arc dipped below the pencil-line horizon. Then the ball was half-gone, then three-quarters. A red streak blistered the deep blue of the ocean. Vermilion spokes shot into the sky from the hub of the sun, the gaps between the spokes filled with a brassy gold.

The sun flattened and widened, became a horizontal orange line, then disappeared. In its place, for just a moment, I saw, like a gift from the gods, the almost mythical green flash, a phenomenon that occurs when the long, red light waves bounce off the atmosphere, and the short, violet rays are absorbed by it, leaving in the visible spectrum a brief flash of green. I fingered my ring, sighed, swirled the wine in my glass and drained it.

"Bravo!" I said, holding up my empty glass. "More wine."

"Amen, brother." Don drank with gusto, wiped his mouth with his sleeve, and held up his cup. The waiter, a tired, thin man, self-deprecating and defeated by life—though I doubt he was thirty—stood there, hunched, looking balefully at Don's raised glass. With a heavy sigh, he took a bottle off a wooden shelf near the door and walked slowly toward our table.

With the sun gone, the color of the wine in our glass deepened, as one bottle followed another. After exploding briefly into long, torrid flames, the sky retreated to a regal purple with traces of lavender about the edges of the scattered cumulus. The sea, reflecting the red off the backs of the clouds, was briefly the color of our wine, blood-red against the evening sky. A cargo ship moved imperceptibly across the horizon, the same color as the sea. As we sat and drank, light and color left the sky like grand showmen exiting a stage, and a clear midnight blue remained. Venus appeared first, brilliant and alone as a solitaire and the deep blue turned jet-black. Jupiter followed shortly and the two planets sat side by side, joined within minutes by a thousand diamond stars. Don and I spoke of small things. We built camaraderie sentence by sentence and glass by glass, inhaling deeply of the salt air, enjoying a level of conversation not always present on ships. As the wine took effect, Don became serious.

"These goddammed ships really get under my skin." He poured another glass and held it up to look through it at the candle that flickered between us.

"I get on a ship and just hate it. I hate standing on the bridge and staring at the ocean hour after hour. I hate walking on deck, surrounded by babbling longshoremen. I hate sitting alone in my room, listening to the hum of the ventilator fans. I hate chewing fried grease in the company of people I probably wouldn't invite to my home for dinner.

I make a trip or two—occasionally three—then get off and feel like I've been released from prison. I haul my bags down the gangway and carry them out the gate. The kids are bouncing in the back seat of our green Volkswagen bus. My wife has a kind of strange, sad smile on her face She gets out of the car and is gorgeous; wearing a simple dress or blue jeans and a sports jacket with her shirt tucked in. She comes up to me and puts her arms around my neck and holds me real tight. Then she pushes me away and looks me over, head to toe, turns me around and looks me over again. The kids jump out and Peter hugs me sort of self-consciously and Tasha bubbles over with joy and stands shyly, unable to tear her eyes away from my face, till I pick her up and squeeze her. And we're just a goddamned sad little family reunited once again. Behind me, I hear the forklifts roaring and the winches screaming and the longshoremen yelling. Some guy passes me carrying a brown wooden box and I know it's my relief with his sextant. He just walks on by, unless we happen to know each other. At that moment, I realize I am nothing to that ship. It doesn't slow down even a little bit when I leave. No one is there to tell me I did a good job. If I'm real lucky, the captain will shake my hand at payoff and say he'd like to have me back some time, but chances are just as good he won't since most likely I haven't kissed his ass. And you know, the funny thing is, it's the same for the captain. I know it is. Only he has to stick around longer getting relieved. But that ship doesn't miss him. None of us are any more important than a piece of machinery. Maybe less. Someone once said there are three states of being: dead, alive and at sea.

"Shit." He drank again. "Shit shit shit."

"Why don't you quit and do something else?" I could feel the alcohol seeping into those areas of my brain that controlled speech.

Don answered, "I've thought about it. I've—well, I've even tried a couple of things. I think I'd like to study history and be a college professor. Really. I think I'd enjoy seeing curious men and women sitting before me absolutely hanging onto every word I say. I think I'd be good at that; having graduates return to tell me where they've been, or calling from some international capital to ask questions about this or that because they'd know I'd have an opinion based on extensive research and thought. But life at sea ruins you. Makes you comfortable and independent—like suburban housewives. Just goddamned ruins you for doing anything else.

"I worked ashore for Western Gulf for a couple years once, right after getting married. I was what they call a Port Captain—a flunky, really; a messenger boy who trots down to the ships to spy and collect gossip and dispense subtle innuendoes about what the office is saying about a certain Captain. Or maybe some Chief Mate is writing up too much overtime or the Chief Engineer on a sister ship is having more than his share of mechanical problems. Then I'd be sent to another ship and there'd be the guys I'd been talking about, and I'd feel like such a jerk. Just a real jerk." Don filled both our glasses.

"Port Captain. Lowest job in the merchant marine. People on ships hate to see you come aboard and love to see you leave. People in the office resent all the time you spend fucking off on the ships, and joke about how little you have to do around the office. No real responsibility. Just go back and forth, make your inane little walk-around inspection on the ship, dawdle back to the office to write a report no one reads and keep hoping maybe someone will see something in you and make you assistant marine superintendent. I finally quit—got to the point where I wasn't going to the ship or the office, but to an open bar someplace to drink and pass the time. Got so I couldn't stand going to work and didn't like coming home."

"Why didn't you ever raise your license?" I asked.

"Sore subject." Don drank more wine. The waiter set calamari sautéed in red peppers and garlic in front of us. "But since you've been so kind as to ask, and we're feeling all rosy from this wine, I'll tell you. Two reasons. One, I didn't want the responsibility. That captain's job looks pretty good most of the time, but I've seen times when it turns into a monster, when the responsibility settles onto the man's back like a big fucking animal and says 'do something, asshole. You're the captain.' One man I knew, Captain Blaine Richards, stood on the bridge during a typhoon between Hong Kong and Taiwan, white knuckled, seas smashing through the inch-thick porthole glass in the wheelhouse, lifting away ten-ton hatch-covers and ripping wire-reels off the resistor houses. He crumpled from the pressure. Nearly lost his ship and crew. Another time, a guy name of Knight fought like a warrior, made a hard, clear decision, beat off the danger and saved the ship and most of the cargo, but lost two men doing it. One of the men he lost, his chief mate, was a lifelong friend, like a brother, godfather to his oldest son. That captain held on till the ship reached port, then was relieved. I saw him a few weeks ago, just before I came on here. He's gone back to sailing third mate. Said it wasn't worth it. Said he wouldn't do it anymore.

"I've thought about myself a lot. Sometimes, I think I lack courage. 'Grace under pressure' as Hemingway put it. I decided being third mate is good enough. There's times, I despise myself for that decision."

I looked at him puzzled.

"No, I really do. I'm not kidding. But I think it's for the best. The other thing is, when you're a captain, you give your heart and soul to the company. When you're a mate out of the hall, they just get your body."

"Like a whore, right?" I asked.

"Exactly." Don looked over at our sad-sack server. "Say, waiter. We're a little hungry over here." Don's loud voice attracted the attention of people sitting nearby. Mostly, they were young couples, talking quietly, holding hands, looking into each other's eyes, the flame of their candles flickering between them.

"There's another reason—maybe the real reason. I never really understood navigation. Math just isn't my thing. I like philosophy and history, especially the history of ideas. As cadet, I just couldn't come up with consistent three star fixes no matter how hard I tried. Without that, without the confidence I could do that consistently, I never felt I'd make it as second mate. Always believed if I could get past the navigator slot, I'd be a great cargo mate. But you know, it's one foot in front of the other in life. Can't take step two, you don't get to even try step three." Don stared at his glass, swirled the wine in it, then drank.

"No shortcuts," I said.

"Unless you're Raskolnikov." Don laughed. "Let's eat."

I turned slowly toward the waiter, suddenly aware of my advanced state of inebriation. Every movement had to be carefully planned, then even more carefully executed. Another bottle of wine was set on the table, then a bowl of thick brownish-white soup with potatoes and vegetables and big chunks of eel and shellfish. We laughed at our drunkenness, but drank nonetheless. I tried to say things about the soup, which I found delicious, but what came out was as mixed as my thoughts. "Shlups gudfish in the shoup. Ver dec'late. Decilate. Good wine. Vino! Ha. Ha."

I raised my glass as if to toast the accomplishment of the soup, or possibly of my description of the soup when my esophagus opened to the unsubtle knockings of a toxic mix and erupted, spraying a composition of an indescribably vile color—to say nothing of the odor—out over the table, into my bowl and Don's. A piece of half-chewed eel wound up in Don's glass. Don looked up, saw the fish in the glass and said: "Oh, fish with wine. Excellent choice."

My lips strained mightily around an apology while my left hand tipped my full glass onto the tablecloth. My right painstakingly picked up peas, one by one, and set them back into my bowl as if in light of everything else that had happened, the spilled peas were all that truly mattered. Finally, my head slumped forward and my forehead plunged directly into the bowl of soup. I felt tired at that moment, decided the warm soup felt good and stayed there.

I don't know how long it took the waiter to get to our table—I suspect no more than a few seconds. By the time he arrived, it must have looked as if a food-fight had occurred, followed by a knife-fight—the red wine blood-colored on the table-cloth—in which the loser, his head resting in his soup, had died, leaving the victor laughing uncontrollably.

When Don reached for his wallet to pay for the mess and realized he'd forgotten it in his haste to leave the ship, he stopped laughing. Like a dog after fleas, his hands moved from empty pocket to empty pocket. Finally, he lifted my head by the hair, shouting as if the ship was on fire and I was a hundred feet away.

"Do you have any money for Christ's sake? If you don't, they're gonna by God throw us into a jail cell that doesn't even have keys and if you think the captain chewed you out this afternoon, just wait till you hear what he has to say when the ship gets held up and he has to come to the jailhouse at midnight to bail us out."

Images of being at the front in Viet Nam flooded my brain and I learned then that fear can cut through an alcoholic coma. I knew I had nothing in my billfold, not having taken a draw yesterday and having relinquished the forty-five dollars I'd received for the ring. Looking at my empty hands, I noticed the candlelight flicker off my gold ring. Without hesitating, I removed it and handed it to the waiter. His eyes widened and he actually grinned when he saw the 18k stamped on the inside. He took the ring, assisted me and Don to the door and waited with us on the sidewalk until a taxi arrived. Like an obsequious doorman, he ushered both of us into the back seat and paid the driver, happily telling him in Spanish where to take us.

The deck gang was rigging to heave in the gangway as we staggered aboard. Boss Jones, the bosun, stood on deck.

"Go on to your room, there, ka-dett," he said. "We'll get outta this sand-pit without you up on the bow. If the cap'n asks, I'll let him know you be jus' a little under the weather. Sumpin' you eat ashore."

Don, of course, had to go on watch, but that was his problem.

Antofagasta to Valparaiso
August 15

At five the next morning, I felt the heavy thud at my door in the soles of my feet. Simple Simmons, four to eight Ordinary Seaman, usually called me, his light rap barely noticed before the door swung open. The sailors had rotated watches leaving Antofagasta, considering it mid-voyage, and the job of calling me for morning stars had passed to the man known only as Fletcher.

"Star-time, cadet," he said, quickly closing the door.

Simple, who did his best to live up to his name, liked to engage in conversation at that early hour. Not much of a philosopher, he was mostly interested in shipboard facts: he had spotted a whale on lookout or the cook was thawing two twenty-pound turkeys for dinner. He loved relaying news about the gyro compasses: the second mate had switched over to the starboard motor, for example, or the error was now one degree east instead of one degree west. I growled at most early-morning conversation, but had come to enjoy hearing whatever it was Simple had to tell me.

I reached up and toggled on the low wattage reading lamp above my head. For the first time this trip—which made it the first time in my fledgling career—the ship was moving a lot: deep rolls, short, bumpy pitching, a sickening yaw. I struggled to remain conscious, drifted into and out of sleep, and slowly became aware of a horrible ache, beginning at the top of my head, centered in my stomach and ending where the door thuds had resonated.

"What the fuck?" I said to myself, slow to recall the previous evening's activities. I felt like I might be dying.

I touched my head gently. It felt three times its normal size. I suspected that in the process of expanding, blood vessels had burst and brain cells lay scattered like dandruff on my pillow. I could not imagine getting out of that bed. Each heartbeat was followed immediately by a cudgeling to the left side of my head. Limp as I felt, I suddenly became aware of a powerful impulse to make my way as quickly as possible to the toilet where I believed I had considerable and important business. I knew moving those ten feet from bunk to head was not going to be easy. I lifted my right arm experimentally. It went up, but would not stay there. And, really, it didn't feel good down either. Something else was rising though, so I almost involuntarily slipped out of my bunk, slid along the floor like a serpent straight into the head and lifted my head above the toilet just in time for my mouth to erupt in a series of vile-tasting vomitings. Thank Christ it was as dark as it was so I didn't have to actually look at the stuff—or the toilet bowl for that matter.

Wally and I had responsibility for cleaning our own room and although Mr. Hunt threatened to come around to inspect, he had not yet done so. Wally's aim when pissing had not noticeably improved. Because he liked to talk while peeing, I called him a social pisser. For me, a sexually-repressed Catholic, anything done with one's penis was serious business; best done alone and undistracted, certainly without conversation. Pissing was no exception. Early in the voyage, tired of yellow puddles on the floor, I mentioned this to him and even told him I didn't want him to talk while he urinated. He tried to improve, but his need to talk overrode everything else.

Now, too weak to kneel, but vividly conscious of Wally's urine, I slouched, my legs extended, torso relaxed, supported only by my arms. I could have been a sunbather at the beach or a grape-eater at a Roman orgy had my chin not rested on the end of a porcelain oval, my face inches from the foul brown liquid in the bowl.

The ship's yawing seemed ten times worse out of bed. I vomited and flushed, vomited and flushed, my hand moving the stainless flusher in an involuntary continuation of the action of my esophagus. Soon, I was dry—or thought so. Yet the eruptions continued along with the flushing, though nothing more went to the sea via the ship's plumbing except clean water and foul odors. I dry-heaved till my chest and stomach ached, then dry-heaved again.

"Hey, could you hold it down in there?" Wally called out from the other room. "How's a guy supposed to get any sleep? Besides, that flusher isn't built for continuous action. You think I've got nothing better to do with my time than fix toilets?"

I groaned, cursed engineers silently for their lack of empathy, then puked again. Finally, my stomach called a halt to this torture and I rested my head on the toilet bowl. I thought about how I was supposed to be on the bridge shooting stars and agonizingly pulled myself to my feet only to become aware that more liquid demanded to be discharged—this time from the other end of the digestive system. In what I envisioned to be an amazingly coordinated motion, I removed my mouth from the bowl and replaced it with my bottom, the end that rightfully claimed responsibility for waste removal and from which, at that moment, waste exited in an explosive gushing accompanied by rumbling emissions of putrid gas.

"For Christ's sake," said Wally. "Would you cut that out?"

The odor was unbearable and my hand once again reached for the flusher. After several minutes in this position, I actually began to feel better. Still, I sat, afraid to move, wanting to make certain every last drop of anything that wanted to leave my body was gone. Finally, my stomach seemed settled. I pulled myself to the sink and splashed water on my face, then continued into the shower. Water pelting my skin had nearly miraculous results, lifting my feelings from horrible to merely awful. One thing led to another and inch by inch, in spite of the ship rolling and pitching like a carnival ride at a county fair, I found myself on the bridge, rummaging on the settee in the chartroom for my sextant, acting like everything was normal.

"Young man, you look like something hell rejected," said

Frank Potter.

I glanced at him. He actually had what I considered to be a smile on his face.

"Better get out and shoot those stars. You go carousing all night, nearly miss the ship, this is how you pay for it."

"Yes sir," I replied, fumbling for the Nautical Almanac, shocked to hear I had nearly missed the ship. Good lord, I thought, did the captain know? Time to change this destructive behavior before it destroys me. I remembered the ring. It was gone now. Maybe my luck would improve. At least I hadn't missed the ship.

I set the almanac on the chart table and adjusted the directional lamp we navigators used to focus light on certain areas of the chart. I glanced up into the wheelhouse and noticed the anemometer showed strong northwesterlies that caught us broad on the quarter and caused the combination pitching and rolling motion called yawing. I reached for the dog-eared copy of H.O. 249. As I did, the ship made a deep motion where the stern fell into a trough on the starboard side, then lifted sharply as the bow fell into the same trough moments later. This caused the ship to roll heavily to starboard, yaw aft, then pitch forward, then yaw forward and to port. My Almanac flew off the chart table, crashing into the settee where Mr. Potter had secured the wooden sextant boxes with a piece of yellow synthetic.

"Watch yourself in there, cadet," muttered the second mate from the wheelhouse. "Remember, 'one hand for you, one hand for the ship.'"

I hadn't a clue what he was talking about. What I did know was that it was nearly twilight and I wasn't ready to shoot stars. Plus, I felt like hell and my stomach was starting to burp and gurgle.

I retrieved the Almanac and did the calculations to find the First Point of Aries and GHA. With that, I opened H.O. 249 to find the stars I should shoot and copied down their azimuths and altitudes. On a separate sheet of paper, I drew a picture showing the ship's heading, then marked the positions of Antares, Acrux, Rigil Kentaurus, Vega and Arcturus, all first magnitude stars, noting their altitudes and bearings relative to the ship's head on the paper next to the name of the star.

Paper and sextant in hand, bent forward like a mountaineer, I climbed the starboard bridge wing as the ship lunged to port. At the summit, in this case the repeater stand, I strove to steady myself enough to measure the angles the stars made with the horizon. I knew I'd be happy with a two star fix this morning. Even without the hangover, this wouldn't have been easy the way the ship was rolling. Mr. Potter, I noticed, had not even taken his sextant out of its case. The ship rolled twenty degrees to port, then, on a very deep roll, twenty-five degrees to starboard.

The mate had mentioned just yesterday in Antofagasta the heavy ingots being loaded in the hold were going to increase our gm and make us very stiff. I asked him what that meant. He briefly explained that gm stood for metacentric height, and was calculated in feet or meters. It was a measure of the forces acting to keep the ship upright in the water and that too much stability was nearly as dangerous as not enough. In heavy seas, as the ship rolled, a righting arm was created that countered the roll. Higher gm meant a longer righting arm. Too much stability meant the ship would snap-roll since the righting arm was so long and resistance to being pushed away from the upright position so strong.

I stood on the starboard wing, holding onto the repeater pedestal. Always strong in math, my mind did the calculations needed to determine the range of motion I was currently experiencing. I'm at least fifty feet from the centerline of the ship, I thought, rolling through forty-five degrees with a period of ten seconds. Figuring the sine of forty-five at point five times fifty for that arm gave twenty five plus maybe five feet or so equaling around thirty feet each time the ship rolled to port and back to starboard. Five of these rolls per minute meant I was moving one hundred and fifty feet in a mostly vertical direction each sixty seconds. In addition to that, the pitching motion thrust me forward then aft in a sickening hump that was worse than the roll. I tried to take a sight and even succeeded once in getting the star—bright Vega, I believe it was, whose brilliancy fluctuated more than any other star—into my mirror. Bringing it down to the horizon, however, proved impossible.

Finally I slumped against the base of the repeater, my

strength gone, my spirits low, another vomit rising. I glanced
into the wheelhouse and saw the faces of Frank Potter and Bob
Fletcher in the window forward of the door to the wing, watching me carefully. First light was rapidly approaching and I could
make out a well-defined grin on Fletcher's face—as if he were
thoroughly enjoying my discomfort—while Mr. Potter seemed
concerned. I carefully set the old World War II sextant loaned to
me by the Academy down onto the wooden duckboards that
lined the decks of the bridge wings, then leaned out over the rail,
ejecting a clear fluid that held a hint of green as well as a couple
of bright red pieces of pimento from the Sopa de Congria,
directly into the wind. That seemed to be the very last drop of
anything my body had any intentions of getting rid of.
Unfortunately, most of it came back on the wind and now covered my face, neck and arms. I fell to a sitting position at the
edge of the bridge wing, honestly wishing I could just die.

"Feeling poorly, cadet?" The second mate stood, arms folded, countenance stern, not more than five feet away, looking
down. I struggled to my feet, ashamed.

"Yes sir," I said. "Guess it was the fish soup I ate last night.
Just didn't agree with me."

Mr. Potter turned away and coughed enough to muffle what
sounded suspiciously like laughter.

"Might as well drop down to your room. See if you can't
sleep it off a bit."

I appreciated that Mr. Potter wasn't in a mood to moralize.
He had been quite pleasant with me lately—once he figured I
was actually interested in learning how to navigate.

"Better hurry, son. The captain will be up here in five minutes. I'll tell him you tried, but just couldn't keep the stars on
the horizon."

Mention of the captain jerked me to my feet. The ship made
a favorable roll and I hustled downhill into the wheelhouse,
latched my sextant into its box and was down to my room and
into my bed in less than a minute.

At eight in the morning, having skipped breakfast in
order to catch thirty minutes more sleep, I walked out of the
house and headed aft to work with the boatswain. The chief

mate, not knowing of my morning's experiences on the bridge, had called me at 0720 and told me to help the boatswain secure things on deck.

The ship continued its bucking motion. Several sailors were already aft including Fletcher. He had been on Don Campbell's watch before rotating onto the four to eight. More than once, Don had cautioned me to steer clear of him.

"He's a cadet hater," Don had said. "I know you kids have a guardian angel that watches over you, but there are a few bad guys out here. Fletcher is one of them."

I hadn't asked what he meant. Since our initial unpleasant meeting my first day aboard, I'd had little contact with the man. The guy was weird. But then, I'd decided a lot of the people out here were a little abnormal. Now that Fletcher was on the four to eight watch—the watch I normally stood—my time near him would increase.

In some ways, the motion at the stern was worst of all. The wind blew a full gale; the seas rolled in off the starboard quarter, crested then broke. Frank Potter had a lot to say earlier that morning about breaking waves.

"We have breaking waves this morning, cadet," he said. "When a wave is large enough that its tip breaks and the wind blows spray off it, it means it's large enough to damage the ship."

I was too sick to understand what he was trying to tell me, and way to sick to care. Down here on deck, though, I could see the seas were monstrous. Forty feet high, I figured. A cap would form at the crest—like a floppy white nightcap folded over—which the wind would blow ahead of the wave into spray and foam. Smaller waves didn't develop enough to form the caps, which were the part of the wave that broke. Waves large enough to have caps developed enormous energy—exponentially more than their smaller brethren. As a wave formed, it sucked the water ahead of it to form a deep trough into which the ship would fall. The mountainous wave behind that trough, bearing down on the ship from above, looked like a wall of water. As that wave caught our ship, the stern would shoot into the air, only to come crashing down into the trough as the wave passed.

I grabbed the handrail for support. My stomach bubbled.
Boss Jones grabbed my arm with his strong right hand.

"Well, well, ka-dett." His deep voice boomed over the roar
of the ocean with a hint of humor.

"Don' tell me you done found yo'se'f a bottle or two o' that
famous chilano wine last night? You probly even been drivin' the
porcelain bus this mornin', huh?"

I moaned, then leaned over the rail to vomit again. The
word wine and the thought of my arms wrapped around the toilet bowl Wally pissed on regularly was just too much to stomach.

"Ka-dett, y'all jis' go on back to yo' room and lay down a
spell till you feels better. We wa'n't gon' do much today nohow."
His kindly brown eyes sparkled.

"No, boatswain. I want to work. I'm in enough trouble with
the captain already without him thinking I'm a drunk."

Boss Jones studied me then said, "All right, then, young
man. Let us turn to like a band of worthy sailors."

I felt approval in his voice.

"Y'all work with Irving Jackson and Fletcher straightening
the lockers forward."

He rolled his eyes. A giant wave picked up the stern and
shook it.

"Lord, Lord," he said. "I don't know how I can be expected to keep this vessel shipshape when the navigation department
fails to mention forty-foot seas are approaching."

We spent the morning securing stuff that had been thrown
about—blocks and sheaves, chunks of dunnage, tools, spindles
of wire-rope. Fletcher's habit of looking at me out of the corner
of his eye unsettled me. Upper-classmen at school had told stories of bad men, bad women, getting rolled, hustled or beat-up.
With few exceptions, I had been treated well by the people on
this ship and ashore. Even Paul Hunt, the mate, who had sliced
my finger with his knife my first day aboard and later wanted to
tattoo my ankle, turned out to be harmless—to me, at least. Don
Campbell's warnings about Fletcher were very strong though—
he said Fletcher was an evil man—placing Fletcher into a category I had no experience with. I had told no one, not even Don
Campbell, but I would never forget Fletcher's smiling face next
to the British sailor who was shot in the bar in Houston. He

seemed infinitely pleased.

Fletcher normally worked alone since even the sailors, his so-called brothers of the sea, didn't take to him or, even more important on board a ship at sea, trust him. That morning, the boatswain assigned everyone to work in pairs or threesomes. Fletcher spoke only to Mr. Jackson, never to me. He treated me as one so subordinate as to be unworthy of even a moment's attention. Yet, many times during the course of our work, I felt the weight of his eyes on me, as if he were sizing me up somehow or even desired me sexually. It occurred to me this must be how women feel when eyed by lusting males. I didn't particularly like it.

Irving Jackson said: "You watch yo'sef widdat shifty-eyed sum-bitch. Whatever you do, don' bend down in front of him."

By noon, we had secured every locker on the ship. I had vomited another half-dozen times, but by late morning, felt my energy improving. Irving Jackson bid me a good rest as I headed for my room to wash up for lunch. I thought a few crackers and a small bowl of split-pea soup would help. When I walked into the saloon, all the officers, including the Captain, turned toward me and applauded.

Storm
August 16

August the sixteenth dawned with red streaks shooting across the sky: a sailor's warning. The wind blew hard, without gusts. The anemometer, screwed into the wall above the forward wheelhouse windows, was the first thing seen upon walking into the bridge and the last leaving. It was pegged at forty knots relative, as though broken. But it wasn't broken. Since the wind was now aft—it had veered to two points on the starboard quarter sometime after midnight, the forty knots relative added to our ship speed of twenty knots meant the wind was actually blowing sixty. With the swell just abaft the beam and the ship stiff due the ingots in the lower hold, we rolled quickly and deeply. The seas, with the wind, crashed the bulwarks aft and the scuppers gurgled and splashed in their attempt to drain the decks. I watched from the bridge as a green sea climbed up over the starboard side just forward of the house like a big animal hunting, crept inboard and wrenched a forty-ton earthmover manifested for Chile from the wires and chains securing it atop number four like it was a toy. Once the ship shook itself like a dog free of that wall of water, the bright yellow earthmover, now unfettered, crabbed dangerously toward the port side of the hatch, threatening to walk right off the ship. Captain Isenhagen reduced to slow, brought the bow around and hove to with the wind forward of the starboard beam. The chief mate took me, the boatswain and the sailors forward to resecure the big caterpillar.

We worked diligently in the howling wind, threading wire ropes through securing eyes welded to the machine, then fastening the wire ropes with clips.

"Saddle on the standing part," the mate kept repeating—a phrase totally confusing until Irving Jackson patiently explained how the clip had two parts: a saddle—it actually looked like a tiny saddle—and a threaded u-bolt that fit over the wire doubled back on itself, passing through holes in the saddle. Nuts were then attached and wrenched tight, compressing the saddle to the standing part of the wire rope.

The storm continued to advance to the west. Shortly after we hove to, conditions changed. The wind dropped to nearly calm while around us the seas raged like life's own nightmare. In its midst, we experienced a gentle, almost motherly rocking motion. Light airs soothed and refreshed us, and drops of rain fell that gently carried away the sweat from our work. After a day and a half of plunging into deep troughs, climbing up over the tops of mountainous crests, and hearing the wind howl through the masts and backstays, the sailors looked at each other nervously, wondering what was happening and what would come next. Stratus and cumulus raced past the pale yellow ball of the sun like it was the end of the world while I stood on a hatch cover in a state of utter tranquility, observing.

"Eye of the storm," said the mate.

"What?" I said.

"Eye of the storm. We're in the eye of the storm. I'll tell you about it later. Hand me that bar."

The sailors stopped their work from time to time to watch the sky and the seas roiling about them. Boss Jones, shirt off even in this cool weather, muscular upper body glistening with sweat and rain, stopped beating on the end of a four by four with a twelve-pound sledge and cocked his head, eyes clear, every sense alert, anticipating something either very dangerous or extremely wonderful. If I could paint a picture of the coming of The Judgment Day, that would be it: Boss Jones, shirtless, eyes skyward, sledge raised.

Eventually, all the turnbuckles were tightened and a bunch of 4 by 4's sledgehammered in between the machine and the bulwarks and the timbers running along the hatch-cover. I ran up to the bridge and watched the captain maneuver the ship through these mountainous seas. He went to half ahead and slowly came about from the two hundred and fifty-degree heading onto which he had hove to. Our course to the Valparaiso breakwater was one-seventy.

"Watch the barograph as we leave the eye," he said.

I walked into the chartroom. The barograph, an instrument that consists of a delicately-balanced needle rising or falling according to the atmospheric pressure, and which applied purple ink to a drum of paper that turned approximately an eighth inch each hour, recorded continuously. It had been in a freefall for the past twelve hours as the storm approached and was now bouncing along the bottom of the paper near the 960-millibar level. As the captain brought the ship more to the south, the wind keened and whined through the antennas on the flying bridge and the waves once again crashed the starboard bulwark. The barograph needle registered a purple ink uptick as we left the bottom of this depression, fluttered a little, then began its long, slow climb out the other side. On the chart, I stepped off our distance to Valpo. At full speed, we were only three hours from the pilot station. The sailors wanted to stay on deck and prepare for what many considered their home port, but Captain Isenhagen sent word they were to repair inside until the weather abated—which it did within the hour.

When the Gulf Trader called Valparaiso, no one did any work that wasn't essential to the vessel's operation. Everyone who could be spared was permitted ashore. Certain things had to be accomplished, of course: regular meals served, electricity generated, cargo gear maintained in operating status. I was with the sailors when Irving Jackson drew the short straw. He said "Damn, I allays gets that short one." The boatswain later told me the drawing was rigged—that Irving, at age seventy-five or whatever he was, didn't really care to go ashore, but didn't want to volunteer to stay aboard either.

The mate sent me to the bow to help tie up. One of the sailors was feeling poorly, so the forward gang was one man short and I filled in. I had been with the ship for five weeks now and felt confident with what I knew. I even felt comfortable with what I didn't know.

In the midst of all this work, the thought that I should get a letter from Melissa in Valparaiso stayed uppermost in my mind. As days passed and we came and went through the various ports since leaving Panama where I'd received her letter declaring her love for me, I had thought often and fondly of her and of what our life together might be like. I had come to think this voyage was designed to somehow educate me in certain things, but that my destiny lay with Melissa— maybe not in Nebraska, but with her nonetheless. I knew one thing: I liked being loved.

The front passed just before we picked up the pilot. The wind veered sharply to south and the temperature fell ten degrees into the low fifties. I hadn't realized it, but Valparaiso was south of thirty-three degrees—similar in latitude to Los Angeles or Little Rock—and August was dead of winter down here. I wore a jacket when I went to the bow and even Boss Jones had on a tee shirt. Paul Hunt, the chief mate, spoke with the bridge via walkie-talkie and relayed orders to the boatswain and deck gang. Everyone snapped with efficiency. We took a tug on the starboard bow and it immediately pulled full to keep our head from falling off with the wind gusts. Fletcher took advantage of the wind and threw a heaving line further than I thought possible to waiting hands ashore. Spring lines were run, then head lines. A couple of breasting lines were left on the winch drums so the mate on watch could keep the ship alongside without having to call out sailors who probably wouldn't be aboard anyway.

Once all fast, we released the stoppers, dropped rat guards over the tops of the lines outboard of the gunwale and tied them off to securing points on the bulwarks. The gang then headed aft, leaving the ordinary seaman and me on the forecastle to put everything away and lock up.

On the dock, a large, tin-roofed warehouse—the last of three—stood abeam. A Chilean freighter named *El Majado* lay directly ahead. Forklifts were already moving pallets of goods from the warehouse onto the apron, presumably to be loaded aboard our ship. I carried the heaving lines below, down into the line locker where I hung them on their pegs. Simple Simon tossed an armful of stoppers in the corner and left. I had learned from Mr. Potter, though, and didn't leave till the space was ship-shape.

Don Campbell had told me all about Valparaiso. He loved it. He had wanted to move here a couple years earlier, but his wife had said no.

"They export more poetry and art than sugar, oil or fruit," he said.

But over the years, the city had fallen into a cycle of neglect, depression and decadence.

"You want to know who lives here?" he asked. "Fugitives, writers, gun-runners and whores; people escaping pasts they can no longer reconcile, or folks with more passion than money who will forgo security for a chance to be lucky."

The terrain stayed relatively flat for a few blocks near the bay, then rose steeply into the green hills that surrounded the port and made up the city. Large buildings, many a mix of German, Italian and Spanish Colonial, sat like small castles on the green slopes.

"The Spanish arrived in the 18th century," said Don. "By the mid-nineteenth century, shipping and banking interests from London, Genoa and Hamburg moved here building large, classically European buildings. Germans sought anonymity here following the two World Wars. In 1906, an earthquake destroyed much of the city's finest architecture. The real blow came in 1914, though, when the Panama Canal opened and the ships and money flowing into Valparaiso dried up. Bankers moved to Santiago. Art galleries and opera houses; all those places dependent upon wealth's good will, closed their doors. Walk around the old Victorians today and what you'll see are dilapidated hovels."

Four men from ashore entered the house with me. They looked different from other South Americans I had seen. One was tall and broad with black hair oiled back; another had

bronze skin with blue eyes and golden hair; the third was dark
but had freckles and the fourth looked like he'd stepped out of
the post office in my home town.

"These people are a beautiful genetic combination." Don
had said. "The mixture of German, English, Irish, Spanish and
native Indian has produced a sub-race in which both men and
women are beautiful and passionate. Mark my words. Four days
from now, you will stand on the fantail looking back toward
Valparaiso broken-hearted."

Wally had other advice.

"Two things to remember here in Valparaiso, lover-boy," he
said. "One, don't fall in love like a damned fool. Two, don't bed
down with a woman one night, then think you'll poke her best
friend the next. These women form strong attachments real
fast—especially to cadetes."

"I don't think I'm going to fall in love with a whore," I said
smugly.

Wally snorted in his superior way.

"Whores are women."

I laughed, thinking what did he know.

"Hey, wiseass. Ever hear the story of Studs O'Laughlin?" he
asked.

"Not yet."

"Well, you're likely to hear it till you're sick of it while we're
in Valpo. I never knew him, and not sure anyone else did either,
but the story goes like this." Wally struck a pose and began.

"Jack O'Laughlin had black curls and eyes so blue the girls
drowned in them. He wore a Greek sailor's cap and a navy coat
with gold buttons. He bought gifts for the girls and wrote them
poetry. One blustery night Sailor Jack swaggered into Yakko's
Bar and swept sweet Suzanna off her feet. He loved her tender
and he loved her rough all night long. Sweet Suzanna was a
young girl, naïve perhaps, but pretty as any lass who'd ever
walked the rugged slopes of Northern Ireland. She was a-lookin'
for her sweet Jack from Tennessee' and based on O'Laughlin's
one easy smile, a snifter of perfume and a hundred whispered
promises, she thought she'd found him. The next night, swag-
gerin' Jack sauntered into Yakko's with big-breasted Maria.

Sweet Suzanna sat in the corner watching them kiss at the bar, twirling a lock of auburn hair around the index finger of her right hand, drinking straight shots of rum with her left, saying nothing to nobody, just watching Smiling Jack as he fondled the gifted Maria.

"Around eleven, Jack and Maria headed up the stairs, arm in arm, to the seaman's heaven on earth. Sweet Suzanna stopped drinking at twelve, sat calm as a stone while she sobered up, then climbed those same steps around one, a razor in her hand and a glint in her eye. At exactly six minutes after the clock above the bar struck one bell, screamin' Jack stood at the top of the stairs, his right hand at his bloody crotch, his left holding a used and completely severed pair of testicles. Fourteen famous sailors—a real NMU seaman can name them all—sat at the bar when Jack fainted from shock and rolled down the steps, one by one, his right hand never leaving his crotch, his left hanging onto his precious balls. He crumpled in a heap at the bottom. The punch line came from an A.B. named Shockley who turned to Tex, the ship's carpenter and said, "Well, guess we don't have to call O'Laughlin Studs no more."

Wally expected me to laugh but I didn't find violence all that funny. Never had. I even felt like Jack pretty much got what he deserved.

I went directly to my room to wash up before going over to the mate's office. George LeClair, the purser, was closing my door as I approached.

"Mail for the cadets," he smiled. "From the smell of the perfume, I would say it's from a girl."

"Wonderful," I said, grinning.

"Oh, Captain Isenhagen asked me to have you stop by when you get the chance."

"Really? Is he mad at me? I suppose he wants to talk to me about drinking too much the other day."

The purser laughed. "Not this time. He likes Valparaiso as well as everyone else and is in a great mood. Just wants you to stop by."

I showered and changed clothes, figuring to give the captain

time to take care of the officials before I went up to see him. I
had a letter from my sister, Sarah, one from my mother, one
from dad, which surprised me, and one from Melissa. They were
precious—like chocolate— and I wanted to savor them. I read
Sarah's first. She was majoring in Art and Literature at a small
college in central Nebraska. She said she was in love with a guy
a year older than her, and how good it felt and how she just
wanted to marry him and finish college and buy a house in one
of the little towns that dot the Nebraska prairie, get a teaching
job and start raising a family. She'd seen Melissa, she said, and
Melissa was always so friendly. She thought Melissa quite pretty,
found her charming as well, but just a little frightening in how
free she seemed to be with herself. Sara told me about each of
my brothers and sisters and how my mom and dad were. She
became, in the letter, more intimate than she had ever been in
conversation. Part of her letter put into words something I'd
been thinking about.

*I'm really sorry about what happened between you and dad. He
hasn't had a drink since you left, so maybe it was good. I hope you're
doing all right. I know I'll always be content to stay close to the folks
even though at times I think the Plains are like a huge prison
extending for hundreds of miles in each direction from which escape
is really difficult. Yet I like how all my questions are answered here
and how our family and community are so strong. I think about
you in school in New York, or on that ship in South America and
how it sounds kind of romantic and adventuresome, but also lonely and frightening to be so far away. How life is to be lived is so
clear here. People just don't do things that are out of the ordinary.
I wonder what you're doing there. Are you doing things that are
out of the ordinary? Tell me about them, would you?*

Well, yes, I thought, wondering if Sarah might be telepathic. I
have been doing things out of the ordinary and I like it. I opened
my father's letter next. He was a good letter-writer but a poor
speller. Mostly, he reported facts: weather information, the price of
alfalfa, something about a large-mouthed bass someone had
caught at Bowman's Lake. He didn't say anything about the fight
we'd had, or that he'd quit drinking. Mentioned the new business

his dad had helped him buy. Said he had a lot to learn but, for the first time in years, felt he was doing something important. In spite of everything, he'd brought a certain solidity to my life. His feet were planted in the prairie soil and he provided a foundation from which his children could grow. He believed in the Church, in one's duty to his family and his country. His motto was "root, hog, or die" and I loved him.

My Mom's letter, in her tiny, almost unreadable hand had this in it:

I worry about you a lot out there on the ocean, but know you're in God's hands and that eases my mind. Really, I don't know what I would do without faith. I know yours isn't strong, but I pray that God will be merciful to you anyway. He has certainly blessed us many times over. Melissa called one night to get this address. She is really quite friendly and very nice. Still, she's not Catholic and I'm not sure how much guidance she receives at home. We hope you're not too lonely and that you say your prayers. Dad is busy with his new business. Grandpa is over a lot, helping him get started. Not that I think what happened between you and Father Henry and your dad was good, but I don't think dad is drinking right now. And I even think Father Henry is more sensitive to people these days.

So there it was. Some good coming out of something hard, something that had looked bad but had taken courage and had come directly from the inner recesses of my heart. I got up, stretched and walked around my chair a couple of times, then sat back down. This trying to bridge two different worlds was tough. I thought a lot about what Sara had said, how it tied into Don's words that we belonged to a tribe and as long as we lived nearby, we were governed by that tribe. I knew I was different. I wouldn't go along with the tribe. I wouldn't live nearby. I rejected their way and they had told me to leave—and I wasn't planning to return.

Melissa's letter lay in a scented light blue envelope addressed in red ink.

"Dearest Jake,
It's after midnight and I'm sitting alone in the window of our

haymow watching the moon shine on the barn and the orchard and the windbreak, listening to an old owl and a bullfrog and a band crickets and thinking very serious thoughts because, you know, beneath my little girl smiles and giggles, I'm a serious person. I sit here a lot and I think about you on that ship and I think about you that night at the river or I think about my parents or I think about this small-minded stupid little town where guys think they have to drink in order to be men. Sometimes, I remember Christmases from when I was real little and how embarrassed my parents were to have a child in their old age, and not really know what to do with her. They would stand around on Christmas morning watching me open all these sweet little presents they had gotten me, all tiny things like they thought I was and it didn't matter what I ever did, they would never get mad at me. They just cherished me—like I was the Most Precious Thing in their lives.

Sometimes I think about how beautiful and how sad everything is and then I laugh and cry. I think about loving someone. I think about marrying some strong man who doesn't have to drink all the time to show he's a real man. I think about doing adventuresome things with him like wintering in Argentina and sipping coffee in French cafes. But then, I think about how that would mean leaving my parents, and I get really sad and confused, and realize I can never leave my parents. I'm everything to them. I know I am. If I left them, I believe they would just look at each other and look at their empty hands, and maybe cry a little, then go off to die.

When I think about loving a man, I think of you. I remember your dark hair and how ready your brown eyes are to laugh, and how muscley and hairy your legs are. I remember your strong shoulders and how you stutter a little and how that makes me smile and want to tell you it's OK. Just because there aren't that many strong men in the world doesn't mean it isn't OK if you happen to be one, which you just happen to be. I remember you catching a touchdown pass once when I was real young and you were a sophomore, and I thought you must be among the greatest of boys, and that you would be my hero—at least until I was older and knew more.

Well, here I am older and I know more, and you're still my hero and I love you so much my stomach feels like someone punched it. But I think something else about you too. I think you want to do something with your life other than marry a girl just out of high

*school and settle on a farm in Nebraska. I think you want to finish
that college in New York, and captain a huge freighter and lead a
life that I'll never do anything but read about. I think you must
have dreamt many dreams about distant lands and exotic people
and strange cities because it takes lots of dreams to make reality
happen. I doubt you'll ever get over wanting adventure. I think this
will be my last letter to you because I know that, in spite of our
many similar desires, in spite of this love we share, there will always
be an ocean between us, and I could never stand to say good-bye to
my man for even a week, much less months.*

So, my love, my dear heart, source of my most wonderful
fantasies, we must stop before ever started. Good-bye. Good-
bye, good-bye and good-bye. My tears fall freely as I write this,
but I know those ships and the seas they sail on are too big for
my arms and your arms to reach across and so let's say it now
while it isn't so hard and there's only you and me to consider.

Good-bye, my darling. I will not forget you.

Melissa.

I have to admit I cried. I sat there in that metal chair covered
with yellow naughahyde, put my head in my hands and wept
hard. I'm not sure what I was crying about, but frankly, I had a
tough time quitting. My shoulders even shook for a while, which
scared me and made me wonder if I was going nuts. Sure, I cried
because I'd just received a letter from the first girl I'd ever loved
saying adios, sucker, but I think I cried also for my dad's disap-
pointments and my mom's tears and for all the little things that
build up for a young person: the chief mate yelling at me, or seeing a man murdered in a bar in Houston, or hearing all the goofy
stories and wondering just exactly how big was this thing called
life and how did one figure out his place in it anyway.

When I finally finished, I felt better. I went into the head and
splashed water on my face, then got out Melissa's picture and
looked at it for a long time. Her beauty took my breath away. I
reread the letter and wondered if I shouldn't go find a phone,
call her and tell her I'm coming home. I'll be there soon and I
won't be going back to sea. And, oh yeah, wanna get married?

But I didn't. I felt like a man at a crossroads where a tree has
fallen, blocking the path. Someone knocked on my door.

"Come in," I said.

The door opened a crack and Captain Isenhagen poked one big ear and his left eye around the edge and said, "May I enter?"

"Oh, yes sir. Please come in. And sit down. Sorry the room is such a mess. I—I didn't know you were coming and, well, going in and out of port, sir, things just built up a little for me."

"That is fine. I am not here to inspect your room," he said, uncomfortable out of his element. That's when I realized there was literally no place for him to sit. Wally had long ago made it clear he had no use for drawers, that he much preferred the convenience of a dirty pile and a clean pile of clothes sitting on the settee where he and everyone else could see them. I used a dirty clothes bag, and kept most of my clean clothes out of sight on a shelf in my closet. Our drawers were empty except for a couple of old Playboys.

"Actually, sir, most of these clothes belong to my roommate. Let me move them."

I scooped up an armload of the clean clothes, walked over to Wally's closet and dumped them in. Finally, the captain sat.

"I thought perhaps we might talk." He hesitated.

"Yes sir," I said. "I was coming up to your room as soon as I finished reading my mail. I figured that would give you time to deal with the port officials."

He waved his hand.

"Is this a good time to have a conversation?" he asked.

"Oh, yes, sir. This is a very good time."

He cleared his throat. I was kind of surprised to see how nervous he was. It made me like him a lot.

"Do you come from a large family?"

"Y-Yes sir." My stuttering returned at the most inopportune times. " I have eight brothers and sisters, and two parents. Well, I mean, of course everyone has two parents."

"Yes, that is the exact number of parents each of us has. What does your father do to support such a large family?"

"Runs a small business. Works very hard."

"Raising a family that size would require a man to work very hard. How does it happen, Mr. Thomas, that you have selected a life at sea, coming, as you do, from the center of the country?"

"I like to read, sir. When I was fifteen, I read a short story

called *Youth* by Joseph Conrad. I read other stories as well—by
Jack London and Melville and Hardy and Tolstoy and others. I
found myself dreaming of ships and far-away ports. I can still
recite the section from *Youth* that made me want to go to sea."

"Conrad, then?" His eyes gleamed. "You know Conrad? I
would like very much to hear anything by Joseph Conrad."

I cleared my throat and began.

*Ah. The good old time. Youth and the sea. Glamour and the
sea! The good, strong sea, the salt, bitter sea that could whisper to
you and roar at you and knock your breath out of you.*

"May I continue?" asked the Captain. I nodded. The words
sounded strangely authentic in his German accent.

*Wasn't that the best time, that time when we were young at sea;
young and had nothing, on the sea that gives nothing, except hard
knocks—and sometimes a chance to feel your strength.*

He stared out the porthole for a full and uncomfortable
minute before continuing.

"That story ends with a sentence that holds great meaning
for me—and really, I think, for any older man who has been to
sea. It goes: *We nodded at him, our weary eyes looking still for
something out of life, that while it is expected is already gone - has
passed unseen, in a sigh, in a flash - together with the youth, with
the strength, with the romance of illusions.*"

Captain Isenhagen cocked his head in a curious, almost
comical manner and asked: "Do you understand 'romance of
illusions'?"

"Yes," I said, a little surprised by my own confidence. But
then, I knew the line. Anyone who had read Conrad knew
that line.

"When I read that story as a young man," continued the
captain, "I thought perhaps he meant to say 'illusions of
romance'. That he had turned it around. But later, I realized
'romance of illusions' is what he meant—just what he said. I've
come to think most people—including sailors—live their lives
based on illusions. Not having answers makes people uncomfortable. Even if the answers are illusionary, they are better than
constant questioning."

"And are these answers truly illusions?" I asked.

"That is the question thoughtful men and women spend

their lifetimes answering."

He sat again, staring at me, as if considering how much he should say, what I should know, or if maybe he shouldn't prejudice me with his own ideas.

"Sailors are escapists in their hearts," is what he finally said. "Military men are adventurists. Then there are the religious and the atheists, the wealth-seekers, pleasure-seekers, academics and politicians. It is difficult to live without a set of illusions."

I nodded, thinking that sounded right but really, what did I know about all this.

"We try to escape many different things—some not so personal. I left my homeland because of the Nazis."

He was again silent, looking down at his large, bony hands.

"My father drove me and my Jewish mother away from our homeland with his belief in the Nazis. Once it became clear what they were doing, my father shot himself. Now, my only son was killed eight weeks ago. He was shot while on patrol in Viet Nam. He went because we argued. Because I told him he should not question what the American government is doing. That we had a duty. . ." He turned and choked on the words.

I hadn't a clue how to respond.

The Captain's voice grew very soft and his accent thickened.

"I wass never proud of my son. And he worked so to make me proud. I wish I could have been with him when he died. Always, I wass here. I felt these ships could not sail without me. And now, he is gone. My father is gone. And here I am still."

I looked down, intensely uncomfortable.

"Young man, I came here to talk about you. Not me, not my son. I want to tell you that I have been pleased with your progress on the ship. I believe you will make a first-rate officer. I want to tell you also, that however it may appear, this is a difficult life. It is not for everyone. There are unseen dangers and temptations much like the shoals and reefs we are so careful to avoid. Before you commit yourself to a career at sea, you must think about the many things you will give up."

He paused. "And yet, a career at sea is an honorable career. You will not be like a used-car salesman. Safe navigation, delivery of cargo undamaged, managing your vessel in a seamanlike way brings honor and distinction. That is what I wanted to say."

He stood to go. "One thing more. Here is extra money for you to enjoy Valparaiso, maybe to buy gifts for your parents and family."

"Thank you, sir," I said. I suspect my mouth hung open and I looked like I'd just fallen off a hayrack. My door opened and closed and I stood there alone with a hundred-dollar bill in my hand and the weight of the captain's words in my heart, thinking of his son bleeding alone on a battlefield in a land he'd never heard of, of Melissa in her haymow looking at the stars, the same stars I saw every night, deciding to end our relationship. I thought about the impact our decisions have on ourselves and others, the responsibility we carry with us for those decisions and how we deal with the consequences.

In spite of all that, I also saw the next four days and nights stretched in front of me like a magic carpet that ran from where I stood to a distant, unknown horizon.

Valparaiso
August 17

Paul Hunt, the chief mate, walked toward our table from the one he shared with the first engineer. He normally dined alone since the engineer rarely ate any meal in the saloon except breakfast. Mr. Hunt once said, "If the first drank beer in the morning, I'd never see the guy."

As he walked by me, the mate tapped me on the shoulder and said "I won't expect to see you on the ship during the next four days unless your underwear needs changing or you run out of money."

Wally and I looked at each other and smiled—partially at Mr. Hunt's attempt at humor, which we considered feeble—partially at the fact that we were finally in Valparaiso. Wally had to stay aboard that afternoon to help the "fucking first" put the auxiliary feed pump back together. We agreed we'd meet that night for dinner at the Valparaiso Eterno, a restaurant near Sotomayor Plaza, which, according to George LeClair, catered to "bohemians, communists, artists and cadete's."

The sun had burned away the morning clouds and its reflection off the tin sides of the warehouse forced me to shield my eyes as I walked ashore after lunch. The air was chilly and I wore a light jacket for the first time since leaving New Orleans. This place felt like South America, but different—richer, more accommodating to people, better air. The locals were taller and heavier. The trucks and forklifts working the dock areas ran quieter and cleaner. Piles of trash didn't collect in every corner. There was no smell of urine seeping from the asphalt, no pallets of flour spoiling in the rain.

I couldn't get Melissa's Dear John letter out of my mind. I was homesick, heartbroken and depressed, but I also felt strangely liberated. As if Melissa understood what I wanted better than I did. More important, she was willing to act on that understanding. Willing to let me be who I wanted to be.

I walked through the warehouse, then crossed an ancient rail track that deadheaded a short distance to the north. A black locomotive, looking like it belonged in a museum, creaked and groaned toward the very end of the track, steam belching out of every pore. It pulled a flat car on which sat twenty or so men dressed in rough work clothes. The damn thing hissed and coughed, looking and sounding like it was dying. The men jumped off as the engine came to a stop and walked slowly back down the tracks. I stopped and watched, thinking the men most likely were workers of some sort, transported here for the night. After a few minutes, I walked into the *Estacion Puerto*. Mr. LeClair had told Wally and me to expect to be searched leaving the port. He said they looked for guns entering the country and would slam you in a jail you definitely wouldn't want to spend time in if they caught you with one. They didn't care about drugs or liquor or cigarettes. Only guns. They didn't check people returning to the ship.

The only crewmember going through customs when I got there was Fletcher. He stood in khaki trousers and a thick navy sweater, six feet tall and thin with his new mustache and slicked-back hair. His arms were lifted as the customs guy frisked him. He appeared to be staring over the head of the uniformed official until I got close enough to see that his eyes were actually sideways toward me. Something about him—the way he didn't smile maybe—made the hair at the back of my neck stand.

"Welcome to Valparaiso, cadet," he said as the official waved him through.

"Yeah, finally. Going shopping," I said.

"Shopping." He smirked when he said the word—as though it was too middle-class for him to comprehend. "Come with me, gadget. I'll show you shopping."

I passed through the checkpoint and out the door, following Fletcher against my better judgment. I really didn't want anything to do with the man. He walked calmly through traffic across the main road—avenue Errazuriz—walked up a block, then turned onto a small side-street—more of an alleyway—with numbered doors set into the two-story brick building. I followed apprehensively. The alley dead-ended into a brick wall fifty feet ahead. We stopped at door number seven. Fletcher softly beat a series of three quick raps followed by four raps widely spaced. A short, stocky man with a gray beard cracked the door, looked Fletcher up and down, squinted at me, then pulled the door just enough for us to enter. As soon as we were inside, he pulled the door shut and locked it.

We stood in a small, windowless hallway with one dim bulb hanging from the ceiling. Off it were three doors, all painted black. Fletcher spoke quietly but politely with the man. I could hear an occasional English word but most of the conversation was in Spanish. Once the man gestured toward me. Fletcher turned at the hip and told me to wait, then turned back and followed the man through the door on the right, leaving it cracked just enough that I could see the guns and knives hanging on the wall. Pistols, mostly. The man reached for one and handed it to Fletcher who was outside my range of vision because of the door. After a few moments, Fletcher returned the pistol. The man replaced it, then led Fletcher to another section of the room where I could no longer see them.

Ten minutes later, Fletcher reappeared in the hallway followed by the stocky man. Neither said anything although I had the feeling business had been transacted. The man closed the door and locked it carefully, then tested it. He stepped over to the door on the left, opened it, and motioned both of us to follow. We entered a room the size of a bedroom. A row of shelves with glass doors stood along one wall. Most of the glass was darkened with black paint. Again, Fletcher and the swarthy man spoke quietly between themselves. The man opened one of the doors along the wall, stuck his hand back as far as his elbow and removed a small wooden box. He opened the box, removed an envelope with several paper-thin wafers and handed them to Fletcher. Fletcher held the paper up to the light, moved it back and forth, nodded his head slightly and returned it.

"Ever drop acid, gadget?" asked Fletcher suddenly, his voice unexpected and too loud.

"Me?" I said, surprised.

Truth was, at that time in my life, I'd scarcely heard of acid, except to know it was a hallucinogenic drug two upper classmen across the hall from me at school used—dropped—from time to time. Like me, they had been restricted most weekends following Christmas break. Bugsy, Big, Tommy the Mick and I had been caught celebrating Christmas early one night with whiskey in my room. Got six months restriction. Bugsy went nuts and punched out a first-classman May first. Couldn't hold on another month. Just lost it after months of being harassed when the guy stuck him for a tarnished belt buckle. I never did hear what the guys across the hall got restricted for. Sometimes, on Saturday nights, when everyone else was out on liberty, they handed me five bucks to watch for the ROOW (Regimental Officer of the Watch) while they lit incense and burned candles and listened to the Rolling Stones and, probably, dropped acid.

"Well, no." I said. The thought of dropping acid frightened me.

"I'll give you a couple little pills. Take them later. It'll make Valpo even more unforgettable."

I said nothing as he and the short man exchanged money and a number of the wafers and we left. Outside again, we walked away from the ship toward town. Fletcher handed me two flat dark wafers wrapped in tissue.

"Keep these in your wallet where you won't lose them. Take one of them tonight and give one to your buddy."

He spoke matter-of-factly, as if there was to be no question about my desire to use drugs. I took them and carefully placed them in my billfold, not at all sure what I would do with them.

"Ever hear of a girl down here named Rosa?"

"Only a dozen times. Everyone on the ship says she's the most beautiful girl in Valparaiso."

His face lit up with my response.

"You want to go with her while we're down here, I'll pay her fee."

"Sure. Thanks, Fletcher. That'll be great."

Don Campbell had said the best way to forget one woman is to take up with another. Rosa sounded like a woman that would make a man forget his own name.

Fletcher turned, hunched his right shoulder just a little and walked away, his limp worse than usual. I watched him until he turned a corner and disappeared from view. Something strange about that offer. Why that particular woman? I needed to discuss this with Don if I got the chance. Wonder what Don would have to say about dropping acid. The whole thing made me nervous. I was glad Fletcher was gone.

I walked along *Avenue Errazuriz*, past a bronze statue of a soldier on a horse in the middle of a plaza. At the intersection, the street sign said *La Maritima*. Fletcher had turned left. I looked down the way he had gone. There was no sign of him, which didn't surprise me. I turned to follow his path.

La Maritima was only a block long but had the most disjointed architecture I'd ever seen. On one side of the street— the side opposite from me—stood a massive three-story stucco building, egg-yolk yellow, with white marble arches above porticoes on each floor. Chunks of stucco were missing in the side of the building. Three of the third story windows were boarded over and neon signs advertised martinis and naked women. My side of the street looked and felt like a wild west movie set except for two things: one, the street in front was paved with cobblestones; two, the saloons had names that played on English maritime words.

I clattered slowly along the wood sidewalk, trying to take in everything I saw. It was early afternoon and people were at siesta so the streets were mostly empty. I walked by The Flying Bridge with its neon sign of a golden bridge with big white wings attached, all against a blue background. The sign for The Lower Hold made me laugh out loud. It showed a wrestler grasping an opponent around his thighs. Owners of the Rusty Truck Saloon and Delicatessen had set an old beat-up jalopy of a pick-up over the front of the building so half of the truck hung over the edge and looked as if it could fall at any moment. The

Hawse Pipe had a sign showing a dark-haired nude propped on one elbow, holding a pipe to her mouth, a trail of smoke wafting up from its bowl.

A blond woman in blue jeans and a white sweater stood in the doorway of The Fidley, her head bent slightly toward her chest, reading. She glanced up, caught my eye and motioned with a jerk of her head as I passed. I just smiled. I wasn't about to start that stuff yet. I was going shopping. I'd be back here after dinner. I had four days and figured I'd pace myself. I had been surprised when, my first time with Maria in Panama, I'd had to rest awhile between orgasms. It kind of pissed me off that women were always ready—far as I knew anyway.

I thought of Fletcher buying the gun and sensed danger—especially on the Wild West side of the street. I remembered, for some reason, that Melissa both hunted and rode. I'd watched her ride Moses, her palomino stallion, at the county fair. She wore boots and leather chaps and a broad-brimmed hat that flew from her blond head but was caught by the leather strap around her neck. She and Moses were the opening act for a horseshow. She carried real pistols in her holsters and shot blanks in the air as her horse galloped around the arena. She rode like she did everything—with an innocence and joy of living that was missing for me. No question I lived with a fair amount of intensity, but joy wasn't always a part of it.

Across the street, over on the European side, I saw the infamous Yakko's where Studs O'Laughlin had rolled down the stairs, balls in hand. Down from there was the New York Bar, the Roland and the Flamingo Club. Most likely the girls took their clients to the second and third levels for the bedroom business. The place was shoddy, but for some reason, its Old World decadence piqued my curiosity.

The last bar on my side of the street was called the Counter, referring to a type of stern some ships had. Someone with talent and imagination had painted a mural showing a neatly groomed man with a mustache, dressed in brown suit and derby hat, moving coins from one pile to another, his eyes looking off to the side anticipating new customers. In the background of the painting sat four women, lounging, wearing evening gowns of burgundy, black and scarlet.

Past the Counter, I turned right and walked along Serrano Street toward Plaza Echaurren. George LeClair said I could find inexpensive gifts there for everyone in my family. I passed by the Ascensor Cordillera, an elevator that looked like a wooden box kids would slap together in someone's back yard. It ran on near-vertical tracks set into the hillside and carried people from the port up into the residential neighborhood on the hill above. Valparaiso had a dozen or so of these lifts—called funicular rail-ways according to George LeClair.

At the plaza, I passed several open-storefront seafood bars where the vendors shouted and waved bug-eyed fish and snaky eel in the air, and juggled mussels. The market was a jumble of stalls and carts and the back-ends of old trucks offering every-thing from made-in-Japan transistor radios to Alpaca blankets to live chickens. Five men with trimmed beards played Salsa on drums and guitars and the whole marketplace moved with a beat like a cartoon. I walked through the labyrinth of shops, finger-ing the trinkets, touching fabrics, talking to the shopkeepers.

I wanted to buy gifts for my parents, my brothers and sis-ters and a few others. Thoughts of Melissa surfaced every few minutes, accompanied by a sharp pain in my heart. Though she was no longer my girlfriend, I wanted to buy her some-thing. The afternoon passed quickly as I haggled and bartered and walked away and returned, taunting the shop-keepers and flirting. The Chilean women handed me bites of tortilla with beans and melted cheese, and sold glasses of beer for a quarter. A fortyish woman with jet-black hair and a nice figure closed a deal on a pair of earrings for my mother by teaching me a dance-step that ended with my left knee thrust between her legs and her winking. Eventually, my shopping bag was full. I had a serape for one sister, a stunning gold and black poncho for another; moccasins for Robert, a white sweater for John. I bought a Seiko that showed its workings for my father—a gift I later regretted since, when I gave it to him, he said, "Where'd you go? Japan or South America?"

For Shelly, my youngest sister, I got a dark-haired flamenco doll. Little Mark, my baby brother, refused to wear the tiny green and black poncho I gave him, but hung it full shape from a nail on the wall of his bedroom as if it was a work of art. Finished with my family, I went shop to shop looking for Melissa's gift. My feelings about her ranged from anger to depression to remorse to something resembling gratitude. Finally, I bought her dangling gold earrings inlaid with lapis that cost nearly as much as all the other gifts combined.

Leaving the marketplace with a heavy shopping bag in each hand, I turned down Perez Street, pleased with my purchases, looking forward to showering on board and coming ashore again to meet Wally. We would eat in a restaurant, relax with wine, talk about the voyage. I'd tell him about Melissa. He'd laugh, tell me he told me so, that seamen can't have girlfriends. At the corner, looking for a break in traffic, I noticed in a storefront window across the road, the muted reflection of two girls. The girls themselves were blocked by a delivery van, but I could see in the window each had on the white blouse and dark plaid skirt worn by girls back home who attended Central Catholic. They appeared excited and both laughed as they talked. Something about the reflected image of one of them made me catch my breath. Curious, I crossed over to their side of the street, ignoring horns and angry drivers. When I got close I felt as though I'd lost control of my faculties; as if my movements were no longer my own. I would never have guessed I would see a woman this beautiful in my lifetime. I remembered Don Campbell saying that you know you're in love when you want to fuck someone so badly you're willing to eat dirt. Standing there, I decided sex was asking far too much. I'd have been happy to carry her books or just hear her talk. There were no thoughts of love or romance. Just an electric jolt I had never before felt and couldn't walk away from.

I was no more than five feet from her when she sensed me and turned. She was robust with curly red hair. She stood nearly as tall as me, with strong shoulders and breasts that jutted out in a way that defied gravity. She had blue eyes and freckles and a full mouth. She looked at me and her smile disappeared.

"Hello," I said. "I am American. Do you speak English?"

I stuttered on *American* and again on *do*.

The red-haired girl said something in Spanish that made her

friend giggle. Then she stopped talking and looked at me with a serious, but puzzled look.

"Please excuse me," I said. "I—I would like to meet you."

"My name is Ana-Elena. I do not speak English so good."

"No. I mean yes. You speak very well. I am sorry I do not speak Spanish."

"Perhaps you could learn."

"Si. Si. I could learn," I said sincerely. "I will begin lessons next year at school." They both laughed.

"You are studente?"

"I am cadete'. A student on a ship. I am visiting Valparaiso on a ship."

She hesitated, as if wanting to make certain she had this piece of information correct before proceeding.

"Are you at a university in America?"

"I go to a university in New York where I learn to sail on ships."

"So you weel be a capitan?"

I shrugged. "Perhaps one day, with luck. Are you also in school?"

She fingered the top buttons on her blouse and smiled.

"Si. Of course. You think I would wear this ugly clothing if I were not a student? I will graduate this year. Then, maybe, I will go to University."

She glanced at her friend as if they shared a secret.

I smiled and nodded. Nothing else in the world existed. No traffic noise, no friend beside her, no bag of gifts in my hand, nothing.

"I am sorry," she said, looking at me standing there, silent. "I must go." She hesitated again.

"M-may I see you again?" Never before had I been so bold.

"Si. I will give to you my number."

She rummaged in her purse, found paper and a pen, wrote her name and a line of numbers and handed me the paper. Then both of them got into a cab and left. I thought of Bob, the guy in New Orleans who had written his number on a napkin. If Ana-Elena had written a phony number on this napkin, it would be worse than ten Dear John letters from Melissa and a hundred bad numbers from Bob.

I leaned against a lamp pole watching the taxi carry them away. I was out of breath. My heart ached and I needed to sit. I looked about for a bench. Finding none, I walked.

In a daze I made my way back to the ship. Once in my room, I put my gifts on the shelf in my closet and closed the door. With my shoes still on, I lay on my bunk and looked, for at least the twentieth time, at her name and number: Ana Elena McGloughlin-Sanchez. I turned the piece of paper over and over in my hand, smelled it, found nothing to smell, so studied her handwriting. It was distinctly feminine, I thought, strong and artistic—particularly the flourish with which she curled the *S* into and around the word *Sanchez*. It had a sensuousness that fit perfectly with my image of her. The letters were neither small nor tight nor forced. They were unhurried, graceful and confident.

I closed my eyes and did my best to recall her face, but remembered only the full lips pursed into a perplexed smile, the red hair and serious blue eyes with long lashes. I could see her pointing breasts, her small waist and long legs. I couldn't recall her feet, or what type of shoes she had worn. I would have said her complexion was pale, but couldn't be sure.

I worried about when I should call her. Now, perhaps. It was only a few minutes past four. Or maybe at five, to give her time to get home and not appear too eager. I was aware of an ache in my heart that made me want to call and go immediately to her house just to be near her, to have some connection no matter how fragile. I felt heartsick and foolish.

I bolted up out of my bed, hitting my head on the edge of Wally's bunk when I realized there was no phone on the ship. Where would I call from? How would I use the phones in Valparaiso? What coins did they take? I spoke no Spanish. What if I could not get her?

Those thoughts burning in my brain, I showered quickly, changed, and ran to the purser's office. Mr. LeClair told me what to do and where to go. I left immediately and ran most of the way to a phone booth in the Main Post Office on Prat Street, a block from Sotomayor Plaza, my heart pounding like a drum in a salsa band.

Valparaiso
August 17 & 18

Located at the corner of Prat and Senoret streets, a block from Sotomayor Plaza, the Main Post Office in Valparaiso occupied the first floor of a stone ruin of a building with two carved lions—one missing part of its nose, the other a right paw—guarding the massive scarred wood door. Of the three people standing in line to use the single phone, I was hands down the most impatient. Fifteen minutes after arriving, I was alone in the booth, every sense focused on how to work the thing. After three misfires—where the phone went dead with no ring and I'd used the last of my change—I heard a female voice say "Hola!"

"Hello. May I speak with Ana-Elena please?"

"Si! Yes! This is she. Is this my very new Amereecan friend I meet today?"

"Yes. It is me. Jake. How are you?"

"I am—how you say? I am quite heathful."

I couldn't hear her well, which was frustrating, as I wanted to glean every nuance from every word. The phone booth was wooden but the door was missing. The stream of people walking by seemed bent on making as much noise as possible.

"I can't hear you." I said, much too loud. "Can you hear me?"

"You are yelling. Of course I hear you. Where are you?"

"I am at a Post Office downtown. I want to meet you later tonight."

"Yes, maybe we can. What to do then?"

"Just tell me where to meet you. I will be there, with my friend so he can meet your friend."

"In Chile, is impossible. I cannot see you without a chaperone."

"Oh, I did not know that." I could have collapsed. Why hadn't she said something? What did this mean?

"But my parents think I am going to a movie tonight with Alejandra, so you will meet me—we—in the theatre in Munoz Hurtado. It is near the Garden Hotel, only one block from where we met this afternoon. Please to be there by nineteen thirty. We will see the movie together. Is a mystery with a famous Chilean actress named Maria Alvarez. She is most beautiful."

"Ana, I think you are most beautiful." I could scarcely believe I had uttered those words. Men did not pay out compliments to women where I came from. She was silent for a moment.

"You are a nice boy," she said.

* * *

I'd already downed one glass of the Cafe Valparaiso Eterno's house-red and was reading a pamphlet in English detailing the nefarious role of the CIA in Chilean politics when Wally walked in, bright-eyed, looking all around, red hair sticking straight up in the front. He saw me, walked over and sat.

"Wally, did you know our government supports the right-wing political party here in Chile?" Wally always seemed to know a little about most everything, and if he didn't, he pretended like he did.

"Yeah," he said. "There's a guy down here named Allende, leader of the Communist Party. Got a lot of votes in the last election. Our government is worried he'll get elected Presidente' and—I don't know—do whatever it is communists do when they get power."

"I didn't know our government got involved in the politics of other countries."

"What do you think we're doing in Viet Nam, refereeing a soccer match? Christ, don't they have newspapers in Nebraska?"

A man with a guitar walked to the corner of the room. He had long black hair, wore dark clothes and was thin as a stick.

"I feel like I grew up in a fucking cave," I muttered, watching the man set up to play. "People read headlines and listen to Paul Harvey on KMMJ a.m. radio. Goddamn, Wally, I want to learn about the world and know what's going on. If our country's meddling in the affairs of others, that doesn't seem right."

"Well, start reading the paper. Must be a library back there someplace. Read a news magazine."

"We have a library and I'm its most best customer. But I read books, not magazines."

"If you're their best customer, I wonder if the other people in your town know World War II is over."

"By the way, asshole, we have a date tonight. With the most beautiful girl I've ever seen."

"We both have a date with the same girl?"

"I have a date with the most beautiful girl in Chile. You have a date with her friend."

"Who just happens to be a dog. I know how beautiful girls operate."

I laughed. "No, you'll see. Her friend's cute."

"Cute. I get cute. You get beautiful. You're right. We'll see."

I told him how I'd met Ana-Elena, how I'd called from the Post Office, and about the chaperones.

"Sounds like you're in love."

"Like you wouldn't believe."

"Don't let me say I told you so too often."

A blond waiter named Miguel with watery blue eyes served us. Wally ate a firm-fleshed sea bass sautéed in butter with salad and something resembling fried potatoes while I went with beef-steak and fries. The flamenco guitarist called himself Hector Aguas. His fingers looked like bugs running up and down the neck of his small guitar and his straight black hair hung down over his eyes. The sun poured over him through a window and sweat ran down his arms. He finished the piece he was playing by beating the heel of his hand against the body of his guitar and gasping a passionate series of "Ole's". Wally and I had never heard such music. Along with the food and wine, we thought it fabulous and applauded wildly, oblivious to the stares of other patrons who, apparently, had heard flamenco a time or two before.

On or off the ship, Wally couldn't quit talking about the first engineer. Wally was disgusted with the guy. Today's episode of incompetence had to do with losing most the water from the starboard boiler. This meant Wally and the wiper had to take on water tomorrow. I lost interest in the conversation and kept looking at my watch. Eventually, even Wally, engineer that he was, picked up on the blank look in my eyes, laughed a little, and said, "fucking first" one last time. Then we hit onto some fairly interesting topics such as how much money a third mate or third engineer could make in a year, or how long it would take to move up to a chief mate or first engineer position and earn what we considered serious money. Conversation moved into the area of ship gossip: foibles of different crewmembers.

"You know the four to eight fireman?" said Wally. "Guy named Alfredo?"

" Yeah," I said. "Guy with all the chest hair and gold chains."

Wally nodded. "He masturbates behind the boiler every morning around five. Everyone knows he does it, but they just leave him to it—like it was part of his morning rounds."

I shook my head to clear it of Alfredo's image behind the boiler.

"What about the purser?" I asked. "Can you believe the new clothes he's been wearing? No more khakis when that guy goes ashore. Oh no. It's black turtle-necks and linen trousers, and, of course, sunglasses."

"Then there's your buddy, Simple Simon," said Wally, pouring another glass of wine from the carafe. "Looks at everything like it's the first time he ever saw it."

"He's a cool guy. How about Fletcher the A.B.?" I asked.

"Very weird person. I don't even know him since he's not in my department, but whenever I see him, its like he's sneaking a peek at me out of the corner of his eyes. Like he wants to check you out."

"Don Campbell says to watch out for him. That he's a cadet-hater."

"Pff!" said Wally. "As if I give a shit if an A.B. likes me."

* * *

At exactly seven-fifteen, I said we had to go. Wally came along reluctantly, not that excited about going on a blind date in Valparaiso, two blocks from a street of bars full of women begging men to come to their beds. The Valparaiso Eterno Cafe was only three blocks from the movie theater as it turned out but I walked so fast Wally had to run to keep up and we were early. We bought our tickets and walked into the lobby. Scarred wainscoting ran halfway up the wall where it met textured red wallpaper with tiny gold stars, peeling at the seams. Faded Hollywood posters—featuring Hollywood celebrities like Katherine Hepburn and Humphrey Bogart—hung on the wall, spaced four feet apart. An old woman sold coffee and small cakes in a tiny concession stand in one corner.

People stood in groups talking—as if seeing the movie was secondary to seeing each other—at least until the movie started. Some even stood on the sidewalk in front. Mostly, they were teen-agers—boys in one group, girls in another, eyeing each other, pointing and giggling. Wally and I stood there watching when I felt a tap on my shoulder. I turned and she was there, wearing a white mini-skirt and white boots to mid-calf. She wore a soft white sweater that clung to her breasts. Her curls were pulled back into a frizzy, red ponytail that lay across her shoulder and down along her right breast. I found it difficult to get enough oxygen and had to fight the urge to embrace her. Wally, speechless for once, gaped like an idiot.

"Ana-Elena." I choked. "Hola. You are—you are beautiful."

"Am I as pretty as she?" She pointed to a Marylyn Monroe head-shot that showed her mouth open, teeth gleaming white against her red lips.

"Much more beautiful," I said sincerely. She smiled and looked at me carefully.

Disconcerted by her stare, I spoke. "This is Wally, my friend from America. We are *cadete's* on the ship. Wally, please meet Ana-Elena."

Ana Elena introduced Alejandra, also pretty, dark-haired

and shorter. Perfect for Wally, I thought. I saw he was pleased. The two of them struck off almost immediately in earnest conversation.

Even though we had all purchased tickets, the two girls had already seen the movie and since it was in Spanish, we figured we wouldn't understand much of it. Ana-Elena, who seemed accustomed to making decisions, suggested we go to a nearby coffeeshop. Everyone thought this was a fine idea. Ana-Elena took my hand as we walked around the corner and up the street, her touch an electric shock.

The Bote Salvavidas was an open-air café near the pier, only three blocks from the movie theater. The place was full—mostly people our age—drinking coffee or wine, eating fried seafood and sweets, engaged in intense, serious conversation. We pulled bent-iron chairs with small wood seats up close to the rough wood table marked with carved initials. Wally and I liked it because we could see the ship. The girls ordered espresso and Wally and I ordered *vino rosa*. Ana-Elena raised an eyebrow when I said I didn't drink coffee and I wished I'd gone ahead and tried some.

The girls told us they were from strict families and if they were ever caught with young men, unchaperoned, like now, they would be in serious trouble and we could be arrested. People either hired chaperones or used family members. Some chaperones—particularly attractive young aunties—understood the needs of their nieces and turned a blind eye toward handholding and kissing. Ana-Elena held my hand unconsciously, friendly-like, and stared directly into my eyes. She told me about an earthquake they'd had a year ago. My attention was so focused on her, I doubt I'd have noticed an earthquake had it shook the seat I sat on.

Our two movie hours passed in an eye-blink and the girls had to leave to meet Alejandra's mother. We ran the three blocks, weaving our way through the crowd of people at Sotomayor Plaza to the movie-house, shouting to each other as we went. Ana-Elena could get her father's car, she said. She would pick me up the next day at the Bote Salvavidas and we would drive to the Vina del Mar where the gambling casinos were, then we would go to the country for a picnic. She would "make it up," some story for her parents. We were breathless from running and from love when we got to the corner across from the theater. She put her arms around my neck and kissed me hard, then left. I stood and watched as they climbed into a large black Lincoln.

* * *

Wally and I wandered around the theater for thirty minutes after they left. Wally kept asking what was wrong and I couldn't explain it. Just couldn't bring myself to leave the area. Eventually, he grabbed my shoulders and pointed me toward La Maritima Street and the sailor's bars.

It was around eleven when we got there and it was a circus. I had thought the girls of Panama and the girls of Peru were pretty, but the girls of Valparaiso made me gape like a fool. Where the Panamanians had seemed emaciated, these girls strutted around with their handful hips and grapefruit breasts. Where the Peruvian girls stood quietly in the shadows, these ran back and forth, bold as bells, flirting, laughing and carrying on with each other and the men. Nothing escaped their attention; nothing seemed too small to comment on.

We went into the Broken Fluke, a bar where the whores wore schoolgirl uniforms similar to the one Ana-Elena had on when I met her except the skirts were shorter and the heels absurdly high. They all wore nylons attached to garter belts and their trick, so to speak, was to bend over showing off their bottoms. Their blouses were white cotton worn half-unbuttoned, depending on the girl and the abundance of her charms. What really amazed me was how much fun these girls seemed to be having.

Wally and I stood at the bar where two Brits sat complaining about the bad food on their ship and ordered a beer. The place had a number of small, intimate rooms and cozy couches stuffed away into little corners. I didn't want any ship-talk. Meeting Ana-Elena had been too important to follow up with words I now considered mundane. I wanted to talk politics or current events things I knew nothing about.

"Wally, you ever drop acid?"

"Naw. I'm not into that. I've got enough trouble with alcohol. How 'bout you?"

"Nope. But look." I took from my billfold the piece of tissue with the paper-thin wafers. Wally set them in the palm of his right hand and looked at them carefully.

"I've seen them before, but never used them," he said. "You gonna try one?"

"I don't know. What do you think?"

"I'll consider it. Wouldn't mind trying it, I guess. Just to say I've done it. I don't think acid is addictive. Just sort of blows your mind is all."

"Oh, good, no problem then."

"Tell you what," said Wally. "I've thought about it long enough. I'll take one tonight and you take care of me and you take one tomorrow and I'll take care of you."

"Okay by me. Sure you wanna go first?"

In answer, he reached down, picked up one of the purplish wafers and popped it into his mouth. I watched as it dissolved on his tongue. Wally looked at me, crossed his eyes and stuck out his tongue. He looked like Jiminy Cricket. I laughed, but I was plenty nervous.

"So," he said. "I've dropped acid. Let the journey begin."

"Damn," I said. "I hope it's a good one."

We drank another beer and after a bit, Wally was saying "wow" to every girl he looked at. The girls could see he had done something out of the ordinary and gathered around to observe his reactions when they unbuttoned their blouses or hiked up their skirts. Three of them pestered him while a dark-haired beauty named Gabriella attached herself to me. Wally couldn't stop giggling at first but then, as the girls tired of the game, he became morose then angry. I danced with Gabriella a couple times, then sat at a table with her, rejecting her advances on account of my love for Ana-Elena. All the while, I kept a weather eye on Wally. After the girls left him, he lay his head on the bar awhile, then raised it and started saying "fuck" to everything. Next, he was banging his beer bottle on the bar, quietly at first, but loud enough so people near him could hear. The British sailors asked him to knock it off, and I heard him say "fuck off mates." That's when I got up, almost dumping Gabriella off my lap. I reached Wally the same time one of the

Brits did and caught the guy's arm as he cocked to swing at him.

"Sorry, mate," I said. "My friend's had a little too much to drink. I'll take him home."

"Yeah, well, I don't rightly appreciate being told to fuck-off, you know, mate. Specially by such a little twerp as this one."

"He is a little twerp all right," I said. "So leave him alone. I'm taking him the hell out of here." The guy mumbled something and shuffled back over to his buddy. I grabbed Wally's arm and pulled him off the barstool to take him back to the ship. He swung at me, but half-heartedly. I caught his arm, spun him around, pinned both his hands behind his back and guided him out the door.

Outside, the street was loud and raunchy: a carnival of sailors, pimps, whores and I don't know who. "I gotta piss," said Wally. "Jesus, please just let me piss someplace."

I guided Wally around the corner of the building and sort of held him up while he fumbled with his zipper. He kept up a steady stream of conversation while his pee splashed off the brick onto his shoes.

"Jake, you're my pal. You know that. You're a great shipmate. You won't leave me alone, will you? Oh goddamn, I'm real scared."

He went on and on about what a good guy I was, how screwed up he was; how hard his mother had worked raising him, and how he barely remembered his lousy, good-for-nothing father who left when he was four. Finally, he finished peeing and leaned against the building bawling like a baby— loud, pitiful moans from some deep place. I stood there, not knowing what to do. Finally, I walked up to him and put my arm around him.

"Hey, Wally. It's all right. Everybody's got some problem or another. You'll be okay. Just hang in there, man. I'll take you back to the ship. You'll be okay."

"Oooh. Goddamn it. Where's the ship? Where's the fuckin' ship? I want to be in my bed. Why is everything so fucked up?"

He sank to the ground, sitting directly in the pool of urine he'd just made. I grabbed him under his arms and lifted him up.

"C'mon, Wally. We're going to the ship right now."

I put his arm around my neck and we stumbled the four

blocks to the ship. He refused to climb the gangway because he didn't like the "fucking first," so I threw him over my shoulder and carried him up like a sack of flour. Don Campbell was on watch. He walked by as I set Wally down on deck.

"Hey, Jake," he said. "He heavy?"

"Naw," I said, setting him down. "But it wouldn't matter if he was."

He shook my hand. "You're right. This is what cadets do for each other."

"He'd do the same for me."

"Probably. Just remember. This is your first night. You've got to pace yourself in Valparaiso."

I took Wally's hand like he was my little brother and led him to our room. This signifies, I thought.

Valparaiso
August 18

Wally was still grunting and snorting when I left at nine-thirty to meet Ana-Elena. The drug hadn't worn off till nearly daylight. He had tossed and turned, slept some, roused himself and me with nightmares that made him scream, cry, flail with his fists, then drop back to sleep with a clunk. I sat much of the night speaking quietly to him, wiping the sweat from his face and back and feeding him sips of water. I had to restrain him twice and was amazed at how strong he was for being so skinny. Once he threw me across the room, then charged for the door, only to find it opened to the head—a fact that saddened him so profoundly he sank to the floor crying about how he missed his dad and just wished he'd get in touch with him so he could forgive him for being absent most of his childhood and if he had any extra money, his Mom could use a break. What's the point of taking drugs if this is how it is, I thought. I considered tossing out the other wafer, but didn't. Should have, but didn't.

It was strange, nursing someone—a buddy—like that. I was worried about him and afraid for him and wondered if he'd be all right. I said five Our Fathers and five Hail Mary's for him, like penance except it didn't feel at all like penance, around five a.m. when he was at his worst but I never considered getting help. This was his trip and I was here to help him take it. Wiping the sweat from his brow was kind of cool, though. I was glad when he went to sleep around six and his breathing quieted down and a look of peace came over him. I slept some myself. I'll say one thing: in spite of, or probably because of, all the trouble he caused, I grew to love the little shit that night.

I awoke at eight, starving. Nervous about leaving Wally long enough to eat breakfast in the saloon, I ran down the three decks to the galley, stuck my head in the pantry and asked for a plate of ham and over easy and a big glass of orange juice. The cook made it up in a couple minutes and I took the food back to our room.

Wally slept, mouth open and drooling, so I stepped outside to eat. My room was on the offshore side of the ship. I took a chair out and got comfortable with my plate in my lap. A rust-streaked freighter was being pulled from her berth by two old tugs while another ship—I thought I recognized a Norwegian flag on her halyard—all spanking new paint and nice lines—stood at the breakwater like a welcome dinner guest. I liked the climate here. It was cool and moist and called for a jacket. Fog cloaked the hills to the east but at sea level we were beneath the clouds.

I sat just outside my room near my window so I could look in on Wally. Something about mornings in foreign ports, standing on deck on the offshore side in the cool marine air, listening to the shrill cries of seagulls mix with the mournful tone of the foghorns, watching the sun burn off the surface fog, watching tugs work the ships, watching the black smoke puff out of the stacks of the freighters, smelling the salt water, breathing deeply of sea air was almost too fine for words. I finished my food, set my plate down and closed my eyes a few minutes, then returned to my room, feeling about as good as I could imagine.

To meet Ana-Elena, I pulled the camel-colored corduroy sports jacket my folks had bought me for my birthday—the one with the ripped pocket from the mugger in New Orleans—from my closet and shook out the wrinkles. I'd already put on a white shirt and blue jeans. The jacket hadn't been off its hangar since New Orleans. I wished I'd sewed the pocket, then remembered I'd purposely not sewn it so I could brag about getting mugged when I returned to school. I thought briefly how, for me, that memory wasn't one of danger. I felt no fear and would not likely change my habits because of it—even though someone had attacked me with a knife. Rather, it seemed like just another experience—not unlike, say, eating my first quesadilla in Boyd's in Houston, or seeing the green flash on the deck of the café in Antofagasta. Christ, I thought. As amazing as this voyage has been already, I feel like I'm barely sticking a toe into the ocean of life. I transferred the packet of LSD to the breast pocket of that jacket and wondered what experience lay in store for me today.

After eating, I showered, blessed Wally, now sleeping quietly, with a kiss on the forehead and left. I got to the Bote Salvavidas at nine-thirty. Ana-Elena was to be there by ten. The building was stucco, painted bright green and orange with vines creeping up most of one side. On the patio overlooking the harbor—more like a courtyard with its big concrete pavers—long blue and yellow benches were interspersed with the bent-iron chairs and small tables we had sat at the night before. Groups of people wearing sweaters and jackets in the early morning chill, talked and sipped their espresso.

I ordered tea. A group of guys my age and older sitting in the corner of the patio shouted at each other and even stood and jabbed one another in the chest. One of them walked over to ask in broken English if I was American. I said yes. He asked how I felt about the Viet Nam war and I decided then and there to be against it and told him so. He raised his right thumb, clapped me hard on the shoulder and walked back to his table. I felt good, like I'd just made an important decision to stand with my generation, however inadvertently or ill-informed.

I breathed deeply and thought how I loved the air here and that I had to find a climate like this and that I'd never again live more than ten miles from salt water. Green, leafy vines with large purple flowers climbed the wood lattice that ran along each side of the patio, leaving a straight-ahead, flower-framed view of the harbor. A beat-up statue of Venus, both arms broken, stood in a pool of stagnant water in the center. The courtyard felt decadent and old-world, and I decided I liked the feeling. I sat on the

bench, watching for Ana-Elena and listening to the argument in
the corner, wondering what they were talking about, glad I'd
taken my recent political stand even if it differed from that of my
father and most other men in my community.

Ana-Elena had talked last night about Chile's political problems. Communists battled Fascists. The American CIA was on
the side of the Fascists. She was descended from the O'Higgins
family on her mother's side and her great great great grandfather, Bernard O'Higgins was considered to have been a leader in
the Chilean battle for independence in the early eighteen hundreds. Her father, a police official of some importance, "slept
with the fascist military pigs." She spat when she said military.
Her mother clung to the liberal ideals of her childhood, and
slept in the guest bedroom. She and her mother were great
friends and ignored her father's business and late-night absences.
When Ana-Elena talked about politics, her eyes widened and she
looked questioningly into my eyes—as if she wondered how I, an
American—and therefore someone whose opinion mattered—
perceived her country and the political struggles it was going
through. Those almond-shaped blue eyes peering into mine
mostly made me want to touch her face and kiss her, but something else in her passionate outbursts strengthened my desire to
better understand the workings of the world.

A thin young man with large brown eyes and a scar on one
cheek set my cup of tea on the bench in front of me. I'd never
tasted tea without honey and lemon before. This, with cream
and sugar, was better. It was richer and sweeter—like everything
down here. Life itself seemed richer here. Not better maybe, but
richer. There was something about the sea air—how it smelled
and even felt, the intensity of the nearby conversation, and the
anticipation of meeting the woman I loved that made me want
to breathe really deeply; as if life here, my life here, was bursting.

The sun broke through the clouds and I finished my tea. It
was 10:30. Ana-Elena was a half-hour late and I began to worry.
I stood to get more hot water poured over my tea bag when the
door to the courtyard opened and she walked toward me. She
wore a red pleated skirt and a white blouse. Her thick hair was
piled on top of her head in loose red curls. Her lips were shiny
and she had applied just a hint of blue eye shadow. She walked

up to me a little out of breath, a concerned look on her face, chattering off a litany of excuses, half Spanish, half English.

"Senor Jacob, I am so sorry. I am late. My sister did not wake me, then there was no hot water for my bath and my mother gave me the—what do you call it—first degree? Fourth degree? I had not prepared anything to say, because I have not gotten used to lying yet, so I had to invent something to say right there, and it was not so easy because what could I be doing? I am a schoolgirl and I had to think of something they could not, you know, catch up with me for, because my mother will probably check since I think she did some things when she was a girl."

Her nose was two inches from mine as she talked, her eyes searching for any hint of reproach, and suddenly her lips were against my lips, briefly but hard. She said, "You are a handsome boy," and I'd have forgiven her anything, anything at all.

She ordered an espresso, so we sat and talked while she drank it. Her parents suspected something was up. Fortunately, her father was too busy to worry about her, but her mother saw trouble "under every leettle stone."

"Anyway, it does not matter. I have the car. The day is," she gestured toward the bay, smiling, "like a painting. We will have a pinchik. No, pinknic."

She looked at me quizzically.

"Yes, picnic is when people carry food to someplace outdoors and eat it."

"Si. That is what I mean. I have not been on a picnic before, but I have read that you *Norte Amereecanos* go on many picnics, so I want to go on a picnic with you."

She beamed. Her two front teeth had a slight space between them.

We left the Bote and walked to her car, a red convertible. I helped her fold down the black top.

"The police know my father's car," she said, speeding away. "So no one will stop me for driving fast, although they may call my papa."

"Great," I said, wondering again what this day would bring.

Valparaiso, according to Ana-Elena, sat on the sides of forty-two hills. Leaving the café, we drove along Errazuriz Avenue, the road that runs along the waterfront. To our right, the town rose steeply. The houses, a blend of crimsons, yellow, cobalt and green, looked as if they could tumble into the sea. They appeared to have been set on these hills at random—without planning, without roads. No Protestant, left-brain, squared off grid of streets and avenues here. A certain level of chaos seemed acceptable in this city. Like a breeding ground for art, it seemed to me. For a creative life. But what did I know?

We passed the Turri Clock, a four-faced timepiece at a three-way intersection.

"This is the financial district," she said. She turned sharply left, laughing as she missed by inches a large truck offloading bags of concrete, onto Prat Street.

"That is the Stock Exchange."

She pointed to a beautiful stone building that made me think of London—even though I'd never been there.

Prat turned into Esmeralda, which turned into O'Higgins. Ana-Elena commented proudly "this street is named for my Mother's family. It is a famous name in my country." Ahead, she slowed for the Plaza Victoria, drove through a crowd of families, ignored the rude gestures and whistling of some of the men, and pointed to a large church.

"That is my church," she said. "Perhaps we will go there on Sunday."

"That would be nice," I replied. "My mother would approve."

We drove on in silence.

"There are many prostitutes in Valparaiso," said Ana-Elena suddenly, looking over at me. "Do you go with prostitutes?"

She startled me by her directness.

"Once or twice," I said, "in Panama."

"Did you enjoy being with the prostitutes?"

"Well, not as much as I enjoy being with you."

She thought about that for a couple of minutes.

"Do you have a girlfriend in *Norte Amereeca*?" she asked finally.

"I used to," I said. "But we broke up."

"Broke up? What is 'broke up'?"

"She wrote me a letter. Said she does not want to be my girl-friend anymore."

"Ahhhh! And do you feel very sad now?"

"At first I was very sad. Now, I am not so sad."

She smiled. "I think you men are all much alike. As soon as you are with another woman, you are happy again."

"And what about you? Do you have a boyfriend?"

She looked at me and smiled. "Yes, but he is of no conse-quence at this moment."

She pulled the car over and stopped at a dilapidated little store with no windows; just a dirty white awning over the door.

"Please wait," she said. "I will return in a moment."

She swung her legs out of the car, closed the door and ran into the store, the back of her skirt flipping up as she ran. She returned carrying a bag of groceries, set them into the small back seat and we drove on.

In minutes we were in the countryside, winding our way up the coast. We drove out of the fog when we left the town, the ocean a deep azure to our left, hills glowing green to our right. Ana-Elena drove fast and the road curved up into a series of hair-pins that took us high above the ocean, then back down toward a group of sand-colored buildings iridescent in the late morning sun. The colors, like everything else, seemed richer here. Maybe it was the light. Or maybe it was being in love.

Ana-Elena abruptly turned left into a vacant parking lot, her rear wheels kicking up gravel as she swerved. She braked sharply and parked at the far end of a lot on a hill overlooking the ocean. Down to our right, we could see the sand-colored buildings of the Vina del Mar; to our left, the low-lying fog that still covered Valparaiso. We got out of the car and walked to a short stone wall overlooking the sea. The wind blew the loose strands of red hair about her cheeks. Her face was flushed. She reached out and took my hand. Below us the ocean sparkled blue and white in the sun. To our right, the stucco buildings seemed too modern against the sandy beach. In spite of the remarkable vistas before me, all I could think of were Don Campbell's words: "Love is when you want to fuck her so bad, you'd eat dirt."

I made a stab at conversation. "Everything here is beautiful—

even the fields and the sheep and cattle. The colors seem more intense than where I grew up."

"Everything is more intense in Chile." She smiled.

We stood together, watching spray break over rocks, my hand in hers, my senses spinning. This, for God's sake, was new and overwhelming. I sucked in air like a runner, wondering what was happening. Something electric and full of life and both terribly frightening and yet welcome as anything could possibly be, something that could change how I thought and would live. I may have felt something warm toward Melissa, but it was nothing compared with the bolts of electricity surging through me now. If this is what love feels like, I thought, then how do people survive a lifetime of it?

Ana-Elena decided we would picnic here. She released my hand, walked to the back of her car and pulled a blanket from the trunk. I carried the food and we walked down a bushy path onto the green slope. We stopped just past a break of small trees bursting with tiny white blossoms where we had a full view of the ocean and the buildings of Vina del Mar. Ana-Elena spread the blanket in a sunny spot and sat. Her skirt rode nearly to her hips, but like Melissa, she seemed free of the confines of excess modesty. As if to say "my body is like that of every other woman; to understand me, a man needs to look further than up my skirt." I wondered how it felt to be so free. She made a half-hearted gesture at smoothing her skirt, looked up and smiled, then handed me the bottle of wine. I removed the cork with a corkscrew I found in the sack and poured two glasses.

"To my American friend," she said.

"To my beautiful Chilean girl and her wonderful country." I thought that sounded awfully corny after I said it.

The wine was still on our lips when they touched. Then her lips were pressed against mine with the weight of her body behind them. The wine spilled onto the grass as we freed our hands. I fell back, my hands at her hips. She was on me then, our passion a sort of wrestling match. I felt like I was floating, like I had left planet earth, that what was happening had a spiritual dimension.

We rolled on the grass, struggling to rid ourselves of our clothes, when, above us, I heard voices. I freed my mouth from

Ana-Elena's long enough to look up and stared straight into the faces of a gaggle of gray hairs. From one particular spot in the parking lot—the spot at which the driver of the bus had parked—we were "ducks on the pond" as my Dad would have said. I rolled over and looked at the sky.

"God," I said. "Why this?"

Ana-Elena burrowed into my neck and licked my ear. "Fuck them old gringos," she said.

"Hey, look down there," chortled a high-pitched voice that sounded straight off the main street of my hometown. "A couple of local kids making out on the slope. Ha ha. Just like kids everywhere, I guess."

"That asshole," said Ana-Elena in my ear.

I sat up, smiling and buckled my belt.

"Such language." I looked into her eyes. They were slightly crossed, as with passion.

"I apologize—to you, not to those dogs. We will eat."

Once we were buttoned up, we ate the tangy cheese and tore off hunks of the rich, crusty bread and drank the wine. We talked between bites and kissed and told of our families, and kissed again. The first bus had left, but another had come and we realized we were part of the tour. Finally, our stomachs full but ravenous for each other, we packed up and climbed the path to the parking lot. We locked the remains of our picnic in the car and walked to the casino.

The flowers surrounding the Vina del Mar seemed unnaturally bright. Valets in sky-blue and red tended people arriving and leaving. Tuxedoed doormen stood by the ten-foot etched glass doors as we climbed three steps and passed between huge Greek columns into the casino. The floor of the entry was a red carpet thick enough to sleep on. Small trees and a life-sized statue of a nude woman washing herself in a waterfall were the first things we saw. Huge chandeliers sparkled with tiny lights. Past the slot machines, the gaming tables were covered with green velvet and tended by attractive men and women in black and white.

"We will play," said Ana-Elena, reaching into her purse. She pulled out money and exchanged it for chips. She sat on one of the high stools and bet. She drew a twenty against the dealer's seventeen, then a blackjack. On her third hand, she doubled down on eleven and won again.

"Ha," she said. "You bring me luck."

She pushed her pile of chips onto the square, winking at me. She held at eighteen. The dealer hit with a seven showing. He turned over a six, then a king.

"That is enough," said Ana-Elena. "We have more important things to do today."

We zigzagged over to the bank window and cashed in. Ana-Elena peeled off several bills from the roll they handed her and gave them to me. "We are a team." She laughed, all white teeth and sparkling eyes. Her smile glittered, as if filled with enchantment. In a deserted hallway, I kissed her, pressing her body against a wall, but people were nearby.

"Come," she said. "I know where to go. We shall visit the dead."

I looked at her, puzzled. She smiled and nuzzled my ear and neck.

In the car, I placed my hand on the tender skin of her inner thigh. Looking straight ahead, she put her hand on top of mine and moved it up her leg under her skirt and closed her eyes, pressing hard on my hand. Then she removed my hand.

"We go," she said.

The car squealed around the hairpins as we sped along the coast back toward the city. The sun was past the local meridian, the fog gone and the air warm. I had no sense of time passing and couldn't figure out where the day had gone.

"Where will we go to visit the dead?" I asked.

"Cerro Los Placeres. It is a cemetery."

"A cemetery?" I asked. "And what does cerro los placeres mean?"

"Shh!" she said. "Do not speak." She seemed cross.

"Are you angry?" I asked.

"I am not angry."

After driving silently for several minutes, she said. "I am afraid."

I moved so the back of my hand touched the outside of her leg.

Anna-Elena steered the car up into the hills above the town. We drove without speaking for a half hour. Finally, she turned onto Avenida Argentin and parked along the side of the road. She motioned toward the wooden lift with the sign *Ascensor Palonco* painted in four-inch black letters. We walked to the lift. Ana-Elena gave the attendant some pocket change and we stepped into the lift. It carried us, creaking and shrieking on its wires, up through a vertical tunnel.

"This is Cerro Baron," Ana-Elena said at the top. She pointed. "Over there is the cemetery at Cerro Los Placeres."

We walked from one hill to another in silence as I stared at the castle on Cerro Baron. I had never seen a real castle before.

"*Cerro Los Placeres* means 'the hill of pleasures'," she said as we entered the cemetery. Strange name for a cemetery, I thought, but, as I was learning, things were different here.

Ana-Elena smiled as we climbed the steps and took my hand—like a guide. At the top, we walked through a sort of gate guarded by two large, marble angels and a short, dark-skinned man in a brown uniform who made a motion that was halfway between a salute and a doff of his hat.

I was used to simple tombstones surrounding a lonely crucifix rising out of the prairie. Here, the grounds were crowded with marble buildings. Each building had statuary of Mary or Jesus or some saint guarding the doors; angels perched on the rooftops, serpents and dragons—anguish on their reptilian faces—crushed underfoot or run through with a sword. It was a garden party, with a crowd of marble guests. Intricate pathways wound their way in and around the buildings, some of which were nearly hidden by the flowers and blossoms and green bushes which grew everywhere.

"What are those buildings?" I asked, trying to hide my amazement.

"They are houses for the dead. Mausoleum, yes? This is the Italian cemetery. The cemetery of the Blessed Virgin. Italians with much money believe they must create expensive houses in which to be buried."

"Everything here is beautiful," I said.

"You also are beautiful. I am embarrassed about my behavior today. My auntie who chaperones me would be shocked. I

am not like this. I want you to know that we will behave ourselves here. I am not Italian, but I will show you where the families of my friends bury their dead."

"I am sorry you are embarrassed. Why are you embarrassed?"

"Because I am too much attracted to you."

"I am very much attracted to you."

"Is OK. We have a nice time walking in the cemetery. Is very
beautiful."

Ana-Elena led me along a labyrinth of twisted stone pathways guarded by life-sized statues. The hollow eyes of fierce-
faced angels appeared to follow us as we walked deeper into
the cemetery. Saints with eyes rolled heavenward stood,
prayerful and at peace. Vines climbed the stone benches.
Oversized flowers, like explosions of red and yellow and peri-
winkle, leaned across the path. Small bright birds squawked
and scolded, hopping from branch to branch. The sun, low
now, cast long shadows from the statues. As we moved deeper into the cemetery, the foliage became almost impenetra-
ble—as though people rarely came this far. Ana-Elena pulled
me along—it was no longer a pleasant stroll—past gargoyles
perched atop the corners of the mausoleums, or devils fighting to keep their toehold in the middle world.

"Where are you leading me?" I asked, after walking ten minutes or more.

"We are going where I have never been," she answered. She
pointed to a man with a fishnet. "That is St. Peter," she said.
"And over there is St. Francis." She stopped near a large, very
old mausoleum and looked at me. "You know St. Francis, yes?"

I nodded. Her eyes seemed to penetrate mine.

"What religion are you?" She spoke sharply, as if it had suddenly occurred to her I might be a heathen of some sort, or even
a Protestant.

"I'm Catholic. Are you?"

"Of course." She took both my hands, satisfied, then moved
into me, her body softly against mine, her hands holding mine at
my sides.

"Joseph is behind you. And there is the Virgin."

She whispered softly in my ear, so I could barely hear, "Like me."

"What did you say?" I asked.

"Like me. I too am a virgin. You are not, I think. That is as it should be."

I shrugged and pulled her to me. She did not resist. We kissed, lightly at first, then harder, our tongues alive. She broke free and pulled me around the statue of the Virgin to a small plot of green grass where, I guessed, were buried the shirt-tail relation and bastards of Angelo Cerruti, the man whose name was inscribed artfully on the mausoleum. Thick vines formed an enclosure for this plot, guarded on one side by two cherubs on foot-high marble pedestals. At the foot of the plot, a man-sized archangel stood with a raised broadsword. The Virgin herself guarded the head of the plot, her bare feet crushing the serpent-devil.

Ana-Elena knelt before me, unbuckled me and pulled down my jeans. She lay on the grass, her legs slightly apart, her skirt barely covering her white panties. She was breathing heavily.

"Take off your shirt," she said. "I wish to see what kind of man you are."

I removed my shirt, then my shoes and trousers. In the shadow of the virgin, I stood in my underwear.

"Take off." Her eyes were narrow slits. Her breathing was short and quick.

I pulled away my white jockey shorts and let them fall to the ground. I was rigid, unyielding, pitiless. If this is sin, I thought, so be it.

Ana-Elena sighed slightly as she looked. Her hands moved to the buttons of her blouse. She removed it slowly, her lips apart in a half-smile.

I could scarcely breathe.

Valparaiso
August 19-20

Ana-Elena dropped me off near the ship that night shortly after seven. She was nervous about what she would tell her parents but I was no longer earth-bound and couldn't share her concern. I walked through the commotion in the warehouse dazed, boarded the ship, and said a cheery hello to a surprised Mr. Potter, on watch, standing near the door to the house scribbling something in his notebook.

"Good evening, cadet," he nodded my direction. "Surprised to see you aboard."

"Treading the straight and narrow sir," I answered.

"That's a hard path to find in this city," he said. "And harder still to stay on it once you've found it."

I continued into the house, walked to the saloon pantry and ate a sandwich. Then I went to my room, showered and was asleep by nine.

I awoke at six-thirty the next morning, Sunday, humming the Beatles *I Want to Hold your Hand*. Wally hadn't been in the room all night, but I scarcely gave him a second thought. Ana-Elena had shown me Iglesia, the Cathedral near the Plaza Victoria. Her family had belonged to that parish for generations. She said she would go to seven-thirty Mass, expecting her parents to go at eleven, their normal time. She would leave them a note saying she would be spending the day with a friend. In case her parents were with her at early mass, I was to sit just in front of them so she could look at me. If she was alone, I could sit next to her, but I was not to act too familiar since she knew people at the church and if she even looked sideways at a boy, word would get back to her mother.

I showered and put on the jacket I'd worn yesterday and my only tie—a skinny red one with little black dots. I had, for the first time in my life, ironed my wrinkled white shirt and one good pair of khaki trousers the previous evening, humming tunelessly and smiling as I worked. Being parted from Ana-Elena even for a few hours caused my heart to ache. I didn't want to think about sailing away without her. I honestly thought the separation would be unbearable.

Once I was dressed, I left the ship and walked the dozen or so blocks to the Cathedral. It was cavernous and somber, it's towering ceiling supported by massive stone pillars. Bloody reds and royal purples flooded the east stained glass and pressed me spiritually. In spite of the size of the place, I saw her almost immediately. She sat midway toward the altar, on the right. From the vestibule, her red curls looked like ripe fruit on her shoulders. I walked up the aisle, drawn like a fruit fly to apples or iron filings to a magnet, without control or consciousness, unaware of the people sitting next to her. They could have been three generations of her family or a pack of gorillas for all I noticed. I genuflected and knelt beside her. She wore a silky cream blouse and a large-rimmed black hat with a veil that covered her eyes. She looked at me from beneath the hat—apparently in style there as other women wore them—and smiled. She wore no make-up other than bright red lipstick. In the filtered, stained-glass light, her skin was lavender and ruby. With her red hair, she was spectrish and beautiful and completely outside the range of my experience. I wanted to stare but forced my head toward the altar. I mumbled some prayer—a Hail Mary, I think—then sat.

We were early. A priest knelt facing the altar, murmuring a repetitive Spanish litany the congregation answered. The cadence sounded familiar, beginning as it did on a high note, lungs full, getting progressively lower in tone till the air was gone, the response, apparently, complete. I looked around and saw the black rosaries in peoples' hands. When they finished, Ana-Elena nodded toward me with a slight smile and excused herself, crossing in front of me, brushing my legs with hers. She walked over to a side-altar, the Shrine of the Virgin, wearing short heels and a mid-calf gray skirt that clung to her hips and legs. She knelt before the statue of Mary, crossed herself, reached for the long wick and lit three red votives, then knelt there praying, outlined by the flickering candles, hands folded, red curls lying against the black silk blouse.

Eventually, she crossed herself, rose and returned to her seat. The Mass progressed quietly and quickly—as early-morning, low Masses tend to do. No music. Two lonely candles. No homily. The altar boys almost somnambulistic in their atonal Latin—a language I had some knowledge of having served Mass during my early years. The priest raising the host, the server ringing the four-tone chimes—three tones ascending when the priest knelt, three higher tones, also ascending, as he raised the host, three final notes, the second ascending, as he knelt a second time. Just as at St. Jerome's, where I served.

I had little awareness of anything except Ana-Elena. Our bodies touched at different parts—hips or knees or shoulders or ankles. When we stepped out of our pew for communion, the fingers of my left hand brushed her waist and I felt an electric jolt. When I knelt at the communion rail next to her and the server slipped the paten beneath my chin in case the host fell, my heart raced like that of a small bird.

Early morning worshippers tend to be a quiet lot. Few kids, no jostling. When the Mass ended, I moved out of the pew without acknowledging her and walked toward the rear of the church where I stood gazing contemplatively at a window of St. Sebastian, seven or eight arrows stuck in his body. I felt about as uncomfortable as he looked. Ana-Elena exchanged quiet greetings with people she knew, then walked toward me, confident and in control. She stopped next to me as if to adjust her hat, smiled and motioned for me to follow.

I walked a few steps behind her into the vestibule—almost to the outside door—when she suddenly turned hard left and disappeared. I passed the small door at first, then backtracked, saw no one was watching me, so opened the door and slipped through, closing it softly behind me. She was there, on a dark landing, waiting. She took my hand and placed it on her breast, reached up, pushed aside her veil, sighed and kissed me. Then, as if temporarily satisfied, she turned and we descended a narrow stairway to the bottom—a musty, dark room with a doorway leading to light. She led me there, whispering the word "catacombs" under her breath. We passed through several small rooms in which shelves were cut out of the reddish rock foundation.

"We keep our archbishops down here," she said. "Others too." I nodded. Each room had one small bulb that cast a pale glow against the red rock. Bones, sometimes piles of them, lay on burial tables. Ana-Elena led me to a large wooden box, grabbed my hand and placed my fingers on a collection of skulls. I started when I touched the cold smooth bone and tried to pull my hand away, but she held it there and looked at me, her face pale behind the veil of her hat.

"Touch the bones," she whispered. "See how smooth. How smooth we are."

She released my hand, and lifted a skull from the box. She turned it over and over, caressing it, a hint of a smile on her lips.

"This is you or me," she said. "This is when our beauty is gone and life has left us. We are smooth and hollow."

"You think that is us?" I asked.

She looked at me with the same half-smile she'd had when we made love.

"It is what remains. When everything else is passed. What we are doing now is more. Love is fire. It laughs at death. Love dances with life."

"And what about sex?" I asked, running my fingers along the holes in the eyes, eyes that once beheld beauty even as mine now beheld Ana-Elena and filled me with desire for her.

"Without sex, love is brittle and hard—like this old bone."

I said nothing more, thought to myself how happy I was to have left home, to have met this woman, to have stood with her, skull in hand, in these musty catacombs, to have heard her speak of sex and love and old bones. She replaced the skull, looked at me and smiled, took my hand and led me deeper into the honeycomb of rooms.

We came to a room where a life-size statue of two women washing Christ's face stood in the center, as though in storage. His eyes were rolled back in agony. The thorns in his head brought forth drops of blood. A huge wooden cross—it seemed much too big—rested on his shoulder. A soldier prodded Christ with a spear. One of the women held a cloth toward his face. Ana-Elena took my hand and led me around behind the statue. She still had not spoken. When I tried to say something, she silenced me with a soft "shh."

"This is how our world is," she said, looking at the statue. "Men inflict pain; women bring comfort."

She stopped and turned towards me, her back against the back of one of the women—Magdalene the prostitute, I believe—and held out her arms. She flung away her hat and lifted her skirt. I pressed her hard against the statue with my body. She was strong and pressed back, our bodies banging against each other, frustrated because we could not press enough. A burial table next to us was clean except for a few small bones—fingers, I think, or possibly children's bones—that clattered on the floor like existential certainties when I swept them off with my arm. I removed my jacket, lifted Ana-Elena to the table, pulled up her skirt and crawled on top of her. Our lovemaking was like wrestling, except thick with pleasure. Ana-Elena screamed once as she bit my hand and I briefly worried the Bishop of Valparaiso might march in, scepter raised. But no one heard. The place was deserted except for the bones of the Archdiocese elite and perhaps an aroused spirit or two.

After being grilled by her mother for being gone all day Saturday with no reasonable excuse, Ana-Elena was unable to spend Sunday with me. From the cathedral—we left during communion at eleven o'clock mass; Ana-Elena could see her parents in their pew—we drove along O'Higgins, parked and rode up the Ascensor Concepcion to the Café Turri. She led me to the third floor balcony where we ate beef with eggs and drank espresso and tea and watched the clouds gather just outside the

breakwater. We talked about life in America and would she like
to go there and what she would study and what were her goals.
As if we were planning our future. I would finish school in New
York; she had heard of Columbia University; perhaps she could
study there. We would rent an apartment. She wanted to sing
like one of her aunts and liked opera—especially Carmen, a role
she identified with because the woman was Spanish and liked
men. I would work. On and on and on. Two lovers planning
their future. Molding their lives through their dreams.

We said goodbye at the table at noon and I watched her get
into the wooden elevator and watched it descend and she was
gone. I looked back at her chair which had been so filled with
both her body and her spirit moments ago. It now sat empty as
if she had never existed. We were to meet at three-thirty tomorrow, Monday, my last day in Valparaiso. She got out of school at
three and we planned to meet at the *Bote* where we had first
gone for coffee. Lonely as I was without her, I don't think I'd
ever been happier. I sat there another hour, sipping tea, looking
out over the world, glad for the breeze, scribbling short phrases
about Love and Life on a napkin.

Finally, I left and returned to the ship. I had new mail—a letter from my draft board reminding me of my low number and
instructing me to notify them immediately if I lost my deferment. In other words, if I got expelled from school. Almost as if
they expected it. The letter went on to say that, because of the
U.S. involvement in Southeast Asia and the need for fighting
men, I should report directly to some place in Georgia for basic
training should my deferment be somehow lost. Don't bother
with formalities. Go directly to the front. I thanked my lucky
stars I'd met Ana-Elena and was now treading the straight and
narrow. I didn't even want to drink. I'd already dealt with the
issue of leaving her when the ship sailed. Our love was established now and we'd laid out plans. I'd return to school. She
would join me soon. We would correspond.

The mate knocked on my door and asked me to go into
number three lower hold to measure available cubic, then to get
some rest. I worked on my Sea Project and did laundry and
wrote letters to my family. I wrote to Melissa, telling her I was
so sorry things had not worked out between us, but it was prob-

ably for the best and blah blah blah. I even decided I'd give Ana-Elena the earrings I'd bought for Melissa. That evening, I sat on the stern, watched the fishermen return from sea and empty their catches. I finished reading *Crime and Punishment*—where Raskolnikov confesses; where he recognizes his need for companionship and that he loves Sonia, even though—poor son of a bitch—he will not see her for the next seven years since he is sent to a Siberian prison. Later, when she follows him to Siberia and convinces him she is willing to wait for his release, he comes to understand love's power. He finds Redemption through Suffering and the Pure Love of a Good Woman. Cool stuff for a reformed Extraordinary Man like myself. I laughed at Raskolnikov now. I was on top of the world—not in some sleazy, street-level apartment.

I walked on deck after finishing *Crime and Punishment.* The air was cool; the afternoon gangs of longshoremen had knocked off; the evening gangs were not yet aboard. I marched around the deck thinking of Ana-Elena and Raskolnikov, exercising my legs and breathing in the fresh air. Mr. Potter was on watch. He motioned for me to stop.

"Surprised you're not ashore, young man," he said.

"I've made some major changes in my life, sir," I said brightly. He looked at me carefully.

"Well, glad someone has." He turned his head up toward the mate's cargo office. Two women were just leaving, one a very young girl—fourteen or so, I guessed. Her arms were wrapped in gauze and she was crying. The older woman hurried her along the deck toward the gangway.

"That girl's hurt," I said.

"Cut, is my guess," he said.

"By the mate?"

"By the mate's knife. The man is sick."

I slept nine hours that night and dreamt a long dream about Ana-Elena and me living on my grandparent's farm in Nebraska. Ana-Elena became my grandmother, a big-boned, sensuous Bohemian woman who butchered chickens in the morning and polkaed in a fur cape that evening. In the shelter belt along the north side of the house, a dark man could be seen from time to time, moving furtively from tree to tree, a large knife in his hand. It was, alternatively, Paul Hunt or Fletcher. While I realized the danger the man posed to our children, Ana-Elena did not—or at least didn't seem to care about it. She only cared about making love. We had children everywhere into everything, yet all Ana-Elena seemed to think about was having sex. I tried to defend my family, knowing the man would hurt my children if he came near, but Ana-Elena kept distracting me with erotic offers. I hated waking, not so much because of the sex but because I felt I had left people I loved defenseless.

Monday morning I hiked up to the *Bellas Artes Museo* and looked at paintings. They'd been done by contemporary local artists. Most of them were of women. Women dressing, undressing, holding babies, washing clothes. Things women do. I noticed none of them had men—almost as if men didn't exist in this artist's vision of a woman's world.

After that, I sat on a bench in Plaza Sotomayor and ate braised beef I'd bought from a vendor. We were scheduled to sail early Tuesday. Around two-thirty, I walked over to the *Bote* to meet Ana-Elena. The clouds we'd seen massing at sea yesterday had moved in low and stayed. Fog covered the city, making it surreal and mysterious. Yet, to me, everything seemed so beautiful: the deeper greens of the vegetation; the muted colors of the flowers. Deep-throated fog-signals sounded from different, unseen points in the bay.

I passed through customs with scarcely a glance from the official, walked the now-familiar path along Errazuriz Avenue up past Plaza Sotomayor. I was early so diverted and walked through the red-light district, feeling like a reformed drinker. It was siesta time and the streets were nearly deserted. I crossed from the American side of the street with the western motif over to the European side. As I passed by the Flamenco Club, the door opened. An attractive woman walked out, nearly hitting me with the door. She wore blue jeans and a long-sleeved red blouse. Her sandy blond hair was tied back in a ponytail. A child followed her out the door, his hand holding hers. The young boy seemed out of place here. He tugged at her arm while she barked at him in rapid Spanish. She looked at me, her expression one of exasperation. We were no more than ten feet apart.

A man stepped out of the bar—an American with a familiar voice. "Rosa, goddamn it. I said get your ass in here now."

I turned and saw Fletcher, an apple in one hand, the black-handled knife with the four-inch blade I had seen him buy a couple of days earlier in the other. He wore khaki pants, a black pullover and sunglasses. He appeared angry.

I looked back over at the woman. So this was Rosa; renowned for her beauty and sensuality. I had tried to visualize her from time to time, usually while lying in bed on the ship at night, wondering what she looked like, expecting her to be more than a mere woman. Something strange about seeing the famous courtesan—I didn't like calling her whore—in the daylight. Full lips, high cheekbones; an easy, sensuous movement—like a great athlete who knows his worth, but acts like he doesn't know, or care.

Rosa looked at Fletcher and said: "I told you I must take my son to see the Doctor. His stomach is unsettled. Later, I will see you."

"Goddamn it, Rosa. I'm in port for four days. Take him to the doc when I'm gone. I want you with me." Fletcher reached out and roughly grabbed her arm. A protective instinct rose in me as in my dream and I stepped toward them.

"Fletcher. How are you?" I said.

He jerked his head toward me, started, then smiled.

"Well, well, well," he said. "The cadet. Cadet, meet Rosa. Known the world over. Most beautiful, most cold-hearted whore you will ever meet. Even in daylight, when most whores lose the illusion of beauty, Rosa becomes more beautiful than ever. Wouldn't you say? Hey, cadet, why don't you fuck Rosa? Here, I'll even give you the ten bucks she charges."

He pulled a roll of bills from his pocket and peeled off a ten. I backed away, holding my hand palm down.

"Thanks, Fletcher, but I'm in love. I'm on my way now to meet her. She's not a whore—" I looked at Rosa after I said that word. "Sorry ma'am. Didn't mean that. Didn't mean anything by it. I meant, you know, she's not a courtesan. And yes, ma'am, you look great in the daytime. Just great."

Rosa looked at me like I was a kid. With Fletcher's attention distracted, she grabbed her son's arm and ran up the street.

"Fuck her," said Fletcher. "I know where she lives."

His laugh was a metallic echo, an inhuman sound. He turned towards me, his eyes bloodshot. He smelled of beer and smoke.

"So you met a real girl and fell in love." He laughed harder, then stopped abruptly. "Just like a seaman. Think you can get an exclusive on fucking some woman. Then along comes some other hard dick when you're gone—sometimes when you're still around, when you're standing there, for Christ's sake, thinking she's just up the street at the doctor's office—and next thing you know your exclusive has her panties down around her knees and some guy's getting his finger sticky. Like that Texas cowboy in the bar in Houston. Figured he needed a gun to keep his exclusive." He laughed until his eyes rolled back in his head.

"I did the same thing once. With Rosa. Fell in love with her. I think that's my kid she drags around. She's the only whore I care to fuck on this god-forsaken run. Only woman I fuck, period, you want to know the truth."

"The truth?" I asked.

Fletcher smiled. "Always more complicated than it seems. Gave up thinking I owned Rosa. She fucks whomever she wants. No man gets an exclusive on a woman like that. Woman so desirable she can't help but have sex."

He looked at me out of the side of his face. "Hey, kid, you take that acid yet?"

"Not yet. I might later though. Or, I'll just give it back." I hated this guy and I sensed he felt it.

"Maybe I'll see you yet tonight, gadget," he said. "These sea-going love affairs have a tendency to not work out. I'll be lookin' for ya."

He slammed the door.

I hurried up the street to the cafe, late now. As I entered, I saw Alejandra, Ana-Elena's friend, sitting alone, a small espresso cup on the table in front of her. I walked over, confident in spite of my unsettling encounter with Fletcher, thinking my life's love was most likely nearby.

"Hola, senor," she said.

"Hola, Alejandra. How are you?"

"Not so good."

"And why is that? It is a beautiful day today."

"I bring bad news from Ana-Elena. That is why I am sad."

What could it be, I thought. Maybe Ana-Elena was lovesick and bedridden. She wanted to marry me now, today, unable to bear the thought of my leaving Valparaiso. Or, she got caught somehow. Her parents knew something was up and she would meet me later.

"She is not able to come today to meet you," said Alejandra.

"I am very sorry. Why is that? When can I see her?"

"She forgot that she had something important to do."

"Important? More important than—? And what would that be?"

"She has an appointment to get fitted for her wedding dress."

"What did you say?"

"Did she not tell you? She is getting married next month. She and her mama are meeting today with the dressmaker."

"Married? There must be a mistake." Had to be a linguistic miscommunication.

"Who is she marrying?"

"Felipe' Reyes. They have been engaged for a year. His father is a banker. It is their destiny to marry."

"Does—does she love him?" I suddenly felt like I was in the middle of a nightmare with no way out.

Alejandra held out her hand palm down and rotated it. "Not so much, I think. But he is fine. He is of the correct class and from a good family. He is not too fat. He has most of his hair. She must do this."

"But, but I love her and I think she loves me."

Alejandra's eyes widened. "You love her? Ah, that is so wonderful, of course, but also most unfortunate. Here in Chile, when our parents are of a certain social class, we must marry who we are told to marry. We do not choose our partner. We do not marry for love. We marry for other reasons. For love, and all those other things that make life worthwhile, we must look outside the marriage. Marriage is for children and family. It is, how do you say, an illusion that couples find happiness in marriage.

Most Chileans no longer even expect it. We find love and pleasure some other place."

I was numb. How would I live?

"Ana-Elena thinks you are a handsome boy. She said your legs are quite shapely," she smiled and glanced down. "She was especially happy to meet you because you do not live here, so you will not be here to cause trouble. Plus, she thinks maybe she will see you when she goes to visit America without her husband. Then you can once again play your bedroom games together." She smiled.

"Cause trouble?"

Alejandra sighed. "We have great difficulty with local men because they think when there is sex with a beautiful woman who is not a *puta,* that it means love. The men get drunk and remember their lover's body and how this was and how that was, and next thing, they are standing outside your window at night with their little guitars and someone must frighten them away or shoot them. It can get very, how do you say, messy. Divorce is not permitted here, so many marriages are annulled when there is trouble. There are financial issues, and questions of honor.

"With you, though, it is no problem. Your ship will sail away and you will be gone. She asked me to tell you she has very much enjoyed herself with you and, furthermore, is grateful for being so gentle her first time." Alejandra glanced up and smiled sweetly, almost a flirt. "She hopes you will return."

I was stunned into silence. We had shared too much to not share more. This could not be happening.

"I can't believe it. I—I thought we were in love."

Alejandra laughed, but politely, as if to not hurt my feelings.

"That is how you men always are and, sometimes, we women too. We are flattered that you choose to fall in love with us, but really, we only wish to be your friend and roll around on the bed with you, then return to our husbands and our homes and our children. Then, in another week or two, to once again enjoy your masculine company. That is called an affair. It is very common. Just, one must not look for more than is there. Unfortunately, we are permitted only one husband."

She dug into her purse as I stood there, speechless.

"Here. Ana-Elena asked me to give you this."

Alejandra handed me a picture. It was of Ana-Elena kneeling, a shaft of light shining on her. Her eyes were closed, her hands folded against her breast. Her face was uplifted as if in prayer. She wore a white sweater and looked angelic in her expression, as if a pure soul emanated from a body that was somehow separate.

"She is so very beautiful." I said softly, my heart falling apart. "Can you wait a moment while I write her a note?"

I honestly didn't know if I could continue living.

I sat in a chair by a window and looked out for a few minutes, the tears rolling down my cheeks. I didn't care what Alejandra thought. Finally, I wrote:

Dearest Ana-Elena,

Alejandra just told me that you are to pick out your wedding dress today. After our two days of happiness, the news that you are marrying another man comes to me like a blow. I do not know what to think or what to believe. I do not know what to say. I would not have believed, did not think it possible to experience such intense pleasure, then say goodbye. You have become a part of me and now I do not know what to do without that part.

I didn't sign it, didn't even end it. I wanted to use the words commitment and love, to tell her how I didn't understand, but I was disoriented.

I wrote my home address on the bottom of the note, folded it, wrote the name Ana-Elena across the front and handed it to Alejandra. Without another word, I walked out of the coffee shop.

Valparaiso to Callao
August 21-22

I walked out of the Valparaiso Eterno Cafe stunned, feeling alone and dejected as a scolded orphan. I crossed Sotomayor Plaza, with people sitting, eating, talking, laughing, onto Cochrane, heading more or less toward the port. The world seemed different now. I had a debilitating sense of loss and couldn't grasp the fact that no one around me shared my suffering or even seemed aware of it. Indians pulled their carts of vegetables and carvings; locals of European descent, dressed in woolen suits, stood at bus stops reading their newspapers; cars moved through the intersection, honking at pedestrians. I felt abandoned and betrayed. I felt like a damned fool.

I don't know how long I walked, but the sun was already low in the west when I shuffled by the Bote Salvavidas Café. I saw Wally and Don Campbell through the lattice on the terrace overlooking the harbor. They sat leaning toward each other, engaged in serious talk, a bottle of wine and two glasses between them. Wally saw me, made a fist, turned it palm toward his face and raised his middle finger, smiling his crooked, freckled smile. I laughed in spite of my misery and walked in.

"Hola! My friend," said Wally, sounding the H. "Come regale us with an adventure of love."

"Give me wine," I said. "Of love at this moment I cannot

speak."

"So bad, he's spouting poetry," chirped Wally. "Well, my son, my son. First of all, I told you not to fall in love. Second, you'll get over her before you grow up. Third, have a glass of Valpo's finest. Priced special for cadets."

Don spoke, "a taste and I'm gone. We set sea watches at midnight." He lifted his glass, swirled the wine in it and drank.

"Whew," he said, his glass half-full when he set it down. "That is one rough drink."

He rose, bowing. "Live and love as though you die at dawn."

"See you," I said.

Don left.

"So, tell me," said Wally.

"Some other time. Hurts too much right now."

Wally drank, then poured more. The waiter came. We ordered beef. Wally's fingers drummed on the tabletop to the beat of the guitarist.

"Hey, thanks for taking care of me the other night," he said. "I remember waking up screaming and you putting a cold washcloth on my face. I s'pose I was a pain in the ass."

"You were a lot of trouble. Yes."

"It was a pretty weird experience. I doubt I'll do it again. On the other hand, I kind of dealt with the issue of my old man. Rotten bastard that he is, I came to realize he didn't exactly leave home because of me—which is what I'd thought before. That I was going to cost too much and be too much trouble. He and my mom appeared in and out of my dreams last night, except it was more than just a dream. It was like they were there. They told me some things—like about him loving me so much and being so scared he'd do what his dad did which was beat up on his kids, so he left. I told him I'd've given anything to have him around. He said he used to come by and watch me go to school, but was too embarrassed to say hello. Now, he wishes he could have a chance and that in spite of everything, he thinks he probably made the right decision; says at least he never beat me up. I told him maybe its not too late. And anyway, that I kind of understand now. It was like a whole world in there. Kind of a tough world, but I guess there were things I needed to hear. I

feel, I don't know, calmer now. You gonna do it tonight?"
"I'm thinking about it. You available to act as my keeper? After watching you, I don't want to go through it alone."
"I'm here, man. I will not abandon you. Let me say that again, I will not leave you alone. Got it, I am with you, man."
The way he said it exactly three times, I had my doubts.

We talked and ate and drank wine, listening all the time to the guitarist pluck his soulful flamenco. When the meal was over, I put my fingers into my jacket pocket for a toothpick, a habit I'd picked up from my father, who I'd been thinking about ever since Wally had talked about his old man. I found instead the folded tissue with the remaining wafer of LSD. I unfolded it, smiled, held it up so Wally could see, set it on my tongue and let it dissolve as we paid and walked out.

As we walked out, I got to thinking about dads. Ignored Wally, ignored the traffic. Tried to ignore my feelings about Ana-Elena, but that wasn't so easy. Decided our culture needs tweaking with regards to dads. Maybe with regard to men in general. Decided the soldiers returning from the Great War couldn't deal with the loss of camaraderie and sense of purpose and danger and adventure and, let's face it, intimacy with other men. Nursing each other, for Christ's sake, like I did Wally last night. Picking lice out of each other's hair; emptying each other's bed pan; dealing with fear of death and fear of life; I don't know what all they did. Returning to their women who wanted a man to give them their babies was fun for a while but it wasn't war, and they got tired of burping the kid and pushing a lawnmower.

The air was brisk now, and, for me, charged with excitement. I sensed danger but recalled Wally had warned me the drug might make me a little paranoid. Streetlights flickered menacingly as evening settled. I grew more and more angry about how Ana-Elena had used me and charged on ahead of Wally, crossing traffic on Errazuriz, until Wally yelled and stopped me.

"Hey, for Christ's sake, slow down. You're walking like a drunk red neck looking for his pick-up truck."

I stopped and waited. We walked up Valdivia to the Mercado Puerto, the area that included La Maritima. Groups of men walked back and forth between the bars, peeing in the alleys, shouting or singing. Muffled red lights glowed from lamps near the doorways. Salsa music spilled out into the street and people danced in the doorways, in the street, in the alleys, their shadows all rhythmic, but maniacal. Beautiful women erotically dressed languished outside the bars, laughing and talking and shouting crude remarks to Wally and me as we walked by. The phrase "responsible adults" played over and over in my mind like a stuck record and I asked myself what that meant and did otherwise responsible adults do things like this when they got the chance, then revert to being responsible later—or what? Another thing, if otherwise responsible adults did this, what did they do when they had a gun in their hands and license to shoot?

We crossed over from the European side of the street to the Wild West side and ducked into the Bitter End. There had been times before when I liked being on my own, but not tonight. Tonight I needed Wally's company. Needed his support. I was depressed about Ana-Elena to the point I wanted to cry. Wally kept doing funny things—even though I don't think he meant to do anything more than shepherd me into a bar—but I couldn't stop laughing at him.

We kicked out a couple bar stools at one of the small sidebars, sat on them, and ordered beers. We talked about lost love and broken hearts. Wally told me about a high school princess named Jenny who had promised him everything, then left him for a big-bellied tackle from West Newton. I laughed like crazy. Wally became angry when I laughed too hard and threatened to walk away—acid or no acid. That initially struck me as hilarious and I laughed even more. Then I got really pouty at the thought of him abandoning me and told him to "get the fuck away from me, I knew you wouldn't stick by me. You're just like your old man. Leave when things get tough. Thanks for nothing, you asshole."

So he walked away, flipping me the finger over his shoulder and I was alone. I shook my head a couple times, then sat pouring beer on the mahogany bar and watching the rivulets run races down toward a herd of blond Norwegians who had crowded in to the small bar, filling the place with their smoke, cursing, singing stupid songs like Northern European sailors do—always in a group; one for all and all for one; ready to fight, and not caring whether it's with each other or someone else. They acted like quarrelsome hogs: farting, making guttural sounds, drinking round after round. At some point, I got pissed and said something—I don't recall what. A couple of them walked over, picked me up, carried me to the door and tossed me into the street like I was a bag of laundry, then followed me out and kicked me a couple of times. I was fixing to go back in and take on the whole bunch when a hand grabbed my shoulder and jerked me up. That really pissed me off until I realized it was Fletcher. Next thing I knew I was in a different bar—one across the street on the European side—with him buying shots, and introducing me to Rosa.

Rosa walked out of a cloud of smoke through a bead curtain wearing a short black dress with spaghetti straps. Even with my brain scrambled, all I could think was how beautiful she was. Her figure was perfect: a narrow waist, pushed-up breasts, a flat stomach. Her sandy-blond hair was up off her neck, with strands falling about her face. She passed her tongue across her bottom lip, painted a whorish red, looked at me, recognized me from the afternoon and smiled. I didn't react immediately. In my drugged state, I was caught by something else about her, some quality I couldn't put my finger on. Something internal and sensual that I had never before seen in a woman; that I could perceive now only because of the drug. I couldn't stop staring at her. In the dim light of the candles burning at each table, she looked the quintessential seductress. This is a woman, I thought. Forget that whore Ana-Elena.

"Go ahead," said Fletcher. "Ask her to dance. If she'll have you, I'll pay."

I walked over, struggling to stay upright and coherent.

"Dance?" I guess I said.

She looked me up and down and nodded slightly and stood. I felt almost powerless.

We danced. She nibbled at my neck, put her hand into the small of my back and pressed me to her. Next I knew, we were upstairs in a bedroom. Fletcher was there and it was very weird. A record was going round and round on a turntable and Jimmy Hendrix or someone played an unfettered guitar. Rosa moved to the music, her eyes closed. She slipped one spaghetti strap off her shoulder, then the other. She shook free of her dress revealing lacy black undergarments and seemed mesmerized by the music and oblivious to us as she unsnapped first one stocking then the other, rolled them down each leg, tossing them. Watching her, I was struck by the power a woman had over a man, and wondered if all women, ordinary housewives say or shop-girls, understood this and used their power when it suited them, or if most women either failed to comprehend this or feared its use the way some men reject the use of authority, preferring others tell them what to do and where to go.

"You love this, don't you, you bitch," Fletcher said. Rosa smiled and nodded, her eyes glazed over.

Then Fletcher undressed and I figured, well, what the hell, so I undressed and we were all naked and the words responsible adults swirled in my muddled brain clockwise like a southern hemisphere drain, and all I could think about was people from my home town wouldn't act like this and for sure not my father, even if he was a drunk and couldn't hold a job and double for sure not father Henry even if he hadn't been ordained. But then the worm of a thought munched its way into my brain that maybe they would act like this; that maybe responsible adults didn't always sit just so, stir their coffee just so, smile and cross their legs just so. Maybe it meant a whole range of things and maybe the fact that I was here with two other people didn't really signify anything other than this is how otherwise responsible adults might behave in certain situations given half a chance.

Fletcher acted like a jealous husband, but also like he wanted to watch us fuck. He obsessed over everything Rosa did. He commented on her underwear and couldn't keep his hands off her butt. Seeing Rosa naked transfixed me. Even with Fletcher there, I felt paralyzed by her beauty and sensuality. The eroticism she brought to the room by unsnapping a garter, bending to remove a heel, or shaking her hair free made my legs wobbly. We had sex, but at the time, it was a lascivious blur I had difficulty making sense of. What I remember is Fletcher, either drunk or on acid himself, walking around and around the bed looking from every angle, singing and dancing with his eyes closed, cigarette in his mouth, hard-on like a cigar and me grossed out and really pissed but fucking Rosa nevertheless, hard and slow, her meeting my thrusts with power, the pleasure like heated syrup, like something surreal, more than any man deserved, building slowly, her fingers doing something, the pleasure building, mounting to a Himalaya of pleasure when I saw the gun, like the gun I'd seen in the bar in Houston; a big, black pistol with a barrel and a trigger and I got scared and cried and wanted to pray and thought I should pray, but couldn't remember any prayers.

I remember screaming with the most intense orgasm of my life the same time the gun flashed and Rosa and I both crumpled forward, but then I remember nothing till I found myself on the street, on my hands and knees, puking. Wally was there, drunk, I suppose, on his knees in the street, bawling about having betrayed my trust, something about his old man, as he wiped my mouth and cradled my head in his lap; everything spinning. Next I know, he's holding me up and we're wobbling toward the ship. The hour seemed very late and everything so different than before. No one was having fun now. People slunk like wraiths and slithered like serpents in the shadows of the fires burning in barrels beside the track and beat-up men sat warming themselves. The old wheezy locomotive puffed past us with its car full of bums who, one by one, jumped down and ran toward us looking like aliens, ran past us and disappeared into the shadows by the fires. One, an old woman, saw us, pointed a gnarled finger and cackled. We passed by the sleeping customs officials and next thing I knew I was walking up the gangway, telling Wally how Rosa had been shot by that fucking Fletcher and that my orgasm was the shot that killed her but Fletcher had pulled the trigger and now I had to kill Fletcher and that I loved Rosa, I loved how her legs looked when she slipped out of her black dress and I loved her lips and that she was not just the most beautiful woman in the world, she was the ALL-TIME most beautiful woman in the world; more beautiful than that cunt Ana-Elena or that other cunt Melissa or this cunt or that cunt and I remember Wally saying something like "if you say that one more time, I'm gonna kick you in the balls" so I quit saying it and apologized like a penitent, wanted to kneel but we were almost to the top of the gangway and it must have been after four a.m. because Mr. Potter stood there on the platform with his arms crossed, looking, as always, like a goddamned Presbyterian minister and it made me think I had to go to confession because I'd killed a whore so I went on and on about needing to confess even though I knew I couldn't since I'd told the priest he was no longer my shepherd and somehow that meant I no longer had the right and Wally pushed me away from Mr. Potter, trying to get me to move down the deck out of earshot into our room. He kept saying, "Yes, for Christ's sake, you can go to confession. In the morning, you can go to confession. Now you gotta go to bed."

Next thing I knew I was standing in the shower with Wally trying to get me to undress. I was so fucking sad about everything. My dad, my mom, my uncles and brothers and sisters striving to live their lives, to get ahead a little, to develop some part of themselves that might earn them a living or provide some little satisfaction; my dad in particular seemed like he'd never really developed anything except his ability to drink whiskey and be everyone's pal, and suddenly I understood why he'd kicked me out. Because all he had left was mom and our family and a fragile position in a tiny community he'd never had the courage to leave and here was me, a young buck with my own ideas, threatening that position, fragile as it was, embarrassing him, making it so he couldn't hold his head up when he walked into Big Al's, slammed a buck on the bar and ordered a Bud. The whole Goddamned world seemed so pitiful. I tried to explain what had happened, but I guess I was hollering because Wally told me to quit making so much noise or the mate would come over and we'd get reported to the Academy.

I got scared about that because of the letter I'd received earlier from my draft board so I quit talking and started crying because it was clear as day to me if I ever got kicked off the ship and out of school, I'd be dead like the captain's son, like the British sailor in the Houston dive, like the bones in the cathedral basement. No more loving women, no adventure, no family. Couldn't stop crying. Felt so bad about having killed Rosa and about Ana-Elena and Melissa and women in general and whores in particular. Then all women were whores—female bodies with little holes for men's cocks and then they were on-a-pedestal untouchable perfect saints, and back and forth and I kept looking for some category in between because I was sure there was one but couldn't find what I was looking for and finally I started yelling at Wally about how it was sad that men just wanted to fuck women and nothing else and I kept telling Wally, "no matter what you learn from this, remember that women are more than just whores. They're REAL PEOPLE." I kept saying that over and over as if it was news. "REAL PEOPLE. REAL PEOPLE. REAL PEOPLE."

Wally again told me to shut up, that he knew women were real people because of how he'd grown up so close to his Mom and he was glad I finally understood that. That pissed me off, because it was suddenly as clear as day that I had known this all along, and that no one knew it as well as I did and I never really wanted to fuck all these whores anyway, just talk to them, but they thought I wanted to fuck them, kept insisting I fuck them, especially that whore Ana-Elena who wanted me to fuck her over and over again like I was some sort of machine, then dumped me like I was the whore, like I was just a hard dick she could jump on and ride, that I had no fucking humanity.

I don't know when all this ended but at some point the demons departed and I slept. Then it was three-thirty in the afternoon and I was called to stand the 4 to 8 watch. I lay there, sleepy, feeling the ship move and realized we were at sea with Valparaiso behind us, a shimmering dream-world with Ana-Elena, with Rosa, with the Bote, and the cemetery and the catacombs and the Wild West bars. And like a dream, all of it now seemed so illusory, the romance of illusions and the illusion of romance.

I got up and peed and a burning pain sent a shudder of fear through my body.

Valparaiso to Callao
August 23-24

The mate stood outside his office, his hands on his hips, looking at the ship's plans on the bulkhead as I stepped out from my room to go up to the bridge. Still influenced by the LSD, I watched him for a time, mesmerized by his motions. He shifted his weight from one foot to another, passing his hand across the glass case that displayed the architectural drawing of the ship's cargo holds as if the movement of his hand would help him locate some hold dimension or ballast tank or whatever it was he was looking for. Instead of seeing his hand move smoothly from one side to another, I saw a series of hands, maybe eight or ten across the three-foot width of the drawing, each stopped in time, like special effects photography, moving first in one direction and then back the other way. Finally, sensing me behind him, he turned and said: "Well, cadet, I have no doubt you committed your share of sins in Valparaiso. I'll put you on Potter's watch so you get the chance to atone for them before we get home."

I smiled and bobbed as if to say, ha ha, good joke, mate, but in my heart I knew what he said was true. My left arm hurt. I had two big purple spots on the right side of my rib cage from the pounding I'd taken at the hands and feet of the Norwegians and I'd skinned both knees and wrists when they'd thrown me out of the bar.

I'd avoided the mate since seeing the young girl exit his cargo office with her arms bandaged. Couldn't really stand the thought of what had happened there, and wanted to avoid the sick bastard. The smart-ass in me wanted to ask him how he planned to atone for his sins but I refrained. This was no time to be throwing stones.

Standing at the windows in the forward part of the wheelhouse, I looked out at the ocean, trying to attend to my duties, but consumed by what was happening inside me. I used the head on the bridge twice to pee. Both times, I started out hopeful, thinking perhaps the pain was not so sharp, that it might actually be going away. Both times that hope was dashed as the burning came on. The second time it was like peeing jalapenos, as though the bacteria were growing and multiplying like yeast. I had a dose of clap and that was that.

Mr. Potter told me to stand a good lookout since there were fishing boats off the coast of Chile and he had work in the chartroom. He said I could tend to navigation and log-keeping later. I had planned to become a consistent three-star fix navigator on the way north. The way I felt now, though, scared and unsure, I figured I'd be lucky to get two stars.

The quartermaster slumped at the wheel, his eyes open but glazed over. From what I could tell, looking down on deck at the boatswain and deck gang dropping loads of rubbish and scraps of dunnage over the side, half the crew was in a stupor.

Fletcher ran the cargo winch at three forward. I watched as he gently dropped the boom into its cradle, released the weight from the falls, then slacked the falls a bit more so a roll of the ship didn't tighten the wires and jerk the boom. A disturbing memory like a really evil spirit tapped at the windows of my consciousness. More troubling even than the certainty of my dose of clap. Feeling the weight of my eyes on him, Fletcher looked up and I remembered those eyes in Rosa's room. I had been there and I knew he had been there too. I couldn't get the memory to come clear, but I had a feeling like a slam to the stomach that something truly bad had happened.

After my watch, I sneaked into the purser's office, looked

through his bookshelf and borrowed his copy of *Ship's Medicine*. I had seen it before at school, in a class called *Sea Year Orientation*. Commander Jankowsky, the instructor, used the pictures of diseased penises from this text in the hope of frightening us into sexual abstinence. I read: *The ordinary symptoms in the male include sudden onset of pain or burning on urination, urgent and frequent urination, and the presence of a white or yellow discharge from the urethra.*

When I showered that night, my shorts had a yellow, pussey discharge. The book said: *In the absence of antibiotics, patient should consume large quantities of water and fruit juices.* I was fairly certain Mr. LeClair had antibiotics in the ship's hospital, but I was afraid to say anything, afraid to admit something this bad had happened to a fresh-faced farm kid like me. Instead, I drank water like a racehorse, peed like an old cow and prayed like the old ladies in the back of the church. For a Catholic, this wasn't just pain; it was punishment, possibly catharsis, but for sure punishment. I drank water by the quart all right, but in my heart I knew all the water in the world wasn't going to wash away what I had. I'd had my fun and I'd sinned getting it. Now there were consequences. Now I had to suffer.

I tossed and turned that entire night; felt like Jacob wrestling the archangel, thinking back over the voyage, what I'd done, hadn't done, who I'd been rude to, opportunities to help someone I passed up. In the morning, the boatswain set me to work with Irving Jackson. I broached the subject with him.

"Irving, you ever have gonorrhea?" We were in the forward part of the forepeak, where the boatswain had his workbench and vise, rigging to throw an eye into a piece of five-eighths inch wire-rope. The water contacting the bow just outside the skin of the ship, even in this nice weather, hummed and gurgled and echoed off the angular metal around us and we had to raise our voices.

"You mean clap?" He measured the two fathom of wire rope he needed for the eye while I screwed a pin into the shackle that would support the bight.

"Yeah. Clap." I tried to sound casual. "I, uh, I need to write something about common diseases at sea for my sea project. Thought I'd write about clap."

"Mmhmm. Das a common one, all right."

He stoked his pipe and cast a suspicious and phlegm-filled eye toward me as he tightened down on the vise clamping the running part to the standing part of the wire rope.

"Sea projeck, huh? Well, you should ask shifty-eyed Fletcher back there, cause he got hisself a real live dose o' it right now, and he could give you the straight dope. Me, I mos' gen'ly kept my pecker in my pants and never had it but three four time and that so long ago, I scarce recall."

"Fletcher has the clap right now?"

"Thas right. Ol' Mr. Cool what never looks square at a man when he talks to him, got hisself a good dose."

Irving hammered an eighteen-inch spike into the top lay of the wire, then moved it back and forth to gain penetration while I sprayed a light lubricant on his work.

"Is he being treated for it?"

"I spec so. Mos' likely won' go 'way itse'f. Some o' dese strains dey got down here don' pay no mind to treatment no more. Jis' eat up dat penercillern and spit it out."

He thrust one of the moused ends of wire into the hole made by the spike, expectorated a tobacco-stained wad into the coffee-can the boatswain made him carry around for just that purpose, then beat the wire till it was flat.

"What if the penicillin doesn't work?"

Irving Jackson's eyes widened and he cocked his head to let me know that was a mighty serious matter.

"Well, they us'ta shove a hot poker up yer thing there and burn the bug out. That worked I guess cept lotsa guys died from the pain. Plus, I ollays figured if it didn't work, I'd tell 'em it did so they wouldn't try it agin."

He took the pipe out of his mouth and scrunched in more tobacco from a small leather pouch he carried on his belt.

"Or, if'n it was a young-un like yourself got a dose, sometimes the cap'n would have him lay his thing on the table like a worm and he'd pound on it a few times with a wood mallet. Never cured nuthin' that way, but it shore gave that boy sumpin' to think about nex' time he contemplate pullin' ol' George out fo' some ho'."

My knees almost buckled at the thought and I felt sweat

running down my face as I watched Irving beat the spliced piece of wire rope into place.

"Yassir," said Irving, passing the spike between the next two strands of wire and twisting it back and forth. "Man ketch a dose today, he better get some good treatment real quick and hope it work, cuz if'n it don', he be in a heap o' trouble."

After lunch, I went to the purser's office and 'fessed up. George LeClair led me directly to the ship's hospital. I sat on the examination bed while George rummaged through the cabinets.

"We've run into real problems treating some of these South American strains," he said.

Now that he engaged in regular sexual activity, he had a new-found compassion for people who came to him with clap.

"Seems like penicillin just won't cure it all the time like it used to. And we don't carry the new wonder drugs. Not allergic to penicillin, I hope?"

"No, sir," I mumbled, numb with fear.

"We'll begin with an oral penicillin program. That cured me. Course, I started the second I felt a burning sensation. If that doesn't work, we'll give you an injection."

He reached into his medical locker and took down a bottle labeled Penicillin G Procaine. He removed the blue twist-off cap and filled a brown glass bottle with enough capsules for eight days, stuck on a label and wrote on it. As he did this, thoughts rose in my mind like gas bubbles, spreading their poison. Would I ever date again? What would my mother say? Would I marry, have a family, father children? Or would I wander the earth with the letters VD branded on my forehead? Must be asylums. Someplace for incurable cases to tell each other their broken dreams.

I took the purser's advice and drank water by the quart, but still found myself holding off till my bladder ached because peeing hurt so much. The yellowish pus seeped like glue from a tube with the cap off. It pasted the head of my penis to my shorts and I either used hot water to separate the cotton from my skin or ripped it away like a band-aid.

George handed over the brown bottle with pills.

"There's another case on the ship I'm treating the same way

276   Joseph Jablonski

with these pills. We'll see what happens."

"That's Fletcher, right."

"It's supposed to be confidential, but, yes, it is Fletcher."

"Rosa was the only whore in Valparaiso I had sex with. Fletcher paid for my time with her. Just gave me ten bucks and told me to use it on Rosa. Fletcher says Rosa is the only woman he ever has sex with. He even . . ." The memory returned like a sledge to the side of the head. I suddenly had a strong, clear image of Fletcher with a gun, going round and round the bed as Rosa and I made love. I remembered a loud report like a gunshot and then weeping uncontrollably at the thought that Rosa had been killed. My legs buckled and I sat back down.

"You all right?" said George.

"Yeah, fine," I said, but I wasn't fine at all.

"I've seen doses of clap show the morning after a one-night stand, so it could be Rosa. Most likely, though, this dose comes from someone you were with earlier in the trip," said George LeClair. "Maybe as far back as the Trockadero. You can't be sure since you've had several sexual partners."

I took the bottle, deciding not to tell him anything about the night with Rosa. I had to sort that out for myself. I considered what he'd said about whom I'd caught the clap from. If I caught it in the Trockadero, that meant I'd given it to Ana-Elena. To me, the more logical idea was Rosa had the dose and passed it on to me and Fletcher. Maybe the Doctor's visit the afternoon we met was for her, not her son. Still, I knew I'd have to write Ana-Elena. My heart ached at the thought I might have infected her even though I couldn't help suspecting cadet-hating Fletcher knew Rosa had gonorrhea when he conned me into going with her—not that I needed much conning.

"Take the first two pills right away," George said. "And no alcohol while you're on this stuff. The thing about gonorrhea and penicillin is, if it works, the symptoms will be gone by morning."

"God, I hope it works."

"No masturbation now. We don't want that area anymore disturbed than it already is." George looked stern.

"Yes sir." I said, thinking he really didn't have to add that on.

That night, I prayed as I had the night my cousin Larry had his accident. I'd had a job the summer of my junior year terracing hillsides for Nebraska Reclamation. Larry, who was a year older, relieved me one day when I had to drive to Omaha for my Navy Physical. My dad and I got home around five that afternoon and I called to see how he'd done and make sure the little John Deere was more or less where I'd left it. Larry wasn't back yet so I drove out. Found him sitting in the dirt behind the tractor staring at his chewed up right hand, turning it over, holding up the left, comparing the two. The endless belt of the tractor, empty now that all the dirt and fingers had been carried away, was flying. I walked over and shut down the tractor, then climbed uphill to where the belt tossed the dirt and dug around till I found the three severed digits, surprised by how small they were. I cleaned them carefully and wrapped them in my handkerchief, then stepped down, put my arms under Larry's shoulders and helped him stand. He didn't cry, didn't pass out, just walked with me to the car, silent. I opened the door for him and he got in. I walked around, got in the driver's side and drove a hundred miles an hour over gravel in to Good Sam. Larry kept his eyes closed the whole way in, didn't make a sound. I pulled my car right up onto the lawn in front of the hospital, crying so hard I could barely see. Felt like it was my fault; that if I hadn't gone to Omaha, Larry would have used his scholarship at the University and pitched, then gone on to the majors. Nobody had a fastball like Larry. I mean nobody. I'd delivered the fingers like they were hosts on a paten, hoping somehow they could be sewed back on. In the hospital chapel, I knelt in the rear pew with my head bowed for an hour, pleading for a miracle. Promised to become a priest if only Larry would get his pitching hand back, which, incidentally, he did. Some of his smoke was gone but he replaced it with a mean stubby finger slider. I, on the other hand, never did pursue the priesthood.

The idea that I was involved with the death of a whore—let's say death of a woman, a woman with a son—was gradually forming. I was afraid to delve too deeply into it. I knew God wouldn't buy the idea of me joining the priesthood after I'd reneged on my promise the first time. To say nothing of all the stuff I'd done in the past couple months. Most likely, wouldn't even want me. This time I told him I just hoped to be a better person—to love people more, to quit lying—especially to myself, to help where I could and not be unkind. And that I was really sorry for whatever had happened.

A new symptom had crept into the disease that prevented me from giving God my full attention. My penis now maintained a permanent half hard-on. The painful process of peeing was drawn out and hurt even more. I couldn't sleep on my stomach because of it, and I believed, in my deepening misery, that it prevented me from sleeping at all. I longed for the release of sleep.

I thought of my childhood and my first tiny male stirrings. My mother explained they were "just little temptations sent by the devil to make you want to touch your penis." Well I'd touched it and more. Now, like a terrified sailor with a devil on his back, I tacked into my religion and anchored there like it was a port in a storm. My ideas of Raskolnikov and how certain men rise above society's rules fled in the face of my dripping penis. I was scared. In bed, I tossed and turned, constantly prevented from repositioning myself on my stomach. When I did sleep, I was haunted by dreams of remorse and punishment, of Sister Mary Angelica, my eighth-grade teacher, tall and stern in black habit and white wimple, circling around me with her wooden pointer, somber as a judge, trying to "whack your pee-pee, you bad bad boy." The effects of the LSD apparently crossed layers of consciousness since even in my dream, Sister Angelica's movements did not flow smoothly; they had a moment by moment motion that broke down my defenses.

At breakfast in the morning, Mr. LeClair reported Fletcher was cured. My penis hurt worse than ever and the idea I'd been involved in a murder settled onto my shoulders like a stone.

Callao, Peru
August 25

I tried to involve myself with the workings of the ship, hoping to take my thoughts away from my trouble. No one but the purser had heard about my dose of clap, but I knew it was only a matter of time before word got around. Mr. Potter took a grandfatherly attitude toward me our first watch out of Valparaiso and gave me additional navigational tasks. I could only assume it was because—far as he knew—I had survived that sinful city intact.

"I know you had some rough moments, cadet, but I'm proud of you," he said. "For how you comported yourself in that terrible city. I've seen young men lose themselves in Valparaiso."

Well, guess what, I thought, nodding and turning away. He had me do a Sailing for this leg of the voyage. That meant finding the shortest route from Valparaiso to Callao and laying down the courses on the charts. Because there was so little longitudinal difference between the two ports, a Great Circle shaved less than a mile off a Mercator Sailing. We settled on the Mercator, which meant I could draw one course line from our point of departure to our point of arrival. We sailed from south latitude thirty-three degrees, east longitude seventy-one degrees forty minutes, (33°-00'S, 71°-40'E) north northwest across the

Tropic of Capricorn to south latitude twelve degrees, east longitude seventy-seven degrees (12°-00'S, 77°-00'E). Thirteen hundred miles all told; every one of them to be painful.

The first night out, I worked hard to achieve my goal of getting an accurate three or four-star fix. The weather was perfect: clear skies, pencil-line horizon. Mr. Potter, my new best friend, was determined I graduate from the two-star level I seemed stuck in.

"You'll have a nice long twilight, being this far from the equator," he said. "The short twilights near the equator have been one of your problems. Just not enough time to get more than two stars, considering your experience level and that primitive sextant they send you out with."

I prepared meticulously that evening: figured time of sunset, checked and rechecked that since I'd made mistakes in the past; then calculated the First Point of Aries and the proper Greenwich Hour Angle (GHA) for my latitude and time. With that information, I went into H.O. 249—even though we were expected to use H.O. 214, an older set of tables. H.O. 214 made getting more than a two-star fix much more difficult since H.O. 214 didn't present seven ideal stars as did H.O. 249 and required additional calculations. I found my page of stars, drew a picture of the ship on a piece of paper, bow north northwest and made a little diagram showing the seven selected stars, their rough altitudes and azimuths for my Latitude and GHA. I had Crux, Sirius, Canopus and Rigel Kentaurus as first magnitude stars; Achernar, Suhail and Aldebaran as second-magnitude stars. I had never yet shot a second-magnitude star and was, frankly, intimidated by how small and dim they appeared in my scope. Crux, appropriately enough, was in the Southern Cross, the constellation Whittier referred to as *the Cross of Pardon*. Perhaps equally appropriate was that Ptolemy and the ancient Greeks considered it part of the hind feet of the constellation Centaur, the half-man, half-horse known for its powerful sexual appetite.

Having four first magnitude stars was good luck though. I truly believed I had a chance of getting a four-star fix tonight.

I started looking for Sirius, the brightest star in the heavens, before Mr. Potter. With the 4-power scope on his shiny black and chrome German Plaith sextant, he could wait a few minutes longer, until the second magnitude stars were out. He liked shooting all seven stars within a four or five minute period because it made plotting adjustments for time that much simpler.

I found Sirius almost right away, counted fourteen seconds as I returned to the chartroom, subtracted those seconds from the lower chronometer, and wrote that time and the latitude in my navigation notebook. I then set my sextant's altitude for Canopus and returned to the bridge wing. Mr. Potter had his sextant out and was standing on the bridge wing looking up. He lifted the sextant to his eye, found the star, made a minor altitude adjustment with the micron wheel, punched a stopwatch, and walked into the chartroom. Seconds later, he was back on the wing.

I looked hard for Canopus, found a star where it should be, brought it to the horizon, then noticed another star, reddish, slightly brighter but not as sparkly, nearby. That turned out to be a planet but I made the mistake of measuring it rather than Canopus. I then got Rigel and tried to get Crux, but got confused with Acrux so nearby and by that time the horizon was blurred and I had two stars and, unknown to me until I did the calculations, Mars instead of Canopus. I solved for that planet— a complex solution that took me forty-five minutes—and actually wound up with three very decent Lines of Position even though only two were stars. It was nine before I finished plotting them.

When the captain came up, he glanced at the chart, saw "Mars" written on one of the LOP's and grunted "Stars are much easier, young man."

I merely nodded, hating the moment the captain would hear of my illness.

Approaching Callao the next morning, Mr. Petrocelli, eight to twelve third mate, reported sighting peaks of the Andes Mountains surrounding Lima when we were still more than two hundred miles off Isla San Lorenzo, the island that guards the entrance to Callao. The entire navigation department panicked.

Ever since we first worked together on deck and I took over his job of operating the controls that open and close the hatch-lids, Mr. Petrocelli had decided I was something of a genius. He'd had little formal education, having come up through the hawse pipe, and although he knew how to work through the navigational tables and formulas, he hadn't the slightest idea as to any theory behind what he was doing. To save face when he had navigation questions, he had gotten into the habit weeks ago of calling me—in spite of the fact I was still at the two-star fix level as a navigator—rather than the second mate or the captain. I would sneak up onto the bridge-deck via the outside ladders on the starboard side, slip into the chartroom, answer his questions—which were usually basic—and slip back off the bridge without anyone else knowing I'd been there. He had long ago decided a third mate's license was the most he could hope for, that even shooting two stars would be difficult. He liked sun-lines. There was only one sun and he knew where it was and what it was.

When Mr. Petrocelli saw the mountains surrounding Lima five hours before he should have, out of habit, he called me instead of calling the captain. I was on deck helping the sailors bring lines up for port when the boatswain came over and said, "You better get your ass up to the bridge ka-dett. That third mate is havin' an awful time over something. Something about mountains dead ahead and the captain's gonna kill him if his position's wrong."

I headed for the bridge thinking this sounded a little strange. When we'd called Callao southbound, the fog and dust had been so thick we couldn't see the mountains even when tied up. This morning was different. The horizon was clear and four or five snowy peaks sat ahead like some Shangri-la. Word had traveled fast about the ship that mountains were visible much too early and the vessel's position was in question. By the time I reached the wheelhouse, half a dozen crewmembers, including Mr. Potter and the Captain were already there. The chief mate had come up just to see what was going on and maybe chuckle a little at Petrocelli's nervousness. Also, I figured he was lonely. Since word came out about the young girl in Valparaiso, no one among the officers or crew would talk to him.

While the professional navigators bent over the chart and the navigation books with dividers, compasses and Mr. Potter's magnifying glass, Mr. Hunt motioned for me to come out to the bridge wing with him. Since he was my boss, I didn't have the luxury of not speaking to him. Besides, I considered myself a fellow sinner. He seemed subdued. I didn't know if it was because his own personal devil had been satisfied or if he felt remorse.

"That is *Huancavelica*," he said, pointing to one of the peaks. "It is seventeen thousand seven hundred feet. *Yauyos*, over there, rises to above twelve thousand. *Cerro Colorado*, further north, is only seventy-one hundred feet."

Knowing where the ship is, is why navigators get paid. Navigators place a lot of stock in predicting exactly when and at what distance they will see a particular lighthouse or prominent charted peak. The need for this knowledge is why the professional navigator must evolve past the two star fix stage into the three, four, five, six and seven-star fix levels. Each additional star provides another Line of Position, which serves to give the experienced navigator that much more confidence in his position.

Mr. Potter explained it like this: "One star gives one Line of Position. That line extends indefinitely. If it is good, your ship lies somewhere on that line. A second star gives a second Line of Position. If both are accurate, they will cross exactly where your ship is located. Usually, though, you want a third LOP to confirm the cross made by the first two. The problem with the third LOP is it usually doesn't fall directly on top of the first two, so what you have is three possibilities for your vessel's position. To decide where you really are in the world, you need at least a fourth LOP and, preferably, a fifth. So, a two-star fix gives you something to go by but it is unconfirmed. A three-star position may confuse you; but should give you a decent indication of your position within a five-mile radius; four stars is much better but a five or six star fix really tells you where the ship is. On the other hand, the best navigators seldom take more than three or four stars because they know precisely when they have a good LOP and when the LOP is questionable and don't waste their time with excess."

In this case, when the mountains were clearly visible four or five hours earlier than expected, it was cause for much consternation and checking and rechecking of navigational data. The second mate had gotten a nice six-star pinwheel that morning and my two-star fix had been only three miles from his.

The captain explained we were experiencing a temperature inversion—a phenomenon where the air grows warmer as the height increases. This, for reasons I couldn't grasp, allowed our vision to travel in an arc so we could see beyond what the captain called the geographic range. A crowd came to the bridge, including Betty, the assistant cook, whom I had never before seen outside the galley.

She said, "When I saw Mr. Potter leave his plate o' scrambled and hightail it to the bridge, I knew something strange was going on."

She looked at the snow-covered peaks. "If I could've seed this far into the future, I'd of never married my old man. Just gotten Mary Louise from him or one of the other ranch hands and raised her myself. Been a lot less trouble."

Standing there looking at those mountains poking up through the layer of clouds lying above the city, all I could think was how miserable I felt. Peeing that morning made me stagger, and I couldn't bring myself to consider the other issue, the issue of violence, the issue I refused to put into words.

Eventually, the navigators settled on a position. Mr. Petrocelli stopped fluttering about blabbing to anyone who would listen how he would never again accept the 4 to 8 watch's D.R. (dead reckoning) position. Mr. Potter left the bridge in disgust. The captain sat in his chair the whole watch, smoking and drinking coffee as we sailed in and boarded the pilot. I went aft with the second mate to tie up. The small tug assisting on the stern, the *Pedro Navarro II*, parted the line it had put up. It was an old nylon rope that recoiled with a loud bang when it broke, nearly hitting Fletcher who stalked off the fantail with a great show of having been wronged. The real damage, though, came when the stern, no longer held off by the tug, closed on the wharf with a sickening thud, denting a couple of plates on the ship and cracking the wood stringer that ran along the face of the dock.

Mr. Potter called me over after we were fast.

"The Captain has to hire a surveyor and file some reports about the damage," he said. "He wants you up in his room to type."

I cleaned up and reported to the captain's office where I typed diligently as directed. Mr. LeClair came to assist when he finished with the officials. The captain, referring to a large spiral notebook of company policies and procedures, called out form numbers. Mr. LeClair pulled them out of the file-drawers and handed them to me and I typed in the blanks—official number, tonnages, ship's name, date, stuff like that.

In spite of this diversion, I thought of almost nothing but my trouble. I figured my most optimistic option was I would spend the rest of my life a sexual cripple. Worst case, rotting in a Chilean prison.

I'd been on antibiotics for three days now. Mr. LeClair had doubled my dosage twenty-four hours earlier. He urged me to "drink more water than you've ever drunk in your life and pee as often as you can stand it."

I thought he could have refrained from suggesting I not visit the Trockadero. Dressed as he was in his dark turtleneck and gabardine slacks, I suspected he wasn't going to be following his own advice. He considered Callao his home-port since he was now—in his mind at least—dating the girl he'd met at the Trockadero on the southbound call. Even talked about coming to Callao during his time off. Ever since his resurrection as a sexually functioning human being, he spent as little time aboard as possible when the ship was alongside. He was a new man: confident, helpful, even warm. He'd gotten his hair cut in Valpo; which, honestly, made him look almost handsome.

After finishing the Captain's typing, I reported back to the Chief Mate. He handed me the cargo plans for the holds forward of the house and gave me several tasks to perform: check the shoring in the lower hold of three; make sure the coffee separations were intact in the upper 'tween deck of two; count mail sacks in the special locker—things like that.

On deck and in the holds, wherever I looked, I saw reminders of my condition: drooping bags of coffee, limp mail-sacks, slumping longshoremen. I was sick, body and soul, and wanted to be cured more than anything I'd ever wanted in my life.

When I first came on deck, standing on the offshore side looking out beyond Isla San Lorenzo, I noticed a dot on the southern horizon. Just another ship, I figured, and went about my afternoon duties. After coffee, I stepped out of the resistor house at the after end of number one and saw the dot had arrived. Standing into port at the breakwater, pennants aflutter, was one of the Santa ships, a group of American-flag passenger/cargo vessels that carried people and goods from New York and Baltimore and Jacksonville down the east coast of South America, through the Straits of Magellan, then up as far north as Callao, and back again. I watched as the gold-painted Santa Magdalena entered the harbor. She passed not more than a good toss of a heaving line away, making for the passenger berth up ahead and around the corner. I stood at the rail gawking at the passengers when I heard my name called. A hundred people or more stood on the decks, waving and pointing and talking to each other. My eyes picked out a dark-haired figure waving both arms and shouting "Over here. Over here."

There was Tony Bissetti, a close friend from the Academy I had gotten into trouble with during plebe year. I waved and shouted, "I'll see you after you're tied up."

"Big time in Callao tonight," he responded, an ear-to-ear smile framing his handsome face.

Two thoughts struck me almost simultaneously. First, I couldn't have a big time in Callao tonight. I couldn't drink and I couldn't have sex, so what else was there? Second and by far most important, the Santa Magdalena would have a real doctor on board, an American doctor with American medicine. I pumped my fist. I would be well by morning. Salvation was at hand. Sure, Fate had thrown a little scare into me; maybe make me think twice before doing something foolish again; get me to mind my manners. Some of my old confidence returned and as long as I refrained from thinking about the possibility that I'd killed someone, I was on top of the world.

My Timex said 4:30. Time to knock off. I wouldn't wait for

Tony. I'd be at the gangway of his ship when he showed up to go ashore. I'd turn him around and march him directly into the infirmary. I'd see that doctor and I'd see him soon.

I almost ran to my room to shower and change. I had another job to do as well. I sat at my desk and wrote a note to Ana-Elena, telling her I had gonorrhea and that even though I believed the bug had entered my body after being with her, I had no way of knowing for sure and she should get checked. Writing it was difficult, yet something about the connection to her, fragile as it was, excited me. I wrote I was ashamed and sorry to have exposed her to bacteria that, while curable, could be troublesome—particularly with a Catholic mother and father to say nothing of a future bridegroom looking over her shoulder.

I apologized as best I could, told her I missed her and wished her well, particularly in light of this development. It occurred to me her emotional strength would see her through this; perhaps even prevent her from getting the disease. My grandmother used to say, "You won't get sick unless you think you deserve to or, for some strange reason, you just want to." I wasn't so sure about that. I put Alejandra's name and address on the envelope with attention to Ana-Elena and dropped it by the purser's office.

The Passenger Ship pier in Callao was different than the old wharf we tied up to. Ours was a dirty, oil-spattered concrete and wood affair smelling of fish-guts, dog-shit and stevedore urine; home to seagulls, crows and mangy dogs; piled with broken crates, cartons with most of the wood stripped away for the shanty-town casas, rotting bags of American hand-shake wheat dated two years earlier plus a rusting, yellow hulk of a Caterpillar delivered by our sister ship, but never received and subsequently stripped. The Termanale de Passegero—where Tony's ship docked—was bright and scrubbed. The concrete was painted egg-yolk with a ten-foot red stripe that curved from the exact spot where the gangway always touched down out through customs onto the street lined with taxis. A small band played Carioca and local artisans hawked their carvings and serapes and "real gold" jewelry. A dozen or so girls wearing white blouses tucked snugly into short black skirts kicked their legs and swayed their hips to the music. Seeing them, I felt the familiar but now painful urging and turned quickly away.

The boarding officials stepped onto the brow and disappeared into the house. After several minutes, the yellow quarantine flag came down, and the announcement "Ship is cleared, ship is cleared" blasted over a loudspeaker.

A cheer arose from the passengers when the sailors lowered the rope guard and suddenly the gangway was flooded with waves of white-haired men and women dressed in pastel pink or green or orange, and mostly pastel white. A grizzled seaman, his Camel cigarette never leaving his lips, stood at the gangway dressed in his blue jeans and tee shirt uniform, scratching his crotch with one hand while the other formed the familiar "V" of the seaman at repose: elbow on the rail, hand supporting the chin. Someone should do a sculpture, I thought.

I stood there, anxious, but as sure as I'd ever been about anything that I was soon to be healed. The initial waves of shore-going passengers dwindled to fifty-ish gentlemen smiling and holding hands with younger women with shapely legs and lots of jewelry.

Then he was there in front of me: Tony Bissetti, wavy black hair, deep tan, thick neck and shoulders. He wore a sky-blue pullover, open at the neck with khaki pants and stood all gleaming white teeth and sparkling eyes, a charmer.

"Jake-boy," he said. "Come aboard. We'll eat here, then go party."

Tony bearhugged me and kissed me on both cheeks, then led me up the gangway. We had known each other only a year but during that time we'd ridden the bench through many freshman basketball games, arguing about who was number eleven and who was number twelve. We became close friends the last six months of the school year marching to musters every two hours on weekends and crawling over the wall when we couldn't stand restriction anymore.

Tony led me to his room and sat on the corner of his desk, dangling his foot while I sat on the settee. His room was smaller than mine and the ship older. Where my room had bright yellow and pale green upholstery, Tony's furniture was gray, almost colorless. I told him about my Valparaiso adventures, leaving out the part about possibly killing Rosa. He snorted when I finished, stood, said, "let's go," and opened the door. I followed him down the narrow corridors to the ship's hospital. A gray-haired man who looked exactly like most of the male passengers except he wore a white medical coat stood in the doorway writing something on a clipboard that sat on a narrow shelf on top of the bottom half of the door.

"Doc," said Tony, putting his hand on the man's shoulder. "This is my best friend in the world. He's a cadet from the *Gulf Trader*. Got to see a doctor. Can you see him? We can pay."

The physician smiled at Tony's direct approach, sighed the way overworked people sigh when presented with one more request at the end of a busy day and opened the lower half of the door to admit Tony and me. I could scarcely contain my exuberance as I told my story. Much as I tried to sound contrite, I suspect all sense of having sinned was gone from my voice. The doctor listened closely, then asked Tony to leave the room while he pulled on latex gloves and examined me. When he was finished, he shook his head, called Tony back into the room and glared at both of us.

"Young men." He looked at me first, then over at Tony, sitting there smiling.

"And I'm talking to you too, Bissetti. Just because this didn't happen to you doesn't mean it couldn't have or won't. You've just been luckier."

Tony tried to not smile while the doctor removed his glasses and wiped them on his tie, then continued.

"I'll be the first to admit there are aspects about young men having their first sexual experiences with prostitutes that are good. Allows the sex while shielding you from the emotional part—the part that can be so much more difficult to deal with. No question many women would benefit from a similar opportunity.

"That said, boys, you don't know the chance you're taking when you go with these girls. Let me tell you a few things I've seen: men from Asia with strains of simple, lovable old gonorrhea in such pain they couldn't think straight. Men wishing they were dead from the pain. I personally know of cases that are incurable. No marriage, no family, no sex life." He hesitated, his eyes scanning face to face.

"Do you think that Academy you go to is going to graduate someone with an incurable dose of clap? You'll be out on your ear so fast you'll get whiplash. They've got no time there for losers. You want to be something, to do something with your life, you've got to have some discipline. Not much, for God's sake, but a little. You must show somebody, sometime, that you've got what it takes: whether that means going over the side to save a life or just keeping your pecker in your pants when some girl hollers 'cadete' and winks."

He paused to let his words penetrate, swiveled on his stool and reached for a bottle of capsules in the cabinet above him. He poured several into a smaller plastic container, wrote on a label and pasted it to the bottle. We sat quietly as he worked.

"I've got something here that will kill that germ you've seen fit to take into your body, young man."

He held the container of pills toward me and rattled them. His thick white eyebrows and dark eyes gave him a manic look— like an old-fashioned medicine man.

"If this stuff doesn't kill you, it will kill the clap. Called Tetracycline. So new it's hardly been tested. Gonococcus hasn't had a chance to become immune to it, but people like you," he pointed at me, "will give it that chance. In two years it won't work either and a new drug will have to be found. Eventually, we'll have diseases we just can't cure. And then what? I don't know, that's what—"

He thrust the bottle toward me. I took it. He turned away.

I was humiliated by his harangue, even thought I should be humbled, but inside, I was dancing. Inside, I laughed and carried on like a drunken fool. The bottle read *tetracycline: one capsule every eight hours for ten days*. I thought they were the most beautiful words I'd ever read.

"Thank you sir," I said quietly. "What do I owe you for this?"

"Just your whole future son. Just your whole future. See you boys later. No alcohol till you're finished with that stuff. Take two now. If it's going to work, your symptoms should be gone by morning. Be sure to take it for a full ten days or the symptoms will return. Understand?" He looked carefully into my eyes.

"I understand."

"No sex, no alcohol. Do something nice for someone. Now, God bless."

He held out his hand, again the smiling Norman Rockwell family physician. My gratitude bubbled and gurgled and my eyes teared. I felt like Lazarus with Christ. We returned to Tony's room. I held up two capsules like they were magic beans, washed them down with water and did a victory dance. Tony and I walked ashore to celebrate.

Callao wasn't much. George LeClair had told me it was the port that serviced Lima, which was a rambling, shack-ridden metropolis populated with aristocratic Spanish landowners on the one hand, and beggars, cripples and whores on the other—and not much in between. In its heyday, it had been an important city through which Spain imported the splendors of Macchu Picchu. Palaces, cathedrals and cabrillos stood now in various states of disrepair.

It was mid-winter here and cool. *Garua*, the thick winter fog the locals woke to most mornings, coated the buildings with a gray sludge that gave them a ghostly pallor. Habit directed our footsteps toward the nearest bar. It was dark and as uninviting as any place I'd seen this trip. A group of scraggly women trying to hustle business on a slow night stood together smoking and dealing cards, bored out of their skulls, at one end of the bar. We walked out back and sat in rickety wicker on a beat-up verandah where the whores tried to leave us alone after we'd shooed them away a couple times, but kept returning, unable to believe two young men could actually resist the temptation of sex. Finally, they started calling us queer boys and names like that. I would neither drink nor flirt. Tony, however, wasn't bound by any such vow and the girls seemed to sense that.

He ordered beers while I drank *chicha morada*, a thick, purple liquid made from corn. It was sweet and I liked it. Around midnight, a young *ambulante*—street-person—came around talking English about Viet Nam and the Beatles and something or other about President Kennedy, long since dead. Tony and I

sat on stools—we had moved inside on account of the chill—at
the small part of the ell of the bar. Tony had the wall on his right.
The small young man—I doubt he weighed a hundred pounds—
stood between us talking, asking us to buy him a beer, when suddenly, Tony was up off his stool, lifting the boy from the floor
and pinning him against the wall.

"Son of a bitch tried to pick your pocket," said Tony. The
boy's feet dangled from the floor as Tony held him with his left
hand—powerful from years of riding his dad's garbage trucks.
Tony cocked his right arm to hit him but I saw the look in the
boy's eyes and put my hand on Tony's shoulder.

"I think he's learned his lesson," I said.

When Tony released him, the young man sunk to the
floor, his eyes large with fear. He reminded me of the boy in
Panama who had led me to his sister—but was maybe a couple years older. I pulled my wallet from my pants and handed
him two small bills of the local currency. It was next to nothing but the boy's eyes lit up. He took the money, murmured
a gracias and ran out.

Tony and I left around two. Though I had drunk no alcohol,
I felt intoxicated being with my close friend. That and the notion
I was cured. I had peed a couple times in the fetid men's room
out back where urine lay in pools on the floor. The pain was bad
as ever, but I was optimistic the gonococcus bacteria were slowly choking on the tetracycline. Outside the bar, a full moon
gleamed over the harbor. Around us, the mountain-tops, impos-
sibly high, glowed in the moonlight while the moldings of the
buildings and window ledges, dripping with sludge, looked like
props in a werewolf movie. A sea breeze blew and the air was
cool and fresh. At Tony's ship, we hugged good-bye. I told him
I was eternally grateful for his help and friendship, then returned
to the *Gulf Trader*. I couldn't wait to wake up in the morning.
I was so sure I'd be healed I didn't even pray.

We sailed at 0900. I got called at seven-twenty but did-
n't get up till nearly eight. When I awoke, the first thing I
became aware of was a raw burning in my penis. I tried to
stay optimistic throughout the day thinking the antibiotic
just needed more time. By evening, in spite of doubling the

dosage, the pain continued. I peed razor blades the following morning and knew the tetracycline had failed.

Callao to Panama: the Doldrums
August 26 - 27

Sitting alone, hunched over my desk, drops of sweat running down my back, I read *they that go down to the sea in ships, that do business in great waters; these see the works of the Lord and his wonders of the deep . . . They mount up to the heaven, they go down again to the depth; their soul is melted because of trouble. They cry unto the Lord in their trouble and he bringeth them out of their distresses. They are glad because they be quiet.*

Being Catholic, I hadn't read much of the Bible before this. Don had dropped his copy of the St. James Version by my room earlier in the day. It had a worn, brown cover with a single black ribbon marker, much like the book I'd seen in the whore's room in the Trockadero. I leafed through it. Its pages were dog-eared, the margins written in, paper scraps with notes stuck out marking readings. I sought solace there, but my despair was such I was unable to cry out to the Lord.

I read this passage over and over, found the tempo of its words soothing and puzzled over their meaning. I thought of the many *works of the Lord* and *wonders of the deep* I had seen in this one brief voyage: standing becalmed in the eye of the storm, a chaos of clouds churning about us; sunsets so glorious I half-expected to see Christ himself emanate from them; Lima's sky-splitting white peaks seen hundreds of miles out to sea; tropical nights on the bridge wing, the air warm against my face, the celestial dome crawling with diamonds. I remembered the green flash like the sparkle of an emerald jewel and the school of dolphins like magic creatures in the purple luminescence.

The next sentence resonated: *They mount up to the heaven, they go down again to the depth; their soul is melted because of trouble.* I'd been to Olympus in my pleasure and in its aftermath, had fallen lower than low, and, dear God, how my soul now melted with my trouble. More than anything, I wanted God to pull me up out of this, but I choked on the prayers I needed to say.

I pondered the last sentence, *they are glad because they be quiet.* As a man in the desert must desire water, I longed for a settled mind, for an inactive mind, a mind at peace. I sensed all the pleasure in the world could not bring contentment; riches could not buy a good night's sleep; fame's exhilaration and fortune's possessions did not encompass serenity.

We made northing now, homebound, speeding like a freight train toward the Canal. We entered that part of the world known as the Doldrums, an airless, desert-like stretch of ocean, and the compressor on the air-conditioner failed. The engineers did not have the part they needed to fix it and the sun became an enemy from which there was no escape. It dominated our world, became omnipotent. The blue-gray of the sky and water became sheet-steel; something metallic that mirrored the burning sun and fried all living things.

Temperatures in the house soared past a hundred and five and all the outside doors were hooked open. The portholes had been sealed when the ship was built—testimony to the design engineer's faith in the invulnerability of technology. People rummaged in their closets and hauled out the wall fans required by the crew labor contracts, hung them on their wall-mounts, plugged them in and ran them on high. They did no more than blow hot air about, but that seemed better than nothing.

Scuttlebutt of my illness spread about the ship sailor by sailor. The purser could not cure it. The miracle drug from the American doctor on the Santa ship had not worked. Men spoke of it in undertones of fear.

"Dis be one a' dem bad strains, dat fo' sure," said Irving Johnson up on the bridge, shaking his wooly head back and forth. "Dis be one a' dem *killer* strains." He spent the watch pacing behind the wheel, the ship on autopilot, mumbling to himself about how the mate had caused this; the mate with his knife and his throwing over the sailors' beer and his unseamanlike manner was the Jonah.

Mr. Potter scarcely acknowledged me when I went to the wheelhouse for morning stars. I could see disappointment etched into his face. He left me alone in the chartroom plotting my meager and, as it turned out, inaccurate two-star fix. When I finished, I walked onto the starboard wing where he stood, arms folded and vigilant: a guardian of a way of life and belief set that did not embrace the sins necessary for gonorrhea to occur. I stood next to him, hoping he would say something, even curse me or scold me, but he remained silent.

The mate, hardly a compassionate man, acknowledged my plight by giving me the day off.

"Hey kid," he said privately at breakfast that morning. "Take the day off. Too damned hot to work. And by the way, I want you to know I respect you for the courage you showed during that Tiny Tim fiasco. Won't ever forget it. Not everyone out here got that kind of courage, but you sure do."

I nodded, grateful, but didn't otherwise respond. After what had happened to the young girl in his office in Valparaiso, I was surprised to even see him, ostracized as he was by everyone from the captain to the messboy. He took his meals in his room and never went on deck; afraid, most likely, of being bagged and tossed over with the evening garbage.

I walked by the purser's office on the way to my room. George Le Clair sat there looking ridiculous in black dress shoes, black socks, khaki shorts and a white dress shirt. He was so engrossed in his task of scouring medical books he didn't notice me standing there until I coughed.

"Hey, Jake," he said. "I keep wondering if there's something in here we haven't tried."

I nodded.

"By the way." He lit a cigarette. "This won't help your condition any, but I want you to know how grateful I am for what you've done for me this trip. I'm a new man."

Bully for you, I thought. I headed for my room.

"Jake," he yelled after me in a tone that made me close my eyes. "The captain wants to talk to you. He asked me to bring you up to his room when you finished eating."

"Great," I said, with sarcasm in my voice. "Let's go."

We climbed the two flights to the Captains office. Even in the heat, Captain Isenhagen looked every bit the master wearing his khaki shirt and shoulder boards. Two fans blew hot air around as he sat at his desk. I noticed an open can of Heinekens on the window ledge behind him. Nine a.m.

"We haff decided to put you ashore in Panama," he said looking directly at me. "No one hass as much experience with South American gonorrhea as the U.S. Navy hospital there. You vill receive good treatment."

"I'm—I'm to be put off the ship?" I asked, astonished. The possibility of this happening had never occurred to me. This was my home. This man with the four gold stripes was my father.

George Le Clair looked at his shoes. Captain Isenhagen nodded.

"We do not like to send you ashore, but are afraid to carry you further. You need some kind of treatment we are not able to provide. We should be negligent to carry you four extra days to New Orleans. You haff done good work aboard my ship. I thank you for that."

I stood there stunned, unable to speak. To my shame, I started crying.

"I'll be kicked out of school."

"I shall not report this to the Academy until I've heard from the Panama agent. Perhaps you can rejoin in New Orleans, healed, and no one will know."

"They will send me to Viet Nam." I was sobbing openly.

Neither of them spoke. The captain lowered his head. I immediately regretted cutting into his raw wound. Finally, George walked over and put his hand on my shoulder.

"It's for the best," he said. "Come to my office. We'll type up your paperwork."

"Mr. Thomas," said the Captain, as I turned to follow the purser out the door. "I too wass young once and did exactly as you. But let me tell you something. There are better ways to spend your time than chasing around with drunks and whores."

"Yes, sir," I said, nodding, assuming that since he was a direct-speaking man, he meant exactly what he said.

I returned to my room in a daze. My dog-eared copy of *Crime and Punishment* sat on the edge of my desk. I picked it up and flung it into my wastebasket. Even though Raskolnikov had come to understand love's saving grace as he sat in his prison cell in Siberia, I hated and resented the ideas I'd taken from that book. I felt I'd been led without guidance down a treacherous path. Don had been right when he'd said, "Forget all that nihilist crap. Do things out of love and kindness and you'll nearly always do right. Do things for any other reason and you'll probably regret it."

After sitting at my desk a few minutes crying, I walked out on deck to find Boss Jones to tell him I wouldn't be working today. He was on the fantail.

"Don' know why this couldn't of happened to someone who deserved it," he said, rubbing his big knife on a stone. "Someone like ol' Fletcher there, who's fucked over ev'y sumbitch he ever met one way or t'other. You ain't never done nuthin but be a young man. You jis' done what you s'pos'd to of done."

Water in the shower was at least as hot as the air surrounding the pipes so it offered no respite. Sometime after eleven, I dragged myself up to the bridge to shoot noon. The thermometers on the bridge wings had already climbed past the one hundred five mark. Mr. Petrocelli refused to budge off a spot just outside the starboard wheelhouse door that provided a square meter of shade but no cool air that I could detect. He had removed both his shirt and trousers and stood in a sleeveless tee-shirt and red striped boxers held up by blue suspenders, an unlit stogy jammed into his mouth. He stared ahead, apparently keeping a lookout, looking dangerously flushed. The captain shot noon with me but didn't have much to say either to me or Mr. Petrocelli. We were both losers. And really, after telling me to get off his ship and why, what else was there to say?

A light breeze blew up from the south but had the effect, when combined with our vessel's motion, of utterly stilling the air about the ship. I set down my noon running fix around 11:45 and did Mr. Petrocelli's log entries. I wrote 106 in the temperature column.

The engineers, besieged and ostracized because of the air-conditioning failure, relieved each other on the hour at the operating platform in the engine room where temperatures spiraled up to above one hundred thirty and became a hazard to life itself. The crew formally filed a lodging claim and the first engineer and the chief retired to the fantail before lunch with a bucket of ice and a case of beer. I went back and had a pop but didn't feel like socializing with a bunch of whining drunks, so left. People's tempers flared with the heat. The captain posted a notice that said any crewmembers caught fighting would be logged and fired and flown home from Panama at their own expense.   The notice said nothing about not drinking, however, and everyone I saw except Mr. Potter carried around either a Heinekens or a Millers—most of which had been taken from the cargo hold southbound—like it was a requirement. The mate had thrown all the Jax over the side earlier in the trip; in my opinion, exactly where it belonged. At lunch, the chief cook refused to light his ovens, just set out cold sandwiches and chips that people carried aft to eat with the beer. For the first time all trip, I skipped a meal.

I was a miserable, guilt-ridden sinner and I felt the hand of God crushing me. I knew in my heart I could not be healed and this seemed to me unalterable and non-negotiable, like the night when I was four or five and heard my parents yelling and heard a body fall to the floor and held my breath in the ensuing silence till my mother stopped sobbing, learning that night things happened in a family home that stayed there—forever. Mistakes were made and every family built small closets for their secrets. This was one of those landmarks—like a beacon of truth—that cuts through the fog of our uncertainties, illuminating a portion of our path, whether we like what we see or not.

I had a clear vision of life as a continuum, a timeline, with disruptions caused by fate or bad judgment or some out-of-control passion. In my anger at Ana-Elena, I'd chosen to drop acid. I'd allowed myself to spin out of control because I couldn't handle the pain of being rejected by a woman I'd chosen to love. Something terrible had happened. At home, offending the parish priest and getting driven out of town by my father was different. It was not sin in a universal sense. It was a relatively minor insult, seen against the enormity of what I had done in Valparaiso. Now I was once again being sent away, not as punishment so much as an associated consequence. The disease was the beginning of my punishment and there would likely be a trial and an incarceration.

On the other hand, I now understood that pleasure is a not an insignificant motivator. Was its pursuit sin? Or was my sin as simple as intimacy with a woman with whom I not only had made no commitment—except perhaps a monetary one—but for whom I had no feeling except lust? Lust, after all, was one of the seven deadly sins. If that alone was my sin, though, why weren't others likewise punished? Men and probably women too experienced lust at some level thousands or even millions of times each day. What about lust within marriage? Was that all right or was that still sin? If one abstained until marriage, did he or she then have the right to do anything sexually, regardless of how his partner felt about it? Or was sin as simple as controlling another's actions? Of forcing another to do something he or she didn't want to do, whether married or not?

Maybe punishment always came for transgressions of this sort. Not as immediate as a slap on a young boy's wrist for raiding a cookie jar, but over time, like how some women are said to be haunted by the whimpering of aborted children, or men who lose potency from the guilt of extramarital affairs. I had read articles about this stuff in the old Playboys in the officer's lounge but really, what did I know—only that, for me, sex was not simple.

I couldn't stand the company back on the fantail, so I made my way back up to my room. I sat there in my underwear drenched in sweat, coming more and more to grips with the idea

I was not only a sinner, but that my condition was hopeless. One thing I knew: I needed a priest at least as much as I needed a doctor. I looked at my clothes and thought, since I would be getting off the ship the next day, I should do some laundry and pack. The last thing I wanted was to be productive, though, so I got up, pulled on some khaki shorts and walked outside where it didn't seem quite so hot. The ship slid noiselessly across the flat metal ocean as if on tracks. I could hear the voices aft growing louder and knew I couldn't party with a bunch of drunken engineers. I walked forward. All the deck-cargo had been discharged, so there weren't a lot of wires and chains and turnbuckles to crawl over. I didn't want to talk to anyone just then. Just wanted to be alone; to sit alone and be miserable alone.

One point was clear: I didn't blame anyone else for my mess. Not like the engineers back there, pointing fingers at the office for not supplying spare parts or at the relieved chief who hadn't ordered something or another. Maybe I could blame it on my youthful libido, or on ideas I'd taken from *Crime and Punishment*. Maybe I was rebelling at having been raised Catholic or growing up hounded by an insecure, authoritative father. But what did any of that change? Far as I could tell, no one besides me was responsible for this mess.

I reached the bow and planted myself on the gray bollard where I'd sat in such bliss reading Melissa's love letter southbound. That seemed a lifetime ago. I thought of her grace and beauty, and how innocent and simple she seemed in her approach to sex. Then her face became Rosa's and I almost gasped. Dead Rosa. Possibly dead by my hand though I was never a fighter. Violence struck me as bestial. Even when there seemed to be no way around it—like the night Ed Maklowski all but called my sister a whore and I had to defend her honor; or the day Hitler invaded Poland and the world started making guns, it seemed a primitive solution. Sitting there, trying my best to keep my fragile grip on a particular image of myself that didn't include violence, I realized I'd blocked that whole drug-violence-death night right out of my consciousness.

No dolphins leaped for the bow today; no flying fish fluttered along the water's surface; no large-winged seabirds followed for the after-meal food-scraps feast. This ocean was

without life and I knew why. I had killed a fellow human—
not knowingly perhaps, but that didn't do Rosa any good.
She was dead, her beautiful body lifeless, a body looked upon
by countless men with the raw desire that makes one catch his
breath, that chases away responsibilities and guides a man's
thoughts into a narrow, animal-like focus, now stiff and pale,
the heat and beauty gone, probably trucked to some desolate
gravesite to rot with thieves and drunkards and other whores;
her young son, alone now, wailing with grief. She was dead as
this burning sun, as this lifeless sea, as this iron hull that carried us. Dead as this whole fucking business.

I sat there remembering for some reason how important the
word *scrupulous* was to me at one point in my life. I was seven,
in church, confessing. I had just passed through the purple velvet curtain, knelt on the worn wooden kneeler, my face barely
reaching the wood mesh on the other side of which was the
huge, monstrously huge head of Father Henry. I finished telling
my little transgressions—venial sins they were called: disobeyed
my mother, cussed twice, stuff like that. Father Henry gave me
my usual penance: five Our Fathers, five Hail Mary's, five Glory
Be's, then droned out the Latin Blessing, crossed me and I left.
Sister Francella, not much taller than me but a hundred pounds
heavier, was there to admonish each of us to "be scrupulous in
the confessional now." I went home, found a dictionary and
looked it up, then did my best to become obsessive about sin
until, in the third grade, kindly Sister Meriam told me being
scrupulous was a sin.

I sat perched like a gull on my bollard thinking and suffering, suffering and maybe wishing. What I did like about the heat
was that I sweat so much I'd pretty much stopped peeing, no
matter how much I drank.

George Le Clair continued to press me to "drink more water
than you've ever drunk in your life," but I was losing heart. I
pissed barbed wire and glass needles now and after any sleep, I'd
wake to a gluey mess in my underwear and have to splash hot
water to unstick it.

Out of the corner of my eye, I noticed Boss Jones, hands on

the rails, pulling himself up the last step onto the port side of the forecastle head. I watched him approach, shirt off as usual, muscles glistening; the most manly man I'd ever met.

"Ka-dett, I done walked up here to tell you sumpin'," his approach, as always, direct. "I knows you sick, and I knows you thinkin' you done sumpin' real bad, but you ain't done nuthin' that ain't been done a million times before. You know I ain't nuthin' but a uneducated bosun, but it seem to me what you done been done by every young man what set foot to a gangway. You go to sea as a young man, you s'posed to get to know them whores. This your training ground so when you get to that marriage bed, you know what you got and what she got and how the two s'posed to fit together. This be part of your job as a young man and your education part of their job as whores. Sometime I think you white boys got the notion you takin' 'vantage of the womenfolk when you go to messin' around down there. Hell, the womenfolk like that stuff too, what I can tell. They probly like it more than us 'cuz they ain't got to worry 'bout the, you know, the manly thing. They kin jus' enjoy theirselves. You ain' doin' nuthin' wrong unless maybe you be like this chief mate what likes to hurt young girls. Then, yeah, you bet, thass wrong. 'Cuz that ain't pleasure. Someone get hurt, anytime someone get hurt, thass bad stuff and I'll be firs' in line to kick your ass, you ever take up that nonsense. Don' matter if you pay or not. Not 'nuff money in de world make up for hurtin' someone."

He looked square at me, his face sincere and his eyes serious. "That cock a' yours ain' no knife you plungin' into those girls. It something good. You jis as well tie a bow around it what says happy birthday. Makes 'em feel like women, like beautiful women."

I never said a word, and he left, muttering to himself, but I appreciated he'd walked all the way to the bow just to say those things. Shortly after four, Don Campbell appeared from around the port side of the anchor windlass, surprising me. He wore khaki shorts and sandals; nothing else. Large beads of sweat ran down through his beard and onto his neck and shoulders.

"Hey. How are ya? Guess what temp I logged at four?" He spoke to me now as an equal.

"One ten," I said.

"One fourteen." He seemed proud of it. "Here's a coke. It's cold."

I took the bottle of soda, opened it with the opener Don handed me and drank most of it at once. I could feel my lower lip quivering and realized I couldn't control it. I turned to face forward, my tears mixing with the sweat. I'd been waiting for Don.

"I know there's not much anyone can say at a time like this," he said softly. "Thinking about you sort of took my mind off the heat. Is it true the captain is putting you ashore in Panama City?"

I nodded without turning.

Don continued. "Tough break getting put off the ship. Probably for the best though. This skipper wouldn't do anything to hurt you."

I calmed down and spoke.

"Don, I'm scared. I know why this is happening to me. I'm being punished and I'm afraid I'll never get well."

When I was a boy, tears sometimes made things better— because of the response adults had to them, I suppose. Now they seemed futile, a sign of weakness without the power to stop something that seemed so adult and permanent.

"Maybe it's not my business," said Don. "But what sin do you feel you've committed that warrants being punished?"

"I don't know where to start," I said. "Shacking up with whores. Screwing in a cathedral. Thinking of women as something to use then forget about."

"You screwed in the cathedral? I didn't know that. Holy shit! That's amazing. You'll be telling that story at class reunions the rest of your life.

"Listen," he said. "Forget about sin. For what you did, anyway. It's one of those behavior modification controls we just accept. In my mind, sin equates to evil and your whoring and carrying on was not evil. Maybe it wasn't treading the straight and narrow, but for someone your age and unmarried besides, it sure as hell wasn't evil. Think about it; turn a boy loose in a candy store and leave him there long enough, nothing you can tell him will keep him from eating a chocolate kiss or a jelly-bean—if he's normal and not all tied up in knots, anyway. He'll eat enough to get a stomachache, then he'll quit. He might get a little sick. Even in his disobedience, if that's involved, he isn't exactly sinning.

"Eventually, what is natural finds its way through all the muck of words and morals and laws. If it doesn't," his voice rose slightly as it did when he felt strongly about something, "there's hell to pay. Either the person goes nuts, like this purser used to be, or worse, someone gets hurt."

He finished his soda, tossed the bottle over the rail and looked out at the horizon.

"And when someone gets hurt, there usually is some sin floating around someplace. The Christian commandments are simple and they're good: Love God. Love and treat your fellow man and woman as you yourself want to be treated. Do that and you're fine."

"All that sounds good," I said. "So how come I'm sick?"

"Nature has its own way of letting us know when we've gone too far. Drink too much, you get drunk or beat up, and sick to boot. You have accidents. You get fired. Your wife leaves you; your credit goes to hell; your kids think you're a loser. Eat too much, you get fat and you can't defend yourself and people laugh at you. Screw too many women instead of settling on one and you wind up with some awful disease. Or you make a baby and have to support it. Nature's pretty simple—very strong on cause and effect." He stopped then and paced back and forth, as if gathering courage.

"Guilt is a different animal though. A dangerous, scary monster with sharp claws that dig into your heart. Rides you like a devil. Never stops, just keeps hurting, keeps doing damage. But you're a Catholic. You been raised to believe in guilt. To believe that guilt is necessary and even good." Don paced back and forth, his eyes on the deck, worked up. He stopped directly in front of me and grabbed my tee shirt, his face inches from mine.

"You listen to me now," he shouted. "Guilt is like a grudge—it eats you from the inside out. Gnaws on your spirit. Leaves you hollowed out, raw, without defenses." He paused, his eyes narrowed.

"Guilt will destroy you, man. You'll get weird diseases; your body will no longer create anything. You won't be able to write

a poem or paint a picture or even screw very well; and when you
do, you won't make enough sperm to make a baby. That's why
Fletcher got well. He doesn't lose any sleep over what he does
and I'll guarantee you that is one man has done some bad shit in
his day." He released my shirt.

"You think this is caused by guilt?" I asked.

"Sure as I'm standing here talking to you."

"How am I supposed to feel?"

"Oh, maybe a little shame, I don't really know what all
you've done."

"What's the difference between guilt and shame?"

"Shame is OK. You can feel ashamed of yourself if you
want. That won't hurt anything. Shame is the rubber bumper
you run into from time to time along the edge of the straight
and narrow."

He stood and walked over to the rail, spit, then walked back.

"Think about the Lord's Prayer. It says 'And lead us not into
temptation.' You know why it says that? Because we're weak sons
of bitches, that's why. Because we can't resist temptation—especially when we're young and full of juice. Look at how folks your
age drink, party, screw and refuse to go to church. Then, when
they turn forty and dry up a little, they get to feeling nervous
about their mortality. They get sanctimonious. They get religion. God be praised. They have seen the light. They come back
to the church with robes on, waving their arms, singin' in the
choir of the Lord, telling their kids and every other swinging
dick how to live. Why? Because that's how it works. You think
its wrong to look at a woman as a sexual object? Particularly a
whore? They're *whores,* for Christ's sake."

I felt a little foolish in the face of this particular bit of logic.

"You're supposed to look at them like that," Don continued.
"If you don't, either they don't make money or you're barking
up the wrong tree.

"Far as non-whores—you know, regular women—think
about this. Let's say you're my age and you're married and you
have a couple of kids and you have a fender-bender in the grocery parking lot. You get out and the driver of the other car is a
looker with long legs. It's summer. She's wearing a short skirt.
She opens her door, swings her legs out and sits there, just a

moment, and makes sure you see pretty far up. You're angry because she pulled out right in front of you. But you look at those legs and if you don't feel at least a whiff of desire, you might need a shot of testosterone. When a normal, healthy adult male sees an attractive female, presumably same species, similar age, that male will have a sexual thought. I guarantee it. And it works for women too. European women—my wife and her sisters do this all the time—are always commenting on one guy's butt or another's nose. A thin nose means a long dong." He touched his own stubby nose, laughing. "Shows what I got to live with.

I touched my own nose, but didn't smile.

"A healthy sexuality is by God OK. It's not a sin."

Don stopped talking and looked at me, his head cocked.

"My wife says American men never really grow up. Never learn to be intimate. Can't get past the Playboy bunny idea that a large-breasted woman running her tongue between her lips wants him. And does this man know this woman? Has he talked to her? No. Hell no. She's a stranger—someone he's never seen, doesn't know, doesn't need to know. My wife says if a man—and this includes husbands—doesn't discuss literature with a woman; if he doesn't come to understand her thoughts and fears and desires; what excites her, all that stuff, that he will never become intimate with her. He'll never really make love to her—just a mindless fuck, roll over and start snoring."

"Sometimes I think I like sex for the wrong reason," I said. "Something about a woman letting me inside makes me feel like I've conquered her. Just some money, and maybe a lie or two."

Don stared at me, a quizzical smile on his face.

"Then I met Ana-Elena and I wanted her so no one else could have her; wanted to live with her and have children with her, but she didn't want that. I don't know if I could screw whores again. I mean I don't know if I want to."

"When you mix sexual pleasure with love, you have the most wonderful thing available to us mortals," said Don. "You fly, man. You float with the angels through those puffy little clouds."

The sea changed from metallic blue to a glassy brown as the

sun dropped in the west. I looked hard at Don.

"I'm afraid I killed Rosa," I whispered. A ship appeared on the horizon—just a dot, about a point to starboard.

"What?" he said.

"I was fucked up on acid so I'm not sure what happened. Fletcher was there but I'm afraid to ask him."

"You think you killed Rosa?" Don's mouth hung open. I wouldn't look at him. "Well, Christ almighty."

Staring at the ship on the starboard bow, I told Don what I remembered, replaying the evening scene by scene. The memory was still hazy, but clearer now than it had been.

"Fletcher was there, in the room, walking around the bed. He was naked and had something in his hand—a gun, I think, but I wasn't paying much attention. Rosa was on her hands and knees. I was behind her, something I'd never done. The drug made the sex different. Slow-motion and intense. I remember thinking I had never before really seen a woman: the way her neck curved into her shoulder; her wide hips and small waist, like a fine instrument built with love and grace. I remember thinking my attraction to her, and the pleasure she gave me, defined me— that her beauty, almost unapproachable, intensified the pleasure and that pleasure was what I now was.

"Something bad happened when I climaxed. A loud pop, like an explosion, went off. Rosa collapsed in front of me. Fletcher grabbed my arm, pulled me to my feet. He seemed angry. He shoved my clothes at me and pushed me out the door. Next thing I remember I was on the street and Wally was helping me dress."

I walked to the rail and threw up. Then I turned, wiping my mouth with the back of my hand.

Don watched me without moving. Finally, he spoke. "Some people lead interior lives. They putz around in their gardens and bake bread and watch the news—nothing much happens. That's not you. Things will happen to you and for you and around you. And you know what? Good for you." Don watched as the ship to starboard closed on us. Something seemed very familiar about it.

"It's a new world today," Don continued. "People are

willing to die for the right to sit in the front of the bus. Harvard graduates are moving to the hills of northern California and learning Transcendental Meditation and how to build A-frames. Some people are even looking for moral freedom, where community, family, home, money, their god-damned identity, everything is at risk."

He paused while the ship to starboard passed close by, less than a mile off. It was our sister-ship, the Latin Trader, identical to us in everything but name, bound for Callao, then Valpo. We watched her go by, could see the guys on the bridge waving—a deck cadet, probably, excited about Valparaiso, listening to scuttlebutt about the famous Rosa. Cadets like Wally and me. Maybe others making their first trip to sea, eyes wide open, hungry for experience.

"You gotta find out what happened that night," Don continued. "You gotta talk to that slimeball Fletcher and find out what happened."

"I can't," I said. "I'm afraid."

Cristobal, Panama
August 28

Banished, expelled, exiled, unwelcome as an ex-lover at a wedding party, I stood at the rail waiting, my green and black plaid handgrip like a puppy by my right foot, packed with underwear, socks, a shirt, a toothbrush and a razor. Sent away for misbehaving, for consorting with whores, drunks, murderers and dopers. Banished while everyone else got to stay though they'd done as bad. I had grown bitter overnight as the pain doubled in intensity.

A low morning haze deepened the greens of the jungle on the small chain of islands sitting like emeralds in the flat gray-blue sea. We slowed as we approached the Panama City pilot station. Our orders were to proceed directly through the canal—no anchoring to await the pilot boat; no mooring for bunkers or cargo. The only transaction the ship had scheduled for this transit was to put me ashore, to get rid of me and move on.

"That is really bad luck," said the purser as he finished typing my documents. "Usually we get twenty-four hours here—sometimes more."

The gleaming white pilot launch approached swiftly, followed at a respectable distance by the wheezy rust-bucket used by the boarding officials. I would go ashore with the officials, appropriately enough. No sleek, polished yacht chatting with American pilots for me. I'd be with the locals, smelling diesel fumes, stale tobacco and urine.

"Do not return with a Not Fit for Duty slip," said the captain sternly at breakfast that morning. He seemed angry. Why, I didn't know.

We are not a hospital ship. We cannot carry around sick people."

I merely nodded, not trusting my quivering lower lip to support the words needed to convey my profound gratitude for everything he'd taught me, and my deep regret for the trouble I'd caused.

George LeClair, the purser, had looked in on my packing. He'd suggested I take the one bag and pick up the rest of my gear in New Orleans. Wally, a better, kinder man after his night with LSD, agreed to help any way he could. I felt like they were presiding over my funeral arrangements and I sensed they did too. No one expected me to return to the ship. The tetracycline had not worked; therefore, according to the wise old salts in the crew mess, my dose was incurable. It was all pretty simple and it was all pretty ugly.

We swung to starboard to shelter the pilot boat from the tiny wavelets and coming out of the west. Two large American pilots clanked up the gangway, confident and jolly, content with each other, ignoring everyone else. I watched them board, both wearing short-sleeve white shirts and dark ties with gold clips, suddenly very jealous of their lives and careers and easy, competent manner. Fucking pilots, I thought. I'd heard they all had drivers and made more money than anyone in Panama except el Presidente. I could tell one thing. They didn't give a shit about anything or anyone except themselves and their goddamned mission of getting these ships through the locks. Nothing like success to make a man seem successful. Guess I'll be with the losers, wherever that is.

Wally ran out in his grimy boiler-suit, his red hair sticking straight up like Dennis the Menace, a splotch of grease on his cheek. He grabbed my hand, threw his arm around my shoulders and hugged me, then stood back. In spite of minor the irritations, we'd done all right as roommates.

"I'll take care of your stuff," he said. "You're going to be all right and then I'll wish I'd never hugged you." We both laughed awkwardly, but I was on the verge of tears, and I knew he could see that.

"Thanks, man," I said. Whatever bitterness I had didn't extend to Wally. He started back toward the house, then stopped and turned toward me once again.

"Hey listen," he said. "Whatever happens, you're not a loser, OK?"

I smiled. "What is a loser, Wally?" I had heard his loser monologue before but wanted to hear it again because it made me laugh.

"You want to know about losers?" He sauntered back toward me, warming to one of his favorite topics. "I'll tell you about losers. They wear faded tee shirts and have beer guts— both the men and the women. The women all have dark roots and try to have affairs. They smoke Old Golds and drink Pabst and Maxwell House. Their kids never get parts in the school play and they give each other bowling shoes for birthdays. Their goal in life is to drive a new red pickup and not one of them finished college. Their closest brush with literature was reading *The Hardy Boys* and they debate the life of Tarzan. The men wear Old Spice on special occasions like their mother's birthday and if they could just get up the down payment, they'd buy on something called a cul-de-sac. Their cars break down; their roofs leak; the men judge each other by the size of their internal combustion engines. They listen to country music and discuss the letters to the editor in their local newspapers. They can all afford to go drinking Saturday nights, but never have quite enough money for child-support payments. They are losers man, L-O-S-E-R-S. I ain't gonna be one and you aren't either."

I laughed out loud when he'd finished and hit him on the arm with my fist. He said, "see ya," and turned quickly away.

Three dark-skinned Panamanian boarding officials with soiled white shirts and frayed black trousers struggled up the gangway, each holding a large, mostly empty black valise—the primary function of which was transporting cigarettes off the ship. I had helped the purser with officials in a couple of ports.

One bag was always placed on the file cabinet nearest the door. While they sat at a table shuffling papers, someone—me or the purser—took the empty briefcase to the slop chest and stuffed ten cartons of Marlboros into it. They would accept nothing else.

Irving Jackson stood beside me as the officials brushed past, headed for the purser's office. Within minutes, they returned, smiling, accompanied by George LeClair.

"Good luck," said George, clapping me on the shoulder. I started out of my daze. It was time for me to go. Irving Jackson, behind him, shuffled and nodded. I could see he was on the verge of tears himself.

So this was it then. This was when I leave the ship.

"Here." The purser handed me an envelope. "Some of us took up a collection. We know you haven't exactly saved money this trip." I looked inside. Five twenties.

"Thanks," I said, stuffing the envelope into my pocket. I hadn't even thought about practical things like money. George looked goofier than ever with his eyes teary behind his coke-bottle glasses. I'd grown to like him a lot, different as he was from the sort of person I usually spent time with.

"Thanks," I said again. "This is really thoughtful of you."

I walked down the gangway and stepped into the old boat with the officials, then looked up at the bridge wing, directly into the eyes of the captain. They gave away nothing—except possibly to say "get along cadet. I've got to move this ship."

I waved. He lifted his arm then dropped it back to his side; as though he realized now he'd backed the wrong horse and needed to cut and run. The boatswain had joined Irving Jackson at the gangway. Fletcher walked up and looked down at me, his face blank. I remembered Don's last words to me, "you need to know what happened that night or you'll never heal. You've got to know the truth."

"Fletcher," I yelled as we pulled away and the gangway began to raise. He heard his name called, lifted his arm in half-wave, then pulled back away from the rail, out of my sight.

"Y'all come back, see us, y'hear," yelled the boatswain from the head of the gangway. I waved, watching as we motored away from the side of my ship. Mr. Potter stood at the rail on the fantail, his khakis perfect. He lifted his arm, palm up, and held it up until I waved. I watched the ship through my tear-blurred vision as it made its way toward the lock, then turned and ducked my head as I entered the small passenger cabin of the boat. I sat on one of the black plank seats that ran along either side, tears running down my cheeks. The floor of the compartment was painted brown and was littered with Styrofoam cups and cigarette butts. The officials stood a few feet away out on the poop deck, smoking Marlboros.

I couldn't bear it. In the past two months, I'd been expelled from my birth-house, driven to the edge of town by my father and left there. Now, here I was dishonorably discharged from my first ship; a fuck-up, maybe a murderer. At best, a whoremonger, a drunk, and a breaker of rules. If the rules didn't suit, I didn't follow them. I didn't deserve to be a midshipman; didn't deserve for people to treat me well. Like Tiny Tim, I didn't deserve a berth on this fine vessel.

I knew I would be expelled from school. They would convene a court martial as they had when I'd gotten caught with beer in my room. Captain Ford, Commandant of Midshipmen, would preside. He would sit at the head of the long, mahogany table with others in navy uniforms with gold bars to act as my judges. I could hire an attorney but face it, my chances were not good. If they could cure me, I'd get sent to Viet Nam where I would undoubtedly get shot. If not, maybe I could go to an asylum for incurable cases of venereal disease. Except, of course, who would pay? And what would my father say, I asked myself the thousandth time. My mother; my little brother Marky. Besides, my parents didn't want me at home healthy. Why should they want me sick? If not home or to school, where would I go? I had no money. I would soon be without friends. Girl friends? Forget it.

I couldn't stand the diesel fumes and engine noise rumbling beneath the deck in the passenger compartment, so I stepped outside. Our boat passed noisily under the Bridge of the Americas. The haziness lingered. Small boats and large ships appeared, then disappeared into the patchy fog. Nothing was clear. We were in such thick fog for a brief period that our boat operator blew his whistle a couple of times.

The officials jabbered in Spanish and puffed away on their precious Marlboros. We passed near a sixty-foot sailing ship anchored just outside the ship channel. A group of rough-looking young men stood on deck glaring at us. They all had spiky blond hair and few wore anything but shorts. The pilot had pointed out this boat on our southbound transit. It had sailed from Norway commanded by professional seamen, carrying a group of young men from a reform school on a training cruise—meant to help rehabilitate these fellows. They had transited the canal, then anchored awaiting orders and supplies. Neither orders nor money was forthcoming. The adults had flown home weeks ago. The boys and their boat were now a tourist attraction. Food and water and medicine was supplied by an international relief group but, according to the pilot, reports of sexual atrocities and violence were making their way ashore. The boat had become a political problem and no one wanted to dirty their hands cleaning up what looked to be a sorry mess. I watched the boys until we passed again into a patch of fog and they disappeared. Perhaps that would be my fate, I thought: exile to a hell-ship.

I wished then I were home; that I'd never heard of ships, that I could click my heels like Dorothy and be in Kansas. I wished I'd obeyed my impulse in the cavernous, echoey train station in Omaha to turn around and take the next locomotive back. I could have apologized to Father Henry and to my parents. I'd have proposed to Melissa. I'd quit reading all those books Henrietta the librarian pushed across her oak desk like they were drugs. I'd be with my family.

Like my dad said though, "If wishes were horses, beggars would ride." He actually said "beggars would fly," but no one really understood what that meant. He'd been a pilot in the war and then bought a share of an airplane which he flew to the little towns where he played baseball on hot summer nights. I always figured it was he would wish for, if wishes were horses. If he could change his life and do whatever he wanted. He'd put on his baseball uniform and fly to the game, land way out in center field, then walk in out of the dark to the mound where he'd pitch the perfect game—over and over and over.

But wishes aren't horses. And regrets for things we didn't do aren't even ponies because they're in the past and time has removed the opportunity.

The operator cut back on his engine and idled up alongside a small concrete wharf covered with a blue tin awning. I stepped ashore. The debarking area was filthy. The walls of the shelter above the long concrete bench were covered with revolting sexual graffiti. Pictures of women speared through every orifice by giant penises, pictures of men defecating on women, peeing on them. I gagged. The space was littered with empty rum bottles and stank of urine. This was where the launches picked up crews of ships about to transit. I'd heard stories of the fabled Panama Canal midnight launch. Balboa was the only stop after the long Pacific crossing and before the long Atlantic crossing.

Don Campbell had said, "otherwise decent men grow horns and bray like goats when their ships anchor in Balboa."

Irving Jackson called it "a nightmare you sho' nuff hope you wakes up from."

I followed the boarding officials up a ramp toward a cluster of peach-colored stucco buildings trimmed white and surrounded by a steel fence. A dark-haired man wearing a creased, short-sleeved white shirt outside his belt, approached.

"Buenos dias, senor. You must be the midshipman from the Gulf Trader."

I nodded.

"I am Senor Fernando Esteban, the agent. I recall meeting you in the purser's office from when you were southbound. We shall go directly to the naval hospital. And how do you feel, my friend?"

The man was sort of obsequious, but I didn't mind. I remembered him escorting Tiny Tim ashore southbound. The purser hadn't told me anyone was going to meet me. I was damn glad for the help.

"Not so good," I said.

"I am sorry. We weel have you at the hospital in no time." He looked at me carefully. "You weel not be returning to the ship, is that correct?"

"I won't know that till I get to the hospital," I said gruffly. "The captain said not to return without a Fit for Duty."

We walked out the gate, the uniformed guard raising his eyes briefly from his newspaper. He and Senor Esteban exchanged a few words in Spanish. I was not asked for any documents. Outside the gate, I walked a couple of steps behind. Though just past eight, the air was already saturated with the moist tropical heat I'd become familiar with. Palm trees and dense foliage appeared everywhere as the fog burned away, exposing a lush, green world.

We reached his car—a Buick matching the peach color of the buildings. We got in and soon were speeding down a boulevard lined on one side by the black iron fences of large Spanish houses. After a time, we turned into a fortified driveway marked UNITED STATES NAVAL HOSPITAL. We stopped at the gate. Senor Esteban handed my documents to a young guard with white MP on a black band around his right arm, white gloves on his hands, black-laced boots and a blue helmet. He looked at my papers, bent and studied my face, returned the documents and motioned for us to enter with a half-salute gesture of his right arm. All I could think was how hot he must be. Took discipline to stand all day in this heat dressed like that. Something I didn't have much of.

The road to the hospital led through manicured grounds filled with large trees and trimmed hedges. No jungle undergrowth here. We approached one of several sand-colored buildings. I had the feeling I was withdrawing permanently from the churning vagaries of life. It's beautiful here, I thought bitterly.

The car stopped in front of the entrance and the agent jumped out, ran around and opened my door. I stepped out heavily, then stood and looked up at the building. It was stone, ranging in color from a dull gray to a brown that made it almost disappear. It was a solid place, but had a temporary feel to it.

The architecture was simple: vertical walls interrupted with boring regularity by large sash windows covered with black bars—placed there to keep people from jumping, I figured. A small awning led from the entrance down a flight of stairs to the street—protection from the drumming rains that fell daily.

So, I thought, is this home? Will they keep me here the next sixty years? At least I'll have a place to live. I felt rejected and abandoned. I already hated the color of the walls.

The agent carried my bag in through the doorway. I followed listlessly, my feet crunching the cinder walkway.

The waiting room was cool and dark; thirty feet wide by sixty long with marble-block floors and rows of plastic blue chairs interrupted occasionally by low desks with red tops that held coverless magazines, coloring books and black ash trays. The ceiling was high—fifteen feet or more—and supported smoky Panama fans deliberately moving air from the ceiling down to the floor.

I dropped into the nearest chair. I had to pee and decided I didn't have the energy to deal with the pain. The agent took my papers to the receptionist while I sat there, elbows on my knees, head down, my vision fixed on the cool nothingness of the marble floor.

"My friend." The agent's officiously cheerful voice interrupted my reverie. "It weel be perhaps one hour before the doctor weel see you. Here ees my card. Have the lady at the desk call me when they have decided your deesposition." He placed his hand on my shoulder. I turned my head up, nodded and returned my gaze to the floor.

"Good luck, amigo." He walked to the door, opened it and left. A man with a life; a future, hope. Fuck it, I thought. Who gives a shit about him?

A wooden clock sat on a mantle above a marble fireplace in the center of the opposite wall. I couldn't believe the Navy had built a fireplace. Likely the only one in the world at this latitude. The room was silent. The fireplace was its heart. I became aware of the tick-tock beating of the clock on the mantle. Unending marking of moments. Incessant ticks. Loud and echoing. The ticks differed from each other—one having a sort of upbeat, seeming to gain energy only to lose it again on the downbeat. Energy gained then lost then gained then lost. The beats echoed in the marble room so the upbeats mixed with the downbeats and energy was lost and regained over and over and over—net effect: zero. The ticking established a place in the recess of my mind and reaffirmed life and the promise of death. Tick-tock, tick-tock; life-death, life-death.

I sat numb, thinking about where and how I would spend the rest of my life. What sort of institution would it be? Would my mom visit? She had never wanted me to go to New York to school anyway, and certainly not to sea. Optimism, pessimism. Tick-tock. Some ancient Catholic European gene blocked hope but I was aware only of the ticking.

Time passed. People entered the waiting room, checked in with the receptionist and sat. Men, women, two young girls with their mom: everyone's shoes clacking annoyingly on the marble floor. They spoke softly, their voices muffled, the sound absorbed in the huge room. I thought again about church and how silence has different dimensions. Today, in this room, it was cavernous, and lonely, and pressed on my heart and made me want to curl into a ball on the floor. Over time, some deep peacefulness wormed its way into my soul as I sat there, head down, eyes closed, dreaming, vaguely aware of the coming and going of humanity, the life-death ticking of the clock, the fwap-fwap of the paddle fans. I descended through layers of consciousness until I noticed Rosa standing at the door of the Broken Fluke, her son in hand, partially hidden in the patchy fog, motionless. She smiled.

"You're all right then?" I asked.

She faded into a swirl of fog and Ana-Elena appeared, wearing her student's plaid skirt and white blouse. She smiled cheerfully and waved.

"Gracias, senor cadete," she said. "I hope to meet you again soon. You are always welcome in my house." She winked. "Just not in the front door please."

Then there was Melissa and my heart raced. She looked to be only thirteen or fourteen; shy, but confident and curious. The fog shifted and all three stood there, radiant and smiling, beautiful sisters, full of life and happy to see me. I found myself weeping like an old, crazy person, though I couldn't have said why.

A voice naming me over a loudspeaker broke through my dream. I rose up out of my meditation like surfacing from a watery depth. Except for having to pee, I felt more relaxed than I had in months. I hadn't slept the night before, and even those few minutes of dreaming had done me good.

The tone of the voice over the loudspeaker grew more insistent. I stood and walked toward the receptionist. She peered at me above her glasses and motioned down a corridor to her right.

"Inoculations," she pointed.

I walked that direction, passing doors identified by white signs with flat green lettering that protruded from the tops of each doorframe like erections. I found a men's room and used it, nearly doubling over from the pain. Three quarters of the way down the corridor, I found *Inoculations* and entered the room. It was small and colorless. Two windows looked out onto the lawn. They were covered by Venetian blinds, the slots admitting light but reflecting the sun's rays. A small metal desk sat off to the right. Next to it a white sink hung from the wall, the faucet handles large-finned, the spout swan-necked and graceful. An ashtray with a handful of lipstick-smeared butts sat on the desk. A black examination table complete with stirrups stood in the center. I sat on the edge of the table.

A door I hadn't noticed burst open and a compact blond exploded into the room. She wore a white nurse's uniform with a name-tag that said *Becca*. A cigarette dangled from her red lips. Except for the smoke, she looked to me like an angel of mercy. She stabbed out her cigarette in the ashtray.

We talked. I humbly pulled down my pants. She donned latex gloves and pulled my sick penis through the separation in the clean shorts I'd just put on—like the Indian girl in Cristobal had done over a month ago.

"Well well well, what have we here?" Her eyes were bright blue and kind. "An unwanted little bug?"

"I don't know how little it is, but it sure is unwanted."

"We'll just have to get rid of it for you." She hesitated, then laughed. "The bug I mean."

She walked to a cupboard above the desk, opened it, rummaged around till she found two huge syringes with needles that looked as if they would be more appropriate in the service of a large-animal veterinary. She held up the needles and smiled over the tops of them.

"See these."

"Yes ma'am."

"They are the largest we have in this entire hospital."

"They look real big."

"I'm gonna use two of them."

"Do they hurt?"

"Mm-hmm."

"Oh."

"But they'll make you well."

She inserted the needle of one into what looked like a quart of milk and pulled the plunger, sucking the liquid into the syringe. My lips curled, imagining the pain. I felt entirely out of control. My Mom was always saying, "Let go, let God." This was that all right.

"Might as well bend over that table and hold on, big boy. I'm just about to stick it to you."

I did as she asked, looking back at her. She laughed as she held the needle in the air and flicked the plunger with her finger causing a few drops of the white fluid to squirt out the end. She looked at the fluid, smiled mischievously, then looked over at me. "You don't have an allergy to penicillin, I hope."

"No ma'am. I've taken a lot of it."

"Well, you're about to get a whole lot more. Now smile."

The pain surprised me. It began as a sharp slap just above the fleshy part of my buttocks and was followed immediately by a stabbing sensation. The needle punched through my skin, penetrated past the subcutaneous area where most needles stop and dove deep into the heavy fat and muscle tissue of my hip. I gasped and the sensation stopped, as if held in abeyance.

"Ready?" came her cheerful voice.

"Ready for what? Jesus Christ, I thought you were finished."

She laughed. "Here comes what you been waitin' for."

The penicillin slowly forced its way into my hip. There wasn't room for it, but with the nurse pushing hard on the plunger with the heel of her right hand, it passed from the syringe into my butt. The pain was dull now, and big, and seemed interminable and inescapable. Moments danced before my eyes like painted balloons, friendly and smiling, lingering, bowing, carrying on conversations with no one in particular before passing on and permitting another to take its place. Eventually, the sensation eased and I felt the needle withdrawing. Then, just when I thought it was over, the pain ramped up. I felt the needle break new tissue as it traveled in an upward arc inside my hip. I cried out: a sigh of relief mixed with a moan of pain.

"Damn," said the nurse. "Needle stuck. Well, don't worry. It's just dangling outside your butt there. I'll get it in a minute. Happens all the time with these big needles."

I felt it grabbed roughly from the outside and jerked out of my body.

"Sorry about that. One down, one to go," she said.

I moaned again. Then, before I could think about relaxing, I felt a *Whack* as she slapped my other buttock. Then a *Stab* as the second needle entered me, followed quickly by a *Push* as the penicillin entered my body. I momentarily lost consciousness as the pain triggered some black-out reflex. Soon enough it was over and the needle was out. The nurse rubbed alcohol over the injection sites and left a small band-aid cross on each. I slumped over the bed, my trousers at my knees, legs apart, balls dangling.

"Pull up them pants, cowboy. You're ready to go again."

I did as she said then turned to look at her.

"How can you be so sure?"

"Listen, there ain't no bacteria known to man can withstand the amount of penicillin I just put into you. It has never in history failed. I'll sign that fit for duty slip and not worry a minute whether or not it'll work."

She cupped my chin in her hand and looked at me carefully. "Kinda hurt, didn't it?"

I was aware of tears, partly from the pain, partly from the utter joy I felt at being rid of the disease. I nodded, tried to smile, wanted to kiss her but only muttered "Thanks."

"Go on out to the desk. They'll take care of you from here. You kinda watch where you stick that thing, OK?" She winked.

I walked out of the room, limping slightly and headed down the hall. A tall man in a black shirt and white collar walked toward me, whistling.

"Excuse me, Father," I said. He stopped and turned toward me. He had a shock of wine-colored hair and brown eyes that sparkled with mischief.

"Top o' the mornin' to ye, lad. And how are we today?"

"Father, I'd like to confess." My direct approach surprised us both.

"Then confess we will," he said. "Come. There's got to be a confessional here somewhere."

He opened the door to a room with a sign that read *X-rays*. It was empty. He sat in one chair and pointed to another. I told him I preferred to stand, that sitting just now would be uncomfortable.

"Then perhaps you could kneel," he said, looking up. "Afraid I'll get a crick in my neck. We Catholics are good kneelers, anyway."

I knelt. "This will be fine, father."

I closed my eyes and told him every single thing that had happened this trip. I didn't care how long it took or if I missed the ship. This was an opportunity I wasn't going to waste. I went all the way back to the New Orleans strippers and what I decided were impure thoughts up through the possibility of murdering Rosa. I told him I hadn't gone to Mass on Sunday; that I regularly used the Lord's name in vain; how I'd lusted, screwed, drank and used drugs. I'd stolen a bottle of Grand Marnier from a bar in Arica, lied to my mother and disobeyed every authority I could name.

His eyes popped open at the word murder. He said "Murder? This is serious then." He questioned me about it. I responded honestly.

"You've got to talk to Mr. Fletcher then, right?" he said. "Even God can only do so much if we're not willing to learn the truth."

When I finished and opened my eyes, he was smiling. He said, "Son, not to make light, but for the first time in my seventeen years as a priest, I've heard a man confess to transgressing every single one of the Ten Commandments. I won't say congratulations, then, but I will thank you for the experience." He leaned toward me, running his hand through his hair.

"I'll bet you're damned glad to get this off your chest."

"You think God can forgive me, Father?"

"Even you, my son, even all this." And with that, he closed his eyes, raised his right hand in a blessing, gave me a penance that included at least one unheralded good deed each day for the remainder of my life and lapsed into the Latin benediction that sounded like a magic incantation.

The Gulf Trader was already in the Mira Flores locks, so the agent drove me to Pedro Miguel where a tug picked me off the corner of the south wingwall and carried me to the lowered gangway while the bow nosed into the lock. The agent had called the ship from the hospital to tell them I was returning.

Once aboard, I delivered the "Fit for duty after one day's rest" slip to the purser and went to bed. Around three in the morning, after sleeping nearly thirteen hours, I woke up, got out of bed and stepped into the head to pee. The bright, yellow stream splashed into the toilet water when I remembered. All sensation was gone. The bug was dead. I was healed. I clenched my fists, gritted my teeth and let out a whoop.

Wally called from the bedroom: "Hey, for Christ's sake, keep it down in there. What're ya doin' anyway? Jerkin' off?"

Panama to New Orleans
August 29

Standing in the head at three a.m., realizing I was well, I permitted myself a brief smile as I looked in the mirror. I closed my eyes and inhaled deeply, then stripped off the clothes I'd slept in and stepped into the shower. The part for the broken compressor had arrived in Panama. The engineers had installed it immediately and the air conditioning was now cranked up so high I was shivering. The hot water in the shower beat against my body warming me. I stood with my eyes closed imagining it washing away the billions of germs my disease had coated me with. Good as the water felt, I knew I wasn't finished with all this yet. I had confessed to a possible murder but the priest had told me, as had Don Campbell, I needed to know the truth. My conscience ached, but I felt a sense of courage I hadn't known before.

Eventually, determined to discover the truth no matter what it took or where it took me, I turned off the water and stepped out of the shower, dried myself and put on my very last pair of clean khaki shorts and a tee shirt. Wally mumbled in his sleep and I didn't work too hard at being quiet as I rummaged around, picking up all the clothes I'd worn while I was sick. I bundled everything, including my towels, into a sheet and slipped quietly out the door.

The ship was still at this early hour as I walked through the decks and passageways to the officer's laundry. I dumped my clothes into the Amana and twisted the control over to extra hot. Then, aware of an enormous hunger, I crossed the foyer to the stairs that lead down to the saloon. Fletcher had just been relieved on the bridge and was walking down to his room. We met on the landing, stopped and stared at each other. He seemed surprised and almost angry to see me.

"Morning, Fletcher," I said.

"Fuck you, cadet," he replied, continuing down the stairs.

"Fuck you too, Fletcher." I ran down after him and grabbed his arm. "Hey asshole. I don't give a shit if you like me or not. I need to talk to you."

"Like I said. Fuck you cadet. I'm going to bed." He continued toward his room.

"What happened that night, in Rosa's room?" I hollered after him. He stopped and turned.

"Whadda ya mean, what happened?"

"What happened to Rosa?" I said. "Did you have a gun? Did you shoot her?"

His face screwed up and he looked at me strangely. Then he laughed, waved me away, turned and walked to his door. He fumbled with the lock, paused, glancing nervously toward me. Finally the key turned. He opened the door. I ran the five steps separating us, pushing him into the room then struggling with him to get myself in the door. I was bigger and stronger and forced him back, closing the door behind me. His mouth was twisted and his eyes grew wide. I had never seen such intense hatred on a man's face.

"No one's ever been in my room," his voice cracked as he choked out the words. He backed against the far wall, lifting his arms as if to hide what was there. I gasped as I looked behind him. The entire wall was covered with pictures of Rosa and the boy. I stepped over to look more closely, ignoring Fletcher who lowered his arms and moved away. The one picture I couldn't stop looking at was an eight by ten close-up of Rosa holding a baby. Her beauty caught me like a hooked bluegill and I couldn't stop staring at the picture. Her hair blew across her face and she wore a simple white blouse with a high-necked collar. Her eyes looked out beyond the photographer, out at some distant thing; maybe something in the future; or maybe just through the camera. Something about her face next to the boy's seemed too incongruous to digest. I could only imagine her thinking, I've got what I needed from a man.

There were a hundred other pictures: pictures of Fletcher and the baby; of Rosa naked in various poses, all possessing an erotic essence. There were pictures of the boy at different ages and of Rosa with her hair down in some, up in others; different clothes, different backgrounds. In all of them, she looked indifferent to what I guessed the photographer—Fletcher, probably—wanted, which was a record of her beauty; an attempt to capture and hold indefinitely that grace and sensuality certain women—and not just beautiful women either—display so effortlessly and which raises the level of desire in men.

"So what do you remember from that night?" asked Fletcher behind me, his voice strangely calm now.

"I remember you were in the room walking around the bed with a gun in your hand. What were you doing there, anyway?"

I heard Fletcher rummaging in a drawer behind me. Suddenly frightened, I turned. Fletcher sat at his desk pointing a gun at me. I raised my hands to my sides, palms out.

"Here is the gun," he said. He handed me the object and I breathed again. It was black and had a barrel protruding from a handgrip. I turned it over, examining the barrel and trigger.

"Camera?" I asked.

"That's right. Got it that morning we went shopping."

I turned it over and over in my hand, wondering why someone would want a camera that looked like a gun. Seemed to me it made more sense to have a gun that looked like a camera. I looked about the room. There were pictures of guns of all sorts—mostly pistols.

"I like pistols," said Fletcher. "They're my thing—pistols and pictures of Rosa. I had this camera built to look like a pistol."

"Why?" I asked. "So you can pretend to kill Rosa every time you take her picture?"

He looked at me as if I'd touched something raw.

"Because I fuckin' well wanted to."

I nodded.

"So what's the deal with you and Rosa?" It occurred to me this guy might be even crazier than some of the others.

"Look, kid. I'm gonna tell you a few things because I think you deserve to know."

He took two beers from a red ice chest sitting on the linoleum-covered deck next to his bed, opened them and handed me one. My first beer in over a week. I sat on his settee and looked around as I took a drink. His room was obsessively neat—nothing appeared out of place. A picture of a stern bald man and a timid, gray-haired woman sat on his desk. On the wall above the desk was a calendar with a winter painting of hunters approaching a downed elk. The calendar said *Winchester Rifles* on it. The brown and white Llama-skin covering his bed looked tight enough to bounce a quarter.

"Rosa is my wife," he said. "We were married a few years ago—just after the kid was born."

He looked at me, silent, waiting to see what reaction that bit of news would bring.

I didn't know what to say. I had fucked another man's wife with him watching.

"So, Rosa is alive, right?"

"Hell, yes. She'll outlive both of us. Rosa is a goddamned survivor."

"Why does Rosa still work as a prostitute if you and she are married?"

"'Cuz it's what she does. She likes sex and she's good at it and I'm not there. Plus, she needs to earn a living. She's got big plans for the kid. College in the States. Wants him to be a doctor for Christ's sake. Anyway, why should I care? I don't own the woman. Besides, it's only sex."

He seemed unsure then, floundering. His head turned right to left to right as though searching for a way out.

"We all prostitute ourselves one way or another, kid. You, me, Rosa, the captain, the owner of this company. We all do things for money we don't want to do. Whether it involves sex or sailing a ship, if we do it only for money, then it ain't, you know, a vocation. We're fucking prostitutes." He paused, closing his eyes for a moment. When he reopened them, he looked square at me and said, "I don't intend to enquire into your

homespun morality and sure as hell don't expect you to ask
about mine."

I raised my eyebrows slightly. As long as Rosa was alive,
whatever else happened that night didn't matter much. I hadn't
killed anyone. I'd been with another man's wife with him watching but that didn't seem any big deal. Being absolved from the
possibility of involvement in a murder brought a new perspective
to all this; made everything else seem like small potatoes—only
way more interesting. And, like Fletcher said, "it's only sex."

"So, you love Rosa?"

"Love? Love? What is that? Affection? Passion? Look, kid,
talk to someone else about love. Too fucking abstract for me.
What matters to me is what people do. I don't even care what
they say, what they talk about. What a man does, what a woman
does is the only thing that signifies anything to me. All the rest
is bullshit. On these ships, you hear 'I'm gonna get my mate's
ticket,' then the years pass and it don't happen. A girl says 'I love
you' but what she wants is something you got—money, maybe
or a shot of sperm."

I nodded, drank a couple more swallows of beer, set down
the can and stood.

"Guess I'll go now," I said.

"Yeah. Go ahead. Get the hell out of here. Go on to your life
of money and success. Leave us peons with our weird lives
behind. What do we mean to youse anyway? Get the fuck out of
here."

I walked out, closing the door behind me, smiling at the
thought of Rosa in her short, black dress, dancing with different
sailors every night at Yakko's, climbing the stairs to her room,
stripping slowly, turning the guy inside out with pleasure. Weird
lives, Fletcher had said. Well, he had that right. And plenty of
weirdness to go around.

I walked down a flight of stairs to the saloon, reeling from
my encounter with Fletcher. Don Campbell sat there, eating his
four a.m. peanut butter sandwich.

"Hey, look who's up." He smiled brightly. "I heard you
came back aboard. How're you feeling?"

"Oh, me? I'm good. Ready to go again, I guess."

"What did they treat you with?"

"Penicillin." I patted both hips. "A lot of it." I sat across the table from him.

"Get a sandwich," he said. "Great peanut butter on this ship. Skippy's."

I smiled. Don's love of peanut butter was legendary. "I will in a minute. I just talked to Fletcher."

"No shit. What'd he say?"

"Rosa's alive. She's fine," I whispered. Like I still couldn't talk about Rosa and breathe at the same time.

"He's got a camera that looks just like a gun. He pointed it at me and I thought he was going to shoot me. Plus, Fletcher says he's married to Rosa. Says that kid is his."

Don smiled out of the side of the mouth. "That's his story. I'd be real surprised if he's got a marriage certificate. Besides, I've talked to other sailors who say that kid is theirs. Fletcher doesn't know for sure. No man ever does. Men grow so hungry for family they'll throw money at the illusion of family. And just keep believing it, regardless of little things like facts to the contrary. You think the motivation for sex is strong, wait a few years till motivation for family kicks in. You forget about sex like it was dirt on the back porch."

I smiled, thinking of being banished from my home, my town and my ship. I knew exactly what he meant—although I figured I was a long way from not wanting sex.

"Maybe we need a few illusions," I said. "Maybe life's too tough without them."

Don looked at me and shrugged. "Men need them. Seems like once a woman's got her kids, she's happy. She'll even follow a man around chasing his illusions. Long as he doesn't fuck with her kids." He wiped grape jam from the corner of his mouth.

I got up, walked over to the pantry and spread honey on a couple pieces of white bread, looked at them, made a face and tossed them into the garbage. I wanted protein. From the refrigerator, I poured milk into a glass, grabbed three hard-boiled eggs and returned to sit with Don.

Don watched, smiling. "Never seen you do that before. Starting to know your own mind, are you?"

I didn't answer.

"So why does Fletcher have such a chip on his shoulder?" I asked, cracking an egg.

Don shrugged. "Who knows. Resentments build up experience by experience. The ordinary seaman who can't read resents the A.B.; the A.B. who can't do trigonometry resents the mate on watch. Just the way it is. Like your buddy Wally says, it doesn't signify—unless you come away thinking you're some kind of Raskolnikov." He smiled again.

"What does signify?" I asked.

He looked at me, nodded just a little, grabbed at his beard and said: "You want to know what signifies? I'll tell you. What signifies is how you feel toward people—people above you, people below you, people of different colors, people of the opposite sex, barbers, poets, car salesmen. You hate a man only because he's black and you're fucked up. You hate women because some cute blond broke your heart when you were a high school senior, and you're really fucked up. Any hatred is bad, but irrational hatred—hating someone you don't know because they fall into a certain group—is worse than bad. It's stupid. For some men, everything they *do*—including sex—grows out of hatred, or at least envy. Certainly not love.

"Same thing applies to choosing your friends. If you like someone just because he or she is Irish-Catholic or lives in a big house or has big tits, you're being stupid. People are more than that. Learn their minds and their hearts. Look at the nature of their spirits and you'll be amazed at how insignificant the size of their house can be."

I thought about that as I salted my egg.

"Wish sex were as simple as two people look at each other and give some sort of sign that says, 'hey, wanta have a good time?' and that would mean they just go someplace and get it on instead of playing a game of cribbage, then both go their merry way without consequence."

Don laughed.

"Damn! Maybe you are a Raskolnikov after all. Without consequence is the tough part. Doesn't seem like that happens much except in whorehouses. And even then there are consequences. Look at your dose of clap you thought you'd never get rid of. Coupling is a game for the gods. We mortals don't understand it, that's for sure."

He took another bite of his peanut butter sandwich, chewed, swallowed, washed it down with milk, then continued.

"Nothing in this world is perfect, including sex, love, friendship and marriage. But it's love keeps kids on the playgrounds and men sailing ships and women singing as they hang their laundry. Now don't get me wrong: fabulous as it is, even love is usually temporary—even if it lasts fifty years. Yet to avoid it because it lacks permanence is nonsense, stupid, cowardly. Sex, on the other hand, is always temporary and avoiding it because it's temporary is ridiculous. We do our best as a society to make marriage permanent—we pass laws and institute tribal rituals—but I suspect happy, fulfilling marriages that last forever are hard to come by.

"So that leaves friendship," I said.

"Yeah, of everything, friendships seem to have the best chance for permanence. Cultivate friendships—especially with your wife. Friendship and humor will see you through the years better than screwing is my bet."

Don paused to bite into his sandwich. He lowered his head for a moment, nodded, then looked up and continued.

"Love and sex are godlike. But they contain the seeds for being *feelthy* as the Panama pimps say; they can make a big man sob; they can splinter a heart like it was made of crystal and can turn us into scruffy French Quarter panhandlers with bloodshot eyes."

He pulled his skin so the space below his eyes showed pink. With his scraggly beard, he looked exactly like a panhandler. I made a face and he continued.

"We have these urges we need to deal with. The irony is: that which can elevate us to a trembling, gasping glimpse of the Divine can just as easily drop us in the gutter."

After Don left I walked back up to the laundry and tossed my clothes into the dryer. I stepped outside the chill of the air-conditioned house and walked forward along the port side to the bow. The warm moist air had the feel of velvet to it. A light breeze blew from forward and the ship rolled slightly in the northwesterly seas. The moon had set earlier and the sky was a warm black cover shot through with holes exposing intense sparkling lights. On the bow, I sat on my favorite bollard and dangled my feet. The sky seemed close and friendly. The water, disturbed by the huge iron knife of a ship, made a friendly, gurgling noise as it repaired itself over and over, immediately forgiving its wound. I sat quietly, as content as though sitting in the hand of God.

I recalled the phrase I'd read in the Bible; the one I hadn't understood: *they are glad because they be quiet*. Was this what kept men returning to sea? Maybe it wasn't the drunken whorehouse bacchanals or the easy money or the escape from a world of lawns to mow and bills to pay. Maybe it was these moments of inner peace, when a person felt close to God, unencumbered by care or fear. I promised myself I'd not soon forget this moment, that it was important, coming as it did at the end of a voyage that would, in some way, define who I was and what kind of man I would be.

I thought of Melissa with her bright smile, and Ana-Elena whose passion made me shudder, and Rosa the quintessential beauty. What I felt for them now and what I had felt for them earlier wasn't hatred. If it was, then this wasn't a world I wanted to live in. For each of them it was love, or, at the very least, desire, and what was so wrong with desire?

I knew I had to go to the bridge and dig out the Nautical Almanac and H.O. 249. I would figure the First Point of Aries and mark up my little diagram of stars and step out to the bridge wing and point my sextant at the heavens. I felt light and strong and fully confident I would shoot a three star fix; one with a perfect pinwheel that would sit precisely on top of Mr. Potter's position.

But I couldn't move. I was caught by the energy that exists just before dawn when the world struggles between darkness and light. The night sky made a vaulted cathedral ceiling. Sitting there on the bow of the ship with the dark water gurgling beneath me and the wind blowing warm across my face, I felt at that moment God was everywhere, roughly in charge, happy with how things were evolving; happy, even, with me, undoubtedly among the worst of His sinners.

Like a crack in a door, a hint of pink appeared in the eastern sky, vertical and narrow, like the intimate part of a woman. I smiled because it reminded me of the Indian girl lying naked in her little room in Panama only a month ago—a month that seemed a lifetime, filled with struggle and seeking, soul-searing love and icy rejection. What did it signify, that hint of pink? That it was time to get up to the bridge to shoot stars, to establish myself as a navigator. And maybe, hopefully, that a dark period in my life was nearly over.

I knew something about desire now, something about the seductiveness of physical pleasure and the permanent satisfaction of a quiet mind. I knew a little about hatred and just the beginning of all there is to know about love. I was still a cadet, but my maiden voyage was nearing its end.

New Orleans
August 30, 1967

We arrived at the pilot station at Southwest Pass around midnight. I saw the pilot aboard at two minutes past and escorted him to the bridge. I knew it was 0002 because I wound up winning the arrival pool. Twenty-five bucks. I needed it. I'd gladly returned the hundred the purser had fronted me when he thought I wouldn't be rejoining and now had exactly four dollars to my name. Monetary considerations aside, I sensed winning the pool was one more sign my luck had changed.

I stayed up on the bridge then, too excited to sleep—channel fever, the mate said. We weaved our way silently through the twists in the Mississippi River, going deep into the bends to meet or pass barges, whistling at them: one blast port to port; two blasts starboard to starboard. The pilot sat at the radar smoking Camels and sipping Folgers, his focus never wavering. He and the watch-mates exchanged tidbits of information from time to time, but the wheelhouse, like the ship and the river, was silent and dark.

I stood on the bridge wing for most of the twelve to four watch, enjoying the wind across my face, watching the headlights of an occasional early-hour driver on the jetty, or looking through the binoculars as we passed by the small towns. Don Campbell tried sending me to bed, but I just smiled and told him I doubted I'd be able to sleep.

At four I left the bridge with Don, went to my room, took off my shirt, lay down and slept till seven-twenty. At eight, I ducked into the pantry, buttered a couple slices of toast and ate them on my way to the bow. The mate and the sailors were already there. We had turned and our ship, assisted by the current and two tugs, was coming alongside the Nashville Avenue docks, exactly where this voyage had begun. Wally and I had done our laundry and packed the night before. We had received a telegram with orders from the Academy Training Representative and were scheduled to get off the Gulf Trader today, after pay-off. I was supposed to schlep my bags up the dock to the Ashley Lykes while Wally had been reassigned to a tanker upriver at a port called St. James. The sun had just broken through the morning haze and the day looked to be muggy. All the sailors wore jeans and white tee shirts and everyone was smiling. The bosun stood at the winch controls shouting an occasional order, but in a gentle, familiar way. Everyone knew who could toss a heaving line the furthest by now, who could set a stopper that wouldn't slip, or who was just in the way. I was full of energy and helped out where I could. The A.B.'s kidded me a lot; the boatswain patted me on the back once. Even the mate was cheery.

After we were fast, I stayed on the bow with Simple Simon, the Ordinary Seaman, to lower the rat guards onto the mooring lines, stow the stoppers, and coil and hang the heaving lines in the boatswain's locker. When we were finished and the Ordinary was gone, I looked around, thinking how well I knew the bow of this ship, and how I would miss it.

Payoff was held in Crew Lounge at ten a.m. sharp. I showered after coming in off the bow and put on my short-sleeve khakis and black dress shoes. I'd pressed my khakis—not sure why—maybe because this was my last day on the Gulf Trader and I wanted to honor these shipmates I'd come to think of as family. Wally and I walked down to the crew lounge together. A half-dozen men sat at the long table that ran along one side of the wall. The captain sat in the center wearing his shoulder boards, stern and tired after the all-night river transit; George

LeClair sat at his right hand with a pile of papers—vouchers and envelopes stuffed with cash. Next to him, according to Wally who acted like he knew everything, sat the Shipping Commissioner: short, balding, with bad teeth and a red nose. He wore a blue uniform with a wrinkled white shirt and stained tie. Customs came next, a younger man, much sharper in light blue with a starched shirt. Then came Immigration, wearing green. Wally figured the last man was the company purser—the guy who brought down the money and settled beefs with the union patrolmen.

We stood in line between the chief engineer and the bosun. I signed my discharge in front of the captain. He grabbed my hand and shook it.

"Come back any time, young man," he said. "And be careful now, you understand."

I shook his hand and nodded, mumbling, "thanks for everything." I couldn't believe this voyage was over. It had been too big and there had been too much for it to simply end.

George LeClair opened an envelope and snapped the seven twenty-dollar bills that wound up being my payoff.

"Good luck, Jake," he said. "I won't forget you or this trip."

I smiled and said goodbye, thinking I'd probably never see George LeClair again.

"See ya," I said. "Thanks for looking after me."

"Wish I could have done more." He pushed his coke-bottle glasses up on his nose and shook his head once. He was getting off for one trip. I wondered if he planned to go to the monastery where he flagellated himself, or if he had other plans for this vacation now that he was reborn womanizer, as Wally called him.

I signed off in front of the Shipping Commissioner who had really foul breath, then skipped the sign-on sheet since I wasn't making next trip. I paid Customs three bucks duty on my souvenirs and showed Immigration my Z-card. Then I was finished. I shook hands with other crewmembers as I made my way out of the lounge.

Mr. Potter stood just outside the door, arms folded, a man who didn't and wouldn't change. He'd been waiting for me.

"Good luck, cadet," he said, extending his hand which I grabbed and shook heartily.

"Thanks for everything, Mr. Potter. I learned an awful lot this trip."

"Here." He handed me a tightly rolled chart.

"What's this?"

"Your first three star fix. A perfect pinwheel. Directly on top of mine. Keep it as a souvenir."

I accepted the chart and nodded my head. I really wanted to hug the man but refrained. He touched my right arm with his hand.

"Good luck now, son. Keep up the good work."

I had a couple of letters from home waiting when I got back to my room. I read the one from my father but didn't have time to think much about it because Wally walked in just as I finished it. This is what it said, though.

Dear Jake,

I'm not much for writing letters, but I plan to get better with you gone from home. You might have heard your granddad and I bought Ed's Market and are now running it. Hasn't given me much chance to drink anymore. Turns out I don't miss the booze or the people I used to drink it with.

The other thing I wanted to say is I'm looking forward to having you home again soon or whenever you get some time off. Real proud of you out there. People ask about you all the time. Your Mom and brothers and sisters are all good except for Mark, who broke his arm riding his bike.

Love, Dad

After lunch, Wally and I hauled our bags down the gangway and stood on the apron talking while he waited for a cab.

"Been a good trip," he said.

"Doubt I'll ever forget it."

"Good luck on the Ashley. I don't know your new sea-partner. He's a class below me."

"Oh, he'll be all right, I suppose," I said. "But he won't be you, Wally. I'll miss you."

"Hey, let's keep the dropping acid to ourselves when we get back to school, OK?"

"No problem."

"One more thing. Sorry I left you alone that night. If I'd stayed with you, you wouldn't have gotten into trouble. And you know what else, you were right when you said I was doing just what my old man would do. I'll never leave anyone again, though. Never. You have my word."

His taxi pulled up. We shook hands one more time, embraced awkwardly and he was gone. I stood there alone, thinking, yeah, this is how it is.

I turned away and walked up the dock slowly, lugging my bags toward the Ashley Lykes. The tears in my eyes gave that ship and the city skyline behind it a watery, surreal appearance. I didn't want to set down my luggage and wipe my eyes, though, so I kept walking and let the breeze dry them. Twice, I stopped and turned to look at the Gulf Trader. She looked so fine sitting there, rolling slightly as her booms picked lifts out of the holds and landed them on the wharf. I was about to turn away for the last time when Don appeared on the gangway with his bags. He ran two steps at a time down onto the dock directly toward a black-haired woman with a child holding each of her hands. He hugged the woman for a long time, then picked up the kids, one at a time and hugged them. He turned just a little then and saw me out of the corner of his eye. He waved.

"Hey Jake," he yelled. "Forget everything I said on the ship. This is what it's all about. This, right here." He gestured toward his family. "Good luck now."

I waved. "Thanks for everything, Don." I swallowed hard and turned to my new ship.

The Ashley Lykes was very different from the Gulf Trader, even though both were freighters, both relatively new. The gangway on the Ashley was narrower, for example, and the house was split with a hatch between the two sections. I found the mate's office with some difficulty, went in and introduced myself. He had black hair slicked back and dark eyes. He wore a large ruby on his right hand and a sign on his desk said *Jules.* He was busy, so he handed me my key and directed me over to my room.

"See you at eight a.m. Monday," he said. "Take tomorrow off. It's Sunday. Go to church or something."

Joseph Jablonski

"Not a bad idea, mate. Where we heading this trip?" I asked.

"Place called Saigon. Been there?"

"No sir," I said. "Heard a lot about it though."

He chuckled. "Lot can happen in Saigon. One of those places you go to you never forget."

I went to my room. Edgar Hill was the name of the engine cadet. I didn't know him at all from school, didn't even recognize his face. There was something about the cut of his jib—a phrase Mr. Hunt had used—I didn't like much. We talked a little. He smirked a lot. Said he'd just made a trip to Northern Europe and our trip to Viet Nam meant a ton of sea-time but when we got there we'd probably have two weeks or more in port. He acted like he'd been going to sea for twenty years when actually, like me, he'd just finished his first trip.

"We're going out to a whorehouse with fancy Cajun women on the edge of LaFitte Bayou if you'd like to go," he said. "Free for cadets."

"Let me think about it. Got some unpacking to do. Plus I'm a little tired from the upriver transit and I haven't called my folks or my girlfriend yet."

"Girlfriend?" He snickered. "Lot of good she's gonna do you when you're out here on a ship."

I nodded. "There's a woman I met here last time in, too. Antoinette. Architecture student. Smart girl with a great sense of humor. Thought I might look her up as well."

"Well, I'm leaving," he said. "These in-port romances don't usually work out, but you can always count on a whore. You're gonna miss a good time."

I smiled and nodded again. "Tell me about it tomorrow," I said, laying my sextant box on the bed next to the rolled up chart with the three star pinwheel, wondering what my dad would say when I told him I was sailing for Saigon.

Joseph Jablonski

Joe Jablonski grew up in Nebraska, graduating from the United States Merchant Marine Academy in Kings Point, New York. He sailed as deck officer, tramping through South America, Africa and the Mediterranean, fighting ice-flows in Alaska and hauling general cargo through Asia. The last ten years of his career was spent as captain of a nine hundred foot containership plying the Pacific and Indian Oceans, and the Arabian Sea. He studied literature and creative writing at the University of Nebraska and has a Master's degree in International Business from Portland State University. Mr. Jablonski lives with his family in Portland, Oregon.